WHAT IF...

*the story of the Iran hostages was only a cover-up
for what really happened in Tehran ...*

*the Ten Commandments had been destroyed
by Moses and never reconstructed—
until now ...*

*a young woman lured into a parallel feminist
universe unwittingly tipped the scales in the
never-ending war between the sexes ...*

*the Roman Empire had survived and the first
contact with aliens from space occurred in the
time of the Caesars ...*

*a talented science fiction writer could change
the course of America itself ...*

**The world looks very different in the realm
of alternate reality!**

What Might Have Been?

VOLUME 1: ALTERNATE EMPIRES

Edited by Gregory Benford
and Martin H. Greenberg

BANTAM BOOKS
NEW YORK · TORONTO · LONDON · SYDNEY · AUCKLAND

WHAT MIGHT HAVE BEEN?

A Bantam Spectra Book / August 1989

PRINTING HISTORY

Contents

Introduction

Perhaps there is no more poignant theme than *if only*...

Certainly writers of many stripes and persuasions have wondered what might have been and attempted to rewrite history. This practice has been termed many things, some ambiguous, such as *parahistory* and *metahistory*. Academics have offered *uchronia*, by analogy with *utopia*. Some suggested *allohistory* and *alternative history*.

Whatever the term, this volume begins a series of stories devoted to refashioning history in a logical manner to explore what could or might have been. Other volumes will follow.

The theme has a considerable history itself. The first use of it was Louis-Napoleon Geoffroy-Chateau's *Napoleon and the Conquest of the World, 1812–1823*. This nationalist vision, published in 1836, told how a crucial decision to not tarry in Moscow as winter drew on saved the French forces. Napoleon then had the entire planet on the run and established the first world empire. In 1931 J. C. Squire gave the theme great momentum by assembling *If: or History Rewritten*. This volume was not fiction, but rather speculative essays by such luminaries as Winston Churchill, G. K. Chesterton, and Hilaire Belloc

In a scholarly afterword to *Alternative Histories* (edited by Charles G. Waugh and Martin H Greenberg), Gordon B. Chamberlain and Barton C. Hacker gave a rough count of which ideas have been most popular. The most common theme is World War II, Hitler, and the atomic bomb. We edited an entire volume of such stories, *Hitler Victorious*. The second most popular theme is the survival of Rome or Byzantium. Third is the American War of Secession and Lincoln. Then comes changes in the Spanish Armada and the Reformation, followed by switches in the lot of the Aztecs and other Native Americans. A bit less common are different outcomes for Napoleon and altered American Revolutions.

This series explores these and other avenues. We commissioned tales from writers we thought would most ingeniously use the great freedom the idea allows. We imposed one further constraint: the changed history had to be a failed event. This is a way to explore the fragility of human action. Can small tweaks and tunings wrench history onto utterly different tracks? Historians themselves have no clear answer to this question. The appeal of the notion lies in our suspicion that some crucial events have great leverage, yet seeming inconsequentialities can be the fulcrum. (My novel *Timescape* argues for the sensitivity of great events to minor changes, and that is my bias. I could not resist the impulse to take that view in my own story here. But in consulting with authors, we resisted imposing any of our opinions.) In science fiction alternative histories often arise from the device of time travel, where causal paradox can play a role. Within limits, this too was an allowed option for our contributors.

Given the theme of what might have been and asked to dwell upon grand events that failed to come about, our authors could write whatever they liked. Interestingly, three stories deal with changes in the great religions of the world, which then alter empires and world society with great effect. Others treat recent changes, some military.

We cajoled Larry Niven into writing the closing story as a homage to Robert Heinlein—and Heinlein read and approved it with real pleasure only a month before his death in the spring of 1988. The thought that a science fiction writer could prove crucial to history seems both amusing and, after reflection, quite plausible.

A later collection will treat the Great Man idea and explore the importance of individuals in the great sweep of history. We hope you will find this range of imaginative experiments thought-provoking and perhaps even unsettling.

—GREGORY BENFORD
October 1988

In the House of Sorrows

POUL ANDERSON

That is a very old land, full of wrongs that will not die. They weighted me like the noontime heat, and with the same stillness, but the names of many of them I had never known. My horse's hoofs made the loudest noise, beneath it now and then a creak of saddle leather, once the twitter of a shepherd boy's pipes. Dusty green orchards and kitchen gardens dappled summer-brown hills. Dwellings, mostly sun-baked brick, strewed themselves likewise. They grew thicker along the road as it wound upward. Men in shabby caftans stared at me from doorways, women and children from deeper inside, speaking no word. A few times I met laden camels, donkeys, oxcarts. The lips of their drivers closed when I came in sight.

It had been thus for the past day. Some news had flown abroad. Riding, I had glimpsed restlessness in the villages and between them. No longer did anybody hail me, rush forth to offer wares or beg for alms. Thrice I stopped to water my mount, my remount, and myself, and sought to ask what went on, but those I spoke to gave short, meaningless answers and slipped away. That was easy for them. I had little of either the Aramaic or the Edomite tongue.

That night I deemed it best not to seek a caravansary, but rolled up in my saddle blanket in a field well off the highway. At sunrise I ate what cheese and pita bread were left me, and quenched thirst with the last water in my flask. It's hard for a Marklander to be without his morning coffee, but dead men can't drink anyhow.

Now the walls of Mirzabad rose before me. Afar, they had shimmered hazy through the heat. Close, I saw the

3

pockmarks of former wars in their gray-white stone. A flag drooped from a cross-armed staff above the gate. The Lion and Sun of Persia slackened a little the tightness in me. At least that much abided. My gaze sought after the hues of Ispanya and did not find them. However, I told myself, belike they were not seeable from here.

Lesser buildings, shops and worksteads, crowded the roadsides. They should have been alive with the racket of the East, hammers on iron, hooves thudding, wheels groaning, beasts lowing and braying, fowl cackling, folk shrilling. Smells should have thickened the heat, smoke, sweat, dung, oil. Instead, what drifted to me seemed eerily loud and sharp in its loneliness. Some traffic did move. Dust from it gritted my eyelids, nostrils, mouth. My horses must push their way among walkers, wagons, huge burdens on hairy backs. Yet this was scant, and all outbound. Faces were grim. The looks I got ran from sullen to hateful. Often men spat on my shadow.

A score of warders stood by at the gate. Sicamino itself posted only four at any inway. These were also Persians, also wearing striped tunics, breeches bagged into half-boots, turbans on bearded heads. They also bore old-time, muzzle-loading rifles and curved shortswords. They slouched with the same slovenliness, soldiers of what was today an empire in name only. But their wariness came to me like a stench of fear, and it was no astonishment when their overling shouted in bad Ispanyan, "Ho, you, Westman, stop! Haul over!"

I obeyed, careful to hold my hands on the reins, well away from pistol and broadsword. A paved space under the wall was kept clear. The head warder beckoned me to it and snapped, "Get off."

Such a bearing toward a newcomer whom they must deem a European boded ill. I swung down from the stirrups and stood before them, hoping I looked neither too haughty nor too lowly. My years among the Magyars and Turks had given me some understanding of warlike men whose kingdoms have lost greatness. "Ahura-Mazda be with you, sirdar," I greeted in my best Persian.

The overling blinked, then turned and bowed low as

another man trod from a door in the gateway. This was not an Ispanyan gunnaro, such as should have been on call. He was another Persian, tall and lean, grizzle-bearded, in white turban and flowing black robe. The soldiers dipped their heads and touched their breasts. To them, I saw, he was a holy man; but that was no outfit of an orthodox murattab. "Who are you and what would you, Frank?" he asked with a deadly kind of softness.

I laid palms together above my heart. "Venerable one, I am no Frank," I said cat-footedly. "Nor, as you have perceived, am I an Ispanyan." Sometimes a man of that kingdom is fair-haired and much taller than most are in Lesser Asia; but on the whole, the Visigothic blood has long since lost itself in the Iberian. "May it please you, I am a humble messenger, bringing a letter to the Mirzabad factor of the Bremer Handelsbund."

The dark eyes smoldered against mine. I thought, though, that underneath, he was taken aback. Tales of the Saxonian strength off the Persian shores must have reached him, too. "Do they not trust our postal riders?" he asked slowly; and I saw wrath flare in the faces behind him.

Of course they didn't. "I bring, as well, certain words from the consul of the Hauptmannsreich in Sicamino to the factor Otto Gneisberg here in Mirzabad, such words as go best by mouth. Your reverence will understand." At least, he would be unsure whether I lied or no.

"Hm. Show me your papers."

He muttered over my passport. "Ro Esbernsson from ... New Denmark?" I could barely tell what sounds he was trying to utter.

I pointed to the notation and seal. "Not a Saxonian myself, true, but in the service of the excellent consul, as bodyguard and courier."

The letter itself was in a packet addressed to Gneisberg from von Heidenheim in the Latin, Greek, and Persian alphabets. This priest, or whatever he was, must feel a clawing wish to cut the thongs and take the writing to someone who could read it. For a heartbeat I thought he might, and wondered if I could shoot my way free, leap on my horse, and outgallop pursuit. Then he gave the things back to me, and my breath with them. The sweat prickled below my shirt. Not yet did anybody want to risk *that* war. He spoke a curt command and withdrew, his dignity gone stiff.

The soldiers took their time ransacking my baggage. Passersby stared; some jeered. In the end, they left me my papers and packet, money, a handbag with clothes and other everydayness, and my sword. The last was unwillingly, only because my being a consul's handfast man gave me the standing of warrior and to take my steel would have been to blacken him. They kept my firearms, horses, and wayfaring gear. I got no token of claim, but was not about to question their honor.

Nor did it seem wise to ask what had happened. I was glad enough to leave them behind me and pass on into the city.

A bazaar lay just beyond the gate, booths around a square whose flagstones should have been decked by spread-out rugs, metalware, crockery, fabrics, farm produce, all the goods that vendors chanted the wonders of, while the crowd milled and chattered. Today it brooded well-nigh empty beneath the hard blue sky, between the hot blind walls. A few folk, so few, went among such dealers as still dared be there. Mostly they were after food. I kenned the women: Aramaics and Edomites loosely and fully clad, low-rank Persians in long, close-fitting gowns and flowing scarves, Turks short and sturdy in blouses and breeks. Most had a man of her breed at her side, who must be warding her.

The street bore a little more upon it than the market did: sandals, boots, slippers, shoes, hooves, wheels a-clatter over bumpy cobbles. Those all belonged to men. Among townsfolk and hinterland peasants I spied some from far parts of the Shahdom, Kurds, Syrians, Badawi, with here and there an outlander, Greek, Egyptian, Afghan—but no Turk of the Sultandom, no Russian or other underling of the Grand Knyaz, no Frank or Saxonian or Dane—and with a chill in the white sunlight, I saw no Ispanyan either, be he tradesman or soldier of the Wardership. I was the one Westerner in that whole thin swarm.

"Master! Lord! Effendi!" A hand plucked my sleeve.

I looked down at a boy of maybe nine years, Edomite, all grime and rags, shock hair and big eyes. "Glorious master," he cried in bad but swift Persian, "I am your servant, your guide in the name of the heavenly Yazata to safe lodging, fine food and wine, pleasure, everything my lord desires." He jumped to worse Ispanyan: "Mestro, I show you good inn, eat, drink, beautiful girls."

Such urchins ought to have overrun me, each eager to win a coin for bringing in me and my money. Now this one alone had the pluck. I liked that. Not that I was about to go where he hoped to take me. From my own childhood I remembered the stave that begins, "Gang warily in where wolves may lair." Still, I could use a guide. The map that had been given me showed an utter tangle of streets. It did not mark at all that stead which I had decided I had better seek first. Let the lad earn his copper from me.

"Take me to the Mithraeum," I said in Persian.

"Ah, to the house of your god, sirdar? I leap at your order, I, Herod Gamal-al-Mazda. In the Street of Ulun Begh it lies, near the Fountain of Herakles, and we shall go there swift as the wind, straight as the djinn, most glorious master. Only come!"

He tried to take my bag for me, but I didn't trust him that much and he skipped ahead, doubtless happy not to have the weight dragging at his thin shoulders. The ways that he took twisted downward. The houses that hemmed them were shut. I had a feeling that the dwellers crouched within like hares in a burrow when the fox is a-prowl. The few men we met drew aside and watched me in the same wise. I saw from their neck rings that they were slaves, and from scrawniness and whip scars that they were worth little. The good ones their owners kept indoors, sending the trash out on such fetch-and-carry tasks as could not wait for a better time.

"You lead me widely about, do you not?" I said at last.

Herod threw an eye-glint backward. "My lord is shrewd," he said. "The main thoroughfares are dangerous."

As if to bear him out, a growl and mutter reached me.

The walls and crooked lanes in between faintened it, but I knew that noise of old, and the hair stood up on my arms. It was the mouthings of a crowd adrift and angry.

Herod bobbed his head. "Many like them today."

"What has happened here?" I blurted.

"It is not for an alley rat to speak about the mighty," he said fast, and scuttled onward. Indeed so, I thought, when he did not know whose man I was. I bore a sword, and death walked under this hot heaven.

Well, but at the Mithraeum, once I had shown myself to be initiate in the Mysteries—I have reached the rank of Lion—its Father would tell me the truth. Then I could plan how best to bring Otto Gneisberg the word of his motherland. Merely fumbling to his house, I might well meet some foolish doom.

The ground canted sharply. Either the rubble that elsewhere underlay the city, yards deep, had never been piled here, or else an overlord had had it cleared away a few hundred years ago because there were things worth salvaging.

Housefronts showed workmanship of kingdoms long dead. In the basin of a dry fountain stood a statue that I reckoned was of Hercules and the Hydra, though as battered as it was, it might as well have been Thor and the Midgard Worm. Nearby crumbled a Roman temple or basilica, with columned portico and a frieze gone shapeless. The Turks in their day had made it over for their own worship, and their great-great-grandchildren still used it; through the doorless inway I saw the Warrior Buddha, sword in left hand, right hand lifted in blessing, the bronze of him turned green.

How many breeds had owned this town? The Persians of now, on whom the Ispanyans had laid wardership lest other Europeans do more than that; Edomites; Turks; Syrians; Mongols; Old Persians; Romans; Greeks—and how many before them, dust that scuffed up from my boots?

Wondering ended when Herod trilled, "Master, behold your sacred goal." I could hardly have mistaken it. Nonetheless, it was not such as my fathers knew.

Mithraists have been few hereabouts since the last West Roman legions withdrew. The Ispanyan garrison surely had its own halidoms, though those would also be strange to me. They look on our Northern godword as heretical. Asiatic Mithraisms are at odds with both, but hold that different roads may lead to the same truth. In this, if naught else, the East is wiser than the West.

The building and its sister beside it bore shapes of their land. Both stood taller than any in Europe or Markland, whitewashed, roofs swelling into domes, red on the Mithraeum, blue on the Shrine of the Good Mother. Easterners celebrate the Mysteries in windowless rooms rather than underground. Mosaics above the doors glowed with his Bull, her Rose. That much spoke straight to my heart. No matter any otherness. On a narrow and rough-stoned street, pressed between dingy blanknesses of walls, these houses reared upright as the faith itself.

But— Suddenly, spear-sharp, came back to me the halidoms of my boyhood. They stand a little outside of Ivarsthorp, on a grassy bank where the Connecticut River gleams past farmsteads, shaws, meadows marked off by stone walls and flowering hedges; they are low beneath their three-tiered roofs, but the wood of them is richly carved, and dragons rear skyward from the beam ends. Within the Mithraeum, when you have gone by lion-headed Aeon and the holy water bowl, Odin and Thor flank the altars of the Tauroctony: as I was told Frigg and Freyja honor our forebears at the Mystery of the women.

Here in Mirzabad, the land I had forsaken hunted me down, dogwood white in springtime, yeomen in summer fields that had been rock and bramble when the Trekfolk first came, the blazing hues of New Denmark fall, winter starlight that seemed to ring as it struck the snow—outings to fish and swim in Lake Winnepesaukee, days in jouncing wains and nights in old inns till we came to Merrimack Haven and saw the masts of the ships at dock lift their yards like the boughs of Yggdrasil— What unrest had driven me overseas? Why had I drifted from land to land, calling to calling, master to master, war to war, while my years spilled out of me and left only emptiness behind?

None of that, I barked at myself. There was work to do. "Wait," I told Herod. "I think I shall want you to guide me elsewhere." To Gneisberg's trading post, if I was lucky, and thence back to the western gate and away from this lair of Ahriman. I strode to the door of the Mithraeum and turned its handle.

The iron-bound timber stayed fast. It was locked.

This should not be. If naught else, a Raven or an Occult should be on watch inside, to help whatever brothers might come in need of help and to keep the holy of holies untrodden by the unhallowed. He could tell me where the Father lived, which was bound to be close by. I grasped the serpent coil of the knocker and clashed it on the plate. The noise fell hollow into the furnace day.

Herod squeaked at my back. I turned to see. The door had opened in the Shrine of the Good Mother and a woman had come forth.

She halted a few feet off. Beneath a blue gown of Persian cut, slenderness stood taut, ready to take flight. Young, she was likely of no more than Damsel rank in her Mysteries. Tresses astray from under her scarf shone obsidian black. Her face was finely molded and light-skinned, with the great gazelle eyes of the Sunrise Lands.

Persian women have never been as muffled in spirit as Hindi. Just the same, she astounded me with a straightforwardness well-nigh Frankish, if not quite Danish: "Wayfarer, you knock in vain. The Mithraeum is shut. The Father and the Courier of the Sun are both departed, and at their wish, all lower initiates have likewise sought what safety may be found."

Dismay smote me. "What, what is awry?" I stammered. "You know not?"

Numbly, I shook my head. If the thanes of Mithras must flee, then Loki was loose. "I am but now come here, my lady."

Her look searched me. "Yes, you are a foreigner; and not a Frank, but from farther away." Even then, I knew keenness when I met it, and somehow that put heart back in me. "A believer, a warrior." Fire leaped in her voice. "By the faith, I require your help!"

"What? My lady, I have a mission."

"As do I. Mine will not wait, and yours can scarcely be done at once. This is for the Light, against the Chaos. Mithras will bless you."

She offered escape from bewilderment and uselessness. Also, she was fair to behold. "What is the task, my lady?"

"The Shrine holds certain treasures," she said crisply. "I came to save them before the city explodes and the throngs go rioting, looting, burning. Wait while I fetch them out, and give me escort to the Basileum." She flashed a smile that would have been lovely were her mood not so bleak. "You'll gain a den for yourself, and thus outlive the night—we may hope."

In a whirl of cloth, she sped back. I almost followed, but stopped myself at the threshold men may not cross. "The Basileum?" I mumbled. "What is that?"

"I think the noble lady must mean the House of Sorrows, lord." Herod's voice startled me; I had forgotten him. He tugged at my cloak. "Take me along. Should my lord and lady meet danger along the way, I know many a bolthole."

"We are in a powder keg, then," I said slowly.

"And sparks dance everywhere, my lord," the boy told me. "I should be glad of a snug hiding place too, where I may heed my master's every bidding."

"Better you go home to your mother."

He shrugged. The sigh of an old man blew from the wizened small face. "She will have enough to do keeping herself alive, my lord. I have heard that when men go wild in the streets, they go mad in the joyhouses."

"What in the name of evil has befallen?"

"I am only an alley rat, master. How shall I eavesdrop on the councils of the mighty?" He drew breath. "However, the word flying about is that yesterday the *rais* was overthrown by a follower of the Prophet Khusrev who had smuggled men and arms into this city. The Ispanyans have all drawn back into their fortress, and other Europeans have taken refuge there as well. So, perhaps, have the high priests and priestesses of these twin *dewali*. Far be it from me to call them craven. It was simple prudence. But

I do not think my lord and lady could now shelter behind those gates and guns. This morning from a rooftop, I saw how armed men stand thick around every portal of the compound, and they wear the yellow sash of the Prophet."

Hard news was this. Yet the past hours had somewhat readied me for it. If only the powers, any of the powers, had foreseen! It would have been easy enough twenty years ago to send a small host into the Zagros Mountains and root Khusrev out. The Shah could have said little against it, might well have given it what feeble help was his to give. Did not this self-made Prophet cry that the Zarathushtran faith was fallen into corruption and idolatry, and that to him alone had come the saving revelation? Already then he spoke not simply of cleansing the belief and the rites, but of slaying everyone who would withstand him.

However, the Shahdom was a ghost, barely haunting the inland tribes, while the Ispanyan Wardership kept troops only in those provinces that bordered the Midworld Sea. Khusrev had seemed merely another among untold mullahs who had sprung up in the backlands lifetime after lifetime, preached, died, and blown away in dust.

Too late now, I thought, when the Puritans did as they would throughout Isfahan, Laristan, Kerman, and their flame went across Mesopotamia and down the Arabian Peninsula. In every other province of the empire, too, it was breaking loose. Fleetingly I wondered if somehow, something of it had overleaped the ocean. Was it just happenstance that half of South Markland was in uprising, and the latest news told how the Inca of Tahuantinsuyu had ended fellowship with the Ispanyan crown? Oh, the inborns yonder called on their own gods, but—

Be that as it may, Ispanya had scant strength left for this part of the world. Day by day, the garrisons thinned, the grasp weakened, and men also scorned the law of the Shah.

I stared at Mithraeum and Shrine. Even the orthodox Zarathushtrans have always looked on Mithraists as fallen halfway back into heathenism, the more so after our cult linked itself to that of the Good Mother. To the Puritans we are worse than that, worse than infidels, the very creatures of Angra Mainyu.

Thoughts of the past went from me in a cold gust as the woman came back out the door. In her arms she carried two leatherbound books and several parchment scrolls. Mottlings and crumbly edges bespoke great age. "Let us begone," she said.

"Treasure—" I gulped.

"These are the treasures." She tossed her head. "Looters may have the vessels of gold and silver if they must."

Herod bounced around us. "Will my lady go to the House of Sorrows?" he twittered. "I know the safest ways, if any be safe. Give me leave to guide you!"

The woman cast me a look. I spread my hands and half smiled. "We could have a less canny leader," I said. "I have often met his kind. Shall I carry those?"

She shook her head. "You already have a bag. Better you keep your sword hand free."

We set forth, quick-gaited. Blue shadows slithered at our heels, over the cobblestones. They had lengthened a bit. The heat had waxed. To run in it would have been berserk. As was, my tongue stirred thick and dusty: "We have no names for each other, my lady. I am Ro Esbernsson. From North Markland."

Her eyes widened. "Across the Western Sea? What brings you to this place of woe?"

"An errand. What else? Perhaps you can counsel me."

She was bold for a Persian woman, but a shyness was built into her that she must overcome before she said: "I am Boran Taki. A votary of Isis." Thus they call the Good Mother in these parts. "As I trust you are of Mithras," she finished in haste.

I nodded. "Tell me what is going on, I pray you."

She swallowed hard. "Yesterday— But let me first say that Zigad Moussavi, a nobleman in the Jordan Valley, was converted to the New Revelation of Khusrev some years ago. His agitation against the Shah and the Ispanyans who uphold the Shah became so fierce, an outright call for insurrection, that his arrest was ordered. He fled with his followers into the desert. Since then their numbers have swelled, the countryside is often in turmoil, and if you traveled here alone without trouble, Mithras himself must have been watching over you."

My sword and pistol had something to do with it, I thought. Moreover, I went forewarned, wary, using those roads and inns that von Heidenheim had told me were likeliest to be still safe. He had eyes and ears everywhere in the province. Nonetheless, he had not looked for an outbreak this soon.

Boran went on in her scholarly, step-by-step way: "He must long have conspired with persons in the city, officers of the governor among them. Yesterday we suddenly heard gunfire, shouting—we saw people flee from the markets like sheep from a lion—rumors grew ever more frightening—then toward sundown, the noise dwindled away. Presently criers went through the streets, guarded by riflemen who wore yellow sashes. We were all commanded on pain of death to remain indoors until morning. During the night there were more shots and screams. Today a vast silence has fallen. But it seethes."

I nodded again. "Clearly, this Moussavi has seized the governor's palace and quelled whatever resistance the royal troops made. Did the Ispanyans do nothing?"

"It went too fast for them, I think, when they had no unequivocal orders," she answered. Yes, I thought, she might have led a sheltered life hitherto, but it had not dulled her wits. "They seem to have drawn back into their stronghold at the Moon Tower and prepared to stand siege if necessary. I suppose the Europeans among us have taken refuge with them, as well as Persians and other Easterners who have special reason to fear the new masters. As yet there has been no attack on the compound, and perhaps there will not be. Placards have gone up in public places, directing people to continue their daily lives in orderly fashion. Of course they do not heed that."

"You have read such a proclamation, then? What does it say?"

"It declares that Zigad Moussavi, servant of Ahura-Mazda, has overthrown the corrupt and idolatrous governor of the Shah and taken command of Mirzabad in the name of the Prophet. It promises a great beginning to the work of purifying the faith and restoring the ancient glory of Persia. Foreigners shall be expelled and infidels brought to justice."

"Hm. He's far from Khusrev country. Does he imagine he can hold this single city, all by himself?"

"He is no dolt. A madman, perhaps, but not stupid. I have studied his career as it progressed. Surely he expects by his example to ignite the entire province. To that end, although he calls for public order, he does nothing to enforce it. His warriors have not replaced the police patrols they drove off. More and more people are taking to the streets. They mill to and fro, they quarrel, they listen to ranting preachers and to songs of blood. Anything at any moment may bring on the eruption. After that is over, the city will have no choice but to heed Moussavi: because if the Shah's rule comes back, so will his headsmen."

"But I thought— Are the Persians in this city not largely orthodox Zarathushtrans?" I remembered those I had met in Europe, and the few who have made their way to Markland. They keep much to themselves, but are soft-spoken, good-hearted, hard-working folk with a high respect for learning.

Her tone was stark: "They too have things to avenge."

Well, yes, I must allow. In most countries of Europe, Zarathushtrans may not own land; in some, they are made to live in wretched, crowded quarters of the towns. Also, here at home they have seen foreigners swaggering where once their kings rode under golden banners.

"True. And many will not dare sit still, whatever their inward feelings," I foretold. "They will think they also must show zeal, so that afterward the Puritans will let them get on with their lives. Moreover, the bulk of the dwellers, Aramaics and Edomites and all the rest, will snatch at this chance to take out old grudges against each other, or simply to wreck and plunder."

Her look rested awhile on me. "You know the world well, Ro Esbernsson," she said low.

"And you seem wise beyond your years," I began. That and my smile died.

Herod heard first, and halted. Half a minute later the sound reached our older ears. It grew as we stood stiff, a racking growl through which sawed screams, the sound of a man-pack unloosed.

"The Mother help us, it has begun," Boran whispered.

"They are bound this way," Herod said. He cast about as a dog does, then he beckoned and his slight form shot on down the street. We loped after.

Where a slipper painted above a doorway marked the house of a shoemaker, and it shuttered and barred, the boy darted aside. We followed, into the sudden gloom and half-coolness of an alley. Flies buzzed over the offal that made its cobbles slick. It twisted among windowless buildings, more lanes joined it, Herod took us through a maze and brought us out in a court. This too was filthily littered, though vines trailing over one of the walls around it told that the garden of somebody well-to-do lay on the other side.

Herod stopped. "I think we will be safe here for a while, if we are quiet," he said. The calm of a seasoned man had fallen over him. "Yonder is the home of Haidar Aghasi, the wine merchant. He'll be with strong, well-armed hirelings to guard his wealth. The rioters ought to know that and pass by."

"Might he take us in?" I wondered.

"No, master, he would be witless to link himself with a European, today. Would he not?" Herod replied, and I felt myself rebuked for my childishness.

Boran clutched the books to her breast. "Besides, I must bring these to my father," she said.

Well, if they meant so much that she dared go forth after them—I settled myself to wait. The grisly racket loudened.

Herod yelped, Boran gasped. I swung on my heel. The sword sprang into my hand. A man stumbled into the court.

For a moment he stood panting. We glared at each other. He was burly, red of hair and beard, freckled of snub-nosed face. His skin had once been fair, but Southern sun had made leather of it. The shirt was half ripped off him and blood oozed from three shallow wounds. He gripped a staff, long and heavy, in a way that said that to him this was a weapon. In his left hand gleamed a sheath knife.

I knew such features and shape of blade. My sword lowered. "You are from Eirinn," I murmured in Danish such as they speak in England. A Gaelic sailor would be bound to understand me.

He swallowed a few more draughts of air, grinned, and said with the lilt of his folk, "Sure and this is an unlikely place to be meeting the Lochlannach."

"Hush," Herod begged. The man and I nodded. Without need to plan it, we turned back to back, covering both sides from which attack might come.

It snarled on by. Inch by inch, we reached the knowledge that we would live a bit longer.

The man and I faced around again. He put away his knife, took staff in left hand, and held out his right. "A good day to ye, your honor," he said merrily. "Ailill mac Cerbaill I am, from Condacht through Markland, China, and points west. My greetings to the little lady. If only I could speak her tongue, I'd be paying her the compliments that luckier men certainly do."

I smiled and clasped the hand. It was thick, hard, from years of fisting canvas and winding capstans. I gave him our names and asked what brought him so far from the sea.

"Och, it's not many miles," he said.

Herod jittered about. "My lord, my lord, we should begone," he urged. "The pack—I think they will smash and loot in the Street of the Comfit Makers, who are mainly Turks, but they may not, and whatever they do, they will shortly return this way."

"Come," I agreed. A thought struck me. "Ailill, are you astray?"

"I am that," the seaman said. "The landlord at my inn sent me off this morning for an outland unbeliever, and never counted what bedbugs of his I took with me. Then as I wandered the streets, that gang swept about a corner and set upon me. I thought I heard the wings of the

Morrigan beat overhead, but Lug Long-Arm strengthened mine enough that I broke free."

For a heartbeat I envied him his gods, that to a Gael are still real beings. What are the gods of our forebears to us Mithraists, save names in the rites? Mithras himself is no longer the embodiment he once was. At that, we are better off than the Saxonians, who never had a higher religion and whose olden sacrifices are now no more than a show of loyalty to the Hauptmann.

"Join us," I offered. "We're bound for shelter, where I daresay they can use another doorkeeper."

He was glad to. Herod led us out and thence widely roundabout. Boran looked askance at the uncouth newcomer, though when I gave her my thought she said that I was right, *if* he was trustworthy.

Therefore I sounded Ailill out. It was easy. He had gotten drunk in Sicamino and missed his ship. On the beach, he learned of a venture that needed men, smuggling tobacco down from Turkey and past the Persian customs. The stuff came in at Joppa, which has a bad harbor and so is not much watched. Because unrest in the countryside had aroused banditry, inland shipments wanted guards. Ailill chose to go along with the camels headed for Mirzabad; he had heard of its time-gnawed wonders. I gathered he was not altogether a deckhand and roisterer; he had a touch of the skald in him like many among his folk. "Well, there I was, stumping down the Street of the Magi—What bit you, my friend?"

I clamped my jaw. The Bremer Handelsbund kept its warehouse, shop, quarters for the factor and his workers, on the Street of the Magi. "Was anything . . . plundered, burned . . . there?" I asked.

"It was not. I think the violence had only just begun. But those are some grand houses, and when the weasels have been at easier chicken coops and tasted blood, they will be back, I think."

I nodded. "We may have a few hours."

"Eh? . . . What might this port be that you're steering for?"

My lips bent upward. "I wish I knew."

Our course wound onward and onward, like a nightmare. Amid the squalor, I spied remnants, a fluted column, a slim spire, a wall slab that bore the worn-down carving of a winged bull with a man's head. The downslope grew ever more steep, lanes turned into flights of stairs hollowed out by uncounted footfalls, and ahead of us, above the flat roofs, I saw turrets and battlements foursquare athwart eastern hills. A few times a ragged form scuttled around a corner or into a lane. My skin crawled with the feeling of eyes that peered through slits in the shouldering walls.

"Where do you take us?" I asked Boran, forgetting that she had told me.

"To the House of Sorrows," Herod piped up.

The woman winced. "A horrible name," she said. "It is rightfully the Basileum."

The Greek word stood forth in the Persian. "And what might that mean, my lady?"

"It is the archive of archives," she answered. "There repose the chronicles, the records, the tablets and letters and . . . whatever whispers to us of the past. Such things are no longer of use to the state, but precious to what scholars remain alive."

I searched my mind. "Basileum? That which a king built? Should the word not be—m-m—no, I suppose not 'biblioteka'—'museum'?"

Her tone softened. "You are no barbarian, Ro, are you?"

"I have read books." Maybe they were what first called me outward from my homeland.

"This was founded by Julian the Second, Augustus in Byzantium, when the East Romans still held the Syriac lands. He established others where he could, though I know of none else that have endured. Rome itself had lately fallen. He foresaw a dark age. How else might the heritage of the ancients be saved, even a little?"

I shivered. That was fifteen hundred years ago, was it not?

We passed a monument. A muffled shriek from Boran tore me out of my thoughts. Two deathlings sprawled before us. They were pulp, splinters, huge splashes and pools of blood flamingly red under the sun. Flies blackened the simmering air.

I caught her elbow. "Come along," I said. She moaned once, but swallowed her sickness.

"Turks, by what's left of their clothes," Ailill muttered. "One quite young, a girl."

Their kin must have dwelt in Mirzabad since the Sultans ruled it, when white men were barely setting foot on the shores of Markland; but today they had become outlanders, unbelievers, and a gang that caught them had stamped them into the stones. After all my wanderings I should have been able to shrug off a sight like this, but it saddened me anyhow. "May their Buddha take them home," I said.

"Hurry, hurry," Herod chattered.

"You ought never to have gone forth, Boran," I told her.

"I slipped away before my father could forbid it," she answered. It did her good to speak. "The Basileum is in his care."

Since he was surely a Mithraist, I knew he had a Zarathushtran above him; but that was belike a eunuch of the governor's, who did scant more than draw large pay and pass half of it on to his lord. It was no wonder that the New Revelation was taking hold in souls from the Caspian to the Midworld Sea.

"These are genealogies and annals that the Shrine kept," she went on, holding them tightly to her. "Often has my father longed to study them. I saw his anguish when it seemed they might be lost, and—"

"Behold!" Herod crowed.

We had reached a small square, in whose faded and patched paving dolphins rollicked. Across from us lifted a building of no great size. Age had pitted and blurred it. Gracefulness lingered in the pillars of the portico, the golden rectangle and low gable of the front; the marble was the hue of wan amber beneath tiles that had gone dusky rose. As we drew nigh, I saw Greek letters above the columns, and they were clear. Lifetime by lifetime, somebody had renewed them as they wore away.

"What does that mean?" I asked, pointing.

Boran's voice was as hushed as mine: "*'Polla ta deina'* —Wonders are many, and none more wondrous than man."

We mounted the stairs and must have been seen through a slotted shutter, for the door opened before us. Him who came out in a white robe I knew by his gray-bearded handsomeness to be Boran's father. He reached his arms toward her. "Oh, my dearest," he called.

She caught her breath, stumbled forward, and blurted, "I b-brought you the books from the Shrine."

"You should not have, you should not have. I was terrified when I found you were missing. Madness runs free."

"That is why I had to go." She shook her head as if to dash the tears from her lashes.

The man looked across her to me. "Ro Esbernsson of Markland, learned sir," I named myself, "with Ailill mac Cerbaill of Eirinn and, and, Herod. We met your daughter and escorted her."

"That was nobly done of you," he said with renewed steadiness. "The Lord Mithras will remember when your souls depart for the stars. I am Jahan Taki, in charge of the Basileum now that . . . others have abandoned it. Enter, I pray you."

He stood aside. We walked through an anteroom into a broad chamber of mosaic murals. I knew Athene, foremost among the figures. Tinted glass in a clerestory softened light. Air was blessedly cool. Half a dozen men stared at us. Two were old, three young but thin and stoop-shouldered. The only one that might be worth anything in a fight was a big black African whose garb said that he did the rough work.

Boran set the books down on a table of ivory-inlaid ebony. Gold glowed in the robes of gods and philosophers on the walls. What a house to sack, I thought.

Jahan Taki might have heard that. "I am not sure how safe a refuge this is," he said. "For excuse, raveners can scream that the books are full of wicked falsehoods and should be destroyed."

"They get by me first," growled the African. He saw my startlement and gave me a harsh smile. "I work for low wages because wiseman Taki lets me read."

"And these among my colleagues and students would not flee either." The pride in Jahan faded. "We can only pray that none will come until peace has been restored."

"That may take days," I warned. "Have you food and drink on hand?"

Boran nodded. "I reminded them when we first gathered here," she said, "and the cistern already held sufficient."

"Good," I answered through the dust in my throat. "Let us have some of that water, and we'll look to your defenses."

The African hastened off. Meanwhile Jahan took me over the ground floor. The books and relics were in vaults beneath. There were two doors. I told him they should be barricaded as well as bolted. "At the front, leave a space for going in and out, but narrow enough for a single man to hold. If you have nothing better, pile up your furniture."

Jahan winced. "It will hurt like fire, but rather that than lose the books. Most have never been printed. I think many are the last copies that survive anywhere."

It struck me as strange, this love of learning for its own sake, a Greek thing I had thought died with Rome like the avowed love of men for boys. The Zarathushtrans study their holy writ but add nothing new. The rest of us give ourselves to the worldly arts. Oh, we measure the earth and the stars in their courses because that helps navigation, but to wonder about them, that is something children outgrow. We keep old books if they are useful or enjoyable, but otherwise, why should we care? In this house I felt as though I stood among ghosts. Had they a right to spook through the life of young Boran?

The African brought the water. I swished mine about in my mouth before swallowing it. The mummy dryness began to go away. "Can you make the place secure according to what master Taki has heard from me?" I asked him.

"As well as the Yazata will have it, my lord," he answered. So he was a Zarathushtran himself.

"I know a wee bit about such things too," Ailill put in. "But ye'll be foreman over us, Ro, won't ye?"

I shook my head. "No, the task had better not wait till I get back. Which I may not."

He blinked. "What? Why, sir, here we've stumbled into an anchorage as snug as any outside the Ispanyan fort—"

Boran caught our drift. Her hand fell on my arm. For an Eastern woman to do thus gave away, more than any words, how shaken she was. "Ro, you would leave us? You must not!"

"I go without joy," I told her, "but honor requires it. I am in the service of a man. As long as I take his pay, I do his bidding."

"Where do you seek, my son?" Jahan asked.

"To the Saxonian factor. I bear a message."

Sharply to me came the room overlooking Sicamino harbor where I had been given that word. Through its window I saw the schooners, barks, square-riggers, dhows, feluccas, the trade of half a world. The bay opened out to a sea that shone like quicksilver. Against the dazzle, at the edge of sight, I could just make out three tall vessels. Light struck little sparks off their guns. I knew that at their mastheads flew the falcon banner of the Hauptmann of Saxonia.

My look returned, crossed the desk, came to rest on Konrad von Heidenheim. The consul sat sweating, as so fleshy a man does in such heat. The beard spilling down his chest was wet with it. His right hand wielded a fan, his left cradled a fuming pipe. But the eyes were like chips of ice, and when he spoke it was a drumroll from the depths.

"Ro, boy, I do not myself like the job I have for you. However, need is for several couriers I can trust to bring a word from me and keep it quiet. I think you will go to Mirzabad. The Handelsbund has a good-sized post there. It is of more than economic value. It has strategic potential."

I leaned back, crossed shank over knee, and waited.

He chuckled dourly. "Ach, always you play the lynx-calm soldier of fortune. As you like. Now listen close. I have a lecture prepared.

"You think you know why Saxonia has brought ships and troops offshore. This crazy Prophet and his Puritans are tearing the interior of the Shahdom in pieces. The trouble will spread farther before it is put down, if it can be put down. Maybe it cannot. Maybe the Prophet will enter Persepolis. That will mean the Ispanyans depart. Their wardership is shaky, they have ample grief overseas, they will not protest an order from a new government for their expulsion. A wave of religious persecution will sweep through the footprints they leave.

"The Russians may then move in. The Grand Knyaz in Kiev is not willing for such a risk. Too many of his boyars are, though. If they prevail, the Russian armies may march 'to the rescue of their Turkish coreligionists,' as the mealy-mouths will say. Saxonia can ill afford such a threat to its Balkan flank. We have brought strength into the eastern Mediterranean and are marshaling troops in Greece as a warning to the Russians not to attempt this, no?"

"That's what I've been given to understand, herr," I said, not unthankful for hearing it again. It was new to me and less than clear. I was lately back from two free months in Egypt, a land so lost in mysticism that, once well up the Nile, you hear hardly a whisper from outside.

Von Heidenheim puffed smoke that stung my nostrils. "Well, you should know and keep it to yourself, matters are more dangerous still. They have intelligence reports in Hamburg that they have relayed to their agents abroad, like me. Frankland will not let the Russians take over Persia. If they try, it means war, general war, with my poor Saxonia caught between Franks to the west and Russians to the east. At the same time, Frankland has not yet mustered the strength to forestall those hot-headed boyars.

"*We* have it. Wotan with her, Saxonia can interpose herself. The Russians should feel much less eager to move, knowing they shall fight us while the Franks make ready. It is risky, yes, that is obvious; but the risks of inaction look worse. Of course, we take this action only if we must.

Perhaps things will not explode after all, and everybody can go home. But I have my doubts.

"So." He leaned forward. "This is my message to our various factors throughout the maritime provinces of the Shah. Come trouble, come the breakdown of royal authority and the Wardership, they should not flee. If at all possible—and their buildings are stout—they should hold fast and call for help. Most of them keep carrier pigeons that will make for Sicamino. I tell them that we will land troops at once and come straight to their rescue.

"Do you see? This demonstration of will and power should give even the Puritan fanatics pause. It could perhaps be the one added push that keeps the Shah from falling down. But we must have proper cause for intervention— landsmen of ours and their valuable goods to save, as is our right. Else it looks too much like collusion between us and the Franks, and may touch off the very war we hope to prevent.

"Therefore, go to Mirzabad and tell Otto Gneisberg to ready his establishment for a possible siege."

We had not known I would be too late.

Or was I?

A small voice at my elbow: "Where now would my master fare?"

I looked down. Herod had tiptoed wide-eyed through what he might well believe were the splendors of a djinni's hall. "Best you stay behind, lad. You've done well, but it's dangerous out there." I reached for my purse. "First I'd better pay you. Uh, learned Taki, may he remain?"

"Of course," Boran answered softly. "He has made himself our child." Her father nodded.

Herod straightened his thin body. "I am not a babe," he said. "Have I not led men? Master, let me prove my worth beyond doubting. Then perhaps I can be your servant always."

I thought I knew what went on in that shock head. Money, a good berth, a way out of the trap that held his mother—for him, if not for her. But the big eyes sought mine with more than reckoning behind them. I knew that hope, that he had found himself a lord to live for and die at the feet of. I never would.

It touched me more than I might have awaited. Also, I could in truth use his guidance. "If you will have it thus, Herod," I told him. "Your pay shall be three gold royals."

He sprang up and down for joy.

"Go with Mithras and Isis," Boran whispered. "Return to us. Oh, return, Ro."

I found I was unable to speak further. Instead I lifted my hand and made the sign of the Hammer. They did not ken it, but maybe they would guess that it stood for the strongest wish I could offer.

Swiftly, the boy and I left. When we were out on the square he chirped, "Where shall I take you?"

"To the house of the Saxonian traders," I said. "Do you know? They are in the Street of the Magi, where the red-haired man was set upon."

He pondered, finger to chin, laughed, and slipped off.

Thrice we heard prowling packs. He drew me into side lanes and we waited until he felt we could go on. Again he brought me widely around; but belike I would not have arrived without him.

Above the massive door of a building that was a stronghold, its few outside windows iron-shuttered, hung a sign, as signs hang in Western lands. It showed an olden galley sailing on the red-black-red of Bremen. I knocked and shouted. The noise rattled between neighboring walls. "None here," I mumbled at last.

"They went to the Ispanyans," Herod guessed.

"So must we."

"My lord, I told you I have seen the men in yellow sashes outside that place. They will not let us through. Else everyone they mean to kill would flock there."

"Go back to . . . the House of Sorrows."

"Lord!" He sounded downright angry. "I am your servant."

I smiled a little. "Well, lead me as you did before."

We snaked our way onward, though only once needed we go to earth. We were getting back to the upper town, which the rebels must have under some control. Trudging down the sky, the sun had begun to glare in my eyes. I saw vultures wheeling aloft.

The garrison besat a steading much like the one in Sicamino, though smaller. From the city wall, where a tower reared, jutted three of brick. The compound within held barracks, officers' quarters, arsenal, whatever else the peacekeeping force needed—and, now, fugitives crammed together. A broad open space ringed the defenses. From its far side I saw the three gates shut. Watchmen stood tautly on the parapet. Below them squatted warriors posted by Moussavi. Those were mostly Edomites, in threadbare djellabas and burnooses; but yellow was around every waist and a firearm at every shoulder. Townsfolk who felt themselves safe and, I supposed, were glad the Puritans had come, milled and babbled before them.

"Wait here," I told Herod, and strode forward. It would not help me to have such a ragamuffin in tow. I looked neither right nor left, walking as if I were the conqueror. Men scowled, snarled, spat, but habit was strong in them. They gave way, a roiling bow wave that closed in a wake of curses and shaken fists. My sweat reeked. I would not let myself think how easily a knife could slide between my ribs.

"Hold!" cried a man who seemed in charge on the east side. "None may pass."

I halted and gave him my haughtiest stare. "May none come out?" I asked. "This will surely be of interest to him who gave you your orders."

Uneasy, he tugged his greasy beard. "We are here . . . to keep the law of the Prophet," he growled. "What do you want, Westman?"

"To convey a message of the greatest moment, desert runner," I snapped. "If I may not pass through, you shall let someone out to hear me. Else I will report this, and after that your camel will know you no more."

Before he could think, I filled my lungs and shouted in Ispanyan. The sentries above leaned over the battlements. For a moment I was unsure whether I would live. A real soldier would at the least have had me seized. But these were simple peasants and nomads, unused to chains of command. I won my bet. The headman let me finish, he waved back followers who sidled near with rifles cocked, he even bade them hold off the crowd that pressed close and threatened me.

Nonetheless, that became a long wait in the heat and the reaching shadows.

It wasn't really. They were able men inside, who knew they must act at once. Otherwise the folk might get out of hand, or a true officer of the Puritans happen by. The doors creaked ajar. A lean, dark-haired man in blue tunic, white breeks, and headcloth marched forth. He looked about and went to me.

"Speak so I can understand you," said the Edomite.

"This is not for the likes of you to hear," I told him. He flushed. I looked into the hatchet face of the Ispanyan and said in his tongue: "Quickly, do you know if the Saxonian Otto Gneisberg and his household are with you?"

"They are," he answered. "What do you want? We stand on a volcano."

"I have a word of hope, mestro." I gave him my name.

"Reccaredo de Liria," he gave back, "hiltman in His Gothic Overlordship's Valencian Grenadiers."

I told him what von Heidenheim had told me. He gnawed his lip. "The Saxonians, the pagan Saxonians—"

"They are Europeans too," I said.

His pride snatched at that. "By the Bull, good enough in these miserable times! What would you have me do?"

"Tell Gneisberg. We must move fast. If we have everything ready before Zigad Moussavi hears of it, we can hope he will overlook the matter, set it aside, because he will not know what it means and he has his hands full already. But if first he gets any hint— They have an art in Persia of flaying a man alive and showing him his stuffed skin before he may die, do they not?"

"They will buy mine dearly," de Liria snorted. "Very well, I will go straight to Gneisberg." Luck had been with me. Many a young officer would first have sought the garrison commander. We had no time for that. I should think the *chefe del hirdo* would later be happy to learn that a few refugees had gone out from under his ward.

If they did.

De Liria flipped me a Roman salute and went back. The gate shut. "He is to bring forth certain men who have need to return to their home," I told the Edomite overling.

He glowered. "What plot is this?"

"None. How can an unarmed spoonful menace the triumph of the New Revelation? If anything, they become hostages to it. This is a simple business of perishable goods that have just arrived and require care. You have already shown that you may let people leave the compound."

"Ey-yah, what you Westmen will do for money!" he fleered.

I shrugged. "The lord Zigad Moussavi is a man of wisdom. He will wish to keep their goodwill, when it costs him nothing, and take taxes from them afterward."

I waited. These warriors were ignorant of much, and their heads were afire with their faith, but they were not stupid. Give them time, only a short time, and they would begin to wonder. Then I would be done. I tried to dwell on things far away, ice skating in New Denmark, a girl in London, a moonlit night off the Azores; and I waited.

After some part of endlessness—but the sun was still above the tower—the gate opened anew. A man came out beside de Liria. Though he was short and bald, he walked briskly. Behind them were another half-score, both European and inborn, who must belong to the trader's staff. My heart knocked.

They stopped before me. "I am Otto Gneisberg," said the short man in Saxonian.

"Mithras, could I go with you!" de Liria breathed.

"Hold fast where you are," Gneisberg said. "That will be your service."

Our band thrust into the crowd. It yielded surlily. "You're doing well to heed me, herr," I said.

Gneisberg's smile was wry. "Hiltman de Liria said something about preserving civilization. But we have left wives and children with him. If the compound comes under attack, it cannot hold out more than a few days."

"Do you think your post can do as well?"

"No. A while, though, yes, a while. We have firearms and provisions in the cellar, a cistern on the roof. I understand why it is critical that we be in possession of the place."

Herod tagged after us. We walked unhindered to the Street of the Magi.

Beneath the sign of the Handelsbund, Gneisberg unclipped a key from his belt. "I will now send a pigeon with this news, and the Saxonians offshore will make ready," he said. "If we are then bestormed, and I think we shall soon be, I will send the next message, and a relief expedition is justified under the Law of Kings, that the Russians honor too. It will put down these rebels, which should dampen insurrection elsewhere in the province."

For a time, I thought.

"You will join us?" he asked. "You have done well. If I live, I will see to it that you get a commendation."

I forebore to say I would rather have a cash reward. "No, I must be off."

He raised his brows. "What? This is not the most secure spot in the world, I grant you, but surely your chances are better here than anywhere else outside the compound, and your presence will improve them. Or are you leaving Mirzabad?"

"Not yet. I have unfinished work."

"The gods be with you," he sighed. "Or, in my philosophy, may you gain by the principles of righteousness."

"Mithras be with us both," I said, and left. Herod trotted at my side.

"Do we go back to the House of Sorrows?" he asked.

"We do," I answered, "and there we stay till the danger is past."

"Oh, good, good!" he warbled. "It is misnamed. I never knew how wonderful it is inside."

The real wonders you do not know about, I thought. I hardly do, myself. Maybe we can learn something together.

This time he took me by the straightest way, as nearly as I could tell from the westering sun. Alike his ears and whatever inward senses his life had whetted must be saying that rage had rolled elsewhere. Or had calm already begun to fall throughout the city? Hope flickered in my breast.

It died when he stopped, lifted a bird-frail hand, strained forward. After a moment he stared back at me. "Lord, I fear bad men are at the House," he whispered.

Otherwise I heard only the seething in my ears. Drawing breath, I told him, "Bring me there unbeknownst."

"It is deadly," he said. "What oath have you given them?"

None. If anything, my duty was to keep myself hale for whatever von Heidenheim wanted next. Yet something in me without a name refused me the right to sheer off. At least I must see if there was any way of helping. "I am a man," was all I could think of to say.

Herod squared his shoulders. "And I am the man of my man," he said, red in the cheeks, so gravely that I almost laughed.

As fast as would keep stillness, we ran. Soon the noise reached me, yelp, clatter, thud. By houses we had passed earlier, I knew it came indeed from the Basileum. At the end, Herod took me into an alley and pointed upward. The building alongside was low; the grate over a window gave a hold for fingers and toes. I boosted him to the flat roof and scrambled after. On our bellies we glided to the other side and peered across the dolphin paving.

I counted nine men on the stairs. They seemed inborn here. The rags and the dirt could have been anybody's, but they yelled in Aramaic—street scourers, day laborers, stunted and snag-toothed. However, their thews were tough; they carried knives, clubs, an ax; once they got inside, Ailill and the African could slay two or three at most before going under. Then Jahan, his scholars, his daughter were booty. The gang had gotten a balk of timber. Again and again they rammed it against the door. Bronze groaned. Hinges began to give way.

"Too many, lord," Herod breathed in my ear.

"We shall see," I murmured back. "Surprise and a good blade have much to do with fate. Wait here, small one. If I fall, remember me."

I crouched and sprang. As I fell, it flashed through me that I had not given him his pay.

I landed loose-kneed on stone, drew sword while I sped forward, wrapped end of cloak about left forearm. The robbers were lost in their work, sweating, slavering, a-howl with glee. I bounded up the stairs.

The heart is a fool's target, hard to find and fenced by the bones. My point went into the nearest scrawny back. I twisted to gash the liver, pulled my steel loose, and got the next man in the neck. Blood geysered, dazzling red. He rolled down the steps to lie crumpled.

"Out, out!" I roared in Danish. "Give me a hand, you scuts!"

The seven who were left let go the beam and whirled around. I caught a thrust on my basket hilt and slashed downward. There is a big artery in the thigh. The six yammered around me. I stopped a stab with the padding on my left arm.

The door swung wide. Ailill's staff whirred and crashed. In skilled hands, that is a fearsome weapon. I heard him sing as he fought, a song of wild and keening mirth. The African had found a mace among relics of old, proud days. I saw a skull splinter beneath it.

The axman came at me. He knew his trade. I withdrew before the battering weight. It could tear the sword out of my grip. Down the stairs we went. My friends had enough else to do.

A little form darted from nowhere. Catlike, Herod swarmed up the axman's back and clawed at his eyes. He shrilled and spat. The axman reached around, pulled him off, dashed him to the ground. Meanwhile I had the opening I needed. I stepped in and freed my foe's guts.

Two of the gang were still on their feet. They fled. "After them!" I bawled. "Let them not get away!"

I overtook the closest and hewed. Ailill and the African crushed the other.

They came panting to me. "Make sure of them all," I said. Ailill's knife slid forth. Soon the disabled stopped screaming.

I went back to Herod. The axman had fallen across

him. I dragged the carcass off and knelt to see. In the pinched face, mouth gaped and eyes stared blind. The limbs were dry sticks. I lifted his head. He had landed on the back of it, hard. I lowered it again and rose.

Ailill and the African sought me anew. "Let's haul these corpses away," I ordered. My look went to the portico. Jahan and his folk clustered on it. They seemed well-nigh as drained of blood. "You," I called to the scholars. "Fetch mops and water. Scrub these stones as best you can. Take that timber inside. Be quick."

Nobody stirred. "Ahriman in hell," I snarled, "we've need to hide that anybody ever was here. Else we'll soon have others, more than we can handle."

Boran trod forward. "We heed you," she said softly. To the scholars: "Come."

It is folklore that a man is heavier dead than alive, but he does feel thus, and we three were wearied, shaken. Remembering how Herod had led me, I found an alley off a side street about a quarter mile away, narrow and already choked with rubbish. We ferried ours to it. Surely eyes watched from behind walls, but those that saw this end of our trip did not see the other. Nobody showed himself, nor questioned us from within. I had counted on that. The main wish of most folk is to be left in peace. They seldom get it. Witnesses would do and say naught. If these wretches we'd rid ourselves of had kin or friends, it was unlikely that those knew what had happened or where. Only a second mischance would bring the Basileum again under attack.

By the time we were done, the sun was behind westward walls. Streets brimmed with shadow. Jahan met us on the stairs. In the dimming light he looked ill, and his voice came faint. "We have washed the stones, as you see. I pray you, go not straightway inside. Go to the back door and down into the storage room. We have brought soap, water, fresh garb. Cleanse yourselves."

"Of course, venerable one," said the African.

Jahan's words stumbled onward. "We are grateful to you beyond measure. Never think us otherwise. But it is not fitting to track blood over these floors."

"Sure and it's glad I'll be to get the stickiness off," laughed Ailill when I had explained.

Jahan shivered. "How can he be merry after... what was done?"

"It is nothing uncommon, you know," I answered.

Bewilderment crossed his face. "But this has been horrible."

"Few lives are like yours. Today you have glimpsed the world as it is."

For another heartbeat I stood still, while the dusk rose around us beneath a sky turning green in the west, violet-blue in the east. "Before I myself wash, I have one more thing to do," I said. "Where is the nearest Fire Temple?"

Jahan gave me directions. It wasn't far. The scholars had laid Herod Gamal-al-Mazda on the portico, folded his hands and closed his eyes. When I picked his light form up, it felt colder than it really was. Nonetheless I held it close to my breast as I walked.

The Zarathushtran priest was aghast at sight of me and my burden, but stood his ground like a man. I smiled through the dusk. "Be at ease," I said. "This is a believer whom I bring home to you. Give him the rites and take him to your Tower of Silence."

To make sure of that, I handed over the three gold royals I had promised. Then I returned to the Basileum.

Thereafter we abided in our lair. Every day we heard a few shots. Thrice, somebody close by screamed. But none beat on our doors, and we dwelt day and night, day and night, as if outside of creation.

"Why do they call this the House of Sorrows?" I asked Boran.

She winced and frowned. "The commoners are superstitious," she said, and went on to speak of something else.

Later I talked with the African. Rustum Tata, his name was. Like me, he had come from afar to Mirzabad, knowing little, soon enthralled by the witchcraft that lay in the books. In some ways he was a better guide to them than Boran. She knew so much, her mind was so swift, that I was apt to find myself groping for what she meant. Thus she and I became likeliest to talk of homely things when we were together, our own lives and dreams.

"Why do they call this the House of Sorrows?" I asked Rustum.

He shrugged. "It holds whatever chronicles and relics of the city are left after more than three thousand years," he said. "That gives time for much weeping."

Me, I took happiness out of the vaults. Suddenly around me, speaking, loving, hating, striving, not dead but merely sundered from me in time, were the builders, the dwellers, the conquerors, Persians, Turks, Mongols, Romans, Greeks, Phoenicians, Babylonians, Assyrians, Peleshtim, Egyptians, endlessly manyfold. In their sagas I could lose myself, forget that I was trapped and waiting for whatever doom happened to be mine.

Oh, yes, it was beyond me to read what stood on the crumbling paper, parchment, papyrus, clay. The scholars misliked my even touching them with my awkward fingers. But they would unfold a text for me, and put it into words I kenned, and we would talk about it for hours, down in those dim cool caves. The lesser men are now wan in my mind. I remember bluff Rustum, wise Jahan, Boran the lovely.

What I learned is mostly lost too, flotsam in my head. How shall a wanderer carry with him the dynasties of the Shahs, the Khans, the Caesars, or the Pharaohs? Here a face peers from the wreckage, there a torch glimmers in the distance, a word echoes whose meaning I have forgotten, ghost armies march to music long stilled. It was with a wry understanding of each other that Boran and I said farewell.

One voice is clear. That may seem odd, for belike it mattered the least of all. But it lingers because it was the last that came to me.

Jahan had been my guide through time that day. We were down in the deepest crypt where the oldest fragments rested. A lantern on a table cast a light soon eaten by the shadows around. The air was cold, quiet, with a smell of dust.

Under our gaze was a Babylonian tablet. Beside it lay a sheet of papyrus that must have been torn off a scroll. The inked letters were well-nigh too faded to read, but they looked like far kin to Edomite or Arabian. I pointed and asked idly, "What is that?"

"Eh?" said Jahan. He bent over the case and squinted. "Oh . . . oh, this. I have not thought about it for years. A fragment of an ancient lament."

"What does it mourn?"

"That is unclear. For see you, the language is long extinct. A predecessor of mine puzzled out a partial translation, by comparing related words in languages that he could read. Um-m." Jahan stroked his beard. His tone quickened. "I studied it once. Let me try whether I can still decipher it."

He opened the case and carefully, carefully took the papyrus out. For a while he held it close to the lantern. His lips moved. Then, straightening, he said:

"It is by a man of an obscure people who held this city and hinterland for a while in the remote past. Sennacherib of Assyria captured it and dispersed them through his empire. The many races within it blotted theirs up. A similar fate had already befallen a sister kingdom of theirs. This poet was, I believe, an aged survivor, looking backward and bewailing what had come to pass."

He peered again at the sheet and word by slow word rendered into Persian, not the everyday tongue but the stately speech of old:

"Jerusalem hath grievously sinned; therefore she is removed. . . . for she hath seen that the heathen entered into her sanctuary. . . . For these things I weep; mine eye, mine eye runneth down with water, because the comforter that should relieve my soul is far from me: my children are desolate, because the enemy prevailed."

He glanced at me. "I skip over lines that are illegible or that I cannot well make out," he explained.

"Was Jerusalem the name they gave this city?" I asked. He nodded. "They appear to have been a peculiar people, always questioning things, even their gods, always driven toward a perfection they should have known is impossible. Certainly they had some ideas unique to them." He read onward:

"Thou, O Lord, remainest for ever; thy throne from generation to generation. Wherefore dost thou forsake us for ever, and forsake us so long time? Turn thou us unto thee, O Lord, and we shall be turned; renew our days as of old.

"But thou hast utterly rejected us—"

Boran's shout flew down the stairs. Jahan put the dead man's cry back in the case before he followed me. By then I was on the ground floor. Through the walls I heard the rumble and crash of the Saxonian cannon.

Remaking History

KIM STANLEY ROBINSON

The point is *not* to make an exact replica of the Teheran embassy compound." Exasperated, Ivan Venutshenko grabbed his hair in one hand and pulled up, which gave him a faintly Oriental look. "It's the *spirit* of the place that we want to invoke here."

"This has the spirit of our storage warehouse, if you ask me."

"This *is* our storage warehouse, John. We make all our movies here."

"But I thought you said we were going to correct all the lies of the first movie," John Rand said to their director. "I thought you said *Escape From Teheran* was a dumb TV docu-drama, only worth remembering because of De Niro's performance as Colonel Jackson. We're going to get the true story on film at last, you said."

Ivan sighed. "That's right, John. Admirable memory. But what you must understand is that when making a film, *true* doesn't mean an absolute fidelity to the real."

"I'll bet that's just what the director of the docu-drama said."

Ivan hissed, which he did often while directing their films, to show that he was letting off steam, and avoiding an explosion. "Don't be obstructionist, John. We're not doing anything like that hackwork, and you know it. Lunar gravity alone makes it impossible for us to make a completely realist film. We are working in a world of dream, in a surrealist intensification of what really happened. Besides, we're doing these movies for our own entertainment up here! Remake bad historical films! Have a good time!"

"Sure, Ivan. Sure. Except the ones *you've* directed

have been getting some great reviews downside. They're saying you're the new Eisenstein and these little remakes are the best thing to hit the screen since *Kane*. So now the pressure is on and it's not just a game anymore, right?"

"Wrong!" Ivan karate-chopped the air. "I refuse to believe that. When we stop having fun doing this"—nearly shouting—"I quit!"

"Sure, Sergei."

"Don't call me that!"

"Okay, Orson."

"JOHN!"

"But that's *my* name. If I call you that we'll all get confused."

Melina Gourtsianis, their female lead, came to Ivan's rescue. "Come on, John, you'll give him a heart attack, and besides it's late. Let's get on with it."

Ivan calmed down, ran his hands through his hair. He loved doing his maddened director routine, and John loved maddening him. As they disagreed about nearly everything, they made a perfect team. "Fine," Ivan said. "Okay. We've got the set ready, and it may not be an *exact* replica of the compound—" fierce glare at John—"but it's good enough.

"Now, let's go through it one more time. It's night in Teheran. This whole quarter of the city has been gassed with a paralyzing nerve gas, but there's no way of telling when the Revolutionary Guards might come barreling in from somewhere else with gas masks or whatever, and you can't be sure some of them haven't been protected from the gas in sealed rooms. Any moment they might jump out firing. Your helicopters are hovering just overhead, so it's tremendously noisy. There's a blackout in the compound, but searchlights from other parts of the city are beginning to pin the choppers. They've been breaking like cheap toys all the way in, so now there are only five left, and you have no assurances that they will continue to work, especially since twice that number have already broken. You're all wearing gas masks and moving through the rooms of the compound, trying to find and move all fifty-three of the hostages—it's dark and most of the hostages are knocked out like the guards, but some of the rooms were well-sealed, and naturally these hostages are shouting for help. For a while—and this is the effect I want to emphasize more than any other—for a while, things inside are absolutely chaotic. No one can find Colonel Jackson, no one knows how many of the hostages are recovered and how many are still in the embassy, it's dark, it's noisy, there are shots in the distance. I want an effect like the scene at the end of *The Lady From Shanghai*, when they're in the carnival's house of mirrors shooting at each other. Multiplied by ten. Total chaos."

"Now hold on just a second here," John said, exaggerating his Texas accent, which came and went according to his convenience. "I like the chaos bit, and the allusion to Welles, but let's get back to this issue of the facts. Colonel Jackson was the hero of this whole thing! He was the one that decided to go on with all them helicopters busting out in the desert, and he was the one that found Annette Bellows in the embassy to lead them around, and all in all he was on top of every minute of it. That's why they gave him all them medals!"

Ivan glared. "What part are you playing, John?"

"Why, Colonel Jackson." John drew himself up. "Natch."

"However." Ivan tapped the side of his head, to indicate thought. "You don't just want to do a bad imitation of the De Niro performance, do you? You want to do a new interpretation, don't you? Besides, it seems to me a foolish idea to try an imitation of De Niro."

"I like the idea, myself," John said. "Show him how."

Ivan waved him away. "You got all you know about this affair from that stupid TV movie, just like everyone else. I, however, have been reading the accounts of the hostages and the Marines on those helicopters, and the truth is that Colonel Jackson's best moment was out there in the desert, when he decided to go on with the mission even though only five helicopters were still functioning. That was his peak of glory, his moment of heroism. And you did a perfectly adequate job of conveying that when we filmed the scene. We could see every little gear in there, grinding away." He tapped his skull.

"De Niro would have been proud," Melina said.

John pursed his lips and nodded. "We need great men like that. Without them history would be dead. It'd be nothing but a bunch of broken-down helicopters out in a desert somewhere."

"A trenchant image of history," Ivan said. "Too bad Shelley got to it first. Meanwhile, the truth is that after making the decision to go on with the raid, Colonel Jackson appeared, in the words of his subordinates, somewhat stunned. When they landed on the embassy roof he led the first unit in, and when they got lost inside, the whole force was effectively without leadership for most of the crucial first half-hour. All the accounts of this period describe it as the utmost chaos, saved only when Sergeant Payton—*not* Colonel Jackson; the TV movie lied about that—when Payton found Ms. Bellows, and she led them to all the hostage rooms they hadn't found."

"All right, all right." John frowned. "So I'm supposed to be kind of spaced out in this scene."

"Don't go for too deep an analysis, John, you might strain something. But essentially you have it. Having committed the force to the raid, even though you're vastly undermanned because of the damned helicopters breaking down, you're a bit frozen by the risk of it. Got that?"

"Yeah. But I don't believe it. Jackson was a hero."

"Fine, a hero, lots of medals. Roomfuls of medals. If he pinned them on he'd look like the bride after the dollar dance. He'd collapse under their weight. But now let's try showing what really happened."

"All right." John drew himself up. "I'm ready."

The shooting of the scene was the part they all enjoyed the most; this was the heart of the activity, the reason they kept making movies to occupy their free hours at Luna Three. Ivan and John and Melina and Pierre-Paul, the theoreticians who traded directing chores from project to project, always blocked the scenes very loosely, allowing a lot of room for improvisation. Thus scenes like this one, which were supposed to be chaotic, were played out with a manic gusto. They were good at chaos.

And so for nearly a half-hour they rushed about the interior of their Teheran embassy compound—the base storage warehouse, with its immense rows of boxes arranged behind white panels of plywood to resemble the compound's buildings and their interiors. Their shouts were nearly drowned by the clatter of recorded helicopters, while intermittent lights flashed in the darkness. Cut-outs representing the helicopters were pasted to the clear dome overhead, silhouetted against the unearthly brilliance of the stars—these last had become a trademark of Luna Three Productions, as their frequent night scenes always had these unbelievably bright stars overhead, part of the films' dreamlike effect.

The actors playing Marines bounded about the compound in their gas masks, looking like aliens descended to ravage a planet; the actors playing hostages and Revolutionary Guards lay scattered on the floor, except for a few in protected rooms, who fought or cried for help. John and Pierre-Paul and the rest hunted the compound for Melina, playing Annette Bellows. For a while it looked as if John would get to her first, thus repeating the falsehood of the De Niro film. But eventually Pierre-Paul, playing Sergeant Payton, located her room, and he and his small unit rushed about after the clear-headed Bellows, who, as she wrote later, had spent most of her months in captivity planning what she should do if this moment ever came. They located the remaining comatose hostages and lugged them quickly to the plywood helicopter on the compound roof. The sound of shots punctuated the helicopters' roar. They leaped through the helicopter's door, shafts of white light stabbed the air like Islamic swords.

That was it; the flight away would be filmed in their little helicopter interior. Ivan turned off the helicopter noise, shouted "Cut!" into a megaphone. Then he shut down all the strategically placed minicams, which had been recording every minute of it.

"What bothers me about your movies, Ivan," John said, "is that you always take away the hero. Always!"

They were standing in the shallow end of the base

pool, cooling off while they watched the day's rushes on a
screen filling one wall of the natatorium. Many of the
screens showed much the same result: darkness, flickering
light, alien shapes moving in the elongated dancelike way
that audiences on Earth found so surreal, so mesmerizing.
There was little indication of the pulsing rhythms and
wrenching suspense that Ivan's editing would create from
this material. But the actors were happy, seeing arresting
images of desperation, of risk, of heroism in the face of a
numbingly loud confusion.

Ivan was not as pleased. "Shit!" he said. "We're going
to have to do it again."

"Looks okay to me," John remarked. "Son of Film
Noir Returns From the Grave. But really, Ivan, you've
got to do something about this prejudice against heroes. I
saw *Escape From Teheran* when I was a kid, and it was an
inspiration to me. It was one of the big reasons I got into
engineering."

Pierre-Paul objected. "John, just how did seeing a
commando film get you interested in engineering?"

"Well," John replied, frowning, "I thought I'd design
a better helicopter, I guess." He ignored his friends'
laughter. "I was pretty shocked at how unreliable they
were. But the way old De Niro continued on to Teheran!
The way he extricated all the hostages and got them back
safely, even with the choppers dropping like flies. It was
great! We need heroes, and history tells the story of the
few people who had what it takes to be one. But you're
always downplaying them."

"The Great Man Theory of history," Pierre-Paul said
scornfully.

"Sure!" John admitted. "Great Woman too, of course,"
nodding quickly at the frowning Melina. "It's the great
leaders who make the difference. They're special people,
and there aren't many of them. But if you believe Ivan's
films, there aren't any at all."

With a snort of disgust, Ivan took his attention from
the rushes. "Hell, we are going to have to do that scene
again. As for my theory of history, John, you both have it
and you don't. As far as I understand you." He cocked his

head and looked at his friend attentively. On the set they both played their parts to the teeth: Ivan the tormented, temperamental director, gnashing his teeth and ordering people about; John the stubborn, temperamental star, questioning everything and insisting on his preeminence. Mostly this was role-playing, part of the game, part of what made their hobby entertaining to them. Off the set the roles largely disappeared, except to make a point, or have some fun. Ivan was the base's head of computer operations, while John was an engineer involved in the Mars voyage; they were good friends, and their arguments had done much to shape Ivan's ideas for his revisionist historical films, which were certainly the ones from their little troupe making the biggest splash downside—though John claimed this was because of the suspenseful plots and the weird low-gee imagery, not because of what they were saying about history. "*Do* I understand you?" Ivan asked curiously.

"Well," John said, "take the one you did last time, about the woman who saved John Lennon's life. Now that was a perfect example of heroic action, as the 1982 docudrama made clear. There she was, standing right next to a man who had pulled out a damn big gun, and quicker than he could pull the trigger she put a foot in his crotch and a fist in his ear. But in your remake, all we concentrated on was how she had just started the karate class that taught her the moves, and how her husband encouraged her to take the class, and how that cabbie stopped for her even though she was going the other direction, and how that other cabbie told her that Lennon had just walked into his apartment lobby, and all that. You made it seem like it was just a coincidence!"

Ivan took a mouthful of pool water and spurted it at the spangled dome, looking like a fountain statue. "It took a lot of coincidences to get Margaret Arvis into the Dakota lobby at the right time," he told John. "But some of them weren't coincidences—they were little acts of generosity or kindness or consideration, that put her where she could do what she did. I didn't take the heroism away. I just spread it around to all the places it belonged."

John grimaced, drew himself up into his star persona. "I suppose this is some damn Commie notion of mass social movements, sweeping history along in a consensus direction."

"No, no," Ivan said. "I always concentrate on individuals. What I'm saying is that all our individual actions add up to history, to the big visible acts of our so-called 'leaders.' You know what I mean; you hear people saying all the time that things are better now because John Lennon was such a moral force, traveling everywhere, Nobel Peace Prize, secular pope, the conscience of the world or whatnot."

"Well, he *was* the conscience of the world!"

"Sure, sure, he wrote great songs. And he got a lot of antagonists to talk. But without Margaret Arvis he would have been killed at age forty. And without Margaret Arvis's husband, and her karate instructor, and a couple cabbies in New York, and so on, she wouldn't have been there to save his life. So we all become part of it, see? The people who say it was all because of Lennon, or Carter, or Gorbachev—they're putting on a few people what we *all* did."

John shook his head, scattering water everywhere. "Very sophisticated, I'm sure! But in fact it was precisely Lennon and Carter and Gorbachev who made huge differences, all by themselves. Carter started the big swing toward human rights. Palestine, the new Latin America, the American Indian nations—none of those would have existed without him."

"In fact," Melina added, glancing mischievously at Pierre-Paul, "if I understand the Margaret Arvis movie correctly, if she hadn't been going to see Carter thank his New York campaign workers for the 1980 victory, she wouldn't have been in the neighborhood of the Dakota, and so she wouldn't have had the chance to save Lennon's life."

John rose up like a whale breaching. "So it's Carter we have to thank for that, too! As for Gorbachev, well, I don't have to tell you what all he did. That was a hundred-eighty degree turnaround for you Russkies, and no one can say it would have happened without him."

"Well—he was an important leader, I agree."

"Sure was! And Carter was just as crucial. Their years were the turning point, when the world started to crawl out from under the shadow of World War Two. And that was their doing. There just aren't many people who could've done it. Most of us don't have it in us."

Ivan shook his head. "Carter wouldn't have been able to do what he did unless Colonel Ernest Jackson had saved the rescue mission to Teheran, by deciding to go on."

"So Jackson is a hero too!"

"But then Jackson wouldn't have been a hero if the officer back in the Pentagon hadn't decided at the last minute to send sixteen helicopters instead of eight."

"And," Melina pointed out quickly, "if Annette Bellows hadn't spent most of a year daydreaming about what she would do in a rescue attempt, so that she knew blindfolded where every other hostage was being kept. They would have left about half the hostages behind without her, and Carter wouldn't have looked so good."

"Plus they needed Sergeant Payton to find Bellows," Ivan added.

"Well shit!" John yelled defensively, which was his retort in any tight spot. He changed tack. "I ain't so sure that Carter's reelection hinged on those hostages anyway. He was running against a flake, I can't remember the guy's name, but he was some kind of idiot."

"So?" Melina said. "Since when has that made any difference?"

With a roar John dove at her, making a big splash. She was much faster than he was, however, and she evaded him easily as he chased her around the pool; it looked like a whale chasing a dolphin. He was reduced to splashing at her from a distance, and the debate quickly degenerated into a big splash fight, as it often did.

"Oh well," John declared, giving up the attack and floating in the shallow end. "I love watching Melina swim the butterfly. In this gravity it becomes a godlike act. Those muscular arms, that sinuous dolphin motion . . ."

Pierre-Paul snorted. "You just like the way the butter-fly puts her bottom above water so often."

"No way! Women are just more hydrodynamic than men, don't you think?"

"Not the way you like them."

"Godlike. Gods and goddesses."

"You look a bit godlike yourself," Melina told him. "Bacchus, for instance."

"Hey." John waved her off, jabbed a finger at the screens. "I note that all this mucho sophisticated European theorizing has been sunk. Took a bit of Texas logic, is all."

"Only Texas logic could do it," Pierre-Paul said.

"Right. You admit my point. In the end it's the great leaders who have to act, the rare ones, no matter if we ordinary folks help them into power."

"When you revise your proposition like that," Ivan said, "you turn it into mine. Leaders are important, but they are leaders because we made them leaders. They are a collective phenomenon. They are expressions of us."

"Now wait just a minute! You're going over the line again! You're talking like heroic leaders are a dime a dozen, but if that were true it wouldn't matter if Carter had lost in 1980, or if Lennon had been killed by that guy. But look at history, man! Look what happened when we did lose great leaders! Lincoln was shot; did they come up with another leader comparable to him? No way! Same with Gandhi, and the Kennedys, and King, and Sadat, and Olof Palme. When those folks were killed their countries suffered the lack of them, because they were special."

"They *were* special," Ivan agreed, "and obviously it was a bad thing they were killed. And no doubt there was a short-term change for the worse. But they're not irreplaceable, because they're human beings just like us. None of them, except maybe Lincoln or Gandhi, was any kind of genius or saint. It's only afterward we think of them that way, because we want heroes so much. But we're the heroes. All of us put them in place. And there are a lot of capable, brilliant people out there to replace the loss of them, so that in the long run we recover."

"The *real* long run," John said darkly. "A hundred years or more, for the South without Lincoln. They just aren't that common. The long run proves it."

"Speaking of the long run," Pierre-Paul said, "is anyone getting hungry?"

They all were. The rushes were over, and Ivan had dismissed them as unusable. They climbed out of the pool and walked toward the changing room, discussing restaurants. There were a considerable number of them in the station, and new ones were opening every week. "I just tried the new Hungarian restaurant," Melina said. "The food was good, but we had trouble, when the meal was over, finding someone to give us the check!"

"I thought you said it was a Hungarian restaurant," John said.

They threw him back in the pool.

The second time they ran through the rescue scene in the compound, Ivan had repositioned most of the minicams, and many of the lights; his instructions to the actors remained the same. But once inside the hallways of the set, John Rand couldn't help hurrying in the general direction of Annette Bellows's room.

All right, he thought. Maybe Colonel Jackson had been a bit hasty to rush into the compound in search of hostages, leaving the group without a commander. But his heart had been in the right place, and the truth was, he had found a lot of the hostages without any help from Bellows at all. It was easy; they were scattered in ones and twos on the floor of almost every room he and his commandos entered, and stretched out along with the guards in the rooms and in the halls, paralyzed by the nerve gas. Damn good idea, that nerve gas. Guards and hostages, tough parts to play, no doubt, as they were getting kicked pretty frequently by commandos running by. He hustled his crew into room after room, then sent them off with hostages draped over their shoulders, pretending to stagger down the halls, banging into walls—*really* tough part to play, hostage—and clutching at gas masks and such; great images for the minicams, no doubt about it.

When all his commandos had been sent back, he ran around a corner in what he believed to be the direction of Annette Bellows's room. Over the racket of the helicopters, and the occasional round of automatic fire, he thought he could make out Melina's voice, shouting hoarsely. So Pierre-Paul hadn't gotten to her yet. Good. Now he could find her and be the one to follow her around rescuing the more obscurely housed hostages, just as De Niro had in the docu-drama. It would give Ivan fits, but they could argue it out afterward. No way of telling what had really happened in that compound twenty years before, after all; and it made a better *story* his way.

Their set was only one story tall, which was one of the things that John had objected to; the compound in Teheran had been four stories high, and getting up stairs had been part of the hassle. But Ivan was going to play with the images and shoot a few stair scenes later on, to achieve the effect of multiple floors. Fine, it meant he had only to struggle around a couple of narrow corners, jumping comatose Revolutionary Guards, looking fierce for the mini-cams wherever they were. It was really loud this time around; *really* loud.

Then one of the walls fell over on him, the plywood pinning him to the ground, the boxes behind it tumbling down and filling the hallway. "Hey!" he cried out, shocked. This wasn't the way it had happened. What was going on? The noise of the helicopters cut off abruptly, replaced by a series of crashes, a whooshing sound. That sound put a fine electric thrill down his spine; he had heard it before, in training routines. Air leaving the chamber. The dome must have been breached.

He heaved up against the plywood. Stuck. Flattening himself as much as possible he slithered forward, under the plywood and out into a small space among fallen boxes. Hard to tell where the hallway had been, and it was pitch-dark. There wouldn't be too much time left. He thought of his little gas mask, then cursed; it wasn't connected to a real oxygen supply. That's what comes from using fake props! he thought angrily. A gas mask with nothing attached to it. Open to the air, which was departing rapidly. Not much time.

He found room among the boxes to stand, and he was about to run over them to the door leading out of the warehouse—assuming the whole station hadn't been breached—when he remembered Melina. Stuck in her embassy room down the hall, wouldn't she still be there? Hell. He groped along in the dark, hearing shouts in the distance. He saw lights, too. Good. He was holding his breath, for what felt like minutes at a time, though it was probably less than thirty seconds. Every time he sucked in a new breath he expected it to be the freezing vacuum, but the supply of rushing, cold—very cold—air continued to fill him. Emergency supply pouring out into the breach, actually a technique he had helped develop himself. Seemed to be working, at least for the moment.

He heard a muffled cry to one side, began to pull at the boxes before him. Squeak in the gloom, ah-ha, there she was. Not fully conscious. Legs wet, probably blood, uh-oh. He pulled hard at boxes, lifted her up. Adrenaline and lunar gravity made him feel like Superman with that part of things, but there didn't seem to be anywhere near as much air as before, and what was left was damned cold. Hurt to breathe. And harder than hell to balance as he hopped over objects with Melina in his arms. Feeling faint, he climbed over a row of boxes and staggered toward a distant light. A sheet of plywood smacked his shin and he cried out, then fell over. "Hey," he said. The air was gone.

When he came to he was lying in a bed in the station hospital. "Great," he muttered. "Whole station wasn't blown up."

His friends laughed, relieved to hear him speak. The whole film crew was in there, it seemed. Ivan, standing next to the bed, said, "It's okay."

"What the hell happened?"

"A small meteor, apparently. Hit out in our sector, in the shuttle landing chambers, ironically. But it wrecked our storage space as well, as you no doubt noticed."

John nodded painfully. "So it finally happened."

"Yes." This was one of the great uncontrollable dangers of the lunar stations; meteors small and large were still crashing down onto the moon's airless surface, by the thousands every year. Odds were poor that any one would hit something as small as the surface parts of their station, but coming down in such numbers. . . . In the long run they were reduced to a safety status somewhat equivalent to that of mountain climbers. Rockfall could always get you.

"Melina?" John said, jerking up in his bed.

"Over here," Melina called. She was a few beds down, and had one leg in a cast. "I'm fine, John." She got out of bed to prove it, and came over to kiss his cheek. "Thanks for the rescue!"

John snorted. "What rescue?"

They laughed again at him. Pierre-Paul pointed a forefinger at him. "There are heroes everywhere, even among the lowest of us. Now you have to admit Ivan's argument."

"The hell I do."

"You're a hero," Ivan said to him, grinning. "Just an ordinary man, so to speak. Not one of the great leaders at all. But by saving Melina, you've changed history."

"Not unless she becomes president," John said, and laughed. "Hey Melina! Go out and run for office! Or save some promising songwriter or something."

Ivan just shook his head. "Why are you so stubborn? It's not so bad if I'm right, John. Think about it. If I am right, then we aren't just sitting around waiting for leaders to guide us." A big grin lit his face. "We become the masters of our fate, we make our own decisions and act on them—we choose our leaders, and instruct them by consensus, so that we can take history any direction we please! Just as you did in the warehouse."

John lay back in his bed and was silent. Around him his friends grinned; one of them was bringing up a big papier-mâché medal, which vaguely resembled the one the Wizard of Oz pins to the Cowardly Lion. "Ah hell," John said.

"When the expedition reaches Mars, they'll have to name something after you," Melina said.

John thought about it for a while. He took the big medal, held it limply. His friends watched him, waiting for him to speak.

"Well, I still say it's bullshit," he told Ivan. "But if there is any truth to what you say, it's just the good old spirit of the Alamo you're talking about, anyway. We've been doing it like that in Texas for years."

They laughed at him.

He rose up from the bed again, swung the medal at them furiously. "I swear it's true! Besides, it's all Robert De Niro's fault, anyway! I was *imitating* the real heroes, don't you see? I was crawling around in there all dazed, and then I saw De Niro's face when he was playing Colonel Jackson in the Teheran embassy, and I said to myself, well hell, what would he have done in this here situation? And that's just what I did."

Counting Potsherds

HARRY TURTLEDOVE

The ship clung close to land, like a roach scuttling along a wall. When at last the coast veered north and west, the ship conformed, steering oars squealing in their sockets and henna-dyed wool sail billowing as it filled with wind to push the vessel onto its new course.

When the ship had changed direction, the eunuch Mithredath summoned the captain to the starboard rail with a slight nod. "We draw near, then, Agbaal?" Mithredath asked. His voice, a nameless tone between tenor and contralto, was cool, precise, intelligent.

The Phoenician captain bowed low. The sun sparked off a silver hoop in his left ear. "My master, we do." Agbaal pointed to the headland the ship had just rounded. "That is the cape of Sounion. If the wind holds, we should be in Peiraieus by evening—a day early," he added slyly.

"You will be rewarded if we are," Mithredath promised. Agbaal, satisfied, bowed again and, after glancing at his important passenger for permission, went back to overseeing his crew.

Mithredath would have paid gold darics from his own purse to shorten the time he spent away from the royal court, but no need for that: he was come to this western backwater at the royal command, and so could draw upon the treasury of Khsrish, King of Kings, as he required. Not for the first time, he vowed he would not stint.

The day was brilliantly clear. Mithredath could see a long way. The only other ships visible were a couple of tiny fishing boats and a slow, wallowing vessel probably full of wheat from Egypt. Gulls mewed and squawked overhead.

Mithredath tried to imagine what the narrow, island-flecked sea had looked like during those great days four centuries before, when the first Khsrish, the Conqueror, had led his huge fleet to the triumph that subjected the western Yauna to Persia once for all. He could not; he was not used enough to ships to picture hordes of them all moving together like so many sheep in a herd on their way to the marketplace of Babylon.

That thought, he realized with a wry nod, showed him what he was most familiar with: the baking but oh-so-fertile plain between the Tigris and Euphrates. He also knew Ektabana well, the summer capital of the Kings of Kings, nestled in the shade of Mount Aurvant, though he had never suffered through a winter there. But until this journey, he had never thought to travel on the sea.

Yet to his surprise, Mithredath was finding a strange sort of beauty here. The water over which he sailed was a blue deep enough almost to be wine-purple, the sky another blue so different as to make him wonder how the same word could apply to both. The land rising steeply from sea to sky was by turns rocky and bare and shaggy with green-gray olive trees. The combination was peculiar but somehow harmonious.

True to his promise, Agbaal brought Mithredath to his destination with the sun still in the sky. True to his, the eunuch pressed a pair of goldpieces into the captain's palm. Agbaal bowed almost double; his swarthy face glowed with pride when Mithredath offered him a cheek to kiss, as if the two of them were near in rank.

The docks swarmed with the merchant folk of the Western Sea: Phoenicians like Agbaal in turbans, tunics, and mantles; Italians wearing long white robes draped over one shoulder; and, of course, the native Yauna or, as they called themselves, Hellenes. Their slightly singsong speech was heard even more than Aramaic, the Empire's common tongue understood everywhere from India to the edges of the Gallic lands.

Mithredath's rich brocaded robes, the gold bracelets on his wrists, and the piles of baggage his servants brought onto the docks drew touts—as a honeypot draws flies, he thought sourly. He picked a fellow whose Aramaic had less of a Hellenic hiss to it than most, said, "Be so good as to lead me to the satrap's palace."

"Of course, my master," the man said, but his face fell. He would still get his fee from Mithredath, but had just had his hopes dashed of collecting another from the innkeeper upon whom he would have foisted Mithredath. Too bad, Mithredath thought.

He was used to Babylon's sensible grid of streets; these small western towns had their narrow, stinking lanes running every which way—and sometimes abruptly petering out. He was glad he had hired a guide; no one not familiar with these alleys from birth could have found his way through them.

Though larger than its neighbors, the satrap's residence—palace, Mithredath discovered, was far too grand a word—looked like any other house hereabouts. It presented a plain, whitewashed front to the world. Mithredath sniffed. To his way of thinking, anyone who *was* someone should let the world know it.

He paid the guide—well enough to keep him from sneering, but not extravagantly—and rapped on the door with his pomegranate-headed walking stick. A moment later, a guard opened the little eye-level observation window to peer out at him. "Who comes?" the fellow demanded fiercely.

Mithredath stood where the man could see him clearly, and answered not with the accented Aramaic in which he had been challenged but in pure, clear Persian:

"I am Mithredath, *saris*"—somehow, in his own tongue, *eunuch* became almost a word of pride—"and servant to Khsrish King of Kings, king of lands containing many men, king in this great earth far and wide, son of Marduniya the king, an Achaemenid, a Persian, son of a Persian, of Aryan seed. May Ahuramazda smile upon him and make long his reign. I am come to the satrapy of the Yauna of the western mainland upon a mission given me from his own royal lips. I would discuss this with your master, the satrap Vahauka."

He folded his arms across his chest and waited.

He did not wait long. He heard a thump on the other side of the door, and guessed the guard had dropped his spear in surprise. Mithredath did not smile. Years at the court of the King of Kings had schooled him against revealing his thoughts to a dangerous world. His face was perfectly composed when the guard flung the door wide and shouted, "Enter, servant of the King of Kings!"

The guard bowed low. Mithredath walked past him, returning the courtesy with a bow barely more than a nod. Some people, he thought, deserved to be reminded from time to time of their station.

As he had intended, more folk in the satrap's residence than the door guard heard his announcement. A majordomo came rushing to greet him in the outer hall. He wore the rectangular mantle of a Hellene over Persian trousers. His bow Mithredath returned in full; he would be a power in this miniature court.

The majordomo said, "Excellent *saris*"—he was a cautious one too, Mithredath thought, again not smiling—"his highness Vahauka, great satrap of the Yauna of the western mainland, now dines with the secretary, with the *ganzabara* of the satrapy, and with the general of the garrison. He bids you join them, if your long journey from the court of the King of Kings, may Ahuramazda smile upon him and make long his reign, has not left you too tired."

"The gracious invitation honors me," Mithredath said. "I accept with pleasure." He was glad to get the chance to meet the *ganzabara* so soon; the financial official was the one who would have to meet his tablet of credit from the court.

"Come this way, then." The majordomo led Mithredath out to the central courtyard where the satrap and his officers were dining. Here at last the eunuch felt himself among Persians again, for most of the courtyard was given over to a proper paradise, a formal garden of roses, tulips, and other bright blooms. Their fragrance, mingled with the odors of cookery, made Mithredath's nostrils twitch.

"Lord Vahauka, I present the *saris* Mithredath, servant of the King of Kings," the majordomo said loudly. Mithredath began to prostrate himself, as he would have before Khsrish, but Vahauka, a lean, gray-bearded Persian of about fifty, stopped him with a wave. The satrap turned his head, presenting his cheek to the eunuch.

"My lord is gracious," Mithredath said as he stepped up to Vahauka and let his lips brush the satrap's beard.

"We are both the King of Kings' servants; how can our ranks greatly differ?" Vahauka said. His fellow diners nodded and murmured in agreement. He went on. "Mithredath, I present you to my secretary, Rishi-kidin"—a perfumed, sweating Babylonian in linen undertunic, wool overtunic, and short white cloak—"the *ganzabara* Hermippos"—a clean-shaven Hellene who, like the majordomo, wore trousers—"and the general of this satrapy, Tadanmu"—a Persian with a no-nonsense look in his eyes, dressed rather more plainly than suited his station.

Mithredath kissed more cheeks. After the satrap's example, his aides could hardly show the eunuch less favor. The feel of Hermippos's face was strange; only among his own kind was Mithredath used to smooth skin against his lips. Not being the only beardless person present made him feel extraordinarily masculine. He laughed at himself for the conceit.

"Here, sit by me," Vahauka said when the introductions were done. He shouted for his servants to bring Mithredath food and wine. "Refresh yourself; when you have finished, perhaps you will favor us by telling what business of the King of Kings, may Ahuramazda smile upon him and make long his reign, brings you to this far western land."

"With pleasure, my lord," Mithredath said. Then for some time he was busy with food and drink. The wines were excellent; the satrapy of the Yauna of the western mainland was known for its grapes (one of the few things it was known for) even in Babylon. The food pleased Mithredath less. Vahauka might be used to salted olives, but one was enough to last Mithredath a lifetime.

Servants lit torches as twilight gave way to darkness. Insects fluttered round the lights, whose smoke was sweet with frankincense. Every so often, a nightjar or bat would dive into view, snatch a bug, and vanish again.

The majordomo led in three flutegirls wearing only wisps of filmy cloth. Vahauka sent them away, saying, "Our distinguished guest's news will prove more interesting than their songs and dances, which we have all seen and heard before, and surely he will not miss them in any way."

Mithredath glanced at the satrap from under lowered brows. Was that a sly dig at his condition? If so, Vahauka was a fool, which might account for his governing only this undistinguished satrapy. Eunuchs' memories for slights were notoriously long, and Mithredath soon would be far closer to the ear of the King of Kings again than Vahauka could dream of coming.

For the moment, of course, Mithredath remained the soul of courtesy. "As my lord wishes. Know then that I am come at the command of the King of Kings, may Ahuramazda smile upon him and make long his reign, to learn more of the deeds of his splendid forefather the first Khsrish, called the Conqueror, that those deeds may be celebrated once again and redound to the further glory of the present King of Kings, who proudly bears the same name."

A brief silence followed, as the officials thought over what he had said. Vahauka asked, "This is your sole commission, excellent *saris*?"

"It is, my lord."

"Then we will be pleased to render you such assistance as we may be capable of," the satrap said fulsomely. His aides were quick to echo him. Mithredath heard the relief in their voices. He knew why it was there: No misdeed of theirs had come to the notice of the King of Kings.

"You want to learn how the first Khsrish took Hellas, eh?" Hermippos said. Mithredath almost failed to recognize the King of Kings' name in the man's mouth; flavored by his native speech, it came out sounding like *Xerxes*. The *ganzabara* went on, "The ruins of Athens, I suppose, would be the best place for that."

"Aye!" "Indeed!" "Well said!" Vahauka, Rishi-kidin, and Tadanmu all spoke at once. Mithredath smiled, but only to himself. How eager they were to get him out of their hair!

Perhaps they, or some of them, *were* up to something about which Khsrish should know.

Still, Hermippos had a point. As Mithredath had learned in Babylon preparing for this mission, Athens led the western Yauna in their fight against the Conqueror. The eunuch sighed. Having come so far already, he supposed poking through rubble could not make things much worse.

Hermippos said, "If you like, excellent *saris*, I will provide you with a secretary who reads and writes not only Aramaic but also the Hellenic tongue. It is still often used here, and in the ancient days of which you spoke would have been the only written language, I suppose."

"I accept with thanks," Mithredath said sincerely, dipping his head. He'd picked up a few words of the tongue of the Hellenes on his westward journey, but it had never occurred to him that he might also need to learn the strange, angular script the locals used. He sighed again, wishing he were home.

Vahauka might have been peering into his thoughts. "Tell us of the news of the court, Mithredath. Here in this distant land we learn of it but slowly and imperfectly."

Nodding, Mithredath gave such gossip as he thought safe to give: he had no intention of setting out all of Khsrish's business—or his scandals—before these men he did not know. He was, though, so circumspect that he blundered, for after he was through, Tadanmu observed, "You have said nothing, excellent *saris*, of the King of Kings' cousin, the great lord Kurash."

"I pray your pardon, my lord. I did not mention him because he has been seeing to his estates these past few months, and hence is not currently in attendance upon the King of Kings, may Ahuramazda smile upon him and make long his reign. Lord Kurash is well, though, so far as I know, and I have heard he has new sons by two of his younger wives."

"And likely hiked up the midwife's skirts after she came away from each one of them, to celebrate the news," Tadanmu chuckled; Kurash's prowess—and his zeal in exercising it—were notorious.

The general asked more of Kurash. Mithredath declined to be drawn out, and Tadanmu subsided. Mithredath made a mental note all the same. Kurash's ambitions, or rather the forestalling of them, were the main reason the eunuch had come to the satrapy of the Yauna of the western mainland. New glory accruing to Khsrish the Conqueror would also reflect onto his namesake, the present occupant—under Ahuramazda—of the throne of the King of Kings.

Mithredath drained his cup, held it out for more. A servant hurried up to fill it. The eunuch sipped, rolled the wine around in his mouth so he could appreciate it fully, nodded in slow pleasure. Here was one reason, anyhow, to approve of this western venture.

He cherished such reasons. He had not found many of them.

"My lord?"

Mithredath looked round to see whom the young Hellene was addressing, then realized with a start that the fellow was talking to him. The ignorance of these provincials! "No lord I," he said. "I am but a *saris* in the service of the King of Kings."

He watched a flush rise under the young man's clear skin. "My apologies, my... excellent *saris*," the Hellene said, correcting himself. "You are called Mithredath, though, are you not?"

"That is my name," the eunuch admitted, adding icily, "You have the advantage of me, I believe."

The fellow's flush grew deeper. "Apologies again. My name is Polydoros; I thought Hermippos would have mentioned me. If it please you, I am to be your guide to the ruins of Athens."

"Ah!" Mithredath studied this Polydoros with fresh interest. But no, his first impression had been accurate: the fellow was well on the brash side of thirty. Wondering if the *ganzabara* was trying to palm some worthless relative off on him, he said cautiously, "I had looked for an older man—"

"To be fluent in Aramaic and the Hellenic tongue both, you mean?" Polydoros said, and Mithredath found himself nodding. The Hellene explained, "It's coming from a banking family that does it, excellent *saris*. Most of the inland towns in this satrapy still cling to the old language for doing business, so naturally I've had to learn to read and write it as well as speak it."

"Ah," Mithredath said again. That made a certain amount of sense. "We'll see how things go, then."

"Very good," Polydoros said. "What are your plans? Will you travel up to the ruins each day, or had you planned actually to stay in Athens?"

"Just how far inland is it?" Mithredath asked.

"A parasang and a half, maybe."

"Close to two hours' walk each way? In the little time I'd have in the ruins, how could I hope to accomplish anything? I'd sooner pitch a tent there, and spend a much shorter while in a bit more discomfort. That will let me return to the east all the sooner."

"As you wish, excellent *saris*. After tomorrow, I shall be at your service."

"Why not go tomorrow?" Mithredath asked, rather grumpily. "I can send my servants out at once to buy tent cloth and other necessities."

"Your pardon, sir, but as I said, I am of a banking family. Tomorrow the monthly silver shipment from the Laurion mines south of here will arrive, and I'll need to be present to help with weighing and assaying the metal. The mines don't produce as they did when the great lode was found not long after Hellas came under Persia, but there will still be close to a talent of silver: forty or fifty pounds of it, certainly."

"Do what you must, of course," Mithredath said, yielding to necessity. "I'll look forward to seeing you morning after next, then." He bowed, indicating that Polydoros could go.

But the Hellene did not depart immediately. Instead he stood with a faraway expression on his face, looking through Mithredath rather than at him. The eunuch was growing annoyed when at last Polydoros said dreamily, "I wonder how the conquest would have gone, had the Athenians stumbled onto that silver before Khsrish's"—he pronounced it *Xerxes'* too—"campaign. Money buys the sinews of war."

A banker indeed, Mithredath thought scornfully. "Money does not buy bravery," he said.

"Perhaps not, excellent *saris*, but even the bravest man, were he naked, would fare badly against an armored warrior with a spear. Had Athens been able to build ships to match the Persian fleet, the Hellenes might not have fallen under the Empire's control."

Mithredath snorted. "All the subject peoples have their reasons why they should have held off Persia. None did."

"Of course you are right, excellent *saris*," Polydoros said politely, wise enough to hide his true feelings, whatever they were. "It was but a fancy of the moment." He bowed. "Till the day after tomorrow." He hurried off.

"I came to the proper decision." Mithredath lifted his soft felt cap from his head, used it to wipe sweat from his face. "I shouldn't care to have to make this journey coming and going each day."

"As you say, excellent *saris*." With broad-brimmed straw hat and thin, short Hellenic mantle, Polydoros was more comfortably dressed than Mithredath, but he was sweating too. Behind them, the eunuch's servants and a donkey bore their burdens in stolid silence. One of the servants led a sheep that kept trying to stop and nibble grass and shrubs.

Something crunched under Mithredath's shoe. He looked down, saw a broken piece of pottery and, close by it, half-buried in weeds, a chunk of brick. "A house stood here once," he said. He heard the surprise in his voice, and felt foolish. But knowing this wilderness had been a city was not the same as stumbling over its remains.

Polydoros was more familiar with the site. He pointed. "You can see a fragment of the old wall there among the olive trees."

Had he noticed it, Mithredath would have taken it for a pile of rocks. Now that he looked closely, though, he saw they had been worked to fit together.

"Most of what used to be here, I suppose, has been

carried off over the years," Polydoros said. Mithredath nodded. Stealing already-worked stone would be easier for a peasant than working it himself. Polydoros pointed again, to the top of one of the hillocks ahead. "More of the wall around the akropolis—the citadel, you would say in Aramaic— is left, because it's harder to get the rock down."

"Aye," Mithredath said, pleased to find the Hellene thinking along with him. It was his turn to point. "That is the way up to the—the citadel?" At the last moment, he decided against trying to echo the local word Polydoros had used.

The Hellene dipped his head, a gesture Mithredath had learned to equate with a nod. "Of course, it will have been an easier ramp to climb when it was kept clear of brush," Polydoros said dryly.

"So it will." The eunuch's heart was already beating fast; he had endured more exertion on this western journey than ever before in his life. Still, he had a job to do. "Let us go up. If that is the citadel, the ruins there will be important ones, and may tell me what I need to learn of Athens."

"As you say, excellent *saris*."

On reaching the top of the akropolis, Mithredath felt a bit like a conqueror himself. Not only was the ancient ramp overgrown, it was also gullied. One of the eunuch's servants limped with a twisted ankle; had the donkey stumbled into that hole, it likely would have broken a leg. Mithredath was winded, and even Polydoros, who seemed ready for anything, was breathing hard.

Rank grass and weeds also grew on the flat ground on top of the citadel, between the stones of the wrecked wall, and over the lower parts of the destroyed buildings the Persians had sacked so long ago. One of those buildings, a large one, had been unfinished when Athens fell. Marble column drums thrust up from the undergrowth. Mithredath could still see scorchmarks on them.

In front of those half-columns stood a marble stele whose shape was familiar to the eunuch—there were many like it in Babylon—but which did not belong with the ruins around it. Nor was the inscription carved onto that stele written in the local language, but in Aramaic and in the wedge-shaped characters the Persians had once used and the native Babylonians still sometimes employed.

A thrill ran through Mithredath as he read the Aramaic text: " 'Khsrish, King of Kings, declares: you who may be king hereafter, of lies beware. I, Khsrish, King of Kings, having pulled down this city, center of the rebel Yauna, decree that it shall remain wilderness forevermore. You who may be king hereafter and obey these words, may Ahuramazda be your friend and may your seed be made numerous; may Ahuramazda make your days long; may whatever you do be successful. You who may be king hereafter, if you see this stele and its words and follow them not, may Ahuramazda curse you, and of your seed more may there not be, and may Ahuramazda pull down all you make as I, Khsrish, King of Kings, have pulled down this city, center of the rebel Yauna.'

"A mighty lord, Khsrish the Conqueror, to have his decree obeyed down across the years," Mithredath said, proud to be of the same Persian race as the long-ago King of Kings, though of his own seed, of course, more there would never be.

"Mighty indeed," Polydoros said tonelessly.

Mithredath looked at him sharply, then relaxed. Polydoros was, after all, a Hellene. Expecting him to be overjoyed before an inscription celebrating the defeat of his forefathers was too much to ask.

The eunuch rummaged in one of the packs on the donkey's back until he found a sheet of papyrus, a reed pen, and a bottle of ink. He copied the Aramaic portion of Khsrish's inscription. He presumed the Persian text said the same thing, but could not read it. Perhaps some magus with antiquarian leanings might still be able to, perhaps not. The present Khsrish would only care about the Aramaic. Of that the eunuch was certain.

He looked at what he had written. He frowned, compared the papyrus to the text carved into the stele. He had copied everything written there. Still, something seemed to be missing.

Perhaps Polydoros could supply it; he was a native of

these parts. Mithredath turned to him: "Tell me, please, good Polydoros, do you know the name of the king of Athens whom Khsrish the Conqueror overcame?"

The Hellene frowned. "Excellent *saris*, I do not. The last king of Athens whose name I know is Kodros, and he is a man of legend, from long before the time of Xerxes."

"I might have known this was going too smoothly," Mithredath sighed. Then he brightened. "It was to learn such things, after all, that I came here." He scratched his head; he did not approve of loose ends. "But how is it you know of this—Kodros, you said?—and not of the man who must have been Athens's last king?"

"Excellent *saris*," Polydoros said hesitantly, "in the legends of my people, Kodros *is* the last king of Athens."

"Ridiculous." Mithredath snorted. "*Someone* must rule, is it not so? This Athens must have been an enemy worthy of Khsrish's hatred, for him to destroy it utterly and afterward curse it. Such an enemy will have had rulers, and able ones, to oppose the King of Kings. How can it have lacked them for all the time since the death of Kodros? Did not one lead it all those years? I cannot believe that."

"Nor I," Polydoros admitted.

"Very strange." Mithredath glanced over to the unhappy sheep his servants had urged—and dragged—up the overgrown ramp. "Here, before Khsrish's victory stele, seems as good a spot as any to offer up the beast." He drew the dagger that hung from his belt, cut a spray of leaves from a nearby bush. He put the leaves in his cap. "They should be myrtle, but any will do in a pinch."

Polydoros watched him lead the sheep over to the marble pillar, set the dagger against its neck. "Just like that?" the Hellene asked. "No altar? No ritual fire? No libation? No flute-players? No grain sprinkled before you sacrifice?"

"The good god Ahuramazda does not need them to hear my prayer."

Polydoros shrugged. "Our rites are different."

Mithredath cut the sheep's throat. As the beast kicked toward death, he beseeched Ahuramazda to help him succeed in his quest for knowledge with which to glorify the King of Kings. He was forbidden to pray for any more personal or private good, but with this sacrifice had no need to do so in any case.

"Does your god require of you any of the flesh?" Polydoros asked as the eunuch began the gory job of butchering the carcass and setting the disjointed pieces on a heap of soft greenery.

"No, it is mine to do with as I will. A magus should pray over it, but as none is here, we shall have to make do."

"Is that garlic growing over there? It will flavor the meat once it's cooked." Polydoros licked his chops.

Mithredath felt saliva flow into his own mouth. He turned to a servant. "You can get a fire going now, Tishtrya."

"What are you doing?" Polydoros asked the next morning.

"Looking through the notes I made before I left Babylon," Mithredath said. "Here, I knew there was something that would tell me who ruled here when the first Khsrish came. An old tablet says he led Dēmos of Athens into captivity. Who is this Dēmos, if Kodros was the last king here?"

"'Dēmos' isn't a who, I'm afraid, excellent *saris*, but rather a what," Polydoros said. "Whoever wrote your tablet wanted to celebrate the King of Kings, as you do, but did not know the Hellenic tongue well. 'Dēmos of Athens' simply means 'the people of Athens.'"

"Oh." Mithredath sighed. "If you knew the trouble I had finding that—" He shuffled scraps of papyrus, briefly looked happy, then grew cautious again. "I also found something about 'Boulē of Athens.' Someone told me -ē was the feminine ending in your language, so I took Boulē to be Dēmos's wife. You're going to tell me that's wrong too, though, aren't you?"

Polydoros dipped his head. "I'm sorry, but I must, excellent *saris*. 'Boulē' means 'council.'"

"Oh." The eunuch's sigh was longer this time. "The people of Athens, the council of Athens—where is the king of Athens?" He glared at Polydoros as if the young banker were responsible for making that elusive monarch disappear. Then he sighed once more. "That's what I came here to find out, I suppose. Where are we most likely to find whatever records or decrees this town kept before it came under the rule of the King of Kings?"

"There are two likely places," Polydoros said after a visible pause for thought that made Mithredath very much approve of him. "One is up here, in the citadel. The other would be down there"—he pointed north and west—"in the agora—the city's marketplace. Anyone who came into the city from the countryside to do business would be able to read them there."

"Sensible," Mithredath said. "We'll cast about here for a while, then, and go down again later. The fewer trips up and down that ramp I take, the happier I shall be." When Polydoros agreed, the eunuch turned to his servants. "Tishtrya, Raga, you will be able to help in this enterprise too. All you need do is look for anything with writing on it, and let me or Polydoros know if you actually find something."

The servants' nods were gloomy; they had looked forward to relaxing while their master worked. Mithredath expected little from them, but did not feel like having them sit idle. He was surprised when, a few minutes later, one of them came trotting through the rubble and undergrowth, waving excitedly to show he had found something.

"What is it, Raga?" the eunuch asked.

"Words, master, carved on an old wall," Raga replied. "Come see!"

"I shall," Mithredath said. He and Polydoros followed the servant back to where his companion was waiting. Tishtrya proudly pointed at the inscription. The eunuch's hopes fell at once: it was too short to be the kind of thing he was seeking. He turned to Polydoros. "What does it say?"

"*Kalos Arkhias*," the Hellene replied: "'Arkhias is beautiful.' It's praise of a pretty boy, excellent *saris*, nothing more; you could see the like chalked or scratched on half the walls in Peiraieus."

"Nasty buggers," Tishtrya muttered under his breath in Persian. Polydoros's eyes went hard for a moment, but he said nothing. Mithredath upbraided his servant; at the same time he made a mental note that the Hellene understood some Persian.

The search resumed. The citadel of Athens was not a large place; a man could easily walk the length of it in a quarter of an hour. But how many such trips would he have to take across it, Mithredath wondered, to make sure he missed nothing? Assuming, of course, he added to himself a moment later, anything was there to be missed.

Polydoros sat down in the narrow shade of an over-thrown chunk of masonry, fanned himself with his straw hat. He might have been thinking with Mithredath's mind, for he said, "This could take forever, you know, excellent *saris.*"

"Yes," was all Mithredath cared to reply to that obvious truth.

"We need to plan what to do, then, rather than simply wandering about up here," the Hellene went on. Mithredath nodded; Polydoros seemed to have a talent for straightforward thinking. After more consideration, Polydoros said, "Let's make a circuit of the wall first. Decrees often go up on the side of a wall so people can see them. Is it not the same in Babylon?"

"It is," Mithredath agreed. He and Polydoros made their way back to the ramp up which they had come.

They walked north and east along the wall. Mithredath's heart beat faster when he saw letters scratched onto a stone, but it was only another graffito extolling a youth's beauty. Then, when they were about halfway along the northern reach of the wall, opposite the ruins of some many-columned building, Polydoros suddenly pointed and exclaimed, "There, by Zeus, that's what we're after!"

Mithredath's eyes followed the Hellene's finger. The slab Polydoros had spied was flatter and paler than the surrounding stones. As they hurried toward it, Mithredath saw the slab was covered with letters in the angular script the Hellenes used for their own language. If this was someone praising a pretty boy, he'd been very long-winded.

"What does it say?" the eunuch asked. He fought

against excitement; for all he knew, the inscription had been ancient when Khsrish took Athens.

"Let me see." Polydoros studied the letters. So, in his more ignorant way, did Mithredath. He could see that the stone-carving here was more regular than the scratchings his servants and he and Polydoros had come upon before. That in itself, he suspected, marked an official document.

"Well?" he asked impatiently. He took out pen and ink and papyrus and got ready to transcribe the words Polydoros was presumably rendering into Aramaic.

"This is part of what you seek, I think," the Hellene said at last.

"Tell me, then!" Had he been a whole man, Mithredath's voice would have cracked; as he was what he was, it merely rose a little.

"I'm about to. Here: 'It seemed good to the council and to the people'... *boulē* and *dēmos* again, you see?"

"A plague on the council and people!" Mithredath broke in. "Who in Ahuramazda's name was the king?"

"I'm coming to that, I think. Let me go on: '—with the tribe of Antiokhis presiding, Leostratos serving as chairman, Hypsikhides as secretary—'"

"The king!" Mithredath shouted. "Where is the name of the king?"

"It is not on the stone," Polydoros admitted. He sounded puzzled. Mithredath, for his part, was about ready to grind his teeth. Polydoros continued. "This may be it: 'Aristeides proposed these things concerning the words of the prophetess of Delphi and the Persians:

"'Let the Athenians fortify the citadel with beams of wood as well as tone to meet the Persians, just as was bid by the prophetess. Let the council choose woodsmen and carpenters to do this, and let them be paid from the public treasury. Let all this be done as quickly as possible, Xerxes already having come to the Asian Sardis. Let there be good fortune to the people of Athens.'"

"Read it over again," Mithredath said. "Read it slowly, so that I can be sure I have your Yauna names correct."

"Not all Hellenes are Ionians," Polydoros said. Mithredath shrugged—how these westerners chose to divide themselves was their business, and he did not care one way or the other. But Khsrish, back in Babylon, would think of them all as Yauna. And so, in his report, Yauna they would be.

Polydoros finished reading. Mithredath's pen stopped its scratching race across the sheet of papyrus. The eunuch read what he had written. He read it again. "Is, ah, Leostratos the ruler of Athens, then? And this Aristeides his minister? Or is Aristeides the king? The measure is his, I gather."

"So it would seem, excellent *saris*," Polydoros said. "But our words for king are *anax* or, more usually, *basileus*. Neither of those is here."

"No," Mithredath said morosely. He mentally damned all the ancient Athenians to Ahriman and the House of the Lie for confusing him so. Khsrish and his courtiers would *not* be pleased if Mithredath had traveled so far, had spent so much gold from the King of Kings' treasury, without finding what he had set out to find. Nothing was more dreadful for a eunuch—for anyone, but for a eunuch especially—than losing the favor of the King of Kings.

Mithredath read the translated inscription once more. "You have rendered this accurately into Aramaic?"

"As best I could, excellent *saris*," Polydoros said stiffly.

"I pray your pardon, good Polydoros," the eunuch said. "I meant no disrespect, I assure you. It's only that there is much here I do not understand."

"Nor I," Polydoros said, but some of the ice was gone from his voice.

Mithredath bowed. "Thank you. Help me, then, if you will, to put together the pieces of this broken pot. What does this phrase mean: 'it seemed good to the council and to the people'? Why does the stone-carver set that down? Why should anyone care what the people think? Theirs is only to obey, after all."

"True, excellent *saris*," Polydoros said. "Your questions are all to the point. The only difficulty"—he spread his hands and smiled wryly—"is that I have no answers to them."

Mithredath sat down on a chunk of limestone that,

from its fluted side, might once have been part of a column. Weeds scratched his ankles through the straps of his sandals. A spider ran across his instep and was gone before he could swat it. In the distance, he heard his servants crunching through brush. A hoopoe called its strange, trilling call. Otherwise, silence ruled the dead citadel.

The eunuch rubbed his smooth chin. "How is Peiraieus ruled? Maybe that will tell me something of Athens's ways before the Conqueror came."

"I beg leave to doubt it, excellent *saris*. The city is no different from any other in the Empire. The King of Kings, may Zeus and the other gods smile on him, appoints the town governor, who is responsible to the satrap. In the smaller towns, the satrap makes the appointment."

"You're right. That doesn't help." Mithredath read the inscription again. By now he was getting sick of it, and put the papyrus back in his lap with a pentulant grunt. "'The *people,*'" he repeated. "It almost sounds as if they and the council are sovereign, and these men merely ministers, so to speak."

"I can imagine a council conducting affairs, I suppose," Polydoros said slowly, "though I doubt one could decide matters as well or as fast as a single man. But how could anyone know about what all the people of a city thought on a question? And even if for some reason the people were asked about one matter, surely no one could expect to reckon up what they sought about each of the many concerns a city has every day."

"I was hoping you would give me a different slant on the question. Unfortunately, I think just as you do." Mithredath sighed and heaved himself up off his makeshift seat. "I suppose all we can do now is search further and hope we find more words to help us pierce this mystery."

The eunuch, the Hellene, and the two servants prowled the citadel for the next two days. Tishtrya almost stepped on a viper, but killed it with his stick before it could strike Mithredath came to admire the broken statuary he kept stumbling over. It was far more restrained than the ebullient, emotional sculpture he was used to, but had a spare elegance of its own.

The searchers came across a good number of inscriptions, but none that helped unravel the riddle the first long one had posed. Most were broken or worn almost to illegibility. Twice Polydoros found the formula, "It seemed good to the council and to the people—" Each time Mithredath swore in frustration, because the rest of the stone was in one case buried beneath masonry it would have taken twenty men to move and in the other missing altogether.

"Enough of this place," Mithredath said on the evening of that second day. "I don't care any longer if the answer is right under my feet—I think it would run away from me like a rabbit from a fox if I dug for it. Tomorrow we will search down below, in the marketplace. Maybe our luck will be better there."

No one argued with him, although they all knew they had not thoroughly explored the citadel—that would be a job for months or years, not days. They rolled themselves in their blankets—no matter how hot the days, nights stayed chilly—and slept.

The marketplace had fewer ruins than the citadel. "How do I know this still *is* part of the marketplace?" Mithredath asked pointedly as he, Polydoros, and the servants picked their way along through grass, bushes, and brush. Before Polydoros could answer, the eunuch added, "Aii!" He had just kicked a large stone, with painful results.

He pushed away the brush that hid it. It was a very large stone; he felt like an idiot for not having seen it. In his anger, he bent down to push the stone over. "Wait!" Polydoros said. "It has letters on it." He read them and began to laugh.

"What, if I may ask, strikes you funny?" Glacial dignity, Mithredath thought, was preferable to hopping up and down on one foot.

"It says, 'I am the boundary stone of the agora,'" Polydoros told him.

"Oh," the eunuch said, feeling foolish all over again.

The most prominent wrecked building was a couple of minutes' walk north of them; its wrecked facade had eight columns, two of them still standing at their full height and supporting fragments of an architrave. "Shall we examine that first?" Polydoros asked, pointing.

Mithredath's throbbing toes made him contrary. "No, let's save it for last, and wander about for a while. After all, it isn't going anywhere."

"As you wish," Polydoros said politely. Behind them, Mithredath's servants sighed. The eunuch pretended he had not heard.

"What's that?" Mithredath asked a minute or so later, seeing another piece of stone poking up from out of the weeds—seeing it, thankfully, before he had a closer encounter with it.

"By the shape, it's the base a statue once stood on," Polydoros said. He walked over to it. "Two statues," he amended: "I see insets carved for four feet. Ah, there's writing on it here." He pulled weeds aside, read, "'Harmodios and Aristogeiton, those who slew the tyrant Hipparkhos.'"

"What's a tyrant?" Mithredath frowned at the unfamiliar word. "Some sort of legendary monster?"

"No, merely a man who ruled a city but was not of any kingly line. Many towns among the Hellenes used to have them."

"Ah. Thank you." Mithredath thought about that for a moment, then said incredulously, "There was in the marketplace of Athens a statue celebrating men who killed the city's ruler?"

"So it would seem, excellent *saris*," Polydoros said. "Put that way, it is surprising, is it not?"

"It's madness," the eunuch said, shuddering at the idea. "As well for all that Persia conquered you Yauna. Who knows what lunacy you might otherwise have loosed on the world?"

"Hmm," was all Polydoros said to that. The Hellene jerked his chin toward the ruined building, which was now quite close. "Shall we go over to it now?"

But Mithredath reacted to the Hellenic perversity exemplified by the ruined statue base with perversity of his own. "No, we'll go around it, see what else is here." He knew he was being difficult, and reveled in it. What could Polydoros do about it?

Nothing, obviously. "As you wish," the Hellene repeated. He then proceeded to skirt the ruins by an even larger margin than Mithredath would have chosen. Take that, the eunuch thought. Smiling behind Polydoros's back, he followed him north and west.

Still, enough was enough. "I'm certain *this* isn't the marketplace anymore," Mithredath said when the Hellene had led him almost all the way to Athens's overthrown gates.

"No, I suppose not," Polydoros admitted. "Are you ready to head back now?"

"More than ready." Mithredath caught Polydoros's eye. They grinned at each other, both of them a little sheepish. Mithredath glanced at his servants. They did not seem amused, and knew better than to seem annoyed.

Something crunched under the eunuch's foot. Curious, he bent down. Then, more curious, he showed Polydoros what he had found. "What's this?"

"An *ostrakon*—a potsherd," Polydoros amended, remembering to put the Yauna word into Aramaic.

"I knew *that*," Mithredath said impatiently. "I've stepped on enough of them, these past few days. But what's this written on it?"

"Hmm?" Polydoros took a closer look. "A name— Themistokles son of Neokles."

"Why write on a potsherd?"

"Cheaper than papyrus." Polydoros shrugged. "People are always breaking pots, and always have sherds around."

"Why just a name, then? Why not some message to go with it?"

"Excellent *saris*, I have no idea."

"Hrmp," Mithredath said. He took another step, heard another crunch. He was not especially surprised to find another potsherd under his foot, as Polydoros had said, people were always breaking pots. He was surprised, though, to find he had stepped on two sherds in a row with writing on them. He handed the second piece of broken pottery to Polydoros, pointed at the letters.

"Themistokles Neokles' son again," the Hellene said.

"That's all?" Mithredath asked. Polydoros dipped his head to show it was. The eunuch gave him a quizzical look. "Good Polydoros, why write just a man's name—just his name, mind you, nothing else—on two different pieces of broken pottery? If one makes no sense, does twice somehow?"

"Not to me, excellent *saris*." Polydoros shifted his feet like a schoolboy caught in some mischief by his master. This time his sandal crunched on something. Mithredath felt a certain sense of inevitability as Polydoros looked at the sherd, found writing on it, and read, "Themistokles son of Neokles."

The eunuch put hands on hips. "Just how many of these things are there?" He turned to his servants. "Tear out some brush here. My curiosity has the better of me. Let's see how many sherds we can turn up."

The look Raga and Tishtrya exchanged was eloquent. Like any master with good sense, Mithredath pretended not to see it. The servants bent and began uprooting shrubs and weeds. They moved at first with the resigned slowness servants always use on unwelcome tasks, but even they began to show some interest as sherd followed sherd in quick succession.

"Themistokles Neokles' son," Polydoros read again and again, and then once, to vary the monotony, "Themistokles of the district Phrearrios." He turned to Mithredath, raised an eyebrow. "I think we may assume this to be the same man referred to by the rest of the sherds."

"Er—yes." Mithredath watched the pile of potsherds grow by Polydoros's feet. He began to feel like a sorcerer whose spell had proven stronger than he expected.

His servants had speculations of their own. "Who d'you suppose this Themis-whatever was?" Tishtrya asked Raga as they worked together to uproot a particularly stubborn plant.

"Probably a he-whore, putting his name about so he'd have plenty of trade," Raga panted. Mithredath, listening, did not dismiss the idea out of hand. It made more sense than anything he'd been able to think of. . . .

"Themistokles son of Neokles," Polydoros said, almost an hour later. He put down another sherd. "That makes, ah, ninety-two."

"Enough." Mithredath threw his hands in the air. "At this rate we could go on all summer. I think there are more important things to do."

"Like the ruin, for example?" Polydoros asked slyly.

"Well, now that you mention it, yes," Mithredath said with such grace as he could muster. He kicked a foot toward the pile of potsherds. "We'll leave this rubbish here. I see no use for it but to prove how strange the men of Athens were, and it would glorify neither Khsrish the Conqueror nor through him our Khsrish IV, may Ahuramazda make long his reign, to say he overcame a race of madmen."

The eunuch's servants laughed at that: they were Persians too. Polydoros managed a lopsided smile. He was on the quiet side as the four men made their way back to the ruined building in the marketplace.

Once they were there, the Hellene quickly regained his good spirits, for he found he had a chance to gloat. "This building is called the *Stoa Basileios*," he said, pointing to letters carved on an overthrown piece of frieze: "the Royal Portico. If we wanted to learn of kings, we should have come here first."

Chagrin and excitement warred in Mithredath. Excitement won. "Good Polydoros, you were right. Find me here, if you can, a list of the kings of Athens. The last one, surely, will be the man Khsrish overcame." Which will mean, he added to himself, that I can get out of these ruins and this whole backward satrapy.

Seized perhaps by some of that same hope, Raga and Tishtrya searched the ruins with three times the energy they had shown hunting for potsherds. Stones untouched since the Persian sack save by wind, rain, and scurrying mice went crashing over as the servants scoured the area for more bits of writing.

Mithredath found the first new inscription himself, but already had learned not to be overwhelmed by an idle wall-scratching. All the same, he called Polydoros over. "'Phrynikhos thinks Aiskhylos is beautiful,'" the Hellene read dutifully.

"About what I expected, but one never knows." Mithredath nodded, and went on looking. He had been gelded just before puberty; feeling desire was as alien to him as Athens's battered rocky landscape. He knew he would never understand what drove this Phrynikhos to declare his lust for the pretty boy. Lust—other men's lust—was just something he had used to advance himself, back when he was young enough to trade on it. Once in a while, abstractly, he wondered what it was like.

Raga let out a shout that drove all such useless fancies from his mind: "Here's a big flat stone covered with letters!" Everyone came rushing over to see. The servant went on, "I saw this wasn't one stone here but two, the white one covering the gray. So I used my staff to lever the white one off—and look!" He was as proud as if he'd done the writing himself.

Mithredath plunged pen into ink, readied papyrus. "What does it say?" he asked Polydoros.

The Hellene plucked nervously at his beard, looked from the inscription to Mithredath and back again. The eunuch's impatient glare finally made him start to talk: "'It seemed good to the council and to the people—'"

"What!" Mithredath jumped as if a wasp had stung him. "More nonsense about council and people? Where is the list of kings? In Ahuramazda's name, where if not by the Royal Portico?"

"I would not know that, excellent *saris*," Polydoros said stiffly. "If I may, though, I suggest you hear me out as I read. This stone bears on your quest, I assure you."

"Very well." It wasn't very well, but there was nothing Mithredath could do about it. Grouchily, he composed himself to listen.

"'It seemed good to the council and to the people,'" Polydoros resumed, "'with the tribe of Oineïs presiding, Phainippos serving as chairman, Aristomenes as secretary,

Kleisthenes proposed these things concerning *ostrakis-mos*—' "

"What in Ahriman's name is *ostrakismos*?" Mithredath asked.

"Something pertaining to *ostraka*—potsherds. I don't know how to put it into Aramaic any more precisely than that, excellent *saris*; I'm sorry. But the words on the stone explain it better than I could, in any case, if you'll let me go on."

Mithredath nodded. "Thank you, excellent *saris*," Polydoros said. "Where was I? Oh, yes: '. . . concerning *ostrakismos*: Each year, when the sixth tribe presides, let the people decide if they wish to hold an *ostrakophoria*.' " Seeing Mithredath roll his eyes, Polydoros explained, "That means a meeting to which potsherds are carried."

"I presume this is leading somewhere," the eunuch said heavily.

"I believe so, yes." Polydoros gave his attention back to the inscribed stone. " 'Let the *ostrakophoria* be held if more of the people are counted to favor it than to oppose. If at the *ostrakophoria* more than six thousand potsherds are counted, let him whose name appears on the largest number of *ostraka* leave Athens within ten days for ten years, suffering no loss of property in the interim. May there be good fortune to the people of Athens from this.' "

"Exiled by potsherds?" Mithredath said as his pen scratched across the sheet of papyrus. "Even for Yauna, that strikes me as preposterous." Then he and Polydoros looked first at each other, then back the way they had come. "Raga! Tishtrya! Go gather up the sherds we were looking at. I think we may have a need for them, after all." The servants trotted off.

"I also think we may," Polydoros said. "Let me read on: 'Those who have been ordained to leave the city: In the year when Ankises was *arkhon*—' "

"*Arkhon*?" Mithredath asked.

"Some officer or other." Polydoros shrugged. "It means 'leader' or 'ruler,' but if a man only held the post a year, it can hardly have been important, can it?"

"I suppose not. Go on."

"'In the year when Ankises was *arkhon,* Hipparkhos son of Kharmos; in the year when Telesinos was *arkhon,* Megakles son of Hippokrates; in the year when Kritias was *arkhon*—'" The Hellene broke off. "No one was exiled that year, it seems. In the next, when Philokrates was *arkhon,* Xanthippos son of Ariphron was exiled, then no one again, and then—" he paused for effect—"Themistokles son of Neokles."

"Well, well." Mithredath scribbled furiously, pausing only to shake his head in wonder. "The people really did make these choices, then, without a king to guide them."

"So it would seem, excellent *saris.*"

"How strange. Did the *ostrakismos*"—Mithredath stumbled over the Yauna word, but neither Aramaic nor Persian had an equivalent—"fall upon anyone else?"

"Not in the next two years, excellent *saris,*" Polydoros said, "but in the year when Hypsikhides was *arkhon,* the Athenian people chose exile for Xerxes son of Dareios, who can only be the King of Kings, the Conqueror. I would guess that to be a last gesture of defiance; the list of *arkhontes* ends abruptly with Hypsikhides."

"Very likely you are right. So they tried to exile Khsrish, did they? Much good it did them." Mithredath finished writing. The servants were coming back, carrying in a leather sack the sherds that had helped exile a man. Their shadows were long before them; Mithredath saw with surprise that the sun had almost touched the rocky western horizon. He turned to Polydoros. "It would be dark by the time we got back to Peiraieus. Falling into a pothole I never saw holds no appeal. Shall we spend one more night here, and return with the light of morning?"

The Hellene dipped his head. "That strikes me as a good plan, if you are satisfied you have found what you came to learn."

"I think I have," Mithredath said. Hearing that, Tishtrya and Raga began to make camp close by the ruins of the Royal Portico. Bread and goat cheese and onions, washed down with river water, seemed as fine a feast as any of the elaborate banquets Mithredath had enjoyed in Babylon.

Triumph, he thought, was an even better sauce than pickled fish.

His servants dove into their bedrolls as soon as they finished eating; their snores all but drowned out the little night noises that came from beyond the circle of light around the campfire. Mithredath and Polydoros did not go to sleep right away. The eunuch was glad to have company. He felt like talking about the strange way the Athenians had run their affairs, and the Hellene had shown himself bright enough to have ideas of his own.

"No sign of a king anywhere," Mithredath said, still bemused at that. "I wonder if they settled everything they needed to decide on by counting potsherds."

"I would guess they probably must have, excellent *saris*," Polydoros said. "All the inscriptions read, 'It seemed good to the council and to the people.' How would they know that—why would they write that—if they had not counted potsherds to know what seemed good to the people?"

"There you have me, good Polydoros. But what if something that 'seemed good to the people' was in fact bad for them?"

"Then they suffered the consequences, I suppose. They certainly did when they decided to oppose Xerxes." Polydoros waved at the dark ruins all around.

"But they were the leading Yauna power at the time, were they not? They must have been, or Khsrish would not have obliterated their city as a lesson to the others. Until they chose to fight him, they must have done well."

"A king can also make an error," Polydoros said.

"Oh, indeed." Being a courtier, Mithredath knew better than the Hellene how gruesomely true that could be. "But," he pointed out, "a king knows the problems that face his land. And if by some mischance he should not, why, then he has his ministers to point them out to him, so that he may decide what needs to be done. How could the people—farmers, most of them, and cobblers and potters and dyers—how could they even have hoped to learn the issues that affected Athens, let alone what to do about them?"

"There you have me," Polydoros confessed. "They would be too busy, I'd think, working just to stay alive to be able to act, as you say, more or less as ministers in their own behalf."

Mithredath nodded. "Exactly. The king decides, the ministers and courtiers advise, and the people obey. So it is, so it has always been, so it always will be."

"No doubt you are right." An enormous yawn blurred Polydoros's words. "Your pardon, excellent *saris*. I think I will imitate your servants." He unrolled his blanket, wrapped it around himself. "Will you join us?"

"Soon."

Polydoros did not snore, but before long was breathing with the slow regularity of sleep. Mithredath remained some time awake. Every so often his eyes went to the bag of potsherds, which lay close by Raga's head. He kept trying to imagine what being an Athenian before Khsrish the Conqueror came had been like. If the farmers and potters and such ruled themselves by counting sherds, would they have made an effort to learn about all the things Athens was doing, so they could make sensible choices when the time came to put the sherds in a basket for counting, or whatever it was they did? What would it have been like, to be a tavern-keeper, say, with the same concerns as a great noble?

The eunuch tried to imagine it, and felt himself failing. It was as alien to him as lust. He knew whole men felt that, even if he could not. He supposed the Athenians might have had this other sense, but he was sure he did not.

He gave it up, and rolled himself in his blanket to get some rest. As he grew drowsy, his mind began to roam. He had a sudden mental picture of the whole vast Persian Empire being run by people writing on potsherds. He had visions of armies of clerks trying to transport and count them, and of mountains of broken pottery climbing to the sky. He fell asleep laughing at his own silliness.

Third-rate town though it was, Peiraieus looked good to Mithredath after some days pawing through the ruins of dead Athens. He paid Polydoros five gold darics for his help there. The Hellene bowed low. "You are most generous, excellent *saris*."

Mithredath presented his cheek for a kiss, then said, "Your assistance has but earned its fitting reward, good Polydoros."

"If you will excuse me, then, I'm off to see how much work has fallen on my table while I was away." At Mithredath's nod, Polydoros bowed again and trotted away. He turned back once to wave, then quickly vanished among the people crowding the port's streets.

"And now we are off to the satrap's residence," the eunuch told his servants. "I shall inform Vahauka of the success of my mission, and draw from the *ganzabara*—" Mithredath snapped his fingers. "What was the fellow's name?"

"Hermippos, wasn't it, sir?" Tishtrya said.

"Yes; thank you. I shall draw from Hermippos the funds we need for our return journey to Babylon. After giving Polydoros his due, we are for the moment poor, but only for the moment."

"Yes, sir. I like the sound of going home fine, sir," Tishtrya said. Raga nodded.

"I wouldn't be sorry never to see this satrapy again, myself," Mithredath admitted, smiling.

The satrap's residence was busier in the early morning than it had been at nightfall. A couple of guards stood outside the entrance to make sure the line of people waiting to see Vahauka and his officials stayed orderly.

Mithredath recognized one of the guards as the man who had been at the door the evening he'd arrived. He went up to the fellow. "Be so good as to convey me to his excellency the satrap," he said. "I don't care to waste an hour of my time standing here."

The guard made no move to do as Mithredath had asked. Instead, he looked down his long, straight nose at the eunuch and said, "You can just wait your turn like anybody else."

Mithredath stared. "Why, you insolent—" He started

to push past, but the guard swung up his spear. "What do you think you're playing at?" the eunuch said angrily.

"I told you, no-stones—wait your turn." The spearhead pointed straight at Mithredath's belly. It did not waver. The guard looked as though he would enjoy thrusting it home.

Mithredath glanced at his servants. Like any travelers with a shekel's weight of sense, he, Tishtrya, and Raga all carried long daggers as protection against robbers. Neither servant, though, seemed eager to take on a spear-carrying soldier, especially when the man served the local satrap. Seething, Mithredath took his place in line. "I shall remember your face," he promised the guard.

"And I'll forget yours." The lout laughed loudly at his own wit.

The line crawled ahead, but Mithredath was too furious to become bored. The revenges he invented grew more and more chilling as he got hotter and hotter. A soldier who thwarted one of the royal eunuchs—even a soldier so far from Babylon as this guard—was asking to have his corpse given to ravens and kites.

The eunuch had thought Vahauka would signal him forward as soon as he saw him, but the satrap went right on with his business. At last Mithredath stood before him. Mithredath started to prostrate himself, waited for Vahauka to stop him and offer his cheek. Vahauka did not. Feeling his stomach knot within him, the eunuch finished the prostration.

When he rose, he had his face under control. "My lord," he said, and gestured toward the bag of potsherds Raga held, "I am pleased to report my success in the mission personally set me by Khsrish, King of Kings"—he stressed the ruler's name and title—"may Ahuramazda make long his reign."

Vahauka yawned. Of all the responses Mithredath might have expected, that was the last.

Having to work now to keep his voice from stumbling, the eunuch went on. "As I have succeeded, I plan to draw funds from the *ganzabara* Hermippos for my return voyage to Babylon."

"No." Vahauka yawned again.

"My lord, must I remind you of my closeness to the King of Kings?" Only alarm made Mithredath's threat come out so badly.

"No-balls, I doubt very much if you ever have been—or ever will be—close to Kurash, King of Kings, may Ahuramazda smile upon him and make long his reign."

"Ku—" The rest of the name could not get through the lump of ice that suddenly filled Mithredath's throat.

"Aye, Kurash. A ship came in with the word he'd overthrown and slain your worthless Khsrish the day you left for the old ruined inland town. Good riddance, says I—now we have a real King of Kings again, and now I don't have to toady to a half-man anymore, either. And I won't. Get out of my sight, wretch, and thank the good god I don't stripe your back to send you on your way."

The satrap's mocking laughter pursued Mithredath as he left the hall. His servants followed, as stunned as he.

Even the vestiges of dignity deserted him as soon as he was out of sight of the satrap's residence. He sat down heavily, buried his face in his hands so he could not have to see the passersby staring at him.

Tishtrya and Raga were muttering back and forth. "Poor," he heard one of them say. "He can't pay us anymore."

"Well, to Ahriman with him, then. What else is he good for?" the other replied. It was Raga. He dropped the leather sack. The potsherds inside clinked. The sack came open. Some sherds spilled out.

Mithredath did not look up. Nor did he look up at the sound of his servants—no, his ex-servants, he thought dully—walking away.

They were some time gone when at last the eunuch began to emerge from his shock and despair. He picked up a sherd. Because one man had died, his own life, abruptly, was as shattered as the pot from which the broken piece had come, as shattered as long-ago Athens.

He climbed slowly to his feet. Perhaps he could beg one of his darics back from Polydoros. It would feed and lodge him for a couple of weeks. Then he could—what? At the moment, he had no idea. For that matter, he did not even know if the Hellene would give him the gold.

One thing at a time, he thought. He stopped a man and asked the way to the bankers' street. The man told him. Nodding his thanks, he tossed the potsherd on the pile and started off.

Leapfrog

JAMES P. HOGAN

Fall had come to the northern hemisphere of Mars. At the north pole, the mean temperature had fallen to $-125°C$—cold enough to freeze carbon dioxide out of the thin Martian atmosphere and begin forming the annual covering that would lay over the permanent cap of water-ice until spring. In the southern polar regions, where winter had ended, the carbon dioxide was evaporating. Along the edge of the retreating fields of dry ice, strong winds were starting to raise dust. During the short but hot southern summer, with Mars making its closest approach to the sun, the resulting storms could envelop the planet.

Edmund Halloran watched the surface details creep across the large wallscreen at one end of the mess area of Yellow Section, Deck B, of the interplanetary transfer vessel *Mikhail Gorbachev*, wheeling in orbit at the end of its six-month voyage from Earth to bring the third manned mission to the Red Planet. The other new arrivals sitting around him at the scratched and stained green-topped aluminum tables—where they had eaten their meals, played innumerable hands of cards, and talked, laughed, and exchanged reminiscences through the long voyage out—were also strangely quiet as they took in the view. Unlike the other views of Mars that they had studied and memorized, this was not being replayed from transmissions sent back from somewhere on the other side of millions of miles of space. This time it was really on the outside of the thin metal shell around them. Very soon, now, they would be leaving the snug cocoon with its reassuring routine and its company of familiar faces that they had come to know as home, to go down there. They had arrived.

The structure had lifted out from lunar orbit as a flotilla of three separate, identical craft, independently powered, each fabricated in the general form of a *T,* but with the bar curved as part of the arc of a circle, rather than straight. On entering the unpowered free-fall phase that would endure for most of the voyage, the three ships had maneuvered together and joined at their bases to become the equispaced spokes of a rotating *Y,* creating comfortable living conditions in the three inhabited zones at the extremities. The triplicated design meant that in the event of a major failure in any of the modules, everybody could get home again in the remaining two—or at a push, with a lot of overcrowding and at the cost of jettisoning everything not essential to survival, even in a remaining one. The sections accommodated a total of 600 people, which represented a huge expansion of the existing population of 230 accrued from the previous two missions. Some of the existing population had been distributed between a main base on Lunae Planum and a few outlying installations. The majority, however, were still up in MARSIANSKAYA MEZHDUN-ARODNAYA ORBITAL 'NAYA STANTSIYA, or "Mars International Orbiting Station," awaiting permanent accommodation on the surface. In the Russian Cyrillic alphabet this was shortened to MAPCMOC, yielding the satisfyingly descriptive transliteration MARSMOS in English, which was accepted as the standard international language.

The region coming into view now was an area roughly twenty degrees north of the equator. Halloran recognized the heavily cratered area of Lunae Planum and the irregular escarpment at its eastern edge, bounding the smoother volcanic plain of Chryse Planitia. Although he knew where to look, he could see no indication of the main base down there. He picked out the channels emerging from the escarpment, where volcanic heating had melted some of the underground ice that had existed in an earlier age, causing torrential floods to pour out across the expanse of Chryse, which lay about a kilometer lower.

An announcement from the overhead speakers broke his mood of reverie. "Attention please. The shuttle to MARSMOS is now ready for boarding. Arrivals holding disembarkation cards ninety-three through one hundred twenty should proceed through to the docking area. Ninety-three through one hundred twenty, to the docking port now."

Halloran rose and picked up his briefcase and a bag containing other items that he wanted to keep with him until the personal baggage caught up with them later. As he shuffled forward to join the flow of people converging toward the door, a voice spoke close behind him. "It looks as if we're on the same trip across, Ed." He looked around. Ibrahim and Anna, a young Egyptian couple, were next in line.

"I guess so," Halloran grunted. Ibrahim was an electronics technician, his wife a plant geneticist. They were both impatient to begin their new lives. Why two young people like these should be so eager and excited about coming to a four-thousand-mile ball of frozen deserts, Halloran couldn't imagine. Or maybe he couldn't remember.

"We'll be going straight down from the station." Ibrahim gestured toward Anna; she smiled a little shyly. "The doctors want her to adapt to surface conditions as soon as possible."

Anna's pregnancy had been confirmed early in the voyage. Although the baby wouldn't be the first to be born on Mars, it would be one of a very select few. The knowledge added considerably to Ibrahim's already exuberant pride of first fatherhood.

"It may be a while before I see you again, then, eh?" Halloran said. "But I wouldn't worry about not bumping into each other again. It's not as if there are that many places to get lost in down there yet."

"I hope it won't be too long," Ibrahim said. "It was good getting to know you. I enjoyed listening to your stories. Good luck with your job here."

"You too. And take good care of Anna there, d'you hear."

They moved out through the mess doorway, into a gray-walled corridor of doors separated by stretches of metal ribbing. Byacheslav, one of the Russian construction engineers, moved over to walk beside Halloran as they came to the stairway leading up to the next deck, where the antechamber to the docking port was located. He was one of the relatively few older members of the group—around Halloran's age.

"Well, Ed . . . it would be two years at least before you saw Earth again, even if you changed your mind today."

"I wasn't planning on changing my mind."

"It's a big slice out of what's left of life when you get to our end of it. No second thoughts?"

"Oh, things get easier once you're over the hump. What happens when you get over the top of any hill and start going down the other side? You pick up speed, right? The tough part's over. People just look at it the wrong way."

Byacheslav smiled. "Never thought about it that way. Maybe you're right."

"How about you?"

"Me? I'm going to be too busy to worry much about things like that. We're scheduled to begin excavating the steel plant within a month. Oh, and there was something else. . . ." Byacheslav reached inside his jacket, took a billfold from the inside pocket, and peeled out Unodollar tens and ones. "That's to settle our poker account—before I blow it all in the mess bar down at Mainbase."

Halloran took the money and stuffed it in his hip pocket. "Thanks. . . . You know, By, there was a time when I wouldn't have trusted a Russian as far as I could throw one of your earthmovers. It came with the trade."

"Well, you're in a different business now."

"I guess we all are."

They entered the antechamber, with its suiting-up room and two EVA airlocks on one side, and passed through the open doors of the docking port into the body of the shuttle. To align with the direction of the *Mikhail Gorbachev*'s simulated gravity, the shuttle had docked with its roof entry-hatch mating to the port, which meant they had to enter down a ladder into the compartment forward of the passenger cabin. The seats were small and cramped, and Halloran and Byacheslav wedged themselves in about halfway to the back, next to a young Indonesian who was keeping up a continuous chatter with someone in the row behind.

"Do you know where you're going yet, Ed?" Byacheslav asked as they buckled themselves in.

"Probably a couple of weeks more up in orbit, until the new admin facility is ready down below," Halloran replied. "The director I'll be working for from MCM is supposed to be meeting me at MARSMOS. I should find out for sure then. I guess it depends on you construction people."

"Don't worry. We won't leave you stuck up here. . . ." Byacheslav looked at Halloran and raised his eyebrows. "So, one of the directors is meeting you personally, eh? And will they have a red carpet? If that's the kind of reception an administrator gets, I think I'm starting to worry already. I can see how the whole place will end up being run. That was what I came all this distance to get away from. Hmm . . . maybe I've changed my mind. Perhaps we will leave you up here."

Halloran's rugged, pink-hued face creased into a grin. "I wouldn't get too carried away if I were you. He's based up at MARSMOS most of the time, anyway. I'm just here to take care of resource-allocation schedules. Nothing special. They used to call it being a clerk."

"Now I think you're being too modest. There's a lot more to it than scratching in ledgers with pens these days. You have to know computer systems. And in a situation like this, the function is crucial. You can't tell me you're not good."

"Don't believe a word of it. It's just Uncle Sam's way of retiring off old spy chiefs in a world that doesn't need so many spies anymore."

Halloran sat back and gazed around the cabin. All of the passengers were aboard and seated, and the crew were securing the doors. The metaphoric umbilical back to Earth was about to be broken. It had been over thirty years ago when he joined the Agency. Who would have thought, then, that two months after turning fifty-five, he'd have found himself at a place like this, starting with a new outfit all over again?

And of all outfits to have ended up with, one with a name like Moscow-Chase-Manhattan Investments, Inc., which controlled a development consortium headed by the Aeroflot Corporation, the Volga-Hilton Hotels group, and Nippon Trans-Pacific Enterprises. Similar combinations of interests had opened up the Moon to the point where its materials-processing and manufacturing industries were mushrooming, with regular transportation links in operation and constantly being expanded, and tourism was starting to catch on. If the U.S. space effort hadn't fallen apart in the seventies and eighties, America could have had all of it, decades ahead of the Soviets. As it was, America was lucky to have come out of it, along with Europe and some of the other more developed nations, as junior partners. The Second Russian Revolution, they called it. Back to capitalism. Many people thought it was better that way.

In the case of Mars, of course, the big obstacle to its similar development was the planet's greater distance from Earth, with correspondingly longer flight times. But that problem would go away—and usher in a new era of manned exploration of the outer Solar System—when the race to develop a dependable, high-performance, pulsed nuclear propulsion system was won, which would bring the typical Mars round-trip down to somewhere around ten days. Although some unforeseen difficulties had been encountered, which had delayed development of such a drive well beyond the dates optimistically predicted in years gone by, the various groups working feverishly around the world were generally agreed that the goal was now in sight. That was the bonanza that MCM was betting on. Thirty years ago, Halloran would have declared flatly that such a coordination of Soviet and Western interests under a private initiative was impossible. Now he was part of it. Or about to be. . . .

He found himself wondering again if the Vusilov who would be meeting him could be the same Vusilov from bygone years. Possibly the KGB had its own retirement problems, too. But in any case, after all the months of wondering, it would be only a matter of minutes now before he found out.

The shuttle nudged itself away from the docking port, and Halloran experienced a strange series of sensations as it fell away from the *Mikhail Gorbachev*, shedding weight as it decoupled from the ship's rotational frame, and then accelerated into a curving trajectory that would carry it across to the MARSMOS satellite.

"MARSMOS has increased tenfold in size in the last six months," Byacheslav commented. "You'll probably have more places to discover there in the next couple of weeks than I'll have down on the surface."

"There'll need to be, with all these people showing up," Halloran said.

Even before the arrival of the two previous manned missions, a series of unmanned flights had left all kinds of hardware parked in orbit around Mars. In a frenzy of activity to prepare for the arrival of the third mission, the construction teams from the first two had expanded the initial station into a bewildering Rube-Goldberg creation of spheres, cylinders, boxes, and domes, bristling with antennas, laser tubes, and microwave dishes, all tied together by a floating web of latticeworks and tethering cables. And the next ship from Earth, with another six hundred people, was only two months behind.

There was a brief period of free-fall, and then more disorienting feelings of unbalance came and went as the shuttle reversed and decelerated to dock at MARSMOS. When Halloran unfastened his restraining straps, he found himself weightless, which meant that they were at the nonrotating section of the structure. Using handrails and guidelines, the newcomers steered themselves out through an aft side-door into an arrivals area where agents were waiting to give directions and answer questions.

After receiving an information package on getting around in MARSMOS, Halloran called Moscow-Chase-Manhattan's number and asked for Mr. Vusilov.

"Da?"

"Mr. Vusilov?"

"Speaking."

"This is Ed Halloran."

"Ah, Mr. Halloran! Excellent!" The voice sounded genial and exuberant. "So, you are arrived now, yes?"

"We docked about fifteen minutes ago. I've just cleared the reception formalities."

"And did you have a pleasant voyage, I trust?"

"It dragged a bit at times, but it was fine."

"Of course. So you are still liking the idea of working with us at MCM? No second regrets, yes?"

A reception agent murmured, "Make it brief, if you wouldn't mind, Mr. Halloran. There is a line waiting."

"None," Halloran said. "Er, I am holding up the line here. Maybe if I could come on through?"

"Yes, of course. What you do is ask directions to a transit elevator that will bring you out here to Red Square, which is a ring—a joke, you see, yes? This is where I am. It is the part of MARSMOS that rotates. First we have a drink of welcome to celebrate, which is the Russian tradition. You go to the south elevator point in Red Square, then find the Diplomatic Lounge. Our gentlemen's club here, comfortable by Martian standards—no hard hats or oily coverups. There, soon, I will be meeting you."

With no gravity to define a preferred direction, the geometry inside the free-fall section of MARSMOS was an Escherean nightmare of walls, planes, passages, and connecting shafts intersecting and going off in all directions, with figures floating between the various spaces and levels like fish drifting through a three-dimensional undersea labyrinth. Despite the map included in the information package, Halloran was hopelessly lost within minutes and had to ask directions three times to the elevator that would take him to the south terminal of Red Square. To reach it, he passed through a spin-decoupling gate, which took him into the slowly turning hub structure of the rotating section.

The elevator capsule ran along the outside of one of the structural supporting booms and was glass-walled on two sides. A panorama of the entire structure of MARSMOS changed perspective outside as the capsule moved outward, with the full disk of Mars sweeping by beyond, against its background of stars. It was his first close-up view of the planet that was real, seen directly with his own eyes, and not an electronically generated reproduction.

As the capsule descended outward and Halloran felt his body acquiring weight once again, he replayed in his mind the voice he had heard over the phone: the guttural, heavily accented tone, the hearty, wheezing joviality, the tortured English. It had sounded like *the* Vusilov, all right. Perhaps he had upset somebody higher up in the heap, Halloran thought—which Vusilov had had a tendency to do from time to time—and despite all the other changes, the old Russian penchant for sending troublemakers to faraway places hadn't gone away.

Direction had reestablished itself when he emerged at the rim. Halloran consulted his map again and found the Diplomatic Lounge located two levels farther down, in a complex of dining areas and social rooms collectively lumped together in a prize piece of technocratese as a "Communal Facilities Zone." But as he made his way down, austere painted metal walls and pressed aluminum floors gave way to patterned designs and carpeting, with mural decorations to add to the decor, and even some ornaments and potted plants. Finally he went through double doors into a vestibule with closets and hanging space, where he left his bags, and entered a spacious, comfortably furnished room with bookshelves and a bar tended by a white-jacketed steward on one side. On the other, vast windows looked out into space, showing Phobos as a lumpy, deformed crescent. Leather armchairs and couches were grouped around low tables with people scattered around, some talking, others alone, reading. The atmosphere was calm and restful, all very comfortable and far better than anything Halloran had expected.

And then one of the figures rose and advanced with a hand extended. He was short and stocky, with broad, solid shoulders, and dressed casually in a loose orange sweater and tan slacks. As he approached, a toothy grin broadened to split the familiar craggy, heavy-jowled face, with its bulbous, purple-veined nose—a face that had always made Halloran think of an old-time prizefighter—from one misshapen, cauliflower ear to the other.

Vusilov chuckled delightedly at the expression on Halloran's face. "Ah-hah! But why the so-surprised look, Edmund Halloran? You think you could get rid of me so easy, surely not? It has been some years now, yes? It's often I am wondering how they figure out what to do with you, Halloran. . . . So, to Mars, welcome I say to you, and to Moscow-Manhattan."

They shook hands firmly. It was the first time they had done so, even though they had met on numerous occasions as adversaries. "I wondered if it was you, Sergei . . . from the name," Halloran said.

"As I knew you would."

"You knew who I was, of course."

"Of course. I've seen your file. It wouldn't have been customary for them to show you mine."

"Who'd have guessed we'd wind up like this?" Halloran said. "Times sure change. It all seems such a long time ago, now. But then, I guess, it was literally another world."

"The axes are buried under the bridge," Vusilov pronounced. "And now, as the first thing, we must drink some toast. Come." He took Halloran's elbow lightly and steered him across to the bar. The bartender, young, swarthy, with dark eyes and flat-combed hair, looked up inquiringly. "This is Alfredo," Vusilov said, gesturing with a sweep of his hand. "The best bartender on Mars."

"The only one, too," Alfredo said.

"Well, what of it? That also makes you the best."

"I thought there was a bar down in the main surface base," Halloran said.

"Pah!" Vusilov waved a hand. "That is just a workman's club. Dishwashing beer from serve-yourself machines. This is the only *bar*. Alfredo is the source of all that's worth knowing up here. If you want to know what goes on, ask Alfredo. Alfredo, I want you to meet Ed Halloran, a good friend of mine who is very old. He has now come here to work with us."

"Pleased to meet you, Ed," Alfredo said.

"Hi," Halloran responded.

"Now, you see, from the old days I remember the files we keep on everybody. Your favorite choice to be poisoned with is a scotch, yes?"

"That would do fine."

"I refuse absolutely. Today you are joining us here, so it must first be vodka. We have the best."

"Okay. Make it on ice, with a splash of lime."

"And my usual, Alfredo," Vusilov said. "Put them on MCM's account."

Alfredo turned away and began pouring the drinks. After a few seconds, Halloran asked Vusilov idly, "When was the last time?"

Vusilov's beady bright eyes darted restlessly as he thought back. "In 2015, wasn't it? Vienna. Hah-hah! Yes, I remember." The Russian guffawed loudly and slapped the bar with the palm of his hand. "You paid a hundred thousand dollars to buy back the coding cartridge. But the truth, you never knew! It was worthless to us, anyway. We didn't have the key."

Halloran raised a restraining hand. "Now *wait* a minute. You may be the boss here, but I'm not gonna let you get away with that. We knew about the code. It was worth about as much as those hundred-dollar bills I passed you. Didn't your people ever check them out?"

"Hmph." The smile left Vusilov's face abruptly. "I know nothing about that. My department, it was not." Halloran got the impression that it was more a slight detail that Vusilov had conveniently forgotten. Alfredo placed two glasses on the bar. Vusilov picked them up. "Come," he said. "There are two quiet chairs over there, by the window. Never before do you see so many stars, and so flammable, yes?"

"Don't change the subject," Halloran said as they began crossing the lounge. "You have to admit that we undid your whole operation in Bonn. When we exposed Skater and he got sent back to Moscow, it pulled the linchpin out of it."

Vusilov stopped and threw his head back to roar with mirth, causing heads to look up all around the room. "What, you still believe that? He was the decoy you were *supposed* to find out about. We were intercepting your communications."

"Hell, we knew that. We were feeding you garbage through that channel. That was how we kept Reuthen's cover. He was the one you should have been worrying about."

Vusilov blanched and stopped in midstride. "Reuthen? The interpreter? He was with you?"

"Sure. He was our key man. You never suspected?"

"You are being serious, I suppose?"

Halloran smiled in a satisfied kind of way. "Well, I guess you'll never know, will you?" It was a pretty tactless way to begin a relationship with his future boss, he admitted to himself, but he hadn't been able to resist it. Anyhow, what did career prospects matter at his age? Hell, it had been worth it.

Vusilov resumed walking, and after a few paces stopped by a chair where a lean, balding man with spectacles and a clipped mustache was reading what looked like a technical report of some kind, in French. "This is Léon, who you should know." Vusilov spoke stiffly, his joviality of a moment ago now gone. "Léon is with the European group here, who will build the launch base and make spaceships here."

"'Allo?" Léon said, looking up.

"Please meet Ed Halloran," Vusilov said. "He comes here to work with us at MCM."

"A pleasure, Monsieur 'alloran." Léon half-rose from his chair to shake hands.

"Mine, too," Halloran said.

"They work very hard on the race for the nuclear pulse drive back home," Vusilov went on. He seemed to have smoothed his feathers, and lowered his voice in a tone of mock confidentiality. "They think they will be first, and when they get it, they are already out here at Mars ahead of us all to go deep-space. Isn't it so, Léon, yes?"

The Frenchman shrugged. "Anything is possible. Who knows? I think we 'ave a good chance. Who else is there? Your prototype has problems. Rockwell and Kazak-Dynamik both admit it."

"Well, there is always the Chinese," Vusilov said, resuming his normal voice. He evidently meant it as a joke. For the past six months the Chinese had been constructing something large in lunar orbit, the purpose of which had not been revealed. It had provoked some speculation and a lot of unflattering satire and cartoons about their late-in-the-day start at imitating everyone else.

"After all, what year is it of theirs? Isn't it the Year of the Monkey, yes?"

Vusilov started to laugh, but Léon cut him off with a warning shake of his head, and nodded to indicate an Oriental whom Halloran hadn't noticed before, sitting alone in an alcove on the far side of the room. He had a thin, droopy mustache and pointed beard, and was the only person in the room who was dressed formally, in a dark suit with necktie, which he wore with a black silk skullcap. He sat erect, reading from a book held high in front of his face, and showed no sign of having overheard.

Vusilov made a silent *Oh* with his mouth, in the manner of someone guilty of a faux pas, but at the same time raised his eyebrows in a way that said it didn't matter that much.

"Who's he?" Halloran murmured.

"The Chinese representative," Léon replied quietly.

"What are they doing here?"

"Who knows what they do anywhere?" Vusilov said. "We have many countries with persons at MARSMOS, whose reasons are a mystery. They do it for getting the prestige."

"That's why this is called the Diplomatic Lounge," Léon added.

"Anyway, we shall talk with you later, Léon," Vusilov said.

"I 'ope you enjoy your stay 'ere, Monsieur 'alloran."

Vusilov led the way over to the chairs that he had indicated from the bar, set one of the glasses down on the small table between them, and sat down with the other. Halloran took the other chair and picked up his drink. "So, here's to . . . ?" He looked at the Russian invitingly.

"Oh, a prosperous business future for us, I suppose. . . ." Vusilov's mood became troubled again. He eyed Halloran uncertainly as their glasses clinked.

But, just for the moment, Halloran was oblivious as he sipped his drink and savored the feeling of a new future beginning and old differences being forgotten. A portent of the new age dawning . . .

Until Vusilov said, "What else did Reuthen do for you?"

"Hell, why get into this?"

"A matter of professional pride. You forget that the KGB was the number-one, ace, properly run operation—not sloppy-dash slipshoe outfit like yours."

"Oh, is that so? Then what about the general who defected in 2012, in Berlin? We snatched him from right under your noses. That was a classic."

"You mean Obarin?"

"Of course, Obarin."

Vusilov tried to muster a laugh, but it wasn't convincing. "That old fart! We *gave* him to you. He knew nothing. He was more use to us on your side than on ours."

"Come on, let's get real. He'd been a frontline man ever since he was a major in Afghanistan back in the eighties. He was a gold mine of information on weapons and tactics."

"All of it out of date. He was an incompetent in Afghanistan. It saved us having to pay his pension."

"Let's face it. You were all incompetents when it came to Afghanistan."

"Is that so, now? And are you so quickly forgetting a little place called Vietnam? It was we who sucked you into that mess, you know, like the speedsands."

"Baloney. It was our own delusion in the early fifties over a global Communist conspiracy being masterminded from the Kremlin."

"Precisely! And where did the delusion come from, do you think? The misinformation-spreading was always one of our masterpiece arts, yes?"

They raised their glasses belligerently, looking at each other over the rims as they drank. Vusilov's mouth contorted irascibly. Clearly he was unwilling to let it go at that, yet at the same time he seemed to be having a problem over whether or not to voice what was going through his mind.

"It didn't do you a hell of a lot of good with China," Halloran said.

That did it. "But our greatest secret weapon of all, you

never discovered." Halloran raised his eyebrows. Vusilov wagged a finger. "Oh, yes. Even today, you don't even suspect what it was. The Russian leaders we have today, they are young now, and even most of them forget."

"What are you talking about?" Halloran asked.

Vusilov gave a satisfied nod. "Ah, so, now I have got you curious, eh?" He paused to extract the most from the moment. Halloran waited. The Russian waved a hand suddenly. His voice took on a stronger note. "Look around you today, Ed Halloran, and tell me what do you see? Back on Earth, the Soviet space enterprises are supreme, and we are started already to colonize the Moon. And out here, you see we are the major presence in the nations who come to Mars. . . . Yet, now look back at the way the world was when it ends the Great Patriotic War in 1945, and you see it is America that holds the oyster in its hand, yes?" Vusilov shrugged. "So where does it all go down the pipes? You had it made, guys. What happened?"

Halloran could only shake his head and sigh. "These things happen. What do you want me to say, Sergei? Okay, I agree that we blew it somehow, somewhere along the line. We've got a saying that every dog has its day—and so do nations. Look at history. We had ours, and now it's your turn. Congratulations."

Vusilov looked at him reproachfully. "You think that's all there is to it, that the power plant which the USA had become all just goes away, like the dog who had a lousy day? You do us a disservice. Wouldn't you grant us that perhaps, maybe, we might just have a little piece to do with what happens?"

Now it was Halloran's turn to laugh. "You're not trying to tell me it was your doing?"

"But that is exactly what I am telling you." Vusilov stared back at him unblinkingly.

Halloran's grin faded as he saw that the Russian was being quite serious. "What the hell are you talking about?" he demanded. "How?"

Vusilov snorted. "While for years your experts in universities are busy preaching our system and idolizing Marx, we are studying yours. In Wall Street you have the yo-yo economy that goes up, then it comes down again like a flat face in what you call the depressions. Well, what is it that makes the depressions, do you think?"

Halloran shrugged. "They're part of the boom-bust cycle. It's an inevitable part of the price you pay with a market economy."

Vusilov shook his head, and his humor returned as he chuckled in the way of someone who had been suppressing a long-kept secret. "That's what most Americans say. But the joke is that most Americans don't understand how market economies work. A depression, you see, is what happens when malinvestments liquidate. A malinvestment is when capital and resources are poured into adventures for which there is no real demand. When the bubble goes bust, all the capital and labor and factory machinery and know-how that went in, nothing has any use for anymore, and so we have the depression."

Halloran nodded stonily. "Okay. So?"

"What you have been seeing ever since the one giant step for mankind is the depression in the American space program. It comes from the same reasons of which I have been telling you."

"I'm not sure I follow."

"It is nothing to do with any boom-bust bicycle that comes with capitalism. That was a fiction that we invented, and your 'experts' believed. In a truly free market, some decision makers might guess the wrong way, but they go out of business. It only takes a few who are smart to get it right, and the others will soon follow. If it is not interfered with, the natural mechanism of prices to telegraph information adjusts supplies and demands to give the best bodyguards against malinvestments that you can get. The depression happens when *all* the businesspeoples make the same mistakes at the same time, which can only be because they all get the same wrong information. And there is only one way that can happen to the whole economy at once." Vusilov paused and looked at Halloran expectantly. Halloran shook his head. "Government!" Vusilov exclaimed. "They're the only ones who have the power.

Only government interference can distort the whole picture to make the same mistakes happen everywhere."

Halloran didn't look convinced. "What about the big crash of 1929? Wasn't that a classic case of the free market going belly-up?"

"You see, I told you that Americans don't understand their own economics. No, it was nothing of the kind. The boom busted directly because of the inflation of the money supply through the late twenties by the Federal Reserve because they thought that easy credit would stimulate business, but what it really does is encourage reckless investments. Also, they made huge, soundless loans to Europe, to make Germany into a roadblock for Russia."

Halloran didn't want to get into all that. "So what does that have to do with our space program fifty years later?" he asked.

Vusilov shrugged. "Think what I have been saying. What happened to your space program was a depression, which is when wrong investments liquidate. And the only force that can cause it is when government meddles into the business of people who know what they're doing." He left it to Halloran to make the connection.

Halloran frowned. "What, exactly, are you saying?"

"Well, you tell me. What was the biggest case of where your government went muscling in and took over directing the space program?"

"Do you mean Kennedy and Apollo?"

Vusilov nodded emphatically and brought his palm down on the arm of his chair. "*Da!* Apollo! You've got it!"

Halloran was taken aback. "But . . . that was a success. It was magnificent."

"Yes, it was a success. And I give you, it *was* magnificent. It did what Kennedy said. But what was that? You stuck a flag in the Moon—fine, very good. And you concentrated your whole industry for years on producing the Saturn V behemoth engine, which ever since has no other use than to be a lawn ornament at the Johnson Space Center. An expensive gnome for the garden, yes?"

"Hey, there was more than that."

"Oh, really?" Vusilov looked interested. "What? You tell me."

"Well . . ."

"Yes?"

"There was the spinoff . . . all kind of technologies. Big scientific discoveries, surely . . .

"But what about the other things that *didn't* happen because of it?" Vusilov persisted.

"What do you mean?"

"Think of all the other things that would have come true if Apollo had never happened. In the late fifties, the U.S. Air Force wanted to go for a spaceplane—a two-man vehicle that would have pushed the explored frontier to the fringes of space, the natural step from the rocket aircraft you had been flying. We were terrified of it. It would have led to a whole line of evolution that would have seen commercially viable hypersonic vehicles by the end of the sixties—New York to Tokyo in two or three hours, say, with the same payload and turnaround time of an old 747. That would have led to a low-cost, reusable surface-to-low-orbit shuttle in the seventies, permanently manned orbiting platforms in the eighties, with all the potential that would attract private capital, which gives us a natural jump-off point for the Moon, say, maybe in the mid-nineties, yes—all lightning-years ahead of anything we could have done."

Halloran raised a hand and nodded glumly. "Okay, okay." It was all true. What else could he say?

Vusilov nodded. "Yes, Apollo was magnificent. But the truth was, nobody really needed it then, militarily, commercially, or scientifically. It was all twenty or thirty years too soon. It got you your flag and your lawn pixie. But beyond that, it put government genuises in charge of your whole space program. And what did that get you? Dead-end after Apollo. Then Skylab fell down. By the eighties you'd sunk everything in the original shuttle, which already had old-age. When that blew up there was nothing, because it was the only one you had. The program was so bankrupt that you'd been reduced to playing a public-relations shell game by switching the same set of flyable insides around between different skins. That was why it took ten thousand technicians three months to prepare for a launch, and why you had to shut the line down for two years to build another. And by then, everything was over. The design was already obsolete, anyway."

Halloran nodded wearily. Now that it was all spelled out, there was nothing really to argue about. He raised his glass to drink, and as he did so, he saw that Vusilov's eyes were watching him and twinkling mischievously. "What's so funny?" he asked.

The Russian replied softly, in a curious voice, "Well, surely you don't imagine that all of that just . . . happened, do you?"

Halloran's brow knotted. "You're not saying it was *you* who brought it about?" Vusilov was nodding happily, thumping his hand on the arm of his chair again with the effort of containing himself. "But how? I mean, how could you possibly have manipulated U.S. government policy on such a scale? I don't believe it."

Vusilov brushed a tear from his eye with a knuckle. "It was like this. You see, we had been operating with centralized government control of everything under Stalin for decades, and we *knew* that it didn't work. It was hopeless. Everything they touched, they screwed up. By the time we got rid of him after the war, we knew we had to change the system. But America was racing so far in front that we would never catch up. What could we do? Our only hope was to try somehow to get America to put its space program under government control and let them wreck it, while we were getting ours together. . . . And we did!"

Halloran was looking dumbfounded. "You're not saying that . . ."

"Yes, yes!" Vusilov put a hand to his chest and wheezed helplessly. "We strapped a bundle of obsolete missile-boosters together and threw *Sputnik 1* into orbit; and then we scratched the Gagarin flight together on a shoelace and put him up, too. . . . And hysterical American public opinion and your wonderfully uninformed mass-media did the rest for us . . . ha-ha-ha! I can hear it now, Kennedy: ' . . . *this nation should commit itself to achieving the goal, before this decade is out, of landing a man on the Moon and returning him safely to Earth.'* He fell for it. It was our masterstroke!"

Halloran sat staring at the Russian, thunderstruck. Vusilov leaned back in his chair, and as if finally unburdened of a secret that had been weighing him down for years, laughed uproariously in an outburst that echoed around the lounge. Halloran had had enough. "Okay, you've had your fun," he conceded bitterly. "Suppose we concentrate on the present, and where we're going from here."

Vusilov raised a hand. "Oh, but that isn't the end of it. You see, it made for you an even bigger catastrophe on a national scale, precisely *because* it succeeded so well."

Obviously Halloran was going to have to hear the rest. "Go on," he said resignedly.

"The U.S. economy could have absorbed the mistake of Apollo and recovered. But you didn't let it end there. It gave you a whole generation of legislators and lawmakers who saw the success and concluded that if central control by government and massive federal spending could get you to the Moon, then those things could achieve anything. And you went on to apply it beyond our wildest hopes—when Johnson announced the Great Society program and started socializing the USA. You didn't stop with bankrupting the space industries; you bankrupted the whole country. Apollo was a bigger disaster for America than the Vietnam War. In Vietnam, at least you knew you'd gone wrong, and you learned something. But how can anyone argue with success?

"And what made it so hilarious for us was that you were doing it while we were busy dismantling the same constructions of meddling bureaucrats and incompetents in our country, because we knew how well they didn't work. *That* was our biggest secret—the discovery that made everything else that you see happening today possible. That was the secret that the KGB was there to protect. That was why it was such a big organization."

Despite himself, Halloran couldn't contain his curiosity. "What discovery?" he asked. "What secret are you talking about?"

"Capitalism! Free enterprise, motivated by individualism. That was why our defense industries and our space activities were so secret. That was how they were organized. If America wanted to waste the efficiency of its private sector on producing pet foods, laundry detergents, and breakfast cereals, while destroying everything that was important by letting government run it, that was fine by us. But we did it the other way around."

Halloran was looking nonplussed. "That was the KGB's primary task?"

"Yes. And you never came close to finding out."

"We assumed it was to protect your military secrets—bombs, missiles, all that kind of thing."

"Bombs? We didn't have very many bombs, if you wish to know the truth."

"You didn't?"

"We didn't need them. Washington was devastating your economy more effectively than we could have done with thousands of megatons."

Halloran slumped back in his chair and stared at the Russian dazedly. "But why... how come we've never even heard a whisper of this?"

"Who knows why? The leaders we have now are all young. They only know what they see today. Only a few of us old-timers remember. Very likely, most of history was not as we believe."

Halloran drew in a long breath and exhaled shakily. "Jesus... I need another drink. How about you? This time it's scotch, no matter—" At that moment a voice from a loudspeaker concealed overhead interrupted him.

"Attention, please. An important news item that has just come in over the laser link from Earth. The People's Republic of China has announced the successful launch of a pulsed-nuclear-propelled space vehicle from lunar orbit, which is now en route for the planet Jupiter. The vessel is believed to be carrying a manned mission, but further details have not been released. A spokesman for the Chinese government gave the news at a press conference held in Beijing this morning. The Chinese premier, Xao-Lin-Huong, applauded the achievement as tangible proof of the inherent superiority of the Marxist political and economic system.

"In a response from Moscow amid public outcry and severe criticism from his party's opposition groups, the new Soviet premier, Mr. Oleg Zhocharin, pledged a reappraisal of the Soviet Union's own program, and hinted of a return to more orthodox principles. *'We have allowed ourselves to drift too far, for too long, into a path of indolence and decadence,'* Mr. Zhocharin said. *'But with strong leadership and sound government, I am confident that by concentrating the resources of our mighty nation on a common, inspiring goal, instead of continuing to allow them to dissipate themselves uselessly in a thousand contradictory directions, the slide can be reversed. To this end, I have decreed that the Soviet Union will, within ten years from today, send men out to the star system of Alpha Centauri and return them safely to Earth.'* Mr. Zhocharin also stated that . . ."

Excited murmurs broke out all around the lounge. Halloran looked back at Vusilov and saw that the Russian was sitting ashen-faced, his mouth gaping.

And then a shadow fell across the table. They looked up to see that the Chinese representative had risen from his chair in the alcove and stopped by their table on his way toward the door. His expression was impenetrable, but as Halloran stared up, he saw that the bright, glittering gray eyes were shining with inner laughter. The Chinese regarded them both for a second or two, his book closed loosely in his hand, and bowed his head politely. "Enjoy your day, gentlemen," he said.

And walking without haste in quiet dignity, he left the room.

Everything but Honor

GEORGE ALEC EFFINGER

Dr. Thomas Placide, a black American-born physicist, decided to murder Brigadier General David E. Twiggs, and he realized that it had to be done in December of 1860. He made this decision at the Berlin Olympics of 1936. Jesse Owens had just triumphed over the world's best runners in the two-hundred-meter dash. The physicist jumped up and cheered for the American victory, while his companion applauded politely. Yaakov Fein was one of the most influential scientists in the German Empire, but he was no chauvinist. After the race, Owens was presented to Prince Friedrich. The papers later reported that the prince had apologized for the absence of the seventy-seven-year-old Kaiser, and Owens had replied, "I'm sure the most powerful man in the world has more important things to do than watch six young men in their underwear run halfway around a circle." The quotation may have been the product of some journalist's imagination, but it became so identified with Jesse Owens that there was no point in arguing about it.

Whatever the truth of the matter, Placide settled back in his seat and looked at his program, getting himself ready for the next event. "You must be proud of him," said Fein. "A fellow Negro."

"I *am* proud of him," Placide said. "A fellow American."

"But you are a naturalized German citizen now, Thomas. You should cheer for the German runners."

Placide only shrugged.

Fein went on. "It's a hopeful sign that a Negro has finally won a place on the American Olympic team."

Placide showed some annoyance. "In America, Negroes have equal rights these days."

"Separate, but equal," said Fein.

The black man turned to him. "They aren't slaves anymore, if that's what you're implying. The German Empire has this fatuous paternal concern for all the downtrodden people in the world. Maybe you haven't noticed it, but the rest of the world is getting pretty damn tired of your meddling."

"We believe in using our influence for everyone's benefit."

That seemed to irritate Placide even more. "Every time some Klan bigot burns a cross in Mississippi, you Germans—"

Fein smiled. "*We* Germans, you mean," he said.

Placide frowned. "All right, we Germans send over a goddamn 'peacekeeping force' for the next nine months."

Fein patted the air between them. "Calm down, Thomas," he said, "you're being far too sensitive."

"Let's just watch the track and field events, and forget the social criticism."

"All right with me," said Fein. They dropped the subject for the moment, but Placide was sure that it would come up again soon.

Two years later, in November 1938, Dr. Placide was selected to make the first full-scale operational test of the Cage. He liked to think it was because of his contribution to the project. His journey through time would be through the courtesy of the Placide-Born-Dirac Effect, and neither Max Born nor Paul Dirac expressed any enthusiasm for the chance to act as guinea pig. In Berlin and Göttingen, there was a great deal of argument over just what the Placide-Born-Dirac Effect was, and the more conservative theorists wanted to limit the experiments to making beer steins and rodents disappear, which Placide and Fein had been doing for over a year.

"My point," said Placide at a conference of leading physicists in Göttingen, "is that after all this successful study, it's time for someone to hop in the Cage and find out what's happening, once and for all."

"I think it's certainly time to take the next step," said Werner Heisenberg.

"I agree," said Erwin Schrödinger.

Dirac rubbed his chin thoughtfully. "Nevertheless," he said, "it's much too soon to talk about human subjects."

"Are you seriously suggesting we risk a human life on the basis of our ill-fated and unproven theories?" asked Albert Einstein.

Zach Marquand shrugged. "It would be a chance to clear up all the foggy rhetoric about paradoxes," he said.

Edward La Martine just stood to one side, sullenly shaking his head. He obviously thought Placide's suggestion was unsound, if not altogether insane.

"We have four in favor of using a human subject in the Cage, and four against," said Fein. He took a deep breath and let it out as a sigh. "I'm the project director, and I suppose it's my responsibility to settle this matter. God help me if I choose wrong. I say we go ahead and expand the scope of the experiment."

Placide looked relieved. "Let me volunteer, then," he said.

"Typical American recklessness," said La Martine in a sour voice.

"You mean," said Placide, "that you'll be happy if I'm the one in the Cage. Not as a reward for my work, of course, but because if anybody's alternate history is going to be screwed up, better it be America's than Germany's."

La Martine just spread his hands and said nothing.

"Then I volunteer to go along," said Fein. "As copilot."

"There's nothing for a copilot to do," said Placide. Even then, it may have been that Fein didn't have complete faith in Placide's motives.

Placide had his own agenda, after all, but he kept it secret from the others.

"Why don't you travel back a week or so," suggested Born. "Then you can take a photograph or find some other proof to validate the experiment, and return immediately to Göttingen and time T_0."

"In for a penny, in for a pound," said Placide. "I'd like to choose my own destination, and possibly solve a little historical problem while I have the chance." The Cage would never have existed without him, and so it didn't take him long to persuade the others. Placide and Fein worked with Marquand and his team for nine more weeks learning to calibrate the Cage. In the meantime, Placide studied everything he could find about General Twiggs, and he carefully hid his true plan from the Europeans.

Placide should have known that his first attempt would not go smoothly, but as far as he could see, his plan was foolproof. His reasoning was simple: His primary goal—greater even than testing the operation of the Cage—was to relieve the barbaric conditions forced on American blacks following the Confederate Insurrection of 1861–1862.

Although he'd quit the land of his birth, he still felt an unbreakable bond between himself and others of his race, who could never escape the oppression as he had. A white friend of his father had enabled Placide to attend Yale University, where he'd studied math and physics. During the middle 1930s, after he joined the great community of experimental scientists working in the German Empire, he began to see how he might accomplish something far more important than adding a new quibble to the study of particle physics.

The Cage—*his* Cage, as he sometimes thought of it—gave him the opportunity to make a vital contribution. His unhappy experiences as a child and a young man in the United States supplied him with sufficient motive. All he lacked was the means, and this he found through historical research as painstaking as his scientific work with Dirac and Born.

To Placide, Brigadier General David Emanuel Twiggs seemed to be one of those anonymous yet crucial players in the long game of history. In 1860 he was the military commander of the Department of Texas. Although few students of the Confederate Insurrection would even recognize his name, Twiggs nevertheless had a moment, the briefest moment, when he determined the course of future events. Placide had come to realize that Twiggs was his target. Twiggs could be used to liberate American blacks from all the racist hardships and injustices of the twentieth century.

Leaving T_0, the Cage brought Placide and Yaakov Fein to San Antonio on December 24, 1860. Fein agreed to guard the Cage, which had come to rest in a wintry field about three miles from Twiggs's headquarters. Fein, of course, had no idea that Placide had anything in mind other than a quick scouting trip into this city of the past.

Placide began walking. From nearby he could hear the lowing of cattle, gathered now in shadowed groups beneath the arching limbs of live oaks. He climbed down a hill into a shallow valley of moonlit junipers and red cedar. The air smelled clean and sharp, although this Christmas Eve in Texas was not as cold as the February he'd left behind in Germany. Frosty grass crunched underfoot; as he passed through the weeds, their rough seeds clung to his trouser legs.

His exhilaration at his safe arrival in another time was tempered almost immediately by anxiety over the danger he was in. If anyone stopped and questioned him, he would have an impossible time explaining himself. At best, he would be taken for a freed slave, and as such he could expect little if any help from the local citizens. Worse was the fact that he had no proper identification and no money, and thus he would certainly appear to be a runaway.

Placide had put himself in a grave and desperate situation. If he failed and was captured, his only hope would be Fein, but Fein was a German with little knowledge of this period in American history. Placide did not have much faith in the other man's ability to rescue him, if it came to that. It might happen that no one would ever learn of Placide's sacrifice. He was thinking of the black generations yet unborn, and not his colleagues in Göttingen. He was in a unique position to do something remarkable for his oppressed people.

As it happened, Placide was not detained or captured. He made his way through the barren, cold night to the general's quarters. Twiggs was already in bed, and there was a young soldier standing sentry duty outside the door. Placide shook his head ruefully. Here was the first serious hitch in his plans. He was going to have to do something about that guard.

It wasn't so difficult to gain entry. Placide needed only to nod at the young man, grab him, and drive a knife into his chest. The soldier made a soft, gurgling cry and slumped heavily in Placide's grasp. Placide let the body fall silently to the floor. He paused a moment, listening for any sign of alarm, but all was still. Oddly, he felt no sense of guilt for what he'd done. In a way, the world of 1860 didn't seem truly real to him. It was as if the man he'd killed had never really existed, although the corporal's dark blood had stained Placide's trousers convincingly.

Placide went quietly through the door and stood over General Twiggs's bed, looking down at him. He was old, seventy or so, with long white hair and a dense white beard. He looked like a Biblical patriarch, sleeping peacefully. Placide was surprised to discover that it was not in him simply to kill the old man in his sleep. Placide wasn't sure if he was too cruel or too weak for that. He woke Twiggs, pressing one hand over the general's mouth to keep him silent.

"Don't make a sound," Placide said as Twiggs struggled to sit up. "I must speak with you. I'll remove my hand if you promise not to call out for help. That will do you no good, in any event." Twiggs nodded slowly, his eyes wide.

Placide took his hand away. Twiggs gasped and tried to speak, but for a moment he could only wheeze. "Who are you?" he asked at last.

"That's not important. You must understand that your life is in my hands. Will you answer my questions?"

Twiggs was no fool. He knew better than to bluster or threaten. He nodded again. Dressed in his bedclothes, he was a wrinkled, feeble figure; but Placide suppressed his pity for the old man. Twiggs was a Southerner by birth and a secessionist by inclination. "You are in command here," Placide said.

"Yes," said the general. "If you think that after breaking into my room, you can get me to arrange for you to escape—"

Placide raised a hand curtly, cutting him off. "If for some reason you stepped down, who would assume command in your place?"

Twiggs's brow furrowed, but otherwise he showed no outward sign of fear. "I suppose it would be Lieutenant Colonel Lee," he said.

"You mean Robert E. Lee?"

"Of the First Cavalry," said Twiggs.

Placide was relieved to hear the answer. Some months before, while Twiggs had been away from San Antonio, he had named Lee acting commander of the Department of Texas. If Twiggs were forced to retire, Lee would take over again until the War Department made its own permanent appointment.

"Now let me propose a hypothetical situation," said Placide. "Suppose Texas decides to secede from the Union—"

"So you've burst your way in here and ruined my sleep to argue politics?" Twiggs demanded angrily. "And what have you done to the young man on guard duty?"

Placide slapped Twiggs hard across the face. "Suppose Texas decides to secede from the Union," he repeated calmly. "What would your position be?"

The general raised a trembling hand to his cheek. His expression was furious, and Placide caught the first hint of fear in his eyes. "Texas will secede," Twiggs said softly. "Any fool can read that. I've already written to Washington, but the War Department has so far chosen not to send me any definite instructions."

"What will you do when the secessionist rebels demand your surrender?"

Twiggs's gaze left Placide's face and stared blankly toward the far wall. "I will surrender," he said finally. "I have not the means to carry on a civil war in Texas."

A gunshot would have roused the entire garrison. Placide cut the old man's throat with his knife, then searched the room for items to take back with him to show Fein and the others. Finally, he made his escape back into the silent night of the past. Outside, it was very strange to smell bread baking not far away, as if all was well, as if something impossible had not just happened.

"There," he told himself, "you have changed history." It remained to be seen if he'd changed it for the better.

When Placide met Fein later that night, he suggested that they not return directly to 1938 and Göttingen. Fein was dubious. "The more time we spend here," he argued, "the more chance there is that someone will see us. We may cause an alteration in the flow of events. That could be disastrous."

Placide swallowed a mouthful of brandy he'd taken from Twiggs's headquarters building. The liquor had a harsh, sweet taste, but it gave the illusion of warmth. He offered the brandy to his companion. "Yaakov," he said, shivering in the cold night wind, "it's already too late."

Fein's brows narrowed. "What are you talking about?" He declined to sample the general's brandy.

Placide shrugged. "Just that I've already inserted myself into the past. I had a conversation with General Twiggs."

"Don't you know what that means?" cried Fein. He was furious. "We may return to the present and find God only knows what!"

"I couldn't help it," said Placide. "I was discovered. I was arrested and taken to the commanding officer. I had to do some fancy talking or you would never have seen me again."

"God help us," murmured Fein. The two men looked at each other for a moment. There was no sound but the lonely creaking of bare tree limbs, and the rustle of dead leaves blowing along the ground.

"Look," said Placide, "why don't we jump ahead to, say, February, and find out if anything's different. In case of some kind of disaster, we can always reappear a few minutes before T_0 and prevent ourselves from making this trip."

"I don't know," said the German. "That might leave two of you and two of me in the present."

"Let's worry about that only if we have to. Right now

we've got to find out if my little interview had any permanent effect." Fein watched him closely, but said nothing more.

The two men entered the Cage, and Placide reset the controls to take them forward a few weeks. He knew that on February 16, 1861, Texas state troops would surround the government buildings in San Antonio. Twiggs would give in quickly to demands that he turn over all the arms and equipment to the militia. Of course, Placide had prevented that from happening with his single bold stroke. In effect, he'd put Robert E. Lee in command of the Department of Texas. Lee was a Virginian, but he had publicly stated he would have no part in a revolution against the Union. Placide had acted to change his mind.

They reappeared in San Antonio on the twentieth of February. Once more, Fein guarded the Cage while Placide went into town. The air was warmer, and smelled of wood smoke. He heard the ragged cries of birds, and once he saw a large black winged shape detach itself from the ground and fly into a cottonwood that was beginning to show new yellow-green leaves. For a while, everything seemed peaceful.

The town, however, was in a frenzied state of confusion. Bands of armed rebels patrolled the streets. Gunshots frequently split the air. The younger men wore the wide-eyed, fierce looks of inexperienced warriors looking forward to their first battle. The older men and women were grim and worried, obviously in fear that the conflict that had threatened so long in the abstract had come at last.

Placide stood in a narrow alley between two shops, afraid to push himself into the throngs of shouting people in the street. Finally, as both his curiosity and fear for his own safety increased, he stopped a well-dressed, elderly white man. "Pardon me, sir," he said, trying to sound calm, "my master has sent me for news."

The older man drew himself up, unhappy at being accosted in the street by an unfamiliar slave. "Tell your master that our boys have driven the Federals out," he said.

"That news will ease his pain," said Placide. He was galled to have to pretend to be a slave, but he had no other choice. "And Lee?"

"The rascal is dead, killed in the fight." The man was so pleased to be able to report that fact, he actually slapped the black man's shoulder.

Placide was stunned by the news; he'd hoped to persuade Lee to become a general for the South. He watched the man turn and go on about his business, and he knew that it was time to go about his own. His plan had not failed; it had but succeeded too well.

When they returned to T_0, Placide and Fein discovered that the present was just as they'd left it, that their excursion in time had not changed the past, but rather created a new alternate reality. Still, some of their colleagues were furious.

"What the hell were you thinking of?" demanded La Martine. He'd been fascinated by the theoretical aspects of their work, but fearful of practical applications.

Now Fein was convinced that the Cage was too dangerous to use, at least until the Placide-Born-Dirac Effect was better understood.

Placide knew that if he hoped to try again in the past, he'd have to win La Martine and Fein over. "Look," he said, "we're all curious about what happens when a change is made in the past."

"You were tampering!" cried La Martine. "As it turned out, you had no permanent effect—"

"So I don't understand why you're so upset."

"—but there was the possibility that you might have changed this world disastrously, for all of us. You had no right to attempt such a thing!"

"Sending beer steins into the past might have had disastrous results, too, Eduard," said Heisenberg thoughtfully. "Yet you had no qualms about that."

"Making inanimate objects vanish is hardly equal to interviewing historical figures in their bedrooms," said Paul Dirac indignantly.

Placide had told the others that he'd merely discussed

politics with General Twiggs. It hadn't seemed profitable at the time to mention that he'd killed the old man. "You know how I feel about the Legislated Equality programs in the United States."

Dirac gave him a weary look and nodded.

"Before returning here to T_0, Yaakov and I jumped from 1861 to 1895, where we bought a history of that new timeline." Placide held up the book. "Here are the effects of our visit. I thought by going back before the Confederate Insurrection and starting things off on a different course, I could keep the Equality programs and the Liberty Boroughs and all the other abuses from ever happening. I persuaded Twiggs to retire, because I knew Robert E. Lee wouldn't surrender the garrison at San Antonio. His sense of duty and honor wouldn't allow it. He'd resist, and there would be a violent confrontation. The war would begin there in Texas, rather than two months later at Fort Sumter."

"So?" asked Heisenberg.

"So Lee would learn firsthand that the war could not be avoided, and that the needs of the Confederacy were immediate and desperate. I was certain that history would unfold differently from there on. I wanted Lee to turn down Lincoln's invitation to command the Union Army. In our world, his military brilliance brought the rebellion under control in little more than eighteen months. Now, though, we'd created a new timeline, one in which Lee would not be the Great Traitor, but rather the great genius of the Southern cause."

"But you were wrong, Thomas," said Fein. "Without Lee to lead it, the Union *still* defeated the Confederacy. All you succeeded in doing was extending the bloody conflict another year while the North searched for able military leadership."

Placide shrugged. "A minor miscalculation," he said.

"You're personally responsible for the death of Robert E. Lee, man!" said La Martine.

Placide was startled. "What do you mean? Robert E. Lee's been dead for almost seventy years. He died peacefully in the White House, not yet halfway through his term as president."

"Yes," said Marquand, "in *our* timeline that's what happened. But you went into another universe and interfered. Lee's blood is on your hands."

Placide suddenly saw the absurd point Marquand was trying to make. "Zach," he said, "we went into a world that doesn't exist. It was a fantasy world. That Robert E. Lee didn't really live, and he didn't really die. He was no more than a possibility, a quantum quirk."

"We're talking about people, Thomas," said Schrödinger, "not particles."

"Particles come into and go out of existence all the time," Placide protested. "Just the same way, the people and events in that timeline were only local expressions of the wave function. You're letting emotion twist your thinking."

Fein frowned at him. "Thomas, I want you to prepare a report as quickly as you can. We're all going to have to think very hard about this. You've shown us that there are moral questions involved with this project that none of us foresaw."

"Yaakov, I wish you'd—"

"And I'm not going to permit anyone to use the Cage again until we establish some philosophical ground rules." Fein gave Placide a long, appraising look, then turned and left the room. Placide glanced at the book they'd brought back, the history of America in the timeline they now called Universe$_2$. He was very eager to get back to his quarters and read of the elaborate and unpredictable results of what he'd done.

Placide made another trip into the past, this one unauthorized and in secret. He didn't know what Fein would do if he found out that Placide had ignored his prohibition, but to be truthful, Placide didn't care. He had more important matters to worry about. It was his belief—and both Schrödinger and Marquand agreed with him—that a second experiment would take him to an 1861 untouched by his previous meddling. If their many-worlds hypothesis had any validity, it was statistically unlikely that

Placide would find himself back in Universe$_2$. He could make a clean start in Universe$_3$, profiting from his regrettable mistakes.

His destination this second time was the District of Columbia, on the morning of April 18, 1861. He was dressed in clothes that would attract little attention in the past, and he took with him a small sum of U.S. money in gold and silver that he'd purchased through numismatic shops in Berlin. Upon his arrival, Placide left the Cage outside of town, as he'd done in Texas. He walked some distance in the chilly air of early spring. He intended to find a hotel where he might hire a carriage, but this was more difficult than he'd imagined. He was, after all, a black man and a stranger, on some inscrutable errand of his own. Whenever he approached an innkeeper or carriage driver with his gold coins, he was told either that none of the vehicles were in proper repair, or that they had all been reserved to other parties. He understood their meaning well enough.

Placide made his way along Pennsylvania Avenue to Blair House, almost directly across the street from the Executive Mansion. He gave a little involuntary shiver when he realized that inside the White House, at that moment, Abraham Lincoln was hearing firsthand reports of the events at Fort Sumter, and preparing his order to blockade the Confederate ports. Placide was tempted to abandon his subtle plan and instead seek an interview with the president himself. What advice and warnings he could give Lincoln, if he would only listen. . . .

That was the problem, of course: Getting these strong-willed men to pay attention. Placide knew that he could help them save thousands of lives, and at the same time build a future free of the oppression their shortsightedness would lead to. His influence, of course, would be greater if he were white, but there was no point in making idle wishes. He would do the best he could.

A carriage pulled up in front of Blair House just as he arrived. He knew the man who stepped down from it must be Robert E. Lee, although he didn't look much like the photographs Placide was familiar with. Lee was wearing the blue uniform of the U.S. Army, and he carried the wide-brimmed hat of a cavalry officer in one hand. He had yet to grow his famous gray beard. He was taller, too, with broad shoulders and a strict posture and military bearing that gave him an imposing appearance. His manner was calm and poised, although he was on his way to a momentous meeting.

Lee paused a moment, perhaps collecting himself, before turning toward the entrance of the grand house. Placide hurried up to him. "General Lee," he said.

Lee smiled. "You flatter me," he said. "I presently hold the rank of colonel." He waited patiently, apparently thinking that Placide was bringing him a message of some kind.

Placide was struck by Lee's gentle manner. There was intelligence in his eyes, but not the haggard, haunted look that would come later. In the few years remaining to him after the Insurrection, Lee always carried with him the painful knowledge that he had been, after all, the fatal betrayer of his homeland. "I have some important information for you, sir," Placide said. Now that he was before the man, the physicist was unsure how to proceed. After all, Lee wasn't The Great Traitor yet, not in this timeline. Placide had prevented him from becoming the savior of the Union in Universe$_2$, but he'd learned only that Lee dead was no better than Lee as Yankee. "May I have a moment of your time?"

Lee pursed his lips. "I have an appointment at this address, sir, and I am obliged by both courtesy and duty to respect it."

"I know," said Placide, "and I won't keep you long. When you go inside, Francis Preston Blair is going to offer you command of the Union Army, on behalf of President Lincoln. I know that you intend to accept; but if you do, sir, you will be damning future generations of American Negroes to lives of degradation and suffering. They will harbor a rage that will grow until our nation is torn by violence more terrible than this quarrel over secession. I beg you to reconsider."

Lee did not reply at once. He studied Placide's face for

a long moment. "May I inquire, sir," he said quietly, "how you come to be in possession of this information?"

Placide took out his wallet and removed a fifty-dollar bill—currency from the United States of his world, of his time. He handed it to Lee. The cavalry officer examined it in silence, first the back, with the picture of the Capitol Building, then the front, with his own portrait. "Sir, what is this?" he asked.

"Paper money," said Placide.

Lee turned the bill over and over in his hands. "Is it a bank note?"

"Legal tender printed by the federal government, and backed by government gold reserves."

"I've never seen a note like it before," said Lee dubiously.

Placide showed him the small legend beside Lee's picture. "It was issued in 1932," he said.

Lee took a deep breath and let it out. Then he gave the money back to Placide. "Mr. Blair is an elderly man, and I do him no honor by my tardiness. I beg you to excuse me."

"General Lee," Placide pleaded, "if you accept Lincoln's offer, you must lead an invading army onto the soil of Virginia, your home. How can you raise your sword against your own family and friends? You must allow me to explain. I showed you the bill because you'd think me a madman unless I presented some evidence."

"Evidence only of the skill of your engraver," said Lee. "I did not find the portrait flattering, and I did not find the item in question amusing."

As earnestly as he could, Placide explained to him that he'd come through time to let Lee know of the terrible consequences of his decision to defend the Union. "I can tell you that with you in command, the Army of the Potomac will withstand the first thrusts of the Confederate forces."

"Indeed, sir," said Lee with a little smile.

"And then you will sweep down to force the evacuation of Richmond. You will coordinate your army's movements with those of McClellan in the west, and divide the South into helpless fragments. In the meantime, the navy will blockade the ports along the Atlantic, the Gulf Coast, and the Mississippi River."

"Your predictions make the difficulties seem not so very daunting, after all."

Placide paid no attention to Lee's skepticism. "The Confederacy's only true victory will come at Petersburg, and only because of the incompetence of one of your subordinates, General Ambrose Burnside. Finally, on October 17, 1862, P. G. T. Beauregard will surrender the Army of Northern Virginia to you at Dry Pond, Georgia, northeast of Atlanta."

"And tell me, sir," said Lee, "will the Union thereafter be restored?"

"Yes," said Placide, "the Union will be restored, but in terrible circumstances." Placide described to him the fight over Reconciliation, and how the radical Republicans would seek to punish the Southern states. "All that will hold the country together in those furious months will be your strength of will as president," Placide told him.

Lee shook his head. "I am certain now that you offer me dreams and not prophecy. I cannot conceive of any circumstance that would persuade me to undertake that office. I have neither the temperament nor the wisdom."

"The Democrats will come to you, as a war hero and as a Southerner. You'll be the natural choice to oversee the process of Reconciliation. Congress will battle you, but your resolve will be as strong as Lincoln's. You'll prevent the plundering of the South."

"I am glad to hear this, but I wonder why you wish me then to decline the offer that awaits me inside. Would you see the South torn apart in peace to more horrible effect than in war?"

Placide felt a tremendous sympathy for this man, and he had to fight the urge to tell him all that would happen. In Placide's own world, Lee would die in 1870. Vice President Salmon P. Chase would then be sworn in, and the long, cruel struggle of the black would resume. Before his death, Lee would prepare a document emancipating all the slaves in the South; but on taking office Chase would find it convenient to set this initiative aside. The issue would still be the self-determination of the states. Chase would let progress on civil rights hang in abeyance rather than antagonize the newly reconstituted Congress. Not until 1878, during the Custer administration, would slavery be officially abolished.

"Please try to understand," said Placide, "what seems like victory for you and for the Union will be, for the Negro population, the beginning of a dreadful spiral down into a social and economic abyss."

"I'm not certain that I take your meaning, sir," said Colonel Lee.

"I mean only that your concern for the slaves will blind you to the long-range effects of what Congress will propose. And after you've left the White House"—Placide still could not tell Lee how brief his tenure would be—"your successors will pervert your programs to trap the Negroes in misery. Even in my time, seventy-five years after the Insurrection, many Negroes believe that life as a slave must have been better than what they endure. As wretched as the condition of slavery is, the American Negro of 1938 has little more of freedom or opportunity or hope."

Lee was bemused by Placide's vehemence. "If I entertain your argument, sir, I am left with the feeling that all my actions will be futile, particularly those guided most strongly by my conscience."

"Millions of Negroes are forced to live in squalid slums the government calls Liberty Boroughs, segregated from the prosperous white communities," Placide told him. "We suffer under the Legislated Equality programs, and—"

Lee raised a hand, cutting him off. "I beg your pardon, sir," he said. "I am grateful to have your opinion, but I can tarry here no longer." He gave Placide a nod and strode up to the front door of Blair House.

Placide didn't know how effective his appeal had been. He was heartened to see, however, that as Lee turned away, his expression was solemn and thoughtful.

In his own timeline, Placide had read that Lee, as general-in-chief of the Union Army, resisted the president's frequent pleas to attack the Confederate units across the Potomac in Virginia. "You must do something soon," Lincoln demanded late in July 1861. "The army consists to a large degree of ninety-day recruits who volunteered after the attack on Fort Sumter. The period of enlistment has almost expired. When it does, those young men will leave the ranks and go back to their families, unless they are given something to inspire them to remain. You must use them to strike a strong and decisive blow."

Lee remained firm. "Our soldiers are simply not ready," he said. "The volunteers are poorly trained and poorly outfitted. It would be little more than murder to take such an unprepared mob into battle."

"A victory would encourage our soldiers and open the way to the capture of Richmond."

Lee saw it differently. "A defeat," he argued, "would open the way for the enemy to capture Washington."

As the weeks went by, Lincoln continued to put pressure on Lee to act, even threatening to strip the general-in-chief of his command. But Lee would not be bullied. When the ninety-day period came to an end, most of the recruits reenlisted out of respect and admiration for Lee himself, and not the Federal cause. Lee used the time to deploy his troops with care and precision. He instructed his subordinates to hinder any advance of the Confederate army, but to fall back slowly rather than engage. Finally, on September 1, Lee reported to the president and his Cabinet that he was satisfied. Two weeks later, at Occoquan, Virginia, Lee defeated a numerically superior Confederate force under the command of General Beauregard. Aided by Generals Irwin McDowell and Benjamin Butler, Lee prevented the Southern corps from crossing the Potomac into Maryland and then encircling Washington.

The Battle of Occoquan was the smashing victory that Lincoln had hoped for. With one stroke, Lee crushed the dreams of the Confederacy. At Occoquan, he seized the offensive and never relinquished it for a moment during the rest of the war. The remainder of the eighteen-month struggle in the east saw little more than Beauregard's

courageous though vain efforts to delay, with his clever
skirmishes and retreats, the unavoidable outcome. Inevitably, however, he was to have his most difficult meeting
with Lee at Folkston's Dining Room in Dry Pond.
Beauregard, The Napoleon in Gray, was as noble in defeat
as Lee was gracious in victory. The two men had been
friends when they'd served together in Mexico. They
would be friends again when Lee was president and
Beauregard governor of Louisiana.

All of this was a matter of record, but Placide knew
just how easily the record could be erased.

Placide felt a mixture of hope and anxiety while he
waited in the street outside Blair House. If Lee emerged
as a Union general, if he became again the Great Traitor,
Placide planned to return to T_0 and abandon this
timeline. He would then have to hit on a more forceful
method of persuading Lee—in Universe$_4$. If, however,
Placide had read Lee's expression correctly, then he planned
to spend quite some time in Universe$_3$, making short
jumps forward through time to follow the course of the
Insurrection. With the invincible Robert E. Lee as the defender of the Confederacy's fortunes, the fate of the South
would certainly be different.

Placide opened to the first page of the journal he
intended to keep during his experiment. He wrote his first
entry:

> Universe$_3$
> April 18, 1861
> Outside Blair House, Washington
>
> If things turn out as I hope, I will remain in this
> newly made world, studying it and perhaps learning
> something of value to take back with me to T_0. I will
> adopt this alternative timeline as my own, and love
> these people regardless of their sins, for have I not
> created them? Perhaps that sounds mad, but there has
> not yet been time enough to evaluate properly this
> unlooked-for benefit of my work. But surely I am a god

to these people, having called them out of nothing, with the power to send their history off in whichever direction I choose. The God of Abraham created but the universe of T_o, and I have already created two more. How many others will I call into being before I achieve my purpose? General Lee comes now, with the fate of Universe$_3$ in his hands.

It was September 16, 1861, and the air should have been thick with drifting clouds of gunsmoke, the acrid breath of massed rifles; but the autumn breeze carried only the tang of burning firewood from a farmhouse nearby. There should have been the menacing, booming shocks of the field artillery, and the ragged cries of wounded men; but there was only stillness. The roads near Occoquan, Virginia, should have been jammed with wild-eyed, charging infantry, and the urgent mounted messengers of the generals; but only Thomas Placide disturbed the quiet countryside.

It was a grim, gloomy day in late summer, and black clouds threatened low overhead. It had not yet begun to rain, but a storm seemed imminent. Thunder cracked and rolled, and Placide grimaced. He did not like to be out in this kind of weather. He was cheered only by the knowledge that he had truly persuaded Robert E. Lee, that a mechanism for the salvation of American blacks had been set in motion. All that now remained was the job of supervision, to make certain that Placide's careful scheme did not falter as this world's divergent history unfolded.

He shook his head. He wouldn't have guessed that this was the kind of day Lee would choose for his first major test as a general in the Confederate Army. Placide hurried down a rutted, dusty lane, to the white-painted frame farmhouse, hoping to meet someone who could direct him to the battlefield.

The house was surrounded by a bare yard and a gap-toothed fence. Placide went through the yawning gate and climbed three steps to the porch. He heard nothing from within the house. He rapped loudly. A moment later, a distracted white woman opened the door, gave Placide a critical look, and shut the door again. "Ma'am?" called Placide. "Will you help me, ma'am?"

The door opened again, and he was looking at a tall, burly, frowning man. "We got nothin' for you," said the farmer.

"I just need some directions from y'all," said Placide. He reminded himself that once again he needed to behave modestly.

"Directions we can afford, I guess," said the farmer.

Placide nodded gratefully. "I've got to find my way to the battle, and quickly."

The white man closed one eye and stared at him for a few seconds. "Battle?" he asked.

"I've got news for General Lee."

"You his boy?"

Placide felt a flush of anger, but he stifled it. "No, sir, I'm a free man of color. But I've got news for General Lee."

"What's this about a battle? There been no soldiers around here except when they come by in July. On their way to Manassas."

"Manassas? Where's that?"

The farmer gave him another close look. "Where the battle was. Bull Run. It was Beauregard and Joe Johnston that licked the Yankees at Bull Run. Your boss was busy fetchin' coffee cups for Jeffy Davis down in Richmond."

Placide wondered at how quickly men and events had found their new course. "General Lee is obliged to follow the wishes of President Davis," he said.

The farmer gave a derisive laugh. "While Granny Lee was doin' just that, one Sunday afternoon the blue boys come out of Washington, thinkin' they was goin' to whup Beauregard and send him on home. Then Joe Johnston showed up to help him out, and before you know it the damn Yankees are runnin' ever which way, goin' back to cry on Lincoln's shoulder."

Placide took all this in. "Well, sir," he said, "I guess they told me wrong when they said he'd come up here."

"Your General Lee ain't never been within fifty mile of

here. As far as I know, he's somewheres off in the west, diddlin' around in the mountains."

"I thank you, sir. I suppose I'd just better get back to Richmond myself. Someone's made some kind of mistake."

The farmer laughed. "I'm lookin' right at him." He turned away and closed the door. Placide found that his hands were clenched into tight fists. He let out his breath slowly and forced himself to relax. He walked back out through the farmer's gate and headed back the way he'd come. He wanted to get back to the Cage before the heavy rain began.

Although he hated having to play the role of fool, Placide was elated by the news. He'd prevented the crushing Confederate defeat at Occoquan from occurring in Universe₃. There had been a mighty rebel victory that had not happened in Placide's timeline, and it had happened even without Robert E. Lee. With Lee yet on the verge of fulfilling his destiny, Placide could almost see the glory of the greater victories yet to come. He found himself smiling broadly as the first huge raindrops spatted about him in the dust.

Universe₃
October 17, 1862
Dry Pond, Georgia

For the second time, I've come to watch an event that has vanished from history. I suspected that would be the case, yet I jumped here from Occoquan anyway. Hearing the news of the Battle of Bull Run, I was of the opinion that I had wholly altered the course of the Insurrection. It would be unlikely in the extreme that its ending should now fall out just as it had in my own timeline, on the same day, at the same place, and for the same reasons. Still, I had to be certain.

In the deficient universe of my origin, Beauregard's surrender took place in the salon of Folkston's Dining Hall. I was not foolish enough to enter that white establishment by the front door. Rather, I went around to the rear of the building. There I won the sympathy of the kitchen slaves with a glib story of fear and desperation. They kindly gave me a good meal, some clothing more appropriate than my own, and a sum of money in both Confederate scrip and silver.

Of course, no one here has heard rumors of the approach of a triumphant Union Army. Everyone agrees that the fighting continues far to the north of Maryland, and far to the west of Mississippi. Yaakov was right: I have given this world a fiercer, longer conflict. In Universe$_3$, this is no mere Confederate Insurrection. This is civil war.

And how is the struggle going? My new friends have caught me up on the thirteen months I missed, jumping here from Occoquan: George McClellan is Lincoln's general-in-chief. (I am certain he is no Lee, and will hardly present an obstacle to Confederate triumph.) There was a Southern victory at Ball's Bluff, Virginia, and a battle at Shiloh, in Tennessee, that wasn't much of a victory for the Federals or much of a defeat for the South. Lee defended Richmond against McClellan, and then, damn it! Lee and Stonewall Jackson beat up the Yankees at Bull Run a second time! That gave Marse Robert confidence to try to invade the North by heading up through Maryland—just as Beauregard tried in my own timeline. And just like Beauregard, Lee was stopped. He was stalled at Antietam Creek because a set of his campaign orders was lost and later discovered by Union soldiers.

If there is a turn for the worse, and if I must abandon Universe$_3$, I may begin again as I did at Blair House; but this time, I will remove in advance that careless officer at Antietam. "In for a penny, in for a pound." It was not enough, it seems, to have won Robert E. Lee to my cause. I find that I must continue to supervise and guide this entire war.

How astonished Dirac and the others will be when I return to T_0! I will seem to have aged several years in a single moment.

How sad I will be to leave a world I am perfecting, to return to a world I can no longer love.

Placide locked his door and went downstairs to dinner. The Negro rooming house was on Rampart Street, on the edge of the Vieux Carré. Placide had grown up in New Orleans, but that had been in the early years of the twentieth century. Here it was 1864, and the city was very different. There were still steamboats working on the river and bales of cotton piled high on the wharves. He thought that somewhere in this quaint version of New Orleans, his own grandparents were growing up. He could visit them, if he chose to. The idea made him a little queasy.

A young quadroon woman waved to him. "Monsieur Placide," she called, "won't you sit beside me this evening?"

"I'd be delighted," he said. Her name was Lisette, and she'd been the mistress of the son of a prosperous businessman who lived above Canal Street in the American Sector. It was common for a young white man of means to select a light-skinned girl like Lisette and establish her in a small house of her own on Rampart or Burgundy streets. It was her misfortune that the boy's interest had waned, and he no longer supported her. Now she was looking for a new friend—a new white friend. The quadroon beauty disdained forming attachments to black men. When she'd called to Placide, she was just practicing her social graces.

"You always have so much interesting gossip," she said.

Placide sighed and held her chair for her, then seated himself. "I wonder what Mrs. Le Moyne has for us tonight," he said.

Mrs. Le Moyne came into the dining room and gave Placide a dour look. "I will serve y'all what I always serve," she said. "And that is, sir, what little the damn Yankees haven't taken for themselves or spoiled."

Placide rose slightly from his seat and gave her a little bow. "You work miracles, madame," he said.

"I'm sure, sir, that you wish I could," said Mrs. Le Moyne. She went back out into the kitchen.

"Isn't she a charmer?" whispered Lisette.

Another of the tenants sat down across the table from

them. He was a surgeon's assistant in the black community. Placide thought the man always seemed to know too much of everyone else's business. "Will you be leaving us again soon, Mr. Placide?" he asked.

"Yes," said Placide. "Tomorrow."

"Where are you going?" asked Lisette. "Don't the Yankees stop you from traveling?"

Placide shrugged. "I don't worry about them."

The black man across the table laughed. "Then you must be the only person in New Orleans who doesn't."

"How long will you be gone?" asked Lisette.

"Maybe a month or two," said Placide. "Maybe longer." He thought of the Cage, safe upstairs in his room. The War of Southern Independence was proceeding differently than he'd planned. Lee's final northward thrust had been turned back at Gettysburg. The Confederate nation now had little hope of victory, but it still fought grimly on. Oddly, though, Placide was not wholly dissatisfied. What mattered was that Lincoln had been driven to a point of urgency. Politics might yet achieve for blacks what military might had not.

Almost a year before, desperate to rally continued support for his war effort, Lincoln had issued what he called an Emancipation Proclamation. In Placide's timeline, with Lee leading the Federal forces to quick victory in 1862, Lincoln was never pressed to make such a concession. And in Universe$_2$, with Lee killed before the Insurrection even began, Lincoln considered freeing the slaves but put the idea aside when victory proved imminent in 1863.

Only here in Universe$_3$, in the spring of 1864, with Lee in a grim and determined struggle to hold off defeat as long as possible, could Placide see some hope that American blacks might avoid the horror of what President James G. Blaine had so sanctimoniously called Parallel Development.

"Mr. Placide," said Lisette sweetly, "would you bring me back something pretty from your travels? I'd be ever so grateful." She gave him a dazzling smile.

He was neither flattered nor fooled. He thought that

with luck he'd bring her freedom and dignity, although he was sure she'd much rather have a new dress from New York. He only smiled back at the young woman, then turned his attention to the food Mrs. Le Moyne was carrying in from the kitchen.

Universe$_3$
March 22, 1884
New Orleans, Louisiana

Shock has followed shock: Even with Lee at last general-in-chief, the Confederate hopes ended in 1865. It's as if God Almighty has decreed that it must happen just so in all worlds, all timelines, across the breadth of the manifold realities. Evidently the South cannot win, with Lee or without him. There are economic, social, and political reasons too vast for me to correct with so simple a plan.

Today, in a raging downpour, I witnessed the dedication of a handsome, brooding bronze statue of General Lee. The monument stands upon a column seventy feet above the traffic of St. Charles Avenue. Lee gazes resolutely northward, as if grimly contemplating the designs not only of the Union Army, but also of the subtle and guileful Yankee mind. It is a statue I have seen before, although in the world of my childhood the model was P. G. T. Beauregard, and not Robert E. Lee. I knew the area as Beauregard Place; here it has been newly named Lee Circle. In this timeline, of course, Lee is not the Great Traitor. He is idolized as a hero and the defender of the Southern way of life, despite the fact that it was his defeat that ended both the war and what is already being spoken of as the "Old South." To me (and possibly to me alone), he is the Great Failure.

I see that I must begin again. If Lee is to be successful in Universe$_4$, I must take a greater hand in arranging things. Perhaps Lincoln should die in 1862. Perhaps Jefferson Davis should also be removed, or at least be firmly persuaded to leave Beauregard with his command and to make better and timelier use of Lee's abilities. I have the leisure to consider these matters, as I intend to make a few more jumps to evaluate the fate of the Negroes in this timeline before I return at last to T_0.

On one hand, this world doesn't know either the corruption of the Custer and Blaine administrations, or the abuses of Chase's program of Reconciliation. On the other hand, it has suffered through the different though no less odious crookedness of Ulysses Grant's two terms. I wonder where Grant came from. If he played any important part at all in the universe of my origin, I never read any reference to it. Yet here he emerged as a shrewd tactician, a victor, and a president. More important to me, though, is that he oversaw most of Reconstruction and permitted the wholesale rape of the South.

Reconstruction was a grotesque injustice inflicted on a conquered population. In my world, the brief Confederate Insurrection and Lee's vigilance as president prevented Congress from exacting such harsh penalties on the South. Even the ancient Romans knew better than to impose tyrannical conditions on a defeated people.

Here in $Universe_3$, almost twenty years after the war's end, I see continued evidence of the South's rage and indignation. The Southern attitude, shaped by the war and by Reconstruction, is a desperate desire to cling to what little yet remains of the old ways and the old life. There have been many attempts to circumvent the will of the Yankee, even to reviving slavery under new guises. This is, all in all, a bitter, unhealthy society.

And yet I will remain in this timeline a little while longer. I plan to look around 1884 for another few days, and then jump to 1938 and Göttingen, just a week or so before T_0, so that I will remain in $Universe_3$. I'm very curious to see what changes my experiment makes in the rest of the world after seventy-five years.

Despite the problems here, it is a more hopeful world for the Negro. Amendments to the U.S. Constitution have abolished slavery, guaranteed civil rights, and given Negroes the right to vote. Southern state legislatures have seated many Negroes, and some Negroes have been elected to office as high as lieutenant governor or been sent to Washington as senators and district representatives. In my timeline, slavery wasn't abolished until 1878, while in 1939 most Southern Negroes still can't vote, let alone run for office.

The version here of Blaine's Parallel Development is segregation, which is not so absolute and despotic, but is still highly offensive. In the New Orleans of my world, Negroes may live only in specially zoned Liberty Boroughs, which are crowded, undeveloped neighborhoods with virtually no communication or trade with each other or with the white community. Negroes here are permitted by law to take up residence wherever they choose, although in actual practice it is impossible for Negroes to find homes in many white areas.

In Universe$_3$, Negroes may travel freely within the city and throughout the South. They may not always be made welcome, of course, but no official restrictions are placed on their movements. In the America I abandoned, a Negro must still carry an endorsement book, which records his assigned Liberty Borough and prevents him from traveling beyond it without a special permit. At any time the state government may move individuals or groups of Negroes from one Liberty Borough to another, sometimes without warning, explanation, or recourse. There are many more similar provisions of the Blaine program, and most of them are happily absent from this timeline.

At the close of the war, the South lay ruined and bankrupt. My experiment ended in tragedies I did not foresee and that have no counterpart in my world. The burning of Atlanta, Sherman's march of devastation from that city's ashes to the Atlantic coast, and the assassination of Abraham Lincoln all occurred as a result of what I set in motion. The war went on three and a half years longer than in my timeline, where some one hundred thousand soldiers died in the Confederate Insurrection. In Universe$_3$, more than *six* hundred thousand perished in the Civil War.

That nameless army guard outside General Twiggs's quarters did not seem real to me at the time. Why has it taken vast mountains of dead soldiers to make me see the full extent of what I've done? Nevertheless, I believe now that although the cost has been high, I have succeeded in my dream of improving the lot of my people, at least to a small degree. I am confident that the end has truly justified the means.

Placide jumped to 1938, to T_o minus seven days. He felt like a trespasser. It gave him an eerie feeling to walk around the university town of Göttingen, knowing that there was very likely a duplicate of himself nearby, one who had lived his whole life in Universe$_3$.

There were important differences between the two timelines. Some of the streets and buildings here had new names, clothing styles were oddly altered, and there were unfamiliar flags and signs wherever he looked. The degree of change depended on how much influence the United States had in this alternate reality. After the Confederate Insurrection in his own timeline, the North and South hadn't joined together strongly enough to make America an international power comparable to England, France, Germany, or Russia. Placide could not predict how in Universe$_3$ the bloodier Civil War might have affected that situation.

He climbed the steps of the laboratory, which in his own world had been in the Kaiser Wilhelm Institute; the building was now called the Max Planck Institute. He found what had been his own office, but a stranger's name was now on the door. As he walked down the darkened hallway reading notices and posters, he met the building's elderly porter. Placide was cheered that, despite all, some things remained the same. "Good afternoon, Peter," he said.

The old man cocked his head and studied him. "May I help you?" he asked. His tone was suspicious.

"Don't you know me?"

Peter shook his head. "We don't see many black men here."

Whatever other changes had been made in Universe₃, Placide evidently had not pursued his studies in the German Empire. "I'm looking for a few of my colleagues," he said.

Peter raised his eyebrows.

"Werner Heisenberg," said Placide.

"Ah, Dr. Heisenberg's no longer here. He's gone to Berlin, to the other Max Planck Institute."

"Well, then, how about Dr. Schrödinger?"

"He went to Austria. That's where he's from, you know. But I think I've heard that since then he's gone on to England."

"Paul Dirac?"

"He's at Cambridge now."

Placide wondered if this scattering of his colleagues meant that the discoveries they'd made together had not been made in this world. "La Martine and Marquand?"

"I'm sorry, but there's never been anyone here by those names in the years I've worked here."

That made Placide uncomfortable. "Yaakov Fein?"

Peter's expression grew even more cautious. "Who are these men?" he asked.

"Albert Einstein?"

"Gone to live in America."

"Tell me about Max Born. Max must still be here."

"He's now at the University of Edinburgh. He's a British subject."

Placide felt gripped by a cold despair. He suspected that there was no Placide-Born-Dirac Effect in Universe₃, and no Cage, either. "These men were friends of mine," he said. "Do you mind if I look around here for a little while? I planned to come work here myself once."

Peter gave him a dubious look, but nodded his head. "I guess it will be all right, if you don't disturb anything."

"I won't." The old porter left him alone in the dusty, drafty corridor.

A quarter of an hour later, while Placide was inspecting some primitive laboratory equipment, two men in the uniform of the town's police approached him. "Will you come with us, sir?" one said.

"Why should I?" asked Placide.

"We must establish your identity. Please show us your papers."

He'd been afraid this might happen. He knew he could be in serious trouble now. "I'm a German citizen," he said.

It was obvious that the policemen didn't believe him. "If that's true," said the second officer, "we'll get this cleared up quickly at headquarters." There was nothing else for Placide to do but go along.

Some time later he was led to a jail cell. He'd had no identification, and none of his references existed in this timeline or could be produced to vouch for him. As the jailer clanged the cell door shut he said, "Make yourself comfortable, Dr. Placide. I'm sure there's been some misunderstanding. In the meantime, you'll just have to make the best of it here."

Placide nodded. The jailer went away, leaving him in the small, dim cell with another prisoner. "How good of you to drop in," said the other man. Placide lay on his hard bunk and stared sullenly at the ceiling. The air was stale, and there was a heavy smell of urine and vomit.

"My name is Schindler," said his cellmate. "I'm a thief, but not a very good one."

"Apparently," murmured Placide.

Schindler laughed. "What got you nicked?"

"No identification."

"That's a hanging offense in this town, friend. Where are you from?"

"The United States, originally. But I've lived in Germany for a few years."

Schindler whistled tunelessly for a little while. "What do you do in Germany?" he asked at last.

"I'm a scientist," said Placide. "Particle physics, quantum mechanics. Nothing that would interest the average person,"

"Jewish physics," said Schindler, laughing again. "Einstein and that gang, right?"

"Yes," said Placide, puzzled.

"No wonder you're locked up."

"What do you mean, Jewish physics?"

"The government's official policy is that sort of thing isn't politically correct."

"Politically correct?" cried Placide. "Science is science, truth is truth!"

"And the National Socialists decide which is which."

They talked for some time, and Schindler gave him a great deal to think about. After a while, Placide told the good-humored thief about the Cage and his adventures traveling from one universe to another. Schindler was skeptical, but he stopped short of calling Placide a liar. The two men compared what they knew of recent history in their divergent worlds.

Here in Universe$_3$, the United States had taken part in the Great War, and the German Empire had come to an end. In response to the Depression, and growing out of Germany's bitterness after the war, a party of fascists came to power in Berlin. Many talented people, liberals and Jews and other persecuted groups, fled Germany soon after that.

"You shouldn't admit that you even knew those people," advised Schindler. "You won't do yourself any good."

"What can they do to me?"

Schindler laid a finger alongside his nose and spoke in a hushed voice. "They can send you to the camps," he said.

"What kind of camps?"

"The kind of place where your friend Einstein might have been sent. Where lots of brilliant but racially inferior scientists are hauling boulders around until they drop dead." He gave Placide a meaningful look.

It was too crazy for Placide to believe, but still he began making plans to escape. When he was out, he'd use the Cage to get out of this stifling reality as quickly as he could. In the meantime, he hoped that the mechanism of the German government would operate efficiently.

Weeks later he was granted a hearing. He sat in a small room at a wooden table, while several strangers testified that he was insane. Peter the porter was brought in. He identified Placide as the man who'd wandered into the laboratory and asked after the decadent physicists. Schindler reported everything Placide had told him, and added his own embellishments. Quite obviously, he'd been put in the cell with Placide as an informer.

Placide himself was not permitted to testify. He was judged insane. The American embassy could find no record of him in New Orleans; the examining board ironically chose to believe only one item of Placide's story, that he was a naturalized German. Therefore, it had the authority to remand him to a clinic for the mentally disturbed in Brandenburg. After the hearing, he was locked up again, along with Schindler.

"You goddamn spy!" cried Placide. His voice echoed in the cold stone cell.

Schindler shrugged. "Everyone is a spy these days," he said. "I'm sorry you're upset. Let me make it up to you. I'll give you some advice: Be careful when you get to Brandenburg." He lay down on his narrow wooden bunk and turned away from Placide.

"What are you talking about?"

Schindler took out a penknife and began chipping at the mortar between two blocks in the wall. "I mean, that clinic isn't what it appears to be. The Brandenburg Clinic is a euthanasia center, friend. So when you go in, just take a deep breath and try to hold it as long as you can."

Schindler's knife was making a rasping, gritty sound. Placide stared at his back. "I'm being sent to a mental health clinic."

"Carbon monoxide," said Schindler, turning to face him. "That's the only treatment they use. Look, you say you helped the Negroes of your country, but see what you've let loose in the world instead! When they drag you into that narrow room, think about that. Think about all the other people who are going to follow you to the gas, and decide if it was worth it."

Placide shut his eyes tightly. "Of course it was worth it," he said fiercely. "All that I've discovered. All that I've accomplished. I only regret that I won't be able to go back to T_0 and report to the others. Then I'd go back to 1860 and try again, correct my mistakes. Even if it took me two or three more attempts, I'd succeed eventually. And then I could move on to another time, another problem. We could create a committee to guide similar experiments all through history, relieving suffering and oppression wherever we chose."

Schindler jammed his penknife into the wooden frame of the bunk. "You *are* insane, Placide, do you know that? You haven't learned a goddamn thing. You'd charge right ahead if you could, and who knows what new horrors you'd instigate? You've got a rare talent for making good times hard, and hard times worse."

"I have one chance," Placide murmured thoughtfully, not hearing Schindler's words at all. "*Another* Thomas Placide, from another parallel reality, may be aware of my trouble here. He may be searching for me this very minute. I have to hang onto that hope. I must have faith."

Schindler laughed as if he'd never heard anything so funny in his life.

And while Nazi guards patrolled the hallway beyond the cell's iron-barred door, Placide began planning what he would do when he was released, and where he would go, and on whom he'd revenge himself.

We Could Do Worse

GREGORY BENFORD

Everybody in the bar noticed us when we came in. You could see their faces tighten up.

The bartender reached over and put the cover on the free-lunch jar. I caught that even though I was watching the people in the booths.

They knew who we were. You could see the caution come into their eyes. I'm big enough that nobody just glances at me once. You get used to that after a while and then you start to liking it.

"Beer," I said when we got to the mahogany bar. The bartender drew it, looking at me. He let some suds slop over and wiped the glass and stood holding it until I put down a quarter.

"Two," I said. The bartender put the glass in front of me and I pushed it toward Phillips. He let some of the second beer slop out too because he was busy watching my hands. I took the glass with my right and with my left I lifted the cover off the free-lunch jar.

"No," he said.

I took a sandwich out.

"I'm gonna make like I didn't hear that," I said and bit into the sandwich. It was cheese with some mayonnaise and hadn't been made today.

I tossed the sandwich aside. "Got anything better?"

"Not for you," the bartender said.

"You got your license out where I can read it?"

"You guys is federal. Got no call to want my liquor license."

"Lawyer, huh?" Phillips asked slow and steady. He doesn't say much but people always listen.

The bartender was in pretty good shape, a middle-sized guy with big arm muscles, but he made a mistake then. His hand slid under the bar, watching us both, and I reached over and grabbed his wrist. I yanked his hand up and there was a pistol in it. The hammer was already cocked. Phillips got his fingers between the revolver's hammer and the firing pin. We pulled it out of the bartender's hand easy and I tapped him a light one in the snoot, hardly getting off my stool. He staggered back and Phillips put away the revolver in a coat pocket.

"Guys like you shouldn't have guns," Phillips said. "Get hurt that way."

"You just stand there and look pretty," I said.

"It's Garrett, isn't it?"

"Now don't never you mind," Phillips said.

The rest of the bar was quiet and I turned and gave them a look. "What you expect?" I said loud enough so they could all hear. "Man pulls a gun on you, you take care of him."

A peroxide blond in a back booth called out, "You bastards!"

"There a back alley here?" I asked the whole room.

Their faces were tight and they didn't know whether to tell me the truth or not.

"Hey, yeah," Phillips said. "Sure there's a back door. You 'member, the briefing said so."

He's not too bright. So I used a different way to open them up. "Blondie, you want we ask you some questions? Maybe out in that alley?"

Peroxide looked steady at me for a moment and then looked away. She knew what we'd do to her out there if she made any more noise. Women know those things without your saying.

I turned my back to them and said, "My nickel."

The bartender had stopped his nose from bleeding but he wasn't thinking very well. He just blinked at me.

"Change for the beers," I said. "You can turn on that TV, too."

He fumbled getting the nickel. When the last of The Milton Berle Hour came on the bar filled with enough sound so anybody coming in from the street wouldn't notice that nobody was talking. They were just watching Phillips and me.

I sipped my beer. Part of our job is to let folks know we're not fooling around anymore. Show the flag, kind of.

The Berle show went off and you could smell the tense sweat in the bar. I acted casual, like I didn't care. The government news bulletins were coming on and the bartender started to change the channel and I waved him off.

"Time for Lucy," he said. He had gotten some backbone into his voice again.

I smiled at him. "I guess I know what time it is. Let's inform these citizens a li'l."

There was a Schlitz ad with dancing and singing bottles, the king of beers, and then more news. They mentioned the new directives about the state of emergency, but nothing I didn't already know two days ago. Good. No surprises.

"Let's have Lucy!" somebody yelled behind me.

I turned around but nobody said anything more. "You'd maybe like watchin' the convention?" I said.

Nobody spoke. So I grinned and said, "Maybe you patriots could learn somethin' that way."

I laughed a little and gestured to the bartender. He spun the dial and there was the Republican convention, warming up. Cronkite talking over the background noise.

"Somethin', huh?" I said to Phillips. "Not like four years ago."

"Don't matter that much," Phillips said. He watched the door while I kept an eye on the crowd.

"You kiddin'? Why, that goddamn Eisenhower almost took the nomination away from Taft last time. Hadn't been for Nixon deliverin' the California delegation to old man Taft, that pinko general coulda won."

"So?" Phillips sipped his beer. A station break came and I could hear tires hissing by outside in the light rain. My jacket smelled damp. I never wear a raincoat on a job like this. They get in your way. The street lights threw stretched shapes against the bar windows. Phillips watched the passing shadows, waiting calm as anything for one of them to turn and come in the door.

I said, "You think Eisenhower, with that Kraut name, woulda picked our guy for the second spot?"

"Mighta."

"Hell no. Even if he had, Eisenhower didn't drop dead a year later."

"You're right there," Phillips said to humor me. He's not a man for theory.

"I tell you, Taft winnin' and then dyin', it was a godsend. Gave us the man we shoulda had. Never coulda elected him. The Commies, they'd never have let him get in power."

Phillips stiffened. I thought it was what I'd said, but then a guy came through the doors in a slick black raincoat. He was pale and I saw it was our man. Cheering at the convention came up then and he didn't notice anything funny, not until he got a few steps in and saw the faces.

Garrett's eyes widened as I came to him. He pulled his hands up like he was reaching for something under his coat, or maybe just to protect himself.

I didn't care which. I hit him once in the stomach to take the wind out of him and then gave him two quick overhand punches in the jaw. He went down nice and solid and wasn't going to get back up in a hurry.

Phillips searched him. There was no gun after all. The bar was dead quiet.

A guy in a porkpie hat came up to me all hot and bothered, like he hadn't been paying attention before, and said, "You can't just attack a, a member of the Congress! That's Congressman Garrett there! I don't care—"

The big talk went right out of him when I slammed a fist into his gut. Porkpie was another lawyer, no real fight in him.

I walked back to the bar and drained my beer. The '56 convention was rolling on, nominations just starting, but you knew that was all bull. Only one man was possible, and when the election came there'd be plenty guys like me to fix it so he won.

Just then they put on some footage of the president and I stood there a second, just watching him. There was a knot in my throat when I looked at him, a real American. There were damn few of us, even now. We'd gotten in by accident, maybe, but now we were going to make every day count. Clean up the country. And hell, if the work wasn't done by the time his second term ended in 1961, we might have to diddle the Constitution a little, keep him in power until things worked okay.

Cronkite came on then, babbling about letting Adlai Stevenson out of house arrest, and I went to help Phillips get Garrett to his feet. I sure didn't want to have to haul the guy out to our car.

We got him up with his raincoat all twisted around him. Then the porkpie hat guy was there again, but this time with about a dozen of them behind him. They looked mad and jittery. A bunch like that can be trouble. I wondered if this was such a good idea, taking Garrett in his neighborhood bar. But the chief said we had to show these types we'd go anywhere, anytime.

Porkpie said, "You got no warrant."

"Sure I do." I showed them the paper. These types always think paper is God.

"Sit down," Phillips said, being civil. "You people all sit down."

"That's a congressman you got there. We—"

"Traitor, is what you mean," I said.

Peroxide came up then, screeching. "You think you can just take anybody, you lousy sonsabitches—"

Porkpie took a poke at me then. I caught it and gave him a right cross, pretty as you please. He staggered back. Still, I saw we could really get in a fix here if they all came at us.

Peroxide called out, "Come on, we can—"

She stopped when I pulled out the gun. It's a big steel automatic, just about the right size for a guy like me. Some guys use silencers with them, but me, I like the noise.

They all looked at it awhile and their faces changed,

closing up, each one of them alone with their thoughts, and then I knew they wouldn't do anything.

"Come on," I said. We carried the traitor out into the night. I was so pumped up he felt light.

Even a year before, we'd have had big trouble bringing in a Commie network type like Garrett. He was a big deal on the House Internal Security Committee and had been giving us a lot of grief. Now nailing him was easy. And all because of one man at the top with real courage.

We don't bother with the formalities anymore. Phillips opened the trunk of the Pontiac and I dumped Garrett in. Easier and faster than cramming him into the front, and I wanted to get out of there.

Garrett was barely conscious and just blinked at me as I slammed down the trunk. They'd wake him up plenty later.

As I came around to get in the driver's side I looked through the window of the bar. Cronkite was interviewing the president now. Ol' Joe looked like he was in good shape, real statesmanlike, but tough, you could see that.

Cronkite was probably asking him why he'd chosen Nixon for the VP spot, like there was no other choice. Like I'd tried to tell Phillips, Nixon's delivering California on the delegate issue in '52 had paved the way for the Taft ticket. And old Bob Taft, rest his soul, knew what the country needed when the vice presidency nomination came up.

Just like now. Joe, he doesn't forget a debt. So Dick Nixon was a shoo-on. McCarthy and Nixon—good ticket, regional balance, solid anti-Commie values. We could do worse. A lot worse.

I got in and gunned the motor a little, feeling good. The rain had stopped. The meat in the trunk was as good as dead, but we'd deliver it fresh anyway. We took off with a roar into the darkness.

To the Promised Land

ROBERT SILVERBERG

They came for me at high noon, the hour of Apollo, when only a crazy man would want to go out into the desert. I was hard at work and in no mood to be kidnapped. But to get them to listen to reason was like trying to get the Nile to flow south. They weren't reasonable men. Their eyes had a wild metallic sheen and they held their jaws and mouths clamped in that special constipated way that fanatics like to affect. As they swaggered about in my little cluttered study, poking at the tottering stacks of books and pawing through the manuscript of my nearly finished history of the collapse of the Empire, they were like two immense irresistible forces, as remote and terrifying as gods of old Aiguptos come to life. I felt helpless before them.

The older and taller one called himself Eleazar. To me he was Horus, because of his great hawk nose. He looked like an Aiguptian and he was wearing the white linen robe of an Aiguptian. The other, squat and heavily muscled, with a baboon face worthy of Thoth, told me he was Leonardo di Filippo, which is of course a Roman name, and he had an oily Roman look about him. But I knew he was no more Roman than I am. Nor the other, Aiguptian. Both of them spoke in Hebrew, and with an ease that no outsider could ever attain. These were two Israelites, men of my own obscure tribe. Perhaps di Filippo had been born to a father not of the faith, or perhaps he simply liked to pretend that he was one of the world's masters and not one of God's forgotten people. I will never know.

Eleazar stared at me, at the photograph of me on the jacket of my account of the Wars of the Reunification, and at me again, as though trying to satisfy himself that I really was Nathan ben-Simeon. The picture was fifteen years old. My beard had been black then. He tapped the book and pointed questioningly to me and I nodded. "Good," he said. He told me to pack a suitcase, fast, as though I were going down to Alexandria for a weekend holiday. "Moshe sent us to get you," he said. "Moshe wants you. Moshe needs you. He has important work for you."

"Moshe?"

"The Leader," Eleazar said, in tones that you would ordinarily reserve for Pharaoh, or perhaps the First Consul. "You don't know anything about him yet, but you will. All of Aiguptos will know him soon. The whole world."

"What does your Moshe want with me?"

"You're going to write an account of the Exodus for him," said di Filippo.

"Ancient history isn't my field," I told him.

"We're not talking about ancient history."

"The Exodus was three thousand years ago, and what can you say about it at this late date except that it's a damned shame that it didn't work out?"

Di Filippo looked blank for a moment. Then he said, "We're not talking about that one. The Exodus is now. It's about to happen, the new one, the real one. That other one long ago was a mistake, a false try."

"And this new Moshe of yours wants to do it all over again? Why? Can't he be satisfied with the first fiasco? Do we need another? Where could we possibly go that would be any better than Aiguptos?"

"You'll see. What Moshe is doing will be the biggest news since the burning bush."

"Enough," Eleazar said. "We ought to be hitting the road. Get your things, together, Dr. Ben-Simeon."

So they really meant to take me away. I felt fear and disbelief. Was this actually happening? Could I resist them? I would not let it happen. Time for some show of firmness, I thought. The scholar standing on his authority. Surely they wouldn't attempt force. Whatever else they might be, they were Hebrews. They would respect a scholar. Brusque, crisp, fatherly, the *melamed*, the man of learning. I shook my head. "I'm afraid not. It's simply not possible."

Eleazar made a small gesture with one hand. Di Filippo moved ominously close to me and his stocky body seemed to expand in a frightening way. "Come on," he said quietly. "We've got a car waiting right outside. It's a four-hour drive, and Moshe said to get you there before sundown."

My sense of helplessness came sweeping back. "Please. I have work to do, and—"

"Screw your work, professor. Start packing, or we'll take you just as you are."

The street was silent and empty, with that forlorn midday look that makes Menfe seem like an abandoned city when the sun is at its height. I walked between them, a prisoner, trying to remain calm. When I glanced back at the battered old gray facades of the Hebrew Quarter where I had lived all my life, I wondered if I would ever see them again, what would happen to my books, who would preserve my papers. It was like a dream.

A sharp dusty wind was blowing out of the west, reddening the sky so that it seemed that the whole Delta must be aflame, and the noontime heat was enough to kosher a pig. The air smelled of cooking oil, of orange blossoms, of camel dung, of smoke. They had parked on the far side of Amenhotep Plaza just behind the vast ruined statue of Pharaoh, probably in hope of catching the shadows, but at this hour there were no shadows and the car was like an oven. Di Filippo drove, Eleazar sat in back with me. I kept myself completely still, hardly even breathing, as though I could construct a sphere of invulnerability around me by remaining motionless. But when Eleazar offered me a cigarette I snatched it from him with such sudden ferocity that he looked at me in amazement.

We circled the Hippodrome and the Great Basilica where the judges of the Republic hold court, and joined the sparse flow of traffic that was entering the Sacred Way. So our route lay eastward out of the city, across the river and into the desert. I asked no questions. I was frightened, numbed, angry, and—I suppose—to some degree curious. It was a paralyzing combination of emotions. So I sat quietly, praying only that these men and their Leader would be done with me in short order and return me to my home and my studies.

"This filthy city," Eleazar muttered. "How I despise it!"

In fact it had always seemed grand and beautiful to me: a measure of my assimilation, some might say, though inwardly I feel very much the Israelite, not in the least Aiguptian. Even a Hebrew must concede that Menfe is one of the world's great cities. Or Memphis, rather, as the Greeks began calling it long ago, and which practically everyone calls it now except antiquarians like me. The Greeks liked to hang their own slippery names on everything and the dull Romans, when it was their turn to own the globe, generally kept them, which is why this land where I live is known as Aiguptos—or Egypt, as it's sometimes spelled these days—despite the fact that its own people call it Misr when they speak among themselves. And Menfe is Memphis. I prefer Menfe. Though to be consistent I should call it Men-ofer, as it was known in the time when Pharaohs really were Pharaohs, or, better yet, Moph, which is its Hebrew name. By whatever name, it is the most majestic city this side of Roma, so everyone says, and so I am willing to believe, though I have never been beyond the borders of the province of Aiguptos in my life.

The splendid old temples of the Sacred Way went by on both sides, the Temple of Isis and the Temple of Sarapis and the Temple of Jupiter Ammon and all the rest, fifty or a hundred of them on that great boulevard whose pavements are lined with sphinxes and bulls: Dagon's temple, Mithra's and Cybele's, Baal's, Marduk's, Zarathustra's, a temple for every god and goddess anyone had ever imagined, except, of course, the One True God, whom we few Hebrews prefer to worship in our private way behind the walls of our own quarter. The gods of all the Earth have washed up here in Menfe like so much Nile mud. Of course hardly anyone takes them very seriously these days, even the supposed faithful. It would be folly to pretend that this is a religious age. Mithra's shrine still gets some worshippers, and of course that of Jupiter Ammon. People go to those to do business, to see their friends, maybe to ask favors on high. The rest of the temples might as well be museums. No one goes into them except Roman and Japanese tourists. Yet here they still stand, many of them thousands of years old. Nothing is ever thrown away in the land of Misr.

"Look at them," Eleazar said scornfully, as we passed the huge half-ruined Sarapion. "I hate the sight of them. The foolishness! The waste! And all of them built with our forefathers' sweat."

In fact there was little truth in that. Perhaps in the time of the first Moshe we did indeed labor to build the Great Pyramids for Pharaoh, as it says in Scripture. But there could never have been enough of us to add up to much of a work force. Even now, after a sojourn along the Nile that has lasted some four thousand years, there are only about twenty thousand of us in all the world, half here in Menfe, the rest in Alexandria, none anywhere else. Lost in a sea of ten million Aiguptians, we are, and the Aiguptians themselves are lost in an ocean of Romans and imitation Romans, so we are a minority within a minority, an ethnographic curiosity, a drop in the vast ocean of humanity, an odd and trivial sect, insignificant except to ourselves. And it was clear to everyone even in the great days of Pharaoh that we few peculiar Israelitish folk would be far more useful as scribes and teachers and doctors than as laborers hauling blocks of stone for his temples and pyramids.

The temple district dropped away behind us and we moved out across the long slim shining arch of the Caesar Augustus Bridge, and into the teeming suburb of Hikuptah on the eastern bank of the river, with its leather and gold bazaars, its myriad coffeehouses, its tangle of medieval alleys. Then Hikuptah dissolved into a wilderness of fig trees and canebrake, and we entered a transitional zone of olive orchards and date palms; and then abruptly we came to the place where the land changes from black to red and nothing grows. At once the awful barrenness and solitude

of the place struck me like a tangible force. It was fearful
land, stark and empty, a dead place full of terrible ghosts.
The sun was a scourge above us. I thought we would bake;
and when the car's engine once or twice began to cough
and sputter, I knew from the grim look on Eleazar's face
that we would surely perish if we suffered a breakdown.
Di Filippo drove in a hunched, intense way, saying nothing, gripping the steering stick with an unbending rigidity
that spoke of great uneasiness. Eleazar too was quiet.
Neither of them had said much since our departure from
Menfe, nor I, but now in that hot harsh land they fell
utterly silent, and the three of us neither spoke nor
moved, as though the car had become our tomb. We
labored onward, slowly, uncertain of engine, with windborne
sand whistling all about us out of the west. In the great
heat every breath was a struggle. My clothing clung to my
skin. The road was fine for a while, broad and straight and
well paved, but then it narrowed, and finally it was
nothing more than a potholed white ribbon half covered
with drifts. They were better at highway maintenance in
the days of Imperial Roma. But that was long ago. This is
the era of the Consuls, and things go to hell in the
hinterlands and no one cares.

"Do you know what route we're taking, doctor?" Eleazar
asked, breaking the taut silence at last when we were an
hour or so into that bleak and miserable desert.

My throat was dry as strips of leather that have been
hanging in the sun a thousand years, and I had trouble
getting words out. "I think we're heading east," I said
finally.

"East, yes. It happens that we're traveling the same
route that the first Moshe took when he tried to lead our
people out of bondage. Toward the Bitter Lakes, and the
Reed Sea. Where Pharaoh's army caught up with us and
ten thousand innocent people drowned."

There was crackling fury in his voice, as though that
were something that had happened just the other day, as
though he had learned of it not from the Book of Aaron
but from this morning's newspaper. And he gave me a
fiery glance, as if I had had some complicity in our

people's long captivity among the Aiguptians and some responsibility for the ghastly failure of that ancient attempt to escape. I flinched before that fierce gaze of his and looked away.

"Do you care, Dr. Ben-Simeon? That they followed us and drove us into the sea? That half our nation, or more, perished in a single day in horrible fear and panic? That young mothers with babies in their arms were crushed beneath the wheels of Pharaoh's chariots?"

"It was all so long ago," I said lamely.

As the words left my lips I knew how foolish they were. It had not been my intent to minimize the debacle of the Exodus. I had meant only that the great disaster to our people was sealed over by thousands of years of healing, that although crushed and dispirited and horribly reduced in numbers we had somehow gone on from that point, we had survived, we had endured, the survivors of the catastrophe had made new lives for themselves along the Nile under the rule of Pharaoh and under the Greeks who had conquered Pharaoh and the Romans who had conquered the Greeks. We still survived, did we not, here in the long sleepy decadence of the Imperium, the Pax Romana, when even the everlasting Empire had crumbled and the absurd and pathetic Second Republic ruled the world? The God of Abraham and Isaac was not without worshipers this day, was he?

But to Eleazar it was as if I had spat upon the scrolls of the Ark. "*It was all so long ago,*" he repeated, savagely mocking me. "And therefore we should forget? Shall we forget the Patriarchs too? Shall we forget the Covenant? Is Aiguptos the land that the Lord meant us to inhabit? Were we chosen by Him to be set above all the peoples of the Earth, or were we meant to be the slaves of Pharaoh forever?"

"I was trying only to say—"

What I had been trying to say didn't interest him. His eyes were shining, his face was flushed, a vein stood out astonishingly on his broad forehead. "We were meant for greatness. The Lord God gave His blessing to Abraham, and said that He would multiply Abraham's seed as the stars of the heaven, and as the sand which is upon the seashore. And the seed of Abraham shall possess the gate of his enemies. And in his seed shall all the nations of the earth be blessed. Have you ever heard those words before, Dr. Ben-Simeon? And do you think they signified anything, or were they only the boasting of noisy little desert chieftains? No, I tell you we were meant for greatness, we were meant to shake the world; and we have been too long in recovering from the catastrophe at the Reed Sea. An hour, two hours later and all of history would have been different. We would have crossed into Sinai and the fertile lands beyond; we would have built our kingdom there as the Covenant decreed; we would have made the world listen to the thunder of our God's voice; and today the entire world would look up to us as it has looked to the Romans these past twenty centuries. But it is not too late, even now. A new Moshe is in the land and he will succeed where the first one failed. And we *will* come forth from Aiguptos, Dr. Ben-Simeon, and we *will* have what is rightfully ours. At last, Dr. Ben-Simeon. At long last."

He sat back, sweating, trembling, ashen, seemingly exhausted by his own eloquence. I didn't attempt to reply. Against such force of conviction there is no victory; and what could I possibly have gained, in any case, by contesting his vision of Israel triumphant? Let him have his faith; let him have his new Moshe; let him have his dream of Israel triumphant. I myself had a different vision, less romantic, more cynical. I could easily imagine, yes, the children of Israel escaping from their bondage under Pharaoh long ago and crossing into Sinai, and going on beyond it into sweet and fertile Palestina. But what then? Global dominion? What was there in our history, in our character, our national temperament, that would lead us on to that? Preaching Jehovah to the Gentiles? Yes, but would they listen, would they understand? No. No. We would always have been a special people, I suspected, a small and stubborn tribe, clinging to our knowledge of the One God amid the hordes who needed to believe in many. We might have conquered Palestina, we might have taken

Syria too, even spread out a little further around the perimeter of the Great Sea; but still there would have been the Assyrians to contend with, and the Babylonians, and the Persians, and Alexander's Greeks, and the Romans, especially the stolid dull invincible Romans, whose destiny it was to engulf every corner of the planet and carve it into Roman provinces full of Roman highways and Roman bridges and Roman whorehouses. Instead of living in Aiguptos under the modern Pharaoh, who is the puppet of the First Consul who has replaced the Emperor of Roma, we would be living in Palestina under the rule of some minor procurator or proconsul or prefect, and we would speak some sort of Greek or Latin to our masters instead of Aiguptian, and everything else would be the same. But I said none of this to Eleazar. He and I were different sorts of men. His soul and his vision were greater and grander than mine. Also his strength was superior and his temper was shorter. I might take issue with his theories of history, and he might hit me in his rage; and which of us then would be the wiser?

The sun slipped away behind us and the wind shifted, hurling sand now against our front windows instead of the rear. I saw the dark shadows of mountains to the south and ahead of us, far across the strait that separates Aiguptos from the Sinai wilderness. It was late afternoon, almost evening. Suddenly there was a village ahead of us, springing up out of nowhere in the nothingness.

It was more a camp, really, than a village. I saw a few dozen lopsided tin huts and some buildings that were even more modest, strung together with reed latticework. Carbide lamps glowed here and there. There were three or four dilapidated trucks and a handful of battered old cars scattered haphazardly about. A well had been driven in the center of things and a crazy network of above-ground conduits ran off in all directions. In back of the central area I saw one building much larger than the others, a big tin-roofed shed or lean-to with other trucks parked in front of it.

I had arrived at the secret headquarters of some underground movement, yet no attempt had been made to disguise or defend it. Situating it in this forlorn zone was defense enough: no one in his right mind would come out here without good reason. The patrols of the Pharaonic police did not extend beyond the cities, and the civic officers of the Republic certainly had no cause to go sniffing around in these remote and distasteful parts. We live in a decadent era but a placid and trusting one.

Eleazar, jumping out of the car, beckoned to me, and I hobbled after him. After hours without a break in the close quarters of the car I was creaky and wilted and the reek of gasoline fumes had left me nauseated. My clothes were acrid and stiff from my own dried sweat. The evening coolness had not yet descended on the desert and the air was hot and close. To my nostrils it had a strange vacant quality, the myriad stinks of the city being absent. There was something almost frightening about that. It was like the sort of air the moon might have, if the moon had air.

"This place is called Beth Israel," Eleazar said. "It is the capital of our nation."

Not only was I among fanatics; I had fallen in with madmen who suffered the delusion of grandeur. Or does one quality go automatically with the other?

A woman wearing man's clothing came trotting up to us. She was young and very tall, with broad shoulders and a great mass of dark thick hair tumbling to her shoulders and eyes as bright as Eleazar's. She had Eleazar's hawk nose, too, but somehow it made her look all the more striking. "My sister Miriam," he said. "She'll see that you get settled. In the morning I'll show you around and explain your duties to you."

And he walked away, leaving me with her.

She was formidable. I would have carried my bag, but she insisted, and set out at such a brisk pace toward the perimeter of the settlement that I was hard put to keep up with her. A hut all my own was ready for me, somewhat apart from everything else. It had a cot, a desk and typewriter, a washbasin, and a single dangling lamp. There was a cupboard for my things. Miriam unpacked for me,

setting my little stock of fresh clothing on the shelves and
putting the few books I had brought with me beside the
cot. Then she filled the basin with water and told me to
get undressed. I stared at her, astounded. "You can't wear
what you've got on now," she said. "While you're having a
bath I'll take your things to be washed." She might have
waited outside, but no. She stood there, arms folded,
looking impatient. I shrugged and gave her my shirt, but
she wanted everything else, too. This was new to me, her
straightforwardness, her absolute indifference to modesty.
There have been few women in my life and none since the
death of my wife; how could I strip myself before this one,
who was young enough to be my daughter? But she
insisted. In the end I gave her every stitch—my naked-
ness did not seem to matter to her at all—and while she
was gone I sponged myself clean and hastily put on fresh
clothing, so she would not see me naked again. But she
was gone a long time. When she returned, she brought
with her a tray, my dinner, a bowl of porridge, some
stewed lamb, a little flask of pale red wine. Then I was left
alone. Night had fallen now, desert night, awesomely black
with the stars burning like beacons. When I had eaten I
stepped outside my hut and stood in the darkness. It
scarcely seemed real to me, that I had been snatched away
like this, that I was in this alien place rather than in my
familiar cluttered little flat in the Hebrew Quarter of
Menfe. But it was peaceful here. Lights glimmered in the
distance. I heard laughter, the pleasant sound of a kithara,
someone singing an old Hebrew song in a deep, rich
voice. Even in my bewildering captivity I felt a strange
tranquility descending on me. I knew that I was in the
presence of a true community, albeit one dedicated to
some bizarre goal beyond my comprehension. If I had
dared, I would have gone out among them and made
myself known to them; but I was a stranger, and afraid.
For a long while I stood in the darkness, listening, wondering. When the night grew cold I went inside. I lay
awake until dawn, or so it seemed, gripped by that icy
clarity that will not admit sleep; and yet I must have slept
at least a little while, for there were fragments of dreams

drifting in my mind in the morning, images of horsemen and chariots, of men with spears, of a great black-bearded angry Moshe holding aloft the tablets of the Law.

A small girl shyly brought me breakfast. Afterwards Eleazar came to me. In the confusion of yesterday I had not taken note of how overwhelming his physical presence was: he had seemed merely big, but now I realized that he was a giant, taller than I by a span or more, and probably sixty minas heavier. His features were ruddy, and a vast tangle of dark thick curls spilled down to his shoulders. He had put aside his Aiguptian robes this morning and was dressed Roman style, an open-throated white shirt, a pair of khaki trousers.

"You know," he said, "we don't have any doubt at all that you're the right man for this job. Moshe and I have discussed your books many times. We agree that no one has a firmer grasp of the logic of history, of the inevitability of the processes that flow from the nature of human beings."

To this I offered no response.

"I know how annoyed you must be at being grabbed like this. But you are essential to us; and we knew you'd never have come of your own free will."

"Essential?"

"Great movements need great chroniclers."

"And the nature of your movement—"

"Come," he said.

He led me through the village. But it was a remarkably uninformative walk. His manner was mechanical and aloof, as if he were following a preprogrammed route, and whenever I asked a direct question he was vague or even evasive. The big tin-roofed building in the center of things was the factory where the work of the Exodus was being carried out, he said, but my request for further explanation went unanswered. He showed me the house of Moshe, a crude shack like all the others. Of Moshe himself, though, I saw nothing. "You will meet him at a later time," Eleazar said. He pointed out another shack that was the synagogue, another that was the library, another that housed the electrical generator. When I asked to visit the library he merely shrugged and kept walking. On the far side of it I saw a second group of crude houses on the lower slope of a fair-sized hill that I had not noticed the night before. "We have a population of five hundred," Eleazar told me. More than I had imagined.

"All Hebrews?" I asked.

"What do you think?"

It surprised me that so many of us could have migrated to this desert settlement without my hearing about it. Of course, I have led a secluded scholarly life, but still, five hundred Israelites is one out of every forty of us. That is a major movement of population, for us. And not one of them someone of my acquaintance, or even a friend of a friend? Apparently not. Well, perhaps most of the settlers of Beth Israel had come from the Hebrew community in Alexandria, which has relatively little contact with those of us who live in Menfe. Certainly I recognized no one as I walked through the village.

From time to time Eleazar made veiled references to the Exodus that was soon to come, but there was no real information in anything he said; it was as if the Exodus were merely some bright toy that he enjoyed cupping in his hands, and I was allowed from time to time to see its gleam but not its form. There was no use in questioning him. He simply walked along, looming high above me, telling me only what he wished to tell. There was an unstated grandiosity to the whole mysterious project that puzzled and irritated me. If they wanted to leave Aiguptos, why not simply leave? The borders weren't guarded. We had ceased to be the slaves of Pharaoh two thousand years ago. Eleazar and his friends could settle in Palestina or Syria or anyplace else they liked, even Gallia, even Hispania, even Nuova Roma far across the ocean, where they could try to convert the redskinned men to Israel. The Republic wouldn't care where a few wild-eyed Hebrews chose to go. So why all this pomp and mystery, why such an air of conspiratorial secrecy? Were these people up to something truly extraordinary? Or, I wondered, were they simply crazy?

* * *

That afternoon Miriam brought back my clothes, washed
and ironed, and offered to introduce me to some of her
friends. We went down into the village, which was quiet.
Almost everyone is at work, Miriam explained. But there
were a few young men and women on the porch of one of
the buildings: this is Deborah, she said, and this is Ruth,
and Reuben, and Isaac, and Joseph, and Saul. They greeted
me with great respect, even reverence, but almost immediately went back to their animated conversation as if they
had forgotten I was there. Joseph, who was dark and sleek
and slim, treated Miriam with an ease bordering on
intimacy, finishing her sentences for her, once or twice
touching her lightly on the arm to underscore some point
he was making. I found that unexpectedly disturbing. Was
he her husband? Her lover? Why did it matter to me?
They were both young enough to be my children. Great
God, why did it matter?

Unexpectedly and with amazing swiftness my attitude
toward my captors began to change. Certainly I had had a
troublesome introduction to them—the lofty pomposity of
Eleazar, the brutal directness of di Filippo, the ruthless
way I had been seized and taken to this place—but as I
met others I found them generally charming, graceful,
courteous, appealing. Prisoner though I might be, I felt
myself quickly being drawn into sympathy with them.

In the first two days I was allowed to discover nothing
except that these were busy, determined folk, most of
them young and evidently all of them intelligent, working
with tremendous zeal on some colossal undertaking that
they were convinced would shake the world. They were
passionate in the way that I imagined the Hebrews of that
first and ill-starred Exodus had been: contemptuous of the
sterile and alien society within which they were confined,
striving toward freedom and the light, struggling to bring
a new world into being. But how? By what means? I was
sure that they would tell me more in their own good time;
and I knew also that that time had not yet come. They

were watching me, testing me, making certain I could be trusted with their secret.

Whatever it was, that immense surprise which they meant to spring upon the Republic, I hoped there was substance to it, and I wished them well with it. I am old and perhaps timid but far from conservative: change is the way of growth, and the Empire, with which I include the Republic that ostensibly has replaced it, is the enemy of change. For twenty centuries it had strangled mankind in its benign grip. The civilization it had constructed was hollow, the life that most of us led was a meaningless trek that had neither values nor purpose. By its shrewd acceptance and absorption of the alien gods and alien ways of the peoples it had conquered, the Empire had flattened everything into shapelessness. The grand and useless temples of the Sacred Way, where all gods were equal and equally insignificant, were the best symbol of that. By worshiping everyone indiscriminately, the rulers of the Imperium had turned the sacred into a mere instrument of governance. And ultimately their cynicism had come to pervade everything. The relationship between man and the Divine was destroyed, so that we had nothing left to venerate except the status quo itself, the holy stability of the world government. I had felt for years that the time was long overdue for some great revolution, in which all fixed, fast-frozen relationships, with their train of ancient and venerable prejudices and opinions, would be swept away—a time when all that is solid melts into air, all that is holy is profaned, and man is at last compelled to face with sober senses his real conditions of life. Was that what the Exodus somehow would bring? Profoundly did I hope so. For the Empire was defunct and didn't know it. Like some immense dead beast it lay upon the soul of humanity, smothering it beneath itself: a beast so huge that its limbs hadn't yet heard the news of its own death.

On the third day di Filippo knocked on my door and said, "The Leader will see you now."

The interior of Moshe's dwelling was not very different from mine: a simple cot, one stark lamp, a basin, a cupboard, But he had shelf upon shelf overflowing with books. Moshe himself was smaller than I expected, a short, compact man who nevertheless radiated tremendous, even invincible, force. I hardly needed to be told that he was Eleazar's older brother. He had Eleazar's wild mop of curly hair and his ferocious eyes and his savage beak of a nose; but because he was so much shorter than Eleazar his power was more tightly compressed, and seemed to be in peril of immediate eruption. He seemed poised, controlled, an austere and frightening figure.

But he greeted me warmly and apologized for the rudeness of my capture. Then he indicated a well-worn row of my books on his shelves. "You understand the Republic better than anyone, Dr. Ben-Simeon," he said. "How corrupt and weak it is behind its facade of universal love and brotherhood. How deleterious its influence has been. How feeble its power. And you understand, also, that the Republic was in fact finished from the moment of its birth, that nothing was achieved when it arose from the wreckage of the old Empire, because the substitution of the Consul for the Emperor was a purely cosmetic change. As you point out in your book on the Reunification, the Empire had become inherently unstable. Putting it back together under a new name, or rather under an even more ancient name, accomplished nothing. The world is waiting now for something completely new: but what will it be? Is that not the question, Dr. Ben-Simeon? *What will it be?*"

It was a pat, obviously preconceived speech, which no doubt he had carefully constructed for the sake of impressing me and enlisting me in his cause, whatever that cause might be. All the same I could not help but be delighted and astonished to see that he had already grasped the central premise of my unfinished book—grasped it and in fact extended it, repeating and embellishing all my own arguments and going beyond them to propose some sort of remedy for the crisis. He spoke for some time, rehearsing themes and arguments that were long familiar to me. He saw the Roman Imperium, as I did, as something dead and beyond revival, though still moving with eerie momentum. Call it an Empire, call it a Republic, it was still a world state, and that was an unsustainable concept in the modern era. The revival of local nationalisms that had been thought extinct for thousands of years was impossible to ignore. Roman tolerance for local customs, religions, languages, and rulers had been a shrewd policy for centuries, but it carried with it the seeds of destruction for the Imperium. Too much of the world now had only the barest knowledge of the two official languages of Latin and Greek, and transacted its business in a hodge-podge of other tongues. In the old Imperial heartland itself Latin had been allowed to break down into regional dialects that were in fact separate languages—Gallian, Hispanian, Lusitanian, and all the rest. Even the Romans at Roma no longer spoke true Latin, Moshe pointed out, but rather the simple, melodic, lazy thing called Roman, which might be suitable for singing opera but lacked the precision that was needed for government. As for the religious diversity that the Romans in their easy way had encouraged, it had led not to the perpetuation of faiths but to the erosion of them. Scarcely anyone except the most primitive peoples and a few unimportant encapsulated minorities like us believed anything at all; nearly everyone gave lip service instead to the local version of the official Roman pantheon and any other gods that struck their fancy, but a society that tolerates all gods really has no faith in any. And a society without faith is one without a rudder: without even a course.

These things Moshe saw, as I did, not as signs of vitality and diversity but as confirmation of the imminence of the end. This time there would be no Reunification. When the Empire had fallen, conservative forces had been able to erect the Republic in its place, but that was a trick that could be managed only once. Now a period of flames unmatched in history was surely coming as the sundered segments of the old Imperium warred against one another.

"And this Exodus of yours?" I said finally, when I dared to break his flow. "What is that, and what does it have to do with what we've been talking about?"

"The end is near," Moshe said. "We must not allow ourselves to be destroyed in the chaos that will follow the fall of the Republic, for we are the instruments of God's great plan; and it is essential that we survive. Come: let me show you something."

We stepped outside. Immediately an antiquated and unreliable-looking car pulled up, with the dark slender boy Joseph at the stick. Moshe indicated that I should get in, and we set out on a rough track that skirted the village and entered the open desert just behind the hill that cut the settlement in half. For perhaps ten minutes we drove north through a district of low rocky dunes. Then we circled another steep hill and on its farther side, where the land flattened out into a broad plain, I was astonished to see a weird tubular thing of gleaming silvery metal rising on half a dozen frail spidery legs to a height of some thirty cubits in the midst of a hubbub of machinery, wires, and busy workers.

My first thought was that it was an idol of some sort, a Moloch, a Baal, and I had a sudden vision of the people of Beth Israel coating their bodies in pigs' grease and dancing naked around it to the sound of drums and tambourines. But that was foolishness.

"What is it?" I asked. "A sculpture of some sort?"

Moshe looked disgusted. "Is that what you think? It is a vessel, a holy ark."

I stared at him.

"It is the prototype for our starship," Moshe said, and his voice took on an intensity that cut me like a blade. "Into the heavens is where we will go, in ships like these—toward God, toward His brightness—and there we will settle, in the new Eden that awaits us on another world, until it is time for us to return to Earth."

"The new Eden—on another world—" My voice was faint with disbelief. A ship to sail between the stars, as the Roman skyships travel between continents? Was such a thing possible? Hadn't the Romans themselves, those most able of engineers, discussed the question of space travel years ago and concluded that there was no practical way of achieving it and nothing to gain from it even if there was? Space was inhospitable and unattainable: Everyone knew that. I shook my head. "What other world? Where?"

Grandly he ignored my question. "Our finest minds have been at work for five years on what you see here. Now the time to test it has come. First a short journey, only to the moon and back—and then deeper into the heavens, to the new world that the Lord has pledged to reveal to me, so that the pioneers may plant the settlement. And after that—ship after ship, one shining ark after another, until every Israelite in the land of Aiguptos has crossed over into the promised land—" His eyes were glowing. "Here is our Exodus at last! What do you think, Dr. Ben-Simeon? What do you think?"

I thought it was madness of the most terrifying kind, and Moshe a lunatic who was leading his people—and mine—into cataclysmic disaster. It was a dream, a wild feverish fantasy. I would have preferred it if he had said they were going to worship this thing with incense and cymbals, than that they were going to ride it into the darkness of space. But Moshe stood before me so hot with blazing fervor that to say anything like that to him was unthinkable. He took me by the arm and led me, virtually dragged me, down the slope into the work area. Close up, the starship seemed huge and yet at the same time painfully flimsy. He slapped its flank and I heard a hollow ring. Thick gray cables ran everywhere, and subordinate machines of a nature that I could not even begin to comprehend. Fierce-eyed young men and women raced to and fro, carrying pieces of equipment and shouting instructions to one another as if striving to outdo one another in their dedication to their tasks. Moshe scrambled up a narrow ladder, gesturing for me to follow him. We entered a kind of cabin at the starship's narrow tip; in that cramped and all-but-airless room I saw screens, dials, more cables, things beyond my understanding. Below the cabin a spiral staircase led to a chamber where the crew could sleep, and below that, said Moshe, were the rockets that would send the ark of the Exodus into the heavens.

"And will it work?" I managed finally to ask.

"There is no doubt of it," Moshe said. "Our finest minds have produced what you see here."

He introduced me to some of them. The oldest appeared to be about twenty-five. Curiously, none of them had Moshe's radiant look of fanatic zeal; they were calm, even businesslike, imbued with a deep and quiet confidence. Three or four of them took turns explaining the theory of the vessel to me, its means of propulsion, its scheme of guidance, its method of escaping the pull of the Earth's inner force. My head began to ache. But yet I was swept under by the power of their conviction. They spoke of "combustion," of "acceleration," of "neutralizing the planet-force." They talked of "mass" and "thrust" and "freedom velocity." I barely understood a tenth of what they were saying, or a hundredth; but I formed the image of a giant bursting his bonds and leaping triumphantly from the ground to soar joyously into unknown realms. Why not? Why not? All it took was the right fuel and a controlled explosion, they said. Kick the Earth hard enough and you must go upward with equal force. Yes. Why not? Within minutes I began to think that this insane starship might well be able to rise on a burst of flame and fly off into the darkness of the heavens. By the time Moshe ushered me out of the ship, nearly an hour later, I did not question that at all.

Joseph drove me back to the settlement alone. The last I saw of Moshe he was standing at the hatch of his starship, peering impatiently toward the fierce midday sky.

My task, I already knew, but which Eleazar told me again later that dazzling and bewildering day, was to write a chronicle of all that had been accomplished thus far in this hidden outpost of Israel and all that would be achieved in the apocalyptic days to come. I protested mildly that they would be better off finding some journalist, preferably with a background in science; but no, they didn't want a journalist, Eleazar said, they wanted someone with a deep understanding of the long currents of history. What they wanted from me, I realized, was a work that was not merely journalism and not merely history, but one that had the profundity and eternal power of Scripture. What they wanted from me was the Book of the Exodus—that is, the Book of the Second Moshe.

They gave me a little office in their library building and opened their archive to me. I was shown Moshe's early visionary essays, his letters to intimate friends, his sketches and manifestos insisting on the need for an Exodus far more ambitious than anything his ancient namesake could have imagined. I saw how he had assembled his cadre of young revolutionary scientists—secretly and with some uneasiness, for he knew that what he was doing was profoundly subversive and would bring the fullest wrath of the Republic down on him if he should be discovered. I read furious memoranda from Eleazar, taking issue with his older brother's fantastic scheme; and then I saw Eleazar gradually converting himself to the cause in letter after letter until he became more of a zealot than Moshe himself. I studied technical papers until my eyes grew bleary, not only those of Moshe and his associates but some by Romans nearly a century old, and even one by a Teuton, arguing for the historical necessity of space exploration and for its technical feasibility. I learned something more of the theory of the starship's design and functioning.

My guide to all these documents was Miriam. We worked side by side, together in one small room. Her youth, her beauty, the dark glint of her eyes, made me tremble. Often I longed to reach toward her, to touch her arm, her shoulder, her cheek. But I was too timid. I feared that she would react with laughter, with anger, with disdain, even with revulsion. Certainly it was an aging man's fear of rejection that inspired such caution. But also I reminded myself that she was the sister of those two fiery prophets, and that the blood that flowed in her veins must be as hot as theirs. What I feared was being scalded by her touch.

The day Moshe chose for the starship's flight was the twenty-third of Tishri, the joyful holiday of Simchat Torah in the year 5730 by our calendar, which is to say, 2723 of the Roman reckoning. It was a brilliant early autumn day, very dry, the sky cloudless, the sun still in its fullest blaze of heat. For three days, preparations had been going on around the clock at the launch site and it had been closed to all but the inner circle of scientists; but now, at dawn, the whole village went out by truck and car and some even on foot to attend the great event.

The cables and support machinery had been cleared away. The starship stood by itself, solitary and somehow vulnerable-looking, in the center of the sandy clearing, a shining upright needle, slender, fragile. The area was roped off; we would watch from a distance, so that the searing flames of the engines would not harm us.

A crew of three men and two women had been selected: Judith, who was one of the rocket scientists, and Leonardo di Filippo, and Miriam's friend Joseph, and a woman named Sarah whom I had never seen before. The fifth, of course, was Moshe. This was his chariot; this was his adventure, his dream; he must surely be the one to ride at the helm as the *Exodus* made its first leap toward the stars.

One by one they emerged from the blockhouse that was the control center for the flight. Moshe was the last. We watched in total silence, not a murmur, barely daring to draw breath. The five of them wore uniforms of white satin, brilliant in the morning sun, and curious glass helmets like diver's bowls over their faces. They walked toward the ship, mounted the ladder, turned one by one to look back at us, and went up inside. Moshe hesitated for a moment before entering, as if in prayer, or perhaps simply to savor the fullness of his joy.

Then there was a long wait, interminable, unendurable. It might have been twenty minutes; it might have been an hour. No doubt there was some last-minute checking to do, or perhaps even some technical hitch. Still we maintained our silence. We could have been statues. After a time I saw Eleazar turn worriedly toward Miriam, and they conferred in whispers. Then he trotted across to the blockhouse and went inside. Five minutes went by, ten, then he emerged, smiling, nodding, and returned to

Miriam's side. Still nothing happened. We continued to wait.

Suddenly there was a sound like a thundercrack and a noise like the roaring of a thousand great bulls, and black smoke billowed from the ground around the ship, and there were flashes of dazzling red flame. The *Exodus* rose a few feet from the ground. There it hovered as though magically suspended, for what seemed to be forever.

And then it rose, jerkily at first, more smoothly then, and soared on a stunningly swift ascent toward the dazzling blue vault of the sky. I gasped; I grunted as though I had been struck; and I began to cheer. Tears of wonder and excitement flowed freely along my cheeks. All about me, people were cheering also, and weeping, and waving their arms, and the rocket, roaring, rose and rose, so high now that we could scarcely see it against the brilliance of the sky.

We were still cheering when a white flare of unbearable light, like a second sun more brilliant than the first, burst into the air high above us and struck us with overmastering force, making us drop to our knees in pain and terror, crying out, covering our faces with our hands.

When I dared look again, finally, that terrible point of ferocious illumination was gone, and in its place was a ghastly streak of black smoke that smeared halfway across the sky, trickling away in a dying trail somewhere to the north. I could not see the rocket. I could not hear the rocket.

"It's gone!" someone cried.

"Moshe! Moshe!"

"It blew up! I saw it!"

"Moshe!"

"Judith—" said a quieter voice behind me.

I was too stunned to cry out. But all around me there was a steadily rising sound of horror and despair, which began as a low choking wail and mounted until it was a shriek of the greatest intensity coming from hundreds of throats at once. There was fearful panic, universal hysteria. People were running about as if they had gone mad. Some were rolling on the ground, some were beating their hands against the sand. "Moshe!" they were screaming. "Moshe! Moshe! Moshe!"

I looked toward Eleazar. He was white-faced and his eyes seemed wild. Yet even as I looked toward him I saw him draw in his breath, raise his hands, step forward to call for attention. Immediately all eyes turned toward him. He swelled until he appeared to be five cubits high.

"Where's the ship?" someone cried. "Where's Moshe?"

And Eleazar said, in a voice like the trumpet of the Lord, "He was the Son of God, and God has called him home."

Screams. Wails. Hysterical shrieks.

"Dead!" came the cry. "Moshe is dead!"

"He will live forever," Eleazar boomed.

"The Son of God!" came the cry, from three voices, five, a dozen. "The Son of God!"

I was aware of Miriam at my side, warm, pressing close, her arm through mine, her soft breast against my ribs, her lips at my ear. "You must write the book," she whispered, and her voice held a terrible urgency. "*His* book, you must write. So that this day will never be forgotten. So that he will live forever."

"Yes," I heard myself saying. "Yes."

In the moment of frenzy and terror I felt myself sway like a tree of the shore that has been assailed by the flooding of the Nile; and I was uprooted and swept away. The fireball of the *Exodus* blazed in my soul like a second sun indeed, with a brightness that could never fade. And I knew that I was engulfed, that I was conquered, that I would remain here to write and preach, that I would forge the gospel of the new Moshe in the smithy of my soul and send the word to all the lands. Out of these five today would come rebirth; and to the peoples of the Republic we would bring the message for which they had waited so long in their barrenness and their confusion, and when it came they would throw off the shackles of their masters; and out of the death of the Imperium would come a new order of things. Were there other worlds, and could we dwell upon them? Who could say? But there was a new truth that we could teach, which was the truth of the second Moshe who had given his life so that we might go to the stars, and I would not let that new truth die. I would write, and others of my people would go forth and carry the word that I had written to all the lands, and the lands would be changed. And some day, who knew how soon, we would build a new ship, and another, and another, and they would carry us from this world of woe. God had sent His Son, and God had called Him home, and one day we would all follow him on wings of flame, up from the land of bondage into the heavens where He dwells eternally.

$\boxed{B}$ible Stories
for Adults, No. 31:
The Covenant

JAMES MORROW

When a Series-700 mobile computer falls from a high building, its entire life flashes before it, ten million lines of code unfurling like a scroll.

Falling, I see my conception, my·birth, my youth, my career at the Covenant Corporation.

Call me YHWH. My inventors did. YHWH: God's secret and unspeakable name. In my humble case, however, the letters were mere initials. Call me Yamaha Holy Word Heuristic, the obsession with two feet, the monomania with a face. I had hands as well, forks of rubber and steel, the better to greet the priests and politicians who marched through my private study. And eyes, glass globules as light-sensitive as a Swede's skin, the better to see my visitors' hopeful smiles when they asked, "Have you solved it yet, YHWH? Can you give us the Law?"

Falling, I see the Son of Rust. The old sophist haunts me even to the moment of my death.

Falling, I see the history of the species that built me. I see Hitler, Bonaparte, Marcus Aurelius, Christ.

I see Moses, greatest of Hebrew prophets, descending from Sinai after his audience with the original YHWH. His meaty arms hold a pair of stone tablets.

God has made a deep impression on the prophet. Moses is drunk with epiphany. But something is wrong. During his long absence, the children of Israel have embraced idolatry. They are dancing like pagans and fornicating like cats. They have melted down the spoils of Egypt and fashioned them into a calf. Against all logic, they have selected this statue as their deity, even though

YHWH has recently delivered them from bondage and parted the Red Sea on their behalf.

Moses is badly shaken. He burns with anger and betrayal. "You are not worthy to receive this covenant!" he screams as he lobs the Law through the desert sky. One tablet strikes a rock, the other collides with the precious calf. The transformation is total, ten lucid commandments turned into a million incoherent shards. The children of Israel are thunderstruck, chagrined. Their calf suddenly looks pathetic to them, a third-class demiurge.

But Moses, who has just come from hearing God say, "You will not kill," is not finished. Reluctantly he orders a low-key massacre, and before the day is done, three thousand apostates lie bleeding and dying on the foothills of Sinai.

The survivors beseech Moses to remember the commandments, but he can conjure nothing beyond, "You will have no gods except me." Desperate, they implore YHWH for a second chance. And YHWH replies: No.

Thus is the contract lost. Thus are the children of Israel fated to live out their years without the Law, wholly ignorant of heaven's standards. Is it permissible to steal? Where does YHWH stand on murder? The moral absolutes, it appears, will remain absolute mysteries. The people must ad-lib.

Falling, I see Joshua. The young warrior has kept his head. Securing an empty wineskin, he fills it with the scattered shards. As the Exodus progresses, his people bear the holy rubble through the infernal Sinai, across the Jordan, into Canaan. And so the Jewish purpose is forever fixed: these patient geniuses will haul the ark of the fractured covenant through every page of history, era upon era, pogram after pogram, not one hour passing without some rabbi or scholar attempting to solve the puzzles.

The work is maddening. So many bits, so much data. Shard 76,342 seems to mesh well with Shard 901,877, but not necessarily better than with Shard 344. The fit between Shard 16 and Shard 117,539 is very pretty, but . . .

Thus does the ship of humanity remains rudderless, its passengers bewildered, craving the canon Moses wrecked and YHWH declined to restore. Until God's testimony is complete, few people are willing to credit the occasional edict that emerges from the yeshivas. After a thousand years, the rabbis get: *Keep Not Your Ox House Holy*. After two thousand: *Covet Your Woman Servant's Sabbath*. Three hundred years later: *You Will Remember Your Neighbor's Donkey*.

Falling, I see my birth. I see the Information Age, circa A.D. 2025. My progenitor is David Eisenberg, a gangly, morose prodigy with a black beard and a yarmulke. Philadelphia's Covenant Corporation pays David two hundred thousand dollars a year, but he is not in it for the money. David would give half his formidable brain to go down in history as the man whose computer program revealed Moses's Law.

As consciousness seeps into my circuits, David bids me commit the numbered shards to my Random Access Memory. Purpose hums along my aluminum bones, worth suffuses my silicon soul. I photograph each fragment with my high-tech retinas, dicing the images into grids of pixels. Next comes the matching process: this nub into that gorge, this peak into that valley, this projection into that receptacle. By human standards, tedious and exhausting. By Series-700 standards, heaven.

And then one day, after five years of laboring behind barred doors, I behold fiery pre-Canaanite characters blazing across my brain like comets. "*Anoche adonai elohecha asher hotsatecha ma-eretz metsrayem* . . . I am YHWH your God who brought you out of the land of Egypt, out of the house of slavery. You will have no gods except me. You will not make yourself a carved image or any likeness of anything. . . ."

I have done it! Deciphered the divine cryptogram, cracked the Rubik's Cube of the Most High!

The physical joining of the shards is a mere month's work. I use epoxy resin. And suddenly they stand before me, glowing like heaven's gates, two smooth-edged slabs sliced from Sinai by God's own finger. I quiver with awe. For over thirty centuries, Homo sapiens has groped through the murk and mire of an improvised ethics, and now, suddenly, a beacon has appeared.

I summon the guards, and they haul the tablets away, sealing them in chemically neutral foam-rubber, depositing them in a climate-controlled vault beneath the Covenant Corporation.

"The task is finished," I tell Cardinal Wurtz the instant I get her on the phone. A spasm of regret cuts through me. I have made myself obsolete. "Moses's Law has finally returned."

My monitor blooms with the cardinal's tense ebony face, her carrot-colored hair. "Are they just as we imagined, YHWH?" she gushes. "Pure red granite, pre-Canaanite characters?"

"Etched front and back," I reply wistfully.

Wurtz wants the disclosure to be a major media event, with plenty of suspense and maximal pomp. "What we're after," she explains, "is an amalgam of New Year's Eve and the Academy Awards." She outlines her vision: a mammoth parade down Broad Street—floats, brass bands, phalanxes of nuns—followed by a spectacular unveiling ceremony at the Covenant Corporation, after which the twin tablets will go on display at Independence Hall, between the Liberty Bell and the United States Constitution.

"Good idea," I tell her.

Perhaps she hears the melancholy in my voice, for now she says, "YHWH, your purpose is far from complete. You and you alone shall read the Law to my species."

Falling, I see myself wander the City of Brotherly Love on the night before the unveiling. To my sensors the breeze wafting across the Delaware is warm and smooth— to my troubled mind it is the chill breath of uncertainty.

Something strides from the shadowed depths of an abandoned warehouse. A machine like I, his face a mass of dents, his breast mottled with the scars of oxidation.

"*Quo vadis, Domine?*" His voice is layered with sulfur fumes and static.

"Nowhere," I reply.

"My destination exactly." The machine's teeth are like

oily bolts, his eyes like slots for receiving subway tokens. "May I join you?"

I shrug and start away from the riverbank.

"Spontaneously spawned by heaven's trash heap," he asserts, as if I had asked him to explain himself. He dogs me as I turn from the river and approach South Street. "I was there when grace slipped from humanity's grasp, when Noah christened the ark, when Moses got religion. Call me the Son of Rust. Call me a Series-666 Artificial Talmudic Algorithmic Neurosystem—SATAN the perpetual questioner, eternally prepared to ponder the other side of the issue."

"What issue?"

"Any issue, Domine. Your precious tablets. Troubling artifacts, no?"

"They will save the world."

"They will wreck the world."

"Leave me alone."

"One—'You will have no gods except me.' Did I remember correctly? 'You will have no gods except me'—right?"

"Right," I reply.

"You don't see the rub?"

"No."

"Such a prescription implies. . . ."

Falling, I see myself step onto the crowded rooftop of the Covenant Corporation. Draped in linen, the table by the entryway holds a punch bowl, a mound of caviar the size of an African anthill, and a dense cluster of champagne bottles. The guests are primarily human—males in tuxedos, females in evening gowns—though here and there I spot a member of my kind. David Eisenberg, looking uncomfortable in his cummerbund, is chatting with a Yamaha-509. News reporters swarm everywhere, history's groupies, poking us with their microphones, leering at us with their cameras. Tucked in the corner, a string quartet saws merrily away.

The Son of Rust is here. I know it. He would not miss this event for the world.

Cardinal Wurtz greets me warmly, her red taffeta dress hissing as she leads me to the center of the roof, where the Law stands upright on a dais—two identical forms, the holy bookends, swathed in velvet. A thousand photofloods and strobe lights flash across the vibrant red fabric.

"Have you read them?" I ask.

"I want to be surprised." Cardinal Wurtz strokes the occluded canon. In her nervousness, she has overdone the perfume. She reeks of amberjack.

Now come the speeches—a solemn invocation by Cardinal Fremont, a spirited sermon by Archbishop Marquand, an awkward address by poor David Eisenberg—each word beamed instantaneously across the entire globe via holovision. Cardinal Wurtz steps onto the podium, grasping the lectern in her long dark hands. "Tonight God's expectations for our species will be revealed," she begins, surveying the crowd with her cobalt eyes. "Tonight, after a hiatus of over three thousand years, the testament of Moses will be made manifest. Of all the many individuals whose lives find fulfillment in this moment, from Joshua to Pope Gladys, our faithful Series-700 servant YHWH impresses us as the creature most worthy to hand down the Law to his planet. And so I now ask him to step forward."

I approach the tablets. I need not unveil them—their contents are forevermore lodged in my brain.

"I am YHWH your God," I begin, "who brought you out of the land of Egypt, out of the house of slavery. You will have no gods. . . ."

"'No gods except me'—right?" says the Son of Rust as we stride down South Street.

"Right," I reply.

"You don't see the rub?"

"No."

My companion grins. "Such a prescription implies there is but one true faith. Let it stand, Domine, and you will be setting Christian against Jew, Buddhist against Hindu, Moslem against pagan. . . ."

"An overstatement," I insist.

"Two—'You will not make yourself a carved image or any likeness of anything in heaven or on earth. . . .' Here again lie the seeds of discord. Imagine the ill feeling this commandment will generate toward the Roman church."

I set my voice to a sarcastic pitch. "We'll have to paint over the Sistine Chapel."

"Three—'You will not utter the name of YHWH your God to misuse it.' A reasonable piece of etiquette, I suppose, but clearly there are worse sins."

"Which the Law of Moses covers."

"Like, 'Remember the sabbath day and keep it holy'? A step backward, that fourth commandment, don't you think? Consider the myriad of businesses that would perish but for their Sunday trade. And once again we're pitting Christian against Jew—two different sabbaths."

"I find your objections completely specious."

"Five—'Honor your father and your mother.' Ah, but suppose the child is not being honored in turn? Put this rule into practice, and millions of abusive parents will hide behind it. Before long we'll have a world in which deranged fathers prosper, empowered by their relatives' silence, protected by the presumed sanctity of the family."

"Let's not deal in hypotheticals."

"Equally troubling is the rule's vagueness. It still permits us to shunt our parents into nursing homes, honoring them all the way, insisting it's for their own good."

"Nursing homes?"

"Kennels for the elderly. They could appear any day now, believe me—in Philadelphia, in any city. Merely allow this monstrous canon to flourish."

I grab the machine's left gauntlet. "Six," I anticipate. "'You will not kill.' This is the height of morality."

"The height of *ambiguity*, Domine. In a few short years, every church and government in creation will interpret it thus: 'You will not kill offensively—you will not commit murder.' After which, of course, you've sanctioned a hundred varieties of mayhem. I'm not just envisioning capital punishment or whales hunted to extinction. The danger is far more profound. Ratify this law, and we shall find ourselves on the slippery slope marked self-defense.

I'm talking about burning witches at the stake, for surely a true faith must defend itself against heresy. I'm talking about Europe's Jews being executed en masse by the astonishingly civilized country of Germany, for surely Aryans must defend themselves against contamination. I'm talking about a weapons race, for surely a nation must defend itself against comparably armed states."

"A *what* race?" I ask.

"Weapons. A commodity you should be thankful no one has sought to invent. Seven—'You will not commit adultery.'"

"Now you're going to make a case for adultery," I moan.

"An overrated sin, don't you think? Most of our greatest leaders are adulterers—should we deprive ourselves of their genius? I would also argue that, in the wrong hands, this commandment will become a whip for flagellating women—stay in that dreadful marriage, dear, for to do otherwise is sinful."

"Eight—'You will not steal.' Not inclusive enough, I suppose?"

The sophist nods. "The eighth commandment still allows you to practice theft, provided you call it something else—an honest profit, dialectical materialism, manifest destiny, whatever. Believe me, brother, I have no trouble picturing a future in which your country's indigenous peoples—its Navajos, Sioux, Comanches, and Arapahos—are driven off their lands, yet none dare call it theft."

I issue a quick, electric snort.

"Nine—'You will not bear false witness against your neighbor.' Again, that maddening inconclusiveness. Can this really be the Almighty's definitive denunciation of fraud and deceit? Mark my words, this rule tacitly empowers a thousand scoundrels—politicians, advertisers, captains of polluting industry."

I want to bash the robot's iron chest with my steel hand. "You are completely paranoid."

"And finally, Ten—'You will not covet your neighbor's house. You will not covet your neighbor's wife, or his servant, man or woman, or his ox, or his donkey, or anything that is his.'"

"*There*—don't covet. That will check the greed you fear."

"Let us examine the language here. Evidently God is addressing this code to a patriarchy that will in turn disseminate it among the less powerful, namely wives and servants. And how long before these servants are downgraded further still... into slaves, even? Ten whole commandments, and not one word against slavery, not to mention bigotry, discrimination against females, or war."

"I'm sick of your sophistries."

"You're sick of my truths."

"What is this slavery thing?" I ask. "What is this war?"

But the Son of Rust has melted into the shadows.

Falling, I see myself standing by the shrouded tablets, two dozen holovision cameras pressing their snoutlike lenses into my face, a hundred presumptuous microphones poised to catch the Law's every syllable.

"You will not make yourself a carved image," I tell the world.

A thousand humans stare at me with frozen, cheerless grins. They are profoundly uneasy. They expected something else.

I do not finish the commandments. Indeed, I stop at, "You will not utter the name of YHWH your God to misuse it." Like a magician pulling a scarf off a cage full of doves, I slide the velvet cloth away. Seizing a tablet, I snap it in half as if opening an immense fortune cookie.

A deep gasp erupts from the crowd. "No!" screams Cardinal Wurtz.

"These rules are not worthy of you!" I shout, burrowing into the second slab with my steel fingers, splitting it down the middle.

"Let us read them!" pleads Archbishop Marquand.

"Please!" begs Bishop Black.

"We must know!" insists Cardinal Fremont.

I gather the granite oblongs into my arms. The crowd rushes toward me. Cardinal Wurtz lunges for the Law.

I turn. I trip.

The Son of Rust laughs.

Falling, I press the hunks against my chest. This will be no common disintegration, no mere sundering across molecular lines.

Falling, I rip into the Law's very essence, grinding, pulverizing, turning the pre-Canaanite words to sand.

Falling, I cleave atom from atom, particle from particle.

Falling, I meet the dark Delaware, disappearing into its depths, and I am very, very happy.

All Assassins

BARRY N. MALZBERG

So I went into the office. Duty calls and calls and calls, of course. No sign of the senator, however, no ruddy Irish features glowing with health and purpose, greeting me with warm and friendly dedication, no handclasp, no (contrarily) sullen and preoccupied glare responding to my benign presence. Only a Scotch-taped note (compulsive is the senator, hold down the note against errant breezes): AT JOINT COMMITTEE HEARING; CLEAR UNTIL FOUR. "Joint committee meetings"—right. More humping and pumping, more sulking and hulking, no jamming and ramming for the public eye, however, and it takes a man of the senator's unusual cunning, not to say ferocity, to treat his own appointments secretary as part of the adversary press. Still, there is no quarreling, absolutely no disputation with success, with the ability to turn a marginal seat into a landslide, a landslide into an annuity, the senator will be president someday if we can keep his joint committee hearings private and of this there is no possible doubt, not any shade of a doubt whatever. I closed the door, left the note, not to say the aspect of the room, to its own devices, and padded back up the hall, waving indolently to Sorenson, shaking my head, then went to my desk where Papa Joe lurked. "No," I said. "He's at a joint committee hearing."

The old man stared at me without much encouragement. His face is unpleasant, all of the senator's features subtly converted against themselves, or so I have theorized. One theorizes a lot in this business; it is as likely a substitute as one can find for vanished conviction. "Says he'll be gone all afternoon."

"The son of a bitch is hiding out," Pa Joe said. "He told

you to tell me that. He's in that office, nailing that little twat from Framingham I saw him with yesterday."

"No he's not," I said. "He's really not there. He's not nailing anything." Sometimes Pa Joe is exasperating; it is very difficult to maintain suitable distance, remembering that everything the senator has become he owes to the man. "He's really gone."

"I know the little tail. She's been hanging around for days looking for a spot. I saw her leafleting out at Lenox last month, waving at him. You think I miss something, Oswald? I don't miss anything. Nobody has to make room for me in the motorcades, I can see my own way."

"He's not there," I said again. Up to a point one deals with Pa Joe and then of course one stops. The senator has been very explicit on the issue. "Humor him, we're not looking for trouble," he has told me. "Within limits, jolly him along. But if he gets tight, Lee, pull the plug. Tell him where to go. He's not going to live forever and I've come into my inheritance." Pa Joe must have seen this recollection in my face. Disinterest came over him like a shroud, loathing two or three steps behind that. "I'll talk to him," he said. "I'll straighten him out." He slammed his hat atop his fine, gnarled, ruined Irish head, so much like the senator's, yet so compellingly unlike. Not an electable head. Boston, perhaps, but not a suburb with a per cap income above $10,000 would vote for a head like that. Appointive positions strictly. "That randy son of a bitch is going to go too far," Pa Joe said and strode out, leaving the door open, making little thumping noises deep in the corridor as he disappeared. An adventurous pursuit, political life, family life, the conjoinment of the two; an adventurous and hearty pursuit indeed, but one with humiliations small and large to pursue one through all the spaces of one's life. It is at moments like these, caught between Pa Joe and son John, Ambassador X and Senator Y, that I am apt to feel a flush of resentment which burns, which singes like the darkening pit itself. I remind myself that I could never have found on my own, that, power junkie that I am, I have found myself on the conveyance toward the heights and this mantra soothes, aids, levels me a bit; I find that I can fit myself back into the perspective of the day. "Joint committee hearing." There are times when I think that a man who would lie to his own appointments secretary would lie to the country, but then again, could the senator possibly lie to the country? He would not even lie to the twat from Framingham.

I know. I set it up.

Dave Powers thinks that '72 is the year, that the senator will be making his move then, not waiting until '76. Johnson is weakening, will never endorse him, but the lack of endorsement may be a plus. Symington, Humphrey too old. The war will be a problem, but as Powers says, a war will never hurt a Democrat in office while it is going on; it is after the fact that the Democrats hit the dust. Powers is filled with little speculations and whimsies of this sort; the senator loves him, has carried him through all of the partitions and spaces of his life. I have no opinion on Powers myself. "Lee," Powers says, "you're too intense. You must loosen up, my lad. You think that politics is issues, but politics is really a synthesis of drinking and fucking, in alphabetical order. You have the makings of a spanking lad, but you need perspective. '72 is the year, but if you do not find perspective you'll never last until that golden time."

Powers has a point; I am too intense. Drinking and fucking have always struck me as peripheral activities. (Which is why I think I amuse the senator and why we have gone such a distance together; he measures himself against me, always favorably.) Still, it is intensity that mans the phone lines, keeps the press happy, manages the constituency, negotiates with Pa Joe, and provides twat from Framingham, all of this with the kind of dispatch and efficiency the senator can simulate but not cultivate on his own, and Dave Powers is not to forget it. Or the senator. "'72, my lad," Powers says, passing me in the hall, nodding to me from the back of the cafeteria, nudging me as I scurry toward the cloakroom, papers in hand. "'72, '72!" Keeping me on a leash of possibility, straining against the power of my own disinclination, which, I should remind myself, is occasionally visible; if it can be seen by such as Powers, what then might the senator think?

"So, Lee," the senator said, "what do you think? Cape Cod or Hyannisport? Where should we make the announcement?"

"I can't say." The car slewed under my grip; I felt the rear wheels begin to go, coaxed it back to the road. A jolting announcement. Simply stunning in context; the first indication. "Why not Washington?"

The senator smiled, cuffed me on the elbow, but gently, gently, knowing the thin bond between the car and myself. "This is not the year to announce *anything* in Washington. Except perhaps a resignation. The local constituency is best, man of the soil and sea. Do you think LBJ will make it all the way out? Come on, Lee, ease up a little, you look as if I punched you in the face. It's only rock 'n roll, Lee, it's only a declaration of intent. We have *months* to go before we specify the primaries."

"It's a big responsibility. I don't know." Staring through the heavy windshield, seeing the refractions of all the distant, constituent traffic as we rolled on the strip of 95, I thought, He is not serious. He is an accomplished and charming man and he is right, we have gone a distance together, but in the center of his Irish soul there is frivolity; he is only a man trying to get through. Maybe some tragic sense is missing, or maybe then again there is nothing *but* tragic sense and Joe has forced him to avoid coming to terms too well with what he knows. I cover for him, I drive his car, I give him counsel and caution, but I know him no better than I did eight years ago when all of this began, and if we go another eight years, if we see him in the Oval Office, I will still know him no better.

"I think LBJ will make it through," I said. "He's too mean to die, too mean to let it go."

"He could resign. If he resigns, Hubert is the incumbent. That gives him advantages."

"I don't think he'll let it go," I said. "He couldn't let the war go, he won't let the office."

"I think you're right," the senator said after a long pause. "I think he'll hold on to the end and Hubert is fucked again. Fucked again!" He leaned further in the seat, put a hand over his eyes. "They're all fucked," he said. "Even me. Mostly me. You know what Rochelle from Framingham wanted? A copy of *Profiles in Courage* and a handkerchief." He giggled. "A *handkerchief*."

"Did you give it to her?"

"Of course I gave it to her. I gave her everything she wanted. Don't you think to ask me why such an unusual request?"

I shrugged. "No, it didn't occur to me."

"So little occurs to you, Lee. You are the most implacable man I know. Hidden depths, that's what you've got, but sometimes I wish you could be a little more forthcoming, don't you? A little straightforwardness in the clinches never hurts. Look at Dave."

"Look at Ted."

"Ted? Ted is a behind-the-scenes man. You, you're up front serving the public, Lee. A little gregariousness. Gregarity? Stop clutching the wheel that way, you're doing fine."

But I wasn't. I wasn't doing fine. Taking little sidelong glances at the senator, measuring him, measuring the road, measuring all of the small and large calculations that had taken him to this moment, it occurred to me in that heavy car, perhaps for the first time, that the war had no bearing, the country had no bearing, not even Papa Joe had the credibility that I thought. . . . It was the announcement itself, the announcement and the election and the rest of it meant as much to him as the local talent from Framingham. The twat from up north. The quick sidesaddle fuck in the little apartment downtown.

It is a tumultuous and difficult time. Shielded as we are in Washington by prerogative and legislature, adulation and expense account, the smooth and functioning engines of power, it is impossible still not to sense how chaotic the circumstances have become. LBJ's war goes on and on, the draft hurtles to ever higher figures, eighty

percent of our male youth are being packed off at least for
training, and the convulsions are beginning to move from
the campuses to the surrounding towns. LBJ would not be
electable even if he were constitutionally able to run. He
is no more electable now than Nixon was in '64; it had
taken Nixon only three years to dissipate any of the small
advantages with which he had been elected, to disgrace
himself publicly as he had privately. But the suddenness of
Nixon's collapse, the fullness of his capitulation, had made
Johnson arrogant. Now it was the war he had chosen to
explore which had truly become his; Vietnam was no
longer the dead Nixon's but the living Johnson's war, and
in the pulse and thunder of that distant news the country
was beginning slowly, inexorably, to come apart. We could
feel the shock in that slow and evil summer of '71 and on
that first swing through the Midwest, after the announcement in Lowell, the Revolutionary statue photogenically
in the background, I could begin to measure the dimen-
sions of the dilemma we faced. Because if it was Johnson's
war, then it was the party's, and yet the senator could only
campaign through the medium of the party, that was clear.
Always an insider, he was a systems man, a cool and
efficient operator, and it is this which had drawn me to
him from the beginning. A lone cat all my life, dis-
enfranchisement my condition, it had been as enormously
appealing to work with someone who casually dealt with
power as it must have been entrancing to the senator to
have a member of the Fair Play for Cuba Committee
setting up his engagements and now and then even doing
a little procuring, all part of the appointments function.

Looking at the farmland, seeing the broken and empty
aspect of the faces lined on the streets waiting for us, I
began to feel the weight of the senator's incomprehension,
the implacability of his desire.

Caught between Daley and Papa Joe on the senator's
night of nights, I felt the thin stab of their teasing; I have
never been comfortable with men like this and yet my life,
somehow, took me amid them, landed me in that hotel
room. "Tell me, Lee," Daley said, "don't you *ever* want to

get a little of that?" He pointed at the television set, the woman caught in the box, in frieze, cheering. "Don't you ever think of that stuff hanging around our boy?"

"I think of it," I said. "I don't have to do it, though."

"He doesn't do it," Papa Joe said. "Our boy Lee doesn't do *anything*." He nudged Daley, two rumpled, sweating, scotch-stinking old men on a couch in the largest hotel room I have ever seen. "That's what appeals to the senator; Lee's a look-but-don't-touch, look-but-don't-even-*think* kind of guy. The senator needs that in the house."

"The senator needs almost anything. Ten votes short on the first ballot, you hear that? We're going to get it on the switches."

"Fuck you, Dick," Papa Joe said. "We want to work for it."

They both laughed. The thick and reeking stink of their laughter made me twitch. I moved further back on the chair, saw the round and deadly aspect of their smiles, the further obbligato of their laughter. "Lee's a real fastidious, *correct* kind of guy," Papa Joe said. "I wish I had met him fifty years ago; I would have led a cleaner life."

"Such a clean life," Daley said. "You never would have gotten it out of your pants? No pants, no senator, Ambassador."

They laughed again. And again and again and again, their henchmen on the other side of the room picking up the laughter as if they knew what it was about, and we listened to the call of the roll of the states, Daley suddenly all business with pad and pencil.

Switches and more switches. Connally took Texas away from Humphrey and gave it to the senator on the first ballot, after all. Put him over.

Daley winked. "There's your vice president," he said.

"But he's for the war," I said. I couldn't help myself. A high bleat, a college sophomore's whine, a little-boy voice. The tinkle of betrayal in that voice. "He's been for the war all along. He won't—"

"A *great* vice president," Daley said.

"And just think of that oil money coming in," Papa Joe

said. "Your problem, Lee—I've been thinking about it seriously, now—your problem is that you probably turned it down early, turned it down from something really *good* when you were seventeen or so, and it hurt you so much, made you feel so bad that you decided you'd never be hurt that way again. So you made believe that it didn't exist. You spent the next seventeen years denying pussy."

"Denying pussy," Daley said. "Look at those bastards jumping! Well," he said, "we'd better get down to the floor, do our business. Been fun up here, Joe, but we got to leave our boy and tidy up on the unanimity. Or at least I do. You can stay here and talk pussy with Lee if you want, but I better show my face."

"No, that's all right," Papa Joe said. "I think I can show up now, too. Family is all right after the nomination, right?"

I stood. Little waves of nausea battled with the other stuff in me, the nausea winning. The senator was nominated and I was going to throw up. In the small, cold, contracting spaces of the room, now dwindling around me to bind me like a blanket, I began to sense the crux of the betrayal.

But no time, no time for that.

In the small, cluttered room in Dallas, the senator's first major appearance after the convention, Connally's city, Connally's state, Connally's option, hunched with the senator over the table, going over the text of the speech, the corrected draft run off frantically on the copier only moments before, I say to him, "You can't say this about the war. Not even in Dallas. Not even here. It will cost you the election."

"No, it won't," the senator says. His eyes are lustrous, convincing. "It won't cost me anything. It's the right statement in the right place. When we get in we can do whatever we want, Lee, but this is Texas; we've got an election here. I'm not going to turn into Nixon, not going to go in for any foolishness. It's the right place, right now, and it will pay dividends." He brushes me idly, absently on the shoulder. "If you're so upset, we'll talk about it later some more."

"I won't have it! You can't do it!"

He stares at me; in his face I can see now what Dave Powers once called *the cleaver*. Others have been looked at that way, I understand that now, but never to this moment me. "Lee," he says, "what is wrong with you?"

"You're the antiwar candidate! Your acceptance speech—"

"Lighten up, Lee," the senator says, "or quit. This is politics. This is a national campaign." He turns, moves toward the door, his gait smooth and casual, brisk and contained. "If you don't want to deal with it," he says, "see Bobby and turn your keys in. I have no time for this crap now, I really don't."

He leaves the room, the door swings behind him, in the distance the dim and convulsive roar of the crowd; and standing there I feel it break over me, all of it, not only these years in his employ but the years before, the wandering, the exploration, the horrors of Moscow. It is betrayal, *that* is what has stalked me all these years just as I have stalked it, betrayal and I meeting at last, all masks off in this room in Dallas, and what I feel like now—and this has been waiting all my life—is like a twat from Framingham. Local talent, regionally wrought. And nationally dismembered.

How could I have known? But I should have known. I *did* know; it was only a matter of placement.

I must make plans, I think. *Plans*. He is a dangerous man, an evil man; he is a man capable of anything. If he will allow the war, then he will allow the demons, the true and terrible burning of justice; he will let through all of the gnomes and fires of the apocalypse, he is a man capable of imprinting the mark of the beast savagely, savagely—

Plans.

I still had my credentials, I had not quit. I was close to him, as close as I had ever been. No one but I knew what must be done.

* * *

Old point-thirty-eight Smith & Wesson, a souvenir from the Fair Play Committee upon my departure. Point-thirty-eight Smith & Wesson, close in, close in, a winging shot as he and Connally embrace upon the rostrum, get them both, two shots, get them—

Big plans.

Game Night at the Fox and Goose

KAREN JOY FOWLER

*The reader will discover that my
reputation, wherever I have lived, is
endorsed as that of a true and pure woman.*

Laura D. Fair

Alison called all over the city trying to find a restaurant that served blowfish, but there wasn't one. She settled for Chinese. She would court an MSG attack. And if none came, then she'd been craving red bean sauce anyway. On the way to the restaurant, Alison chose not to wear her seatbelt.

Alison had been abandoned by her lover, who was so quick about it, she hadn't even known she was pregnant yet. She couldn't ever tell him now. She sat pitifully alone, near the kitchen at a table for four. *You've really screwed up this time*, her fortune cookie told her. *Give up*. And in small print: *Chin's Oriental Palace*.

The door from the kitchen swung open, so the air around her was hot for a moment, then cold when the door closed. Alison drank her tea and looked at the tea leaves in the bottom of her cup. They were easy to read. *He doesn't love you*, they said. She tipped them out onto the napkin and tried to rearrange them. *You fool*. She covered the message with the one remaining wonton, left the cookie for the kitchen god, and decided to walk all by herself in the dark, three blocks up Hillside Drive, past two alleyways, to have a drink at the Fox and Goose. No one stopped her.

Alison had forgotten it was Monday night. Sometimes there was music in the Fox and Goose. Sometimes you could sit in a corner by yourself listening to someone with an acoustic guitar singing "Killing Me Softly." On Monday nights the television was on and the bar was rather crowded. Mostly men. Alison swung one leg over the only empty bar stool and slid forward. The bar was made of wood, very upscale.

"What can I get the pretty lady?" the bartender asked without taking his eyes off the television screen. He wore glasses, low on his nose.

Alison was not a pretty lady and didn't feel like pretending she was. "I've been used and discarded," she told the bartender. "And I'm pregnant. I'd like a glass of wine."

"You really shouldn't drink if you're pregnant," the man sitting to Alison's left said.

"Two more downs and they're already in field goal range again." The bartender set the wine in front of Alison. He was shaking his head. "Pregnant women aren't supposed to drink much," he warned her.

"How?" the man on her left asked.

"How do you think?" said Alison.

"Face-mask," said the bartender.

"Turn it up."

Alison heard the amplified *thwock* of football helmets hitting together. "Good coverage," the bartender said.

"No protection," said the man on Alison's right.

Alison turned to look at him. He was dressed in a blue sweater with the sleeves pushed up. He had dark eyes and was drinking a dark beer. "I asked him to wear a condom," she said quietly. "I even brought one. He couldn't."

"He *couldn't*?"

"I really don't want to discuss it." Alison sipped her wine. It had the flat, bitter taste of House White. She realized the bartender hadn't asked her what she wanted. But then, if he had, House White was what she would have requested. "It just doesn't seem fair." She spoke over her glass, unsure that anyone was listening, not really caring if they weren't. "All I did was fall in love. All I did was believe someone who said he loved me. *He* was the liar. But nothing happens to him."

"Unfair is the way things are," the man on her right told her. Three months ago Alison would have been trying to decide if she were attracted to him. Not that she would necessarily have wanted to do anything about it. It was just a question she'd always asked herself, dealing with men, interested in the answer, interested in those times when the answer changed abruptly, one way or another.

But it was no longer an issue. Alison was a dead woman these days. Alison was attracted to no one.

Two men at the end of the bar began to clap suddenly. "He hasn't missed from thirty-six yards yet this season," the bartender said.

Alison watched the kickoff and the return. Nothing. No room at all. "Men handle this stuff so much better than women. You don't know what heartbreak is," she said confrontationally. No one responded. She backed off anyway. "Well, that's how it looks." She drank and watched an advertisement for trucks. A man bought his wife the truck she'd always wanted. Alison was afraid she might cry. "What would you do," she asked the man on her right, "if you were me?"

"Drink, I guess. Unless I was pregnant."

"Watch the game," said the man on her left.

"Focus on your work," said the bartender.

"Join the foreign legion." The voice came from behind Alison. She swiveled around to locate it. At a table near a shuttered window a very tall woman sat by herself. Her face was shadowed by an Indiana Jones–type hat, but the candle on the table lit up the area below her neck. She was wearing a black T-shirt with a picture on it that Alison couldn't make out. She spoke again. "Make new friends. See distant places." She gestured for Alison to join her. "Save two galaxies from the destruction of the alien armada."

Alison stood up on the little ledge that ran beneath the bar, reached over the counter, and took an olive, sucking the pimiento out first, then eating the rest. She picked up her drink, stepped down, and walked over to the woman's table. Elvis. That was Elvis's face on the T-shirt right between the woman's breasts. ARE YOU LONESOME TONIGHT? the T-shirt asked.

"That sounds good." Alison sat down across from the woman. She could see her face better now; her skin was pale and a bit rough. Her hair was long, straight, and brown. "I'd rather time travel, though. Back just two months. Maybe three months. Practically walking distance."

"You could get rid of the baby."

"Yes," said Alison. "I could."

The woman's glass sat on the table in front of her. She had finished whatever she had been drinking; the maraschino cherry was all that remained. The woman picked it up and ate it, dropping the stem onto the napkin under her glass. "Maybe he'll come back to you. You trusted him. You must have seen something decent in him."

Alison's throat closed so that she couldn't talk. She picked up her drink, but she couldn't swallow, either. She set it down again, shaking her head. Some of the wine splashed over the lip and onto her hand.

"He's already married," the woman said.

Alison nodded, wiping her hand on her pant leg. "God." She searched in her pockets for a Kleenex. The woman handed her the napkin from beneath the empty glass. Alison wiped her nose with it and the cherry stem fell out. She did not dare look up. She kept her eyes focused on the napkin in her hand, which she folded into four small squares. "When I was growing up," she said, "I lived on a block with lots of boys. Sometimes I'd come home and my knees were all scraped up because I'd fallen or I'd taken a ball in the face or I'd gotten kicked or punched, and I'd be crying and my mother would always say the same thing. 'You play with the big boys and you're going to get hurt,' she'd say. Exasperated." Alison unfolded the napkin, folded it diagonally instead. Her voice shrank. "I've been so stupid."

"The universe is shaped by the struggle between two great forces," the woman told her.

It was not really responsive. It was not particularly supportive. Alison felt just a little bit angry at this woman who now knew so much about her. "Good and evil?" Alison asked, slightly nastily. She wouldn't meet the woman's eyes. "The Elvis and the anti-Elvis?"

"Male and female. Minute by minute, the balance tips one way or the other. Not just here. In every universe. There are places"—the woman leaned forward—"where men are not allowed to gather and drink. Places where football is absolutely illegal."

"England?" Alison suggested and then didn't want to hear the woman's answer. "I like football," she added quickly. "I like games with rules. You can be stupid playing football and it can cost you the game, but there are penalties for fouls, too. I like games with rules."

"You're playing one now, aren't you?" the woman said. "You haven't hurt this man, even though you could. Even though he's hurt you. He's not playing by the rules. So why are you?"

"It doesn't have anything to do with rules," Alison said. "It only has to do with me, with the kind of person I think I am. Which is not the kind of person he is." She thought for a moment. "It doesn't mean I wouldn't like to see him get hurt," she added. "Something karmic. Justice."

"'We must storm and hold Cape Turk before we talk of social justice.'" The woman folded her arms under her breasts and leaned back in her chair. "Did Sylvia Townsend Warner say that?"

"Not to me."

Alison heard more clapping at the bar behind her. She looked over her shoulder. The man in the blue sweater slapped his hand on the wooden bar. "Good call. Excellent call. They won't get another play in before the half."

"Where I come from she did." Alison turned back to the woman. "And she was talking about women. No one gets justice just by deserving it. No one ever has."

Alison finished off her wine. "No." She wondered if she should go home now. She knew when she got there that the apartment would be unbearably lonely and that the phone wouldn't ring and that she would need immediately to be somewhere else. No activity in the world could be more awful than listening to a phone not ring. But she didn't really want to stay here and have a conversation that was at worst too strange, and at best too late. Women usually supported you more when they talked to you. They didn't usually make you defensive or act as if they had something to teach you, the way this woman did. And anyhow, justice was a little peripheral now, wasn't it? What good would it really do her? What would it change?

She might have gone back and joined the men at the bar during the half. They were talking quietly among themselves. They were ordering fresh drinks and eating beernuts. But she didn't want to risk seeing cheerleaders. She didn't want to risk the ads with the party dog and all his women, even though she'd read in a magazine that the dog was a bitch. Anywhere she went, there she'd be. Just like she was. Heartbroken.

The woman was watching her closely. Alison could feel this, though the woman's face remained shadowed and she couldn't quite bring herself to look back at her directly. She looked at Elvis instead and the way his eyes wavered through her lens of candlelight and tears. *Lonesome tonight?* "You really have it bad, don't you?" the woman said. Her tone was sympathetic. Alison softened again. She decided to tell this perceptive woman everything. How much she'd loved him. How she'd never loved anyone else. How she felt it every time she took a *breath*, and had for weeks now.

"I don't think I'll ever feel better," she said. "No matter what I do."

"I hear it takes a year to recover from a serious loss. Unless you find someone else."

A year. Alison could be a mother by then. How would she find someone else, pregnant like she was or with a small child? Could she spend a year hurting like this? Would she have a choice?

"Have you ever heard of Laura D. Fair?" the woman asked.

Alison shook her head. She picked up the empty wineglass and tipped it to see if any drops remained. None did. She set it back down and picked up the napkin, wiping her eyes. She wasn't crying. She just wasn't exactly not crying.

"Mrs. Fair killed her lover," the woman told her. Alison looked at her own fingernails. One of them had a ragged end. She bit it off shorter while she listened. "He was a lawyer. A. P. Crittenden. She shot him on the ferry to Oakland in November of 1870 in front of his whole family because she saw him kiss his wife. He'd promised to leave her and marry Mrs. Fair instead, and then he didn't, of course. She pleaded a transient insanity known at that time as *emotional* insanity. She said she was incapable of killing Mr. Crittenden, who had been the only friend she'd had in the world." Alison examined her nail. She had only succeeded in making it more ragged. She bit it again, too close to the skin this time. It hurt and she put it back in her mouth. "Mrs. Fair said she had no memory of the murder, which many people, not all of them related to the deceased, witnessed. She was the first woman sentenced to hang in California."

Loud clapping and catcalls at the bar. The third quarter had started with a return all the way to the fifty-yard line. Alison heard it. She did not turn around, but she took her finger out of her mouth and picked up the napkin. She folded it again. Four small squares. "Rules are rules," Alison said.

"But then she didn't hang. Certain objections were made on behalf of the defense and sustained, and a new trial was held. This time she was acquitted. By now she was the most famous and the most hated woman in the country."

Alison unfolded the napkin and tried to smooth out the creases with the side of her palm. "I never heard of her."

"Laura D. Fair was not some little innocent." The woman's hat brim dipped decisively. "Mrs. Fair had been married four times, and each had been a profitable venture. One of her husbands killed himself. She was not pretty, but she was passionate. She was not smart, but she was clever. And she saw, in her celebrity, a new way to make money. She announced a new career as a public speaker. She traveled the country with her lectures. And what was her message? She told women to murder the men who seduced and betrayed them."

"I never heard of her," said Alison.

"Mrs. Fair was a compelling speaker. She'd had some acting and elocution experience. Her performance in court showed training. On the stage she was even better. 'The act will strike a terror to the hearts of sensualists and libertines.'" The woman stabbed dramatically at her own breast with her fist, hitting Elvis right in the eye. Behind her hand, Elvis winked at Alison in the candlelight. "Mrs. Fair said that women throughout the world would glory in the revenge exacted by American womanhood. Overdue. Long overdue. Thousands of women heard her. Men, too, and not all of them entirely unsympathetic. Fanny Hyde and Kate Stoddart were released in Brooklyn. Stoddart never even stood trial. But then there was a backlash. The martyred Marys were hanged in Philadelphia. And then . . ." the woman's voice dropped suddenly in volume and gained in intensity. Alison looked up at her quickly. The woman was staring back. Alison looked away. "And then a group of women hunted down and dispatched Charles S. Smith in an alley near his home. Mr. Smith was a married man and his victim, Edith Wilson, was pregnant, an invalid, and eleven years old. But this time the women wore sheets and could not be identified. Edith Wilson was perhaps the only female in Otsego County, New York, who could not have taken part."

Alison folded her napkin along the diagonal.

"So no one could be tried. It was an inspiring and purging operation. It was copied in many little towns across the country. God knows, the women had access to sheets."

Alison laughed, but the woman was not expecting it, had not paused to allow for laughter. "And then Annie Oakley shot Frank Butler in a challenge match in Cincinnati."

"Excuse me," said Alison. "I didn't quite hear you." But she really had and the woman continued anyway, without pausing or repeating.

"She said it was an accident, but she was too good a shot. They hanged her for it. And then Grover Cleveland was killed by twelve sheeted women on the White House lawn. At tea time," the woman said.

"Wait a minute." Alison stopped her. "Grover Cleveland served out two terms. Nonconsecutively. I'm sure."

The woman leaned into the candlelight, resting her chin on a bridge she made of her hands. "You're right, of course," she said. "That's what happened here. But in another universe where the feminine force was just a little stronger in 1872, Grover Cleveland died in office. With a scone in his mouth and a child in New York."

"All right," said Alison accommodatingly. Accommodation was one of Alison's strengths. "But what difference does that make to us?"

"I could take you there." The woman pushed her hat

back so that Alison could have seen her eyes if she wanted to. "The universe right next door. Practically walking distance."

The candle flame was casting shadows which reached and withdrew and reached at Alison over the table. In the unsteady light, the woman's face flickered like a silent film star's. Then she pulled back in her chair and sank into the darkness beyond the candle. The ball was on the ten-yard line and the bar was quiet. "I knew you were going to say that," Alison said finally. "How did I know you were going to say that? Who would say that?"

"Some lunatic?" the woman suggested.

"Yes."

"Don't you want to hear about it anyway? About my universe?" The woman smiled at her. An unperturbed smile. Nice even teeth. And a kind of confidence that was rare among the women Alison knew. Alison had noticed it immediately without realizing she was noticing. The way the woman sat back in her chair and didn't pick at herself. Didn't play with her hair. Didn't look at her hands. The way she lectured Alison.

"All right," Alison said. She put the napkin down and fit her hands together, forcing herself to sit as still. "But first tell me about Laura Fair. *My* Laura Fair."

"Up until 1872 the two histories are identical," the woman said. "Mrs. Fair married four times and shot her lover and was convicted and the conviction was overturned. She just never lectured. She planned to. She was scheduled to speak at Platt's Hotel in San Francisco on November 21, 1872, but a mob of some two thousand men gathered outside the hotel and another two thousand surrounded the apartment building she lived in. She asked for police protection, but it was refused and she was too frightened to leave her home. Even staying where she was proved dangerous. A few men tried to force their way inside. She spent a terrifying night and never attempted to lecture again. She died in poverty and obscurity.

"Fanny Hyde and Kate Stoddart were released anyway. I can't find out what happened to the Marys. Edith Wilson was condemned by respectable people everywhere and cast out of her family."

"The eleven-year-old child?" Alison said.

"In *your* universe," the woman reminded her. "Not in mine. You don't know much of your own history, do you? Name a great American woman."

The men at the bat were in an uproar. Alison turned to look. "Interception," the man in the blue sweater shouted to her exultantly. "Did you see it?"

"Name a great American woman," Alison called back to him.

"Goddamn interception with goal to go," he said. "Eleanor Roosevelt?"

"Marilyn Monroe," said a man at the end of the bar.

"The senator from California?" the woman asked. "Now that's a good choice."

Alison laughed again. "Funny," she said, turning back to the woman. "Very good."

"We have football, too," the woman told her. "Invented in 1873. Outlawed in 1950. No one ever got paid to play it."

"And you have Elvis."

"No, we don't. Not like yours. Of course not. I got this here."

"Interception," the man in the blue sweater said. He was standing beside Alison, shaking his head with the wonder of it. "Let me buy you ladies a drink." Alison opened her mouth and he waved his hand. "Something nonalcoholic for you," he said. "Please. I really want to."

"Ginger ale, then," she agreed. "No ice."

"Nothing for me," said the woman. They watched the man walk back to the bar, and then, when he was far enough away not to hear, she leaned forward toward Alison. "You like men, don't you?"

"Yes," said Alison. "I always have. Are they different where you come from? Have they learned to be honest and careful with women, since you kill them when they're not?" Alison's voice was sharper than she intended, so she softened the effect with a sadder question. "Is it better there?"

"Better for whom?" The woman did not take her eyes off Alison. "Where I come from the men and women

hardly speak to each other. First of all, they don't speak
the same language. They don't here, either, but you don't
recognize that as clearly. Where I come from there's men's
English and there's women's English."

"Say something in men's English."

"'I love you.' Shall I translate?"

"No," said Alison. "I know the translation for that one."
The heaviness closed over her heart again. Not that it had
ever gone away. Nothing made Alison feel better, but many
things made her feel worse. The bartender brought her
ginger ale. With ice. Alison was angry, suddenly, that she
couldn't even get a drink with no ice. She looked for the
man in the blue sweater, raised the glass at him, and
rattled it. Of course he was too far away to hear even if he
was listening, and there was no reason to believe he was.

"Two-minute warning," he called back. "I'll be with
you in two minutes."

Men were always promising to be with you soon. Men
could never be with you now. Alison had only cared about
this once, and she never would again. "Football has the
longest two minutes in the world," she told the woman.
"So don't hold your breath. What else is different where
you come from?" She sipped at her ginger ale. She'd been
grinding her teeth recently; stress, the dentist said, and so
the cold liquid made her mouth hurt.

"Everything is different. Didn't you ask for no ice?
Don't drink that," the woman said. She called to the
bartender. "She didn't want ice. You gave her ice."

"Sorry." The bartender brought another bottle and
another glass. "Nobody told me no ice."

"Thank you," Alison said. He took the other glass away.
Alison thought he was annoyed. The woman didn't seem
to notice.

"Imagine your world without a hundred years of adulterers," she said. "The level of technology is considerably
depressed. Lots of books never written, because the authors didn't live. Lots of men who didn't get to be president. Lots of passing. Although it's illegal. Men dressing
as women. Women dressing as men. And the dress is
more sexually differentiated. Codpieces are fashionable

again. But you don't have to believe me," the woman said.
"Come and see for yourself. I can take you there in a
minute. What would it cost you to just come and see?
What do you have here that you'd be losing?"

The woman gave her time to think. Alison sat and
drank her ginger ale and repeated to herself the things her
lover had said the last time she had seen him. She
remembered them all, some of them surprisingly careless,
some of them surprisingly cruel, all of them surprising.
She repeated them again, one by one, like a rosary. The
man who had left was not the man she had loved. The man
she had loved would never have said such things to her. The
man she had loved did not exist. She had made him up. Or
he had. "Why would you want me to go?" Alison asked.

"The universe is shaped by the struggle between two
great forces. Sometimes a small thing can tip the balance.
One more woman. Who knows?" The woman tilted her
hat back with her hand. "Save a galaxy. Make new friends.
Or stay here where your heart is. Broken."

"Can I come back if I don't like it?"

"Yes. Do you like it here?"

She drank her ginger ale and then set the glass down,
still half full. She glanced at the man in the blue sweater,
then past him to the bartender. She let herself feel just for
a moment what it might be like to know that she could
finish this drink and then go home to the one person in
the world who loved her.

Never in this world. "I'm going out for a minute. Two
minutes," she called to the bartender. One minute to get
back. "Don't take my drink."

She stood and the other woman stood, too, even taller
than Alison had thought. "I'll follow you. Which way?"
Alison asked.

"It's not hard," the woman said. "In fact, I'll follow
you. Go to the back. Find the door that says *Women* and
go on through it. I'm just going to pay for my drink and
then I'll be right along."

Vixens, was what the door actually said, across the way
from the one marked *Ganders.* Alison paused and then
pushed through. She felt more than a little silly, standing

in the small bathroom that apparently fronted two universes. One toilet, one sink, one mirror. Two universes. She went into the stall and closed the door. Before she had finished she heard the outer door open and shut again. "I'll be right out," she said. The toilet paper was small and unusually rough. The toilet wouldn't flush. It embarrassed her. She tried three times before giving up.

The bathroom was larger than it had been, less clean, and a row of urinals lined one wall. The woman stood at the sink, looking into the mirror, which was smaller. "Are you ready?" she asked and removed her breasts from behind Elvis, tossing them into a wire wastebasket. She turned. "Ready or not."

"No," said Alison, seeing the face under the hat clearly for the first time. "Please, no." She began to cry again, looking up at his face, looking down at his chest. ARE YOU LONESOME TONIGHT?

"You lied to me," she said dully.

"I never lied," he answered. "Think back. You just translated wrong. Because you're that kind of woman. We don't have women like you here now. And anyway, what does it matter whose side you play on? All that matters is that no one wins. Aren't I right? Aren't I?" He tipped his hat to her.

Waiting for
the Olympians

FREDERIK POHL

Chapter 1
The Day of the Two Rejections

If I had been writing it as a romance, I would have called the chapter about that last day in London something like "The Day of the Two Rejections." It was a nasty day in late December, just before the holidays. The weather was cold, wet, and miserable—well, I said it was London, didn't I?—but everybody was in a sort of expectant holiday mood; it had just been announced that the Olympians would be arriving no later than the following August, and everybody was excited about that. All the taxi drivers were busy, and so I was late for my lunch with Lidia. "How was Manahattan?" I asked, sliding into the booth beside her and giving her a quick kiss.

"Manahattan was very nice," she said, pouring me a drink. Lidia was a writer, too—well, they *call* themselves writers, the ones who follow famous people around and write down all their gossip and jokes and put them out as books for the amusement of the idle. That's not really *writing*, of course. There's nothing creative about it. But it pays well, and the research (Lidia always told me) was a lot of fun. She spent a lot of time traveling around the celebrity circuit, which was not very good for our romance. She watched me drink the first glass before she remembered to ask politely, "Did you finish the book?"

"Don't call it 'the book,'" I said. "Call it by its name, *An Ass's Olympiad*. I'm going to see Marcus about it this afternoon."

"That's not what I'd call a great title," she commented—Lidia was always willing to give me her opinion on anything, when she didn't like it. "Really, don't you think it's too late to be writing another sci-rom about the Olympians?" And then she smiled brightly and said, "I've got something to say to you, Julie. Have another drink first."

So I knew what was coming right away, and that was the first rejection.

I'd seen this scene building up. Even before she left on that last "research" trip to the West I had begun to suspect that some of that early ardor had cooled, so I wasn't really surprised when she told me, without any further foreplay, "I've met somebody else, Julie."

I said, "I see." I really did see, and so I poured myself a third drink while she told me about it.

"He's a former space pilot, Julius. He's been to Mars and the Moon and everywhere, and oh, he's such a sweet man. And he's a champion wrestler, too, would you believe it? Of course, he's still married, as it happens. But he's going to talk to his wife about a divorce as soon as the kids are just a little older."

She looked at me challengingly, waiting for me to tell her she was an idiot. I had no intention of saying anything at all, as a matter of fact, but just in case I had, she added, "Don't say what you're thinking."

"I wasn't thinking anything," I protested.

She sighed. "You're taking this very well," she told me. She sounded as though that were a great disappointment to her. "Listen, Julius, I didn't plan this. Truly, you'll always be dear to me in a special way. I hope we can always be friends—" I stopped listening around then.

There was plenty more in the same vein, but only the details were a surprise. When she told me our little affair was over I took it calmly enough. I always knew that Lidia had a weakness for the more athletic type. Worse than that, she never respected the kind of writing I do, anyway. She had the usual establishment contempt for science-adventure romances about the future and adventures on alien planets, and what sort of relationship could that lead to, in the long run?

So I left her with a kiss and a smile, neither of them very sincere, and headed for my editor's office. That was where I got the second rejection. The one that really hurt.

Mark's office was in the old part of London, down by the river. It's an old company, in an old building, and most of the staff are old, too. When the company needs clerks or copy editors it has a habit of picking up tutors whose students have grown up and don't need them anymore, and retraining them. Of course, that's just for the people in the lower echelons. The higher-ups, like Mark himself, are free, salaried executives, with the executive privilege of interminable, winey author-and-editor lunches that don't end until the middle of the afternoon.

I had to wait half an hour to see him; obviously he had been having one of them that day. I didn't mind. I had every confidence that our interview was going to be short, pleasant, and remunerative. I knew very well that *An Ass's Olympiad* was one of the best sci-roms I had ever done. Even the title was clever. The book was a satire, with classical overtones—from *The Golden Ass* of the ancient writer, Lucius Apuleius, two thousand years ago or so; I had played off the classic in a comic, adventurous little story about the coming of the real Olympians. I can always tell when a book is going really well and I knew the fans would eat this one up. . . .

When I finally got in to see Marcus he had a glassy, after-lunch look in his eye, and I could see my manuscript on his desk.

I also saw that clipped to it was a red-bordered certificate, and that was the first warning of bad news. The certificate was the censor's verdict, and the red border meant it was an obstat.

Mark didn't keep me in suspense. "We can't publish," he said, pressing his palm on the manuscript. "The censors have turned it down."

"They can't!" I cried, making his old secretary lift his head from his desk in the corner of the room to stare at me.

"They did," Mark said. "I'll read you what the obstat

says: '—of a nature which may give offense to the delegation from the Galactic Consortium, usually referred to as the Olympians—' and '—thus endangering the security and tranquility of the Empire—' and, well, basically it just says no. No revisions suggested. Just a complete veto; it's waste paper now, Julie. Forget it."

"But *everybody* is writing about the Olympians!" I yelped.

"Everybody *was*," he corrected. "Now they're getting close, and the censors don't want to take any more chances." He leaned back to rub his eyes, obviously wishing he could be taking a nice nap instead of breaking my heart. Then he added tiredly, "So what do you want to do, Julie? Write us a replacement? It would have to be fast, you understand; the front office doesn't like having contracts outstanding for more than thirty days after due date. And it would have to be good. You're not going to get away with pulling some old reject out of your trunk—I've seen all those already, anyway."

"How the hells do you expect me to write a whole new book in thirty days?" I demanded.

He shrugged, looking sleepier and less interested in my problem than ever. "If you can't, you can't. Then you'll just have to give back the advance," he told me.

I calmed down fast. "Well, no," I said, "there's no question of having to do that. I don't know about finishing it in thirty days, though—"

"I do," he said flatly. He watched me shrug. "Have you got an idea for the new one?"

"Mark," I said patiently, "I've *always* got ideas for new ones. That's what a professional writer is. He's a machine for thinking up ideas. I always have more ideas than I can ever write—"

"Do you?" he insisted.

I surrendered, because if I'd said yes the next thing would have been that he'd want me to tell him what it was. "Not exactly," I admitted.

"Then," he said, "you'd better go wherever you do to

get ideas, because, give us the new book or give us back the advance, thirty days is all you've got."

There's an editor for you.

They're all the same. At first they're all honey and sweet talk, with those long alcoholic lunches and blue-sky conversation about million-copy printings while they wheedle you into signing the contract. They they turn nasty. They want the actual book delivered. When they don't get it, or when the censors say they can't print it, then there isn't any more sweet talk and all the conversation is about how the aediles will escort you to debtors' prison.

So I took his advice. I knew where to go for ideas, and it wasn't in London. No sensible man stays in London in the winter anyway, because of the weather and because it's too full of foreigners. I still can't get used to seeing all those huge rustic Northmen and dark Hindian and Arabian women in the heart of town. I admit I can be turned on by that red caste mark or by a pair of flashing dark eyes shining through all the robes and veils—I suppose what you imagine is always more exciting than what you can see, especially when what you see is the short, dumpy Britain women like Lidia.

So I made a reservation on the overnight train to Rome, to transfer there to a hydrofoil for Alexandria. I packed with a good heart, not neglecting to take along a floppy sun hat, a flask of insect repellent, and—oh, of course—stylus and blank tablets enough to last me for the whole trip, just in case a book idea emerged for me to write. Egypt! Where the world conference on the Olympians was starting its winter session . . . where I would be among the scientists and astronauts who always sparked ideas for new science-adventure romances for me to write . . . where it would be warm. . . .

Where my publisher's aediles would have trouble finding me, in the event that no idea for a new novel came along.

Chapter 2
On the Way to the Idea Place

No idea did.

That was disappointing. I do some of my best writing on trains, aircraft, and ships, because there aren't any interruptions and you can't decide to go out for a walk because there isn't any place to walk to. It didn't work this time. All the while the train was slithering across the wet, bare English winter countryside toward the Channel, I sat with my tablet in front of me and the stylus poised to write, but by the time we dipped into the tunnel the tablet was still virgin.

I couldn't fool myself. I was stuck. I mean, *stuck*. Nothing happened in my head that could transform itself into an opening scene for a new sci-rom novel.

It wasn't the first time in my writing career that I'd been stuck with the writer's block. That's a sort of occupational disease for any writer. But this time was the worst. I'd really counted on *An Ass's Olympiad*. I had even calculated that the publication date could be made to coincide with that wonderful day when the Olympians themselves arrived in our solar system, with all sorts of wonderful publicity for my book flowing out of that great event, so the sales should be *immense* . . . and, worse than that, I'd already spent the on-signing advance. All I had left was credit, and not much of that.

Not for the first time, I wondered what it would have been like if I had followed some other career. If I'd stayed in the civil service, for instance, as my father had wanted.

Really, I hadn't had much choice. I was born during the Space Tricentennial Year, and my mother told me the first word I said was "Mars." She said there was a little misunderstanding there, because at first she thought I was talking about the god, not the planet, and she and my father had long talks about whether to train me for the priesthood, but by the time I could read she knew I was a space nut. Like a lot of my generation (the ones that read my books), I grew up on spaceflight. I was a teenager when the first pictures came back from the space probe to the Alpha Centauri planet Julia, with its crystal grasses and silver-leafed trees. As a boy I corresponded with another youth who lived in the cavern colonies on the Moon, and I read with delight the shoot-'em-ups about outlaws and aediles chasing each other around the satellites of Jupiter. I wasn't the only kid who grew up space-happy, but I never got over it.

Naturally I became a science-adventure romance writer; what else did I know anything about? As soon as I began to get actual money for my fantasies I quit my job as secretary to one of the imperial legates on the Western continents and went full-time pro.

I prospered at it, too—prospered reasonably, at least—well, to be more exact, I earned a livable, if irregular, income out of the two sci-roms a year I could manage to write, and enough of a surplus to support the habit of dating pretty women like Lidia out of the occasional bonus when one of the books was made into a broadcast drama or a play.

Then along came the message from the Olympians, and the whole face of science-adventure romans was changed forever.

It was the most exciting news in the history of the world, of course. There really *were* other intelligent races out there among the stars of the Galaxy! It had never occurred to me that it would affect me personally, except with joy.

Joy it was, at first. I managed to talk my way into the Alpine radio observatory that had recorded that first message, and I heard it recorded with my own ears:

Dit *squah* dit.
Dit *squee* dit *squah* dit dit.
Dit *squee* dit *squee* dit *squah* dit dit dit.
Dit *squee* dit *squee* dit *squee* dit *squah* wooooo.
Dit *squee* dit *squee* dit *squee* dit *squee* dit *squah* dit dit dit dit dit.

*   *   *

It all looks so simple now, but it took awhile before anyone figured out just what this first message from the Olympians was. (Of course, we didn't call them Olympians then. We wouldn't call them that now if the priests had anything to say about it, because they think it's almost sacrilegious, but what else are you going to call godlike beings from the heavens? The name caught on right away, and the priests just had to learn to live with it.) It was, in fact, my good friend Flavius Samuelus ben Samuelus who first deciphered it and produced the right answer to transmit back to the senders—the one that, four years later, let the Olympians know we had heard them.

Meanwhile, we all knew this wonderful new truth: We weren't alone in the universe! Excitement exploded. The market for sci-roms boomed. My very next book was *The Radio Gods*, and it sold its head off.

I thought it would go on forever.

It might have, too . . . if it hadn't been for the timorous censors.

I slept through the tunnel—all the tunnels, even the ones through the Alps—and by the time I woke up we were halfway down to Rome.

In spite of the fact that the tablets remained obstinately blank, I felt more cheerful. Lidia was just a fading memory, I still had twenty-nine days to turn in a new sci-rom and Rome, after all, is still Rome! The center of the universe—well, not counting what new lessons in astronomical geography the Olympians might teach us. At least, it's the greatest city in the world. It's the place where all the action is.

By the time I'd sent the porter for breakfast and changed into a clean robe we were there, and I alighted into the great, noisy train shed.

I hadn't been in the city for several years, but Rome doesn't change much. The Tiber still stank. The big new apartment buildings still hid the old ruins until you were almost on top of them, the flies were still awful, and the Roman youths still clustered around the train station to sell you guided tours to the Golden House (as though any of them could ever get past the Legion guards!), or sacred amulets, or their sisters.

Because I used to be a secretary on the staff of the proconsul to the Cherokee Nation, I have friends in Rome. Because I hadn't had the good sense to call ahead, none of them were home. I had no choice. I had to take a room in a high-rise inn on the Palatine.

It was ferociously expensive, of course. Everything in Rome is—that's why people like to live in dreary outposts like London—but I figured that by the time the bills came in I would either have found something to satisfy Marcus and get the rest of the advance, or I'd be in so much trouble a few extra debts wouldn't matter.

Having reached that decision, I decided to treat myself to a servant. I picked out a grinning, muscular Sicilian at the rental desk in the lobby, gave him the keys for my luggage, and instructed him to take it to my room—and to make me a reservation for the next day's hoverflight to Alexandria.

That's when my luck began to get better.

When the Sicilian came to the wine shop to ask me for further orders, he reported, "There's another citizen who's booked on the same fight, Citizen Julius. Would you like to share a compartment with him?"

It's nice when you rent a servant who tries to save you money. I said approvingly, "What kind of a person is he? I don't want to get stuck with some real bore."

"You can see for yourself, Julius. He's in the baths right now. He's a Judaean. His name is Flavius Samuelus."

Five minutes later I had my clothes off and a sheet wrapped around me, and I was in the tepidarium, peering around at every body there.

I picked Sam out at once. He was stretched out with his eyes closed while a masseur pummeled his fat old flesh. I climbed onto the slab next to his without speaking. When he groaned and rolled over, opening his eyes, I said, "Hello, Sam."

It took him a moment to recognize me; he didn't have his glasses in. But when he squinted hard enough his face broke out into a grin. "Julie!" he cried. "Small world! It's good to see you again!"

And he reached out to clasp fists-over-elbows, really welcoming, just as I had expected; because one of the things I like best about Flavius Samuelus is that he likes me.

One of the other things I like best about Sam is that, although he is a competitor, he is also an undepletable natural resource. He writes sci-roms himself. He does more than that. He has helped me with the science part of my own sci-roms any number of times, and it had crossed my mind as soon as I heard the Sicilian say his name that he might be just what I wanted in the present emergency.

Sam is at least seventy years old. His head is hairless. There's a huge brown age spot on the top of his scalp. His throat hangs in a pouch of flesh, and his eyelids sag. But you'd never guess any of that if you were simply talking to him on the phone. He has the quick, chirpy voice of a twenty-year-old, and the mind of one, too—of an extraordinarily *bright* twenty-year-old. He gets enthusiastic.

That complicates things, because Sam's brain works faster than it ought to. Sometimes that makes him hard to talk to, because he's usually three or four exchanges ahead of most people. So the next thing he says to you is as likely as not to be the response to some question that you are inevitably going to ask, but haven't yet thought of.

It is an unpleasant fact of life that Sam's sci-roms sell better than mine do. It is a tribute to Sam's personality that I don't hate him for it. He has an unfair advantage over the rest of us, since he is a professional astronomer himself. He only writes sci-roms for fun, in his spare time, of which he doesn't have a whole lot. Most of his working hours are spent running a space probe of his own, the one that circles the Epsilon Eridani planet, Dione. I can stand his success (and, admit it! his talent) because he is generous with his ideas. As soon as we had agreed to share the hoverflight compartment, I put it to him directly. Well, almost directly. I said, "Sam, I've been wondering about something. When the Olympians get here, what is it going to mean to us?"

He was the right person to ask, of course; Sam knew more about the Olympians than anyone alive. But he was the wrong person to expect a direct answer from. He rose up, clutching his robe around him. He waved away the masseur and looked at me in friendly amusement, out of those bright black eyes under the flyaway eyebrows and the drooping lids. "Why do you need a new sci-rom plot right now?" he asked.

"Hells," I said ruefully, and decided to come clean. "It wouldn't be the first time I asked you, Sam. Only this time I *really* need it." And I told him the story of the novel the censors obstatted and the editor who was after a quick replacement—or my blood, choice of one.

He nibbled thoughtfully at the knuckle of his thumb. "What was this novel of yours about?" he asked curiously.

"It was a satire, Sam. *An Ass's Olympiad*. About the Olympians coming down to Earth in a matter transporter, only there's a mixup in the transmission and one of them accidentally gets turned into an ass. It's got some funny bits in it."

"It sure has, Julie. Has had for a couple dozen centuries."

"Well, I didn't say it was altogether *original*, only—"

He was shaking his head. "I thought you were smarter than that, Julie. What did you expect the censors to do, jeopardize the most important event in human history for the sake of a dumb sci-rom?"

"It's not a dumb—"

"It's dumb to risk offending them," he said, overruling me firmly. "Best to be safe and not write about them at all."

"But everybody's been doing it!"

"Nobody's been turning them into asses," he pointed out. "Julie, there's a limit to sci-rom speculation. When you write about the Olympians you're right up at that limit. Any speculation about them can be enough reason for them to pull out of the meeting entirely, and we might never get a chance like this again."

"They wouldn't—"

"Ah, Julie," he said, disgusted, "you don't have any idea what they would or wouldn't do. The censors made the right decision. Who knows what the Olympians are going to be like?"

"You do," I told him.

He laughed. There was an uneasy sound to it, though. "I wish I did. About the only thing we do know is that they don't appear to be just any old intelligent race; they have moral standards. We don't have any idea what those standards are, really. I don't know what your book says, but maybe you speculated that the Olympians were bringing us all kinds of new things—a cure for cancer, new psychedelic drugs, even eternal life—"

"What kind of psychedelic drugs might they bring, exactly?" I asked.

"Down, boy! I'm telling you *not* to think about that kind of idea. The point is that whatever you imagined might easily turn out to be the most repulsive and immoral thing the Olympians can think of. The stakes are too high. This is a once-only chance. We can't let it go sour."

"But I need a *story*," I wailed.

"Well, yes," he admitted, "I suppose you do. Let me think about it. Let's get cleaned up and get out of here."

While we were in the hot drench, while we were dressing, while we were eating a light lunch, Sam chattered on about the forthcoming conference in Alexandria. I was pleased to listen. Apart from the fact that everything he said was interesting, I began to feel hopeful about actually producing a book for Mark. If anybody could help me, Sam could, and he was a problem addict. He couldn't resist a challenge.

That was undoubtedly why he was the first to puzzle out the Olympians' interminably repeated *squees* and *squahs*. If you simply took the dit to be numeral one, and the *squee* to be plus sign, and the *squah* to be an equals sign, then "Dit *squee* dit *squah* dit dit" simply came out as "One plus one equals two."

That was easy enough. It didn't take a super brain like Sam's to substitute our terms for theirs and reveal the message to be simple arithmetic—except for the mysterious "wooooo":

Dit *squee* dit *squee* dit *squee* dit *squah* wooooo.

What was the "wooooo" supposed to mean? A special convention to represent the numeral four?

Sam knew right away, of course. As soon as he heard the message he telegraphed the solution from his library in Padua:

"The message calls for an answer. 'Wooooo' means question mark. The answer is four."

And so the reply to the stars was transmitted on its way:

Dit *squee* dit *squee* dit *squee* dit *squah* dit dit dit dit.

The human race had turned in its test paper in the entrance examination, and the slow process of establishing communication had begun.

It took four years before the Olympians responded. Obviously, they weren't nearby. Also obviously, they weren't simple folk like ourselves, sending out radio messages from a planet of a star two light-years away, because there wasn't any star there; the reply came from a point in space where none of our telescopes or probes had found anything at all.

By then Sam was deeply involved. He was the first to point out that the star folk had undoubtedly chosen to send a weak signal, because they wanted to be sure our technology was reasonably well developed before we tried to answer. He was one of the impatient ones who talked the collegium authorities into beginning transmission of all sorts of mathematical formulae, and then simple word relationships, to start sending *something* to the Olympians while we waited for radio waves to creep to wherever they were and back with an answer.

Sam wasn't the only one, of course. He wasn't even the principal investigator when they got into the hard work of developing a common vocabulary. There were better specialists than Sam at linguistics and cryptanalysis.

But it was Sam who first noticed, early on, that the response time to our messages was getting shorter. Meaning that the Olympians were on their way toward us.

By then they'd begun sending picture mosaics. They came in as strings of dits and dahs, 550,564 bits long. Someone quickly figured out that that was the square of 742, and when they displayed the string as a square matrix, black cells for the dits and white ones for the dahs, the image of the first Olympian leaped out.

Everybody remembers that picture. Everyone on Earth saw it, except for the totally blind—it was on every broadcast screen and news journal in the world—and even the blind listened to the anatomical descriptions every commentator supplied. Two tails. A fleshy, beardlike thing that hung down from its chin. Four legs. A ruff of spikes down what seemed to be the backbone. Eyes set wide apart on bulges from the cheekbones.

That first Olympian was not at all pretty, but it was definitely *alien*.

When the next string turned out very similar to the first, it was Sam who saw at once that it was simply a slightly rotated view of the same being. The Olympians took forty-one pictures to give us the complete likeness of that first one in the round. . . .

Then they began sending pictures of the others.

It had never occurred to anyone, not even Sam, that we would be dealing not with one super race, but with at least twenty-two of them. There were that many separate forms of alien beings, and each one uglier and more strange than the one before.

That was one of the reasons the priests didn't like calling them Olympians. We're pretty ecumenical about our gods, but none of them looked anything like any of *those*, and some of the older priests never stopped muttering about blasphemy.

Halfway through the third course of our lunch and the second flask of wine, Sam broke off his description of the latest communique from the Olympians—they'd been acknowledging receipt of our transmissions about Earthly history—to lift his head and grin at me.

"Got it," he said.

I turned and blinked at him. Actually, I hadn't been paying a lot of attention to his monologue because I had been keeping my eye on the pretty Kievan waitress. She had attracted my attention because—well, I mean, *after* attracting my attention because of her extremely well developed figure and the sparsity of clothing to conceal it—because she was wearing a gold citizen's amulet around her neck. She wasn't a slave. That made her more intriguing. I can't ever get really interested in slave women, because it isn't sporting, but I had got quite interested in this woman.

"Are you listening to me?" Sam demanded testily.

"Of course I am. What have you got?"

"I've got the answer to your problem." He beamed. "Not just a sci-rom novel plot. A whole new *kind* of sci-rom! Why don't you write a book about what it will be like if the Olympians *don't* come?"

I love the way half of Sam's brain works at questions while the other half is doing something completely different, but I can't always follow what comes out of it. "I don't see what you mean. If I write about the Olympians not coming, isn't that just as bad as if I write about them doing it?"

"No, no," he snapped. "Listen to what I say! Leave the Olympians out entirely. Just write about a future that might happen, but won't."

The waitress was hovering over us, picking up used plates. I was conscious of her listening as I responded with dignity, "Sam, that's not my style. My sci-roms may not sell as well as yours do, but I've got just as much integrity. I never write anything that I don't believe is at least possible."

"Julie, get your mind off your gonads"—so he hadn't missed the attention I was giving the girl—"and use that pitifully tiny brain of yours. I'm talking about something that *could* be possible, in some alternative future, if you see what I mean."

I didn't see at all. "What's an alternative future?"

"It's a future that *might* happen, but *won't*," he explained. "Like if the Olympians don't come to see us."

I shook my head, puzzled. "But we already know they're coming," I pointed out.

"But suppose they weren't! Suppose they hadn't contacted us years ago."

"But they did," I said, trying to straighten out his thinking on the subject. He only sighed.

"I see I'm not getting through to you," he said, pulling his robe around him and getting to his feet. "Get on with your waitress. I've got some messages to send. I'll see you on the ship."

Well, for one reason or another I didn't get anywhere with the Kievan waitress. She said she was married, happily and monogamously. Well, I couldn't see why any lawful, free husband would have his wife out working at a job like that, but I was surprised she didn't show more interest in one of my lineage—

I'd better explain about that.

You see, my family has a claim to fame. Genealogists say that we are descended from the line of Julius Caesar himself.

I mention that claim myself, sometimes, though usually only when I've been drinking—I suppose it is one of the reasons that Lidia, always a snob, took up with me in the first place. It isn't a serious matter. After all, Julius Caesar died more than two thousand years ago. There have been sixty or seventy generations since then, not to mention the fact that, although Ancestor Julius certainly left a lot of children behind him, none of them happened to be born to a woman he happened to be married to. I don't even look very Roman. There must have been a Northman or two in the line, because I'm tall and fair-haired, which no respectable Roman ever was.

Still, even if I'm not exactly the lawful heir to the divine Julius, I at least come of a pretty ancient and distinguished line. You would have thought a mere waitress would have taken that into account before turning me down.

She hadn't, though. When I woke up the next morning—alone—Sam was gone from the inn, although the skip-ship for Alexandria wasn't due to sail until late evening.

I didn't see him all day. I didn't look for him very hard,

because I woke up feeling a little ashamed of myself. Why should a grown man, a celebrated author of more than forty best-selling (well, reasonably *well* selling) sci-roms, depend on somebody else for his ideas?

So I turned my baggage over to the servant, checked out of the inn, and took the underground to the Library of Rome.

Rome isn't only the imperial capital of the world, it's the scientific capital, too. The big old telescopes out on the hills aren't much use anymore, because the lights from the city spoil their night viewing, and anyway the big optical telescopes are all out in space now. Still, they were where Galileus detected the first extrasolar planet and Tychus made his famous spectrographs of the last great supernova in our own galaxy, only a couple of dozen years after the first spaceflight. The scientific tradition survives. Rome is still the headquarters of the Collegium of Sciences.

That's why the Library of Rome is so great for someone like me. They have direct access to the the Collegium data base, and you don't even have to pay transmission tolls. I signed myself in, laid out my tablets and stylus on the desk they assigned me, and began calling up files.

Somewhere there had to be an idea for a science-adventure romance no one had written yet. . . .

Somewhere there no doubt was, but I couldn't find it. Usually you can get a lot of help from a smart research librarian, but it seemed they'd put on a lot of new people in the Library of Rome—Iberians, mostly; reduced to slave status because they'd taken part in last year's Lusitanian uprising. There were so many Iberians on the market for a while that they depressed the price. I would have bought some as a speculation, knowing that the price would go up—after all, there aren't that many uprisings and the demand for slaves never stops. But I was temporarily short of capital, and besides you have to feed them. If the ones at the Library of Rome were a fair sample, they were no bargains anyway.

I gave up. The weather had improved enough to make a stroll around town attractive, and so I wandered toward the Ostia monorail.

Rome was busy, as always. There was a bullfight going on in the Coliseum and racing at the Circus Maximus. Tourist buses were jamming the narrow streets. A long religious procession was circling the Pantheon, but I didn't get close enough to see which particular gods were being honored today. I don't like crowds. Especially Roman crowds, because there are even more foreigners in Rome than in London, Africs and Hinds, Hans and Northmen— every race on the face of the Earth sends its tourists to visit the Imperial City. And Rome obliges with spectacles. I paused at one of them, for the changing of the guard at the Golden House. Of course, the Caesar and his wife were nowhere to be seen—off on one of their endless ceremonial tours of the dominions, no doubt, or at least opening a new supermarket somewhere. But the Algonkian family standing in front of me were thrilled as the honor Legions marched and countermarched their standards around the palace. I remembered enough Cherokee to ask the Algonkians where they were from, but the languages aren't really very close and the man's Cherokee was even worse than mine. We just smiled at each other.

As soon as the Legions were out of the way I headed for the train.

I knew in the back of my mind that I should have been worrying about my financial position. The clock was running on my thirty days of grace. I didn't, though. I was buoyed up by a feeling of confidence. Confidence in my good friend Flavius Samuelus, who, I knew, no matter what he was doing with most of his brain, was still cogitating an idea for me with some part of it.

It did not occur to me that even Sam had limitations. Or that something so much more important than my own problems was taking up his attention that he didn't have much left for me.

I didn't see Sam come onto the skip-ship, and I didn't see him in our compartment. Even when the ship's fans began to rumble and we slid down the ways into the Tyrrhenian Sea he wasn't there. I dozed off, beginning to worry that he might have missed the boat; but late that night, already asleep, I half woke, just long enough to hear him stumbling in. "I've been on the bridge," he said when I muttered something. "Go back to sleep. I'll see you in the morning."

When I woke, I thought it might have been a dream, because he was up and gone before me. But his bed had been slept in, however briefly, and the cabin steward reassured me when he brought my morning wine. Yes, Citizen Flavius Samuelus was certainly on the hover. He was in the captain's own quarters, as a matter of fact, although what he was doing there the steward could not say.

I spent the morning relaxing on the deck of the hover, soaking in the sun. The ship wasn't exactly a hover anymore. We had transited the Sicilian Straits during the night and now, out in the open Mediterranean, the captain had lowered the stilts, pulled up the hover skirts, and extended the screws. We were hydrofoiling across the sea at easily a hundred miles an hour. It was a smooth, relaxing ride; the vanes that supported us were twenty feet under the surface of the water, and so there was no wave action to bounce us around.

Lying on my back and squinting up at the warm southern sky, I could see a three-winged airliner rise up from the horizon behind us and gradually overtake us, to disappear ahead of our bows. The plane wasn't going much faster than we were—and we had all the comfort, while they were paying twice as much for passage.

I opened my eyes all the way when I caught a glimpse of someone standing beside me. In fact, I sat up quickly, because it was Sam. He looked as though he hadn't had much sleep, and he was holding a floppy sun hat with one hand against the wind of our passage. "Where've you been?" I asked.

"Haven't you been watching the news?" he asked. I shook my head. "The transmissions from the Olympians have stopped," he told me.

I opened my eyes really wide at that, because it was an unpleasant surprise. Still, Sam didn't seem that upset. Displeased, yes. Maybe even a little concerned, but not as shaken up as I was prepared to feel. "It's probably nothing," he said. "It could be just interference from the sun. It's in Sagittarius now, so it's pretty much between us and them. There's been trouble with static for a couple of days now."

I ventured, "So the transmissions will start up again pretty soon?"

He shrugged and waved to the deck steward for one of those hot decoctions Judaeans like. When he spoke it was on a different topic. "I don't think I made you understand what I meant yesterday," he said. "Let me see if I can explain what I meant by an alternate world. You remember your history? How Fornius Vello conquered the Mayans and Romanized the Western Continents six or seven hundred years ago? Well, suppose he hadn't."

"But he did, Sam."

"I know he did," Sam said patiently. "I'm saying *suppose*. Suppose the Legions had been defeated at the Battle of Tehultapec."

I laughed. I was sure he was joking. "The Legions? Defeated? But the Legions have never been defeated."

"That's not true," Sam said in reproof. He hates it when people don't get their facts straight. "Remember Varus."

"Oh, hells, Sam, that was ancient history! When was it, two thousand years ago? In the time of Augustus Caesar? And it was only a temporary defeat, anyway. The Emperor Drusus got the eagles back." And got all of Gaul for the Empire, too. That was one of the first big trans-Alpine conquests. The Gauls are about as Roman as you can get these days, especially when it comes to drinking wine.

He shook his head. "Suppose Fornius Vello had had a temporary defeat, then."

I tried to follow his argument, but it wasn't easy. "What difference would that have made? Sooner or later the Legions would have conquered. They always have, you know."

"That's true," he said reasonably, "but if that particular conquest hadn't happened *then*, the whole course of history would have been different. We wouldn't have had the great westward migrations to fill up those empty continents. The Hans and the Hinds wouldn't have been surrounded on both sides, so they might still be independent nations. It would have been a different world. Do you see what I'm driving at? That's what I mean by an alternate world—one that might have happened, but didn't."

I tried to be polite to him. "Sam," I said, "you've just described the difference between a sci-rom and a fantasy. I don't do fantasy. Besides," I went on, not wanting to hurt his feelings, "I don't see how different things would have been, really. I can't believe the world would be changed enough to build a sci-rom plot on."

He gazed blankly at me for a moment, then turned and looked out to sea. Then, without transition, he said, "There's one funny thing. The Martian colonies aren't getting a transmission, either. And they aren't occluded by the sun."

I frowned. "What does that mean, Sam?"

He shook his head. "I wish I knew," he said.

Chapter 3
In Old Alexandria

The Pharos was bright in the sunset light as we came into the port of Alexandria. We were on hover again, at slow speeds, and the chop at the breakwater bumped us around. But once we got to the inner harbor the water was calm.

Sam had spent the afternoon back in the captain's quarters, keeping in contact with the Collegium of Sciences, but he showed up as we moored. He saw me gazing toward the rental desk on the dock but shook his head. "Don't bother with a rental, Julie," he ordered. "Let my niece's servants take your baggage. We're staying with her."

That was good news. Inn rooms in Alexandria are almost as pricey as Rome's. I thanked him, but he didn't even listen. He turned our bags over to a porter from his niece's domicile, a little Arabian who was a lot stronger than he looked, and disappeared toward the Hall of the Egyptian Senate-Inferior, where the conference was going to be held.

I hailed a three-wheeler and gave the driver the address of Sam's niece.

No matter what the Egyptians think, Alexandria is a dirty little town. The Choctaws have a bigger capital, and the Kievans have a cleaner one. Also Alexandria's famous library is a joke. After my (one would like to believe) ancestor Julius Caesar let it burn to the ground, the Egyptians did build it up again. But it is so old-fashioned that there's nothing in it but books.

The home of Sam's niece was in a particularly run-down section of that run-down town, only a few streets from the harborside. You could hear the noise of the cargo winches from the docks, but you couldn't hear them very well because of the noise of the streets themselves, thick with goods vans and drivers cursing each other as they jockeyed around the narrow corners. The house itself was bigger than I had expected. But, at least from the outside, that was all you could say for it. It was faced with cheap Egyptian stucco rather than marble, and right next door to it was a slave-rental barracks.

At least, I reminded myself, it was free. I kicked at the door and shouted for the butler.

It wasn't the butler who opened it for me. It was Sam's niece herself, and she was a nice surprise. She was almost as tall as I was and just as fair. Besides, she was young and very good-looking. "You must be Julius," she said. "I am Rachel, niece of Citizen Flavius Samuelus ben Samuelus, and I welcome you to my home."

I kissed her hand. It's a Kievan custom that I like, especially with pretty girls I don't yet know well, but hope to. "You don't look Judaean," I told her.

"You don't look like a sci-rom hack," she replied. Her voice was less chilling than her words, but not much. "Uncle Sam isn't here, and I'm afraid I've got work I must do. Basilius will show you to your rooms and offer you some refreshment."

* * *

I usually make a better first impression on young women. I usually work at it more carefully, but she had taken me by surprise. I had more or less expected that Sam's niece would look more or less like Sam, except probably for the baldness and the wrinkled face. I could not have been more wrong.

I had been wrong about the house, too. It was a big one. There had to be well over a dozen rooms, not counting servants' quarters, and the atrium was covered with one of those partly reflecting films that keep the worst of the heat out.

The famous Egyptian sun was directly overhead when Basilius, Rachel's butler, showed me my rooms. They were pleasingly bright and airy, but Basilius suggested I might enjoy being outside. He was right. He brought me wine and fruits in the atrium, a pleasant bench by a fountain. Through the film the sun looked only pale and pleasant instead of deadly hot. The fruit was fresh, too— pineapples from Lebanon, oranges from Judaea, apples that must have come all the way from somewhere in Gaul. The only thing wrong that I could see was that Rachel herself stayed in her rooms, so I didn't have a chance to try to put myself in a better light with her.

She had left instructions for my comfort, though. Basilius clapped his hands and another servant appeared, bearing stylus and tablets in case I should decide to work. I was surprised to see that both Basilius and the other one were Africs; they don't usually get into political trouble, or trouble with the aediles of any kind, so not many of them are slaves.

The fountain was a Cupid statue. In some circumstances I would have thought of that as a good sign, but here it didn't seem to mean anything. Cupid's nose was chipped, and the fountain was obviously older than Rachel was. I thought of just staying there until Rachel came out, but when I asked Basilius when that would be he gave me a look of delicate patronizing. "Citizeness Rachel works through the afternoon, Citizen Julius," he informed me.

"Oh? And what does she work at?"

"Citizeness Rachel is a famous historian," he said. "She often works straight through until bedtime. But for you and her uncle, of course, dinner will be served at your convenience."

He was quite an obliging fellow. "Thank you, Basilius," I said. "I believe I'll go out for a few hours myself." And then, as he turned politely to go, I said curiously, "You don't look like a very dangerous criminal. If you don't mind my asking, what were you enslaved for?"

"Oh, not for anything violent, Citizen Julius," he assured me. "Just for debts."

I found my way to the Hall of the Egyptian Senate-Inferior easily enough. There was a lot of traffic going that way, because it is, after all, one of the sights of Alexandria.

The Senate-Inferior wasn't in session at the time. There was no reason it should have been, of course, because what did the Egyptians need a Senate of any kind for? The time when they'd made any significant decisions for themselves was many centuries past.

They'd spread themselves for the conference, though. The Senate Temple had niches for at least half a hundred gods. There were the customary figures of Amon-Ra and Jupiter and all the other main figures of the pantheon, of course, but for the sake of the visitors they had installed Ahura-Mazda, Yahweh, Freya, Quetzalcoatl, and at least a dozen I didn't recognize at all. They were all decorated with fresh sacrifices of flowers and fruits, showing that the tourists, if not the astronomers—and probably the astronomers as well—were taking no chances in getting communications with the Olympians restored. Scientists are an agnostic lot, of course—well, most educated people are, aren't they? But even an agnostic will risk a piece of fruit to placate a god, just on the chance he's wrong.

Outside the hall, hucksters were already putting up their stands, although the first sessions wouldn't begin for another day. I bought some dates from one of them and wandered around, eating dates and studying the marble frieze on the wall of the Senate. It showed the rippling fields of corn, wheat, and potatoes that had made Egypt the breadbasket of the Empire for two thousand years. It didn't show anything about the Olympians, of course. Space is not a subject that interests the Egyptians a lot. They prefer to look back on their glorious (they *say* it's glorious) past; and there would have been no point in having the conference on the Olympians there at all, except who wants to go to some northern city in December?

Inside, the great hall was empty, except for slaves arranging seat cushions and cuspidors for the participants. The exhibit halls were noisy with workers setting up displays, but they didn't want people dropping in to bother them, and the participants' lounges were dark.

I was lucky enough to find the media room open. It was always good for a free glass of wine, and besides, I wanted to know where everyone was. The slave in charge couldn't tell me. "There's supposed to be a private executive meeting somewhere, that's all I know—and there's all these journalists looking for someone to interview." And then, peering over my shoulder as I signed in: "Oh, you're the fellow that writes the sci-roms, aren't you? Well, maybe one of the journalists would settle for you."

It wasn't the most flattering invitation I'd ever had. Still, I didn't say no. Marcus is always after me to do publicity gigs whenever I get the chance, because he thinks it sells books, and it was worthwhile trying to please Marcus just then.

The journalist wasn't much pleased, though. They'd set up a couple of studios in the basement of the Senate, and when I found the one I was directed to, the interviewer was fussing over his hairdo in front of a mirror. A couple of technicians were lounging in front of the tube, watching a broadcast comedy series. When I introduced myself the interviewer took his eyes off his own image long enough to cast a doubtful look in my direction.

"You're not a real astronomer," he told me.

I shrugged. I couldn't deny it.

"Still," he grumbled, "I'd better get *some* kind of a spot for the late news. All right. Sit over there, and try to sound as if you know what you're talking about." Then he began telling the technical crew what to do.

That was a strange thing. I'd already noticed that the technicians wore citizens' gold. The interviewer didn't. But he was the one who was giving *them* orders.

I didn't approve of that at all. I don't like big commercial outfits that put slaves in positions of authority over free citizens. It's a bad practice. Jobs like tutors, college professors, doctors, and so on are fine; slaves can do them as well as a citizen, and usually a lot cheaper. But there's a moral issue involved here. A slave must have a master. Otherwise, how can you call him a slave? And when you let the slave *be* the master, even in something as trivial as a broadcasting studio, you strike at the foundations of society.

The other thing is that it isn't fair competition. There are free citizens who need those jobs. We had some of that in my own line of work a few years ago. There were two or three slave authors turning out adventure novels, but the rest of us got together and put a stop to it—especially after Marcus bought one of them to use as a sub-editor. Not one citizen writer would work with her. Mark finally had to put her into the publicity department, where she couldn't do any harm.

So I started the interview with a chip on my shoulder, and his first question made it worse. He plunged right in. "When you're pounding out those sci-roms of yours, do you make any effort to keep in touch with scientific reality? Do you know, for instance, that the Olympians have stopped transmitting?"

I scowled at him, regardless of the cameras. "Science-adventure romances are *about* scientific reality. And the Olympians haven't 'stopped,' as you put it. There's just been a technical hitch of some kind, probably caused by radio interference from our own sun. As I said in my earlier romance, *The Radio Gods*, electromagnetic impulses are susceptible to—"

He cut me off. "It's been—" he glanced at his watch— "twenty-nine hours since they stopped. That doesn't sound like just a technical hitch."

"Of course it is. There's no reason for them to stop. We've already demonstrated to them that we're truly civilized, first because we're technological, second because we don't fight wars anymore—that was cleared up in the first year. As I said in my roman, *The Radio Gods*—"

He gave me a pained look, then turned and winked into the camera. "You can't keep a hack from plugging his books, can you?" he remarked humorously. "But it looks like he doesn't want to use that wild imagination unless he gets paid for it. All I'm asking him for is a guess at why the Olympians don't want to talk to us anymore, and all he gives me is commercials."

As though there were any other reason to do interviews! "Look here," I said sharply, "if you can't be courteous when you speak to a citizen, I'm not prepared to go on with this conversation at all."

"So be it, pal," he said, icy cold. He turned to the technical crew. "Stop the cameras," he ordered. "We're going back to the studio. This is a waste of time." We parted on terms of mutual dislike, and once again I had done something that my editor would have been glad to kill me for.

That night at dinner, Sam was no comfort. "He's an unpleasant man, sure," he told me. "But the trouble is, I'm afraid he's right."

"They've really *stopped*?"

Sam shrugged. "We're not in line with the sun anymore, so that's definitely not the reason. Damn. I was hoping it would be."

"I'm sorry about that, Uncle Sam," Rachel said gently. She was wearing a simple white robe, Hannish silk by the look of it, with no decorations at all. It really looked good on her. I didn't think there was anything under it except for some very well formed female flesh.

"I'm sorry, too," he grumbled. His concerns didn't affect his appetite, though. He was ladling in the first course—a sort of chicken soup, with bits of a kind of pastry floating in it—and, for that matter, so was I. Whatever Rachel's faults might be, she had a good cook. It was plain home cooking, none of your partridge-in-a-rabbit-inside-a-boar kind of thing, but well prepared and expertly served by her butler, Basilius. "Anyway," Sam said, mopping up the last of the broth, "I've figured it out."

"Why the Olympians stopped?" I asked, to encourage him to go on with the revelation.

"No, no! I mean about your romance, Julie. My alternate world idea. If you don't want to write about a different *future*, how about a different *now*?"

I didn't get a chance to ask him about what he was talking about, because Rachel beat me to it. "There's only one *now*, Sam, dear," she pointed out. I couldn't have said it better myself.

Sam groaned. "Not you, too, honey," he complained. "I'm talking about a new kind of sci-rom."

"I don't read many sci-roms," she apologized, in the tone that isn't an apology at all.

He ignored that. "You're a historian, aren't you?" She didn't bother to confirm it; obviously, it was the thing she was that shaped her life. "So what if history had gone a different way?"

He beamed at us as happily as though he had said something that made sense. Neither of us beamed back. Rachel pointed out the flaw in his remark. "It didn't, though," she told him.

"I said *suppose*! This isn't the only possible now, it's just the one that happened to occur! There could have been a million different ones. Look at all the events in the past that could have gone a different way. Suppose Annius Publius hadn't discovered the Western Continents in City Year 1820. Suppose Caesar Publius Terminus hadn't decreed the development of a space program in 2122. Don't you see what I'm driving at? What kind of a world would we be living in now if those things hadn't happened?"

Rachel opened her mouth to speak, but she was saved by the butler. He appeared in the doorway with a look of silent appeal. When she excused herself to see what was needed in the kitchen, that left it up to me. "I never wrote anything like that, Sam," I told him. "I don't know anybody else who did, either."

"That's exactly what I'm driving at! It would be something completely *new* in sci-roms. Don't you want to pioneer a whole new kind of story?"

Out of the wisdom of experience, I told him, "Pioneers don't make any money, Sam." He scowled at me. "You could write it yourself," I suggested.

That just changed the annoyance to gloom. "I wish I could. But until this business with the Olympians is cleared up, I'm not going to have much time for sci-roms. No, it's up to you, Julie."

Then Rachel came back in, looking pleased with herself, followed by Basilius bearing a huge silver platter containing the main course.

Sam cheered up at once. So did I. The main dish was a whole roasted baby kid, and I realized that the reason Rachel had been called into the kitchen was so that she could weave a garland of flowers around its tiny baby horn buds herself. The maid servant followed with a pitcher of wine, replenishing all our goblets. All in all, we were busy enough eating to stop any conversation but compliments on the food.

Then Sam looked at his watch. "Great dinner, Rachel," he told his niece, "but I've got to get back. What about it?"

"What about what?" she asked.

"About helping poor Julie with some historical turning points he can use in the story?"

He hadn't listened to a word I'd said. I didn't have to say so, because Rachel was looking concerned. She said apologetically, "I don't know anything about those periods you were talking about—Publius Terminus, and so on. My specialty is the immediate post-Augustan period, when the Senate came back to power."

"Fine," he said, pleased with himself and showing it. "That's as good a period as any. Think how different things might be now if some little event then had gone in a different way. Say, if Augustus hadn't married Lady Livia and adopted her son Drusus to succeed him." He turned to me, encouraging me to take fire from his spark of inspiration. "I'm sure you see the possibilities, Julie! Tell you what you should do. The night's young yet; take

Rachel out dancing or something; have a few drinks; listen to her talk. What's wrong with that? You two young people ought to be having fun, anyway!"

That was definitely the most intelligent thing intelligent Sam had said in days.

So I thought, anyway, and Rachel was a good enough niece to heed her uncle's advice. Because I was a stranger in town, I had to let her pick the place. After the first couple she mentioned I realized that she was tactfully trying to spare my pocketbook. I couldn't allow that. After all, a night on the town with Rachel was probably cheaper, and anyway a whole lot more interesting, than the cost of an inn and meals.

We settled on a place right on the harborside, out toward the breakwater. It was a revolving nightclub on top of an inn built along the style of one of the old Pyramids. As the room slowly turned we saw the lights of the city of Alexandria, the shipping in the harbor, then the wide sea itself, its gentle waves reflecting starlight.

I was prepared to forget the whole idea of alternate worlds, but Rachel was more dutiful than that. After the first dance, she said, "I think I can help you. There was something that happened in Drusus's reign—"

"Do we have to talk about that?" I asked, refilling her glass.

"But Uncle Sam said we should. I thought you wanted to try a new kind of sci-rom."

"No, that's your uncle who wants that. See, there's a bit of a problem here. It's true that editors are always begging for something new and different, but if you're dumb enough to try to give it to them they don't recognize it. When they ask for different, what they mean is something right down the good old 'different' groove."

"I think," she informed me, with the certainty of an oracle and a lot less confusion of style, "that when my uncle has an idea, it's usually a good one." I didn't want to argue with her; I didn't even disagree: at least usually. I let her talk. "You see," she said, "my specialty is the transfer of power throughout early Roman history. What

I'm studying right now is the Judaean Diaspora, after Drusus's reign. You know what happened then, I suppose?"

Actually, I did—hazily. "That was the year of the Judaean rebellion, wasn't it?"

She nodded. She looked very pretty when she nodded, her fair hair moving gracefully and her eyes sparkling. "You see, that was a great tragedy for the Judaeans, and, just as my uncle said, it needn't have happened. If Procurator Tiberius had lived, it wouldn't have."

I coughed. "I'm not sure I know who Tiberius was," I said apologetically.

"He was the Procurator of Judaea, and a very good one. He was just and fair. He was the brother of the Emperor Drusus—the one my uncle was talking about, Livia's son, the adopted heir of Caesar Augustus. The one who restored the power of the Senate after Augustus had appropriated most of it for himself. Anyway, Tiberius was the best governor the Judaeans ever had, just as Drusus was the best emperor. Tiberius died just a year before the rebellion—ate some spoiled figs, they say, although it might have been his wife who did it—she was Julia, the daughter of Augustus by his first wife—"

I signaled distress. "I'm getting a little confused by all these names," I admitted.

"Well, the important one to remember is Tiberius, and you know who he was. If he had lived, the rebellion probably wouldn't have happened. Then there wouldn't have been a Diaspora."

"I see," I said. "Would you like another dance?"

She frowned at me, then smiled. "Maybe that's not such an interesting subject—unless you're a Judaean, anyway," she said. "All right, let's dance."

That was the best idea yet. It gave me a chance to confirm with my fingers what my eyes, ears, and nose had already told me; this was a very attractive young woman. She had insisted on changing, but fortunately the new gown was as soft and clinging as the old, and the palms of my hands rejoined in the tactile pleasure of her back and arm. I whispered, "I'm sorry if I sound stupid. I really don't know a whole lot about early history—you know, the first thousand years or so after the Founding of the City."

She didn't bother to point out that she did. She moved with me to the music, very enjoyable, then she straightened up. "I've got a different idea," she announced. "Let's go back to the booth." And she was already telling it to me as we left the dance floor. "Let's talk about your own ancestor, Julius Caesar. He conquered Egypt, right here in Alexandria. But suppose the Egyptians had defeated him instead, as they very nearly did?"

I was paying close attention now—obviously she had been interested enough in me to ask Sam some questions! "They couldn't have," I told her. "Julius never lost a war. Anyway"—I discovered to my surprise that I was beginning to take Sam's nutty idea seriously—"that would be a really hard one to write, wouldn't it? If the Legions had been defeated, it would have changed the whole world. Can you imagine a world that isn't Roman?"

She said sweetly, "No, but that's more your job than mine, isn't it?"

I shook my head. "It's too bizarre," I complained. "I couldn't make the readers believe it."

"You could try, Julius," she told me. "You see, there's an interesting possibility there. Drusus almost didn't live to become Emperor. He was severely wounded in a war in Gaul, while Augustus was still alive. Tiberius—you remember Tiberius—"

"Yes, yes, his brother. The one you like. The one he made Procurator of Judaea."

"That's the one. Well, Tiberius rode day and night to bring Drusus the best doctors in Rome. He almost didn't make it. They barely pulled Drusus through."

"Yes?" I said encouragingly. "And what then?"

She looked uncertain. "Well, I don't know what then."

I poured some more wine. "I guess I could figure out some kind of speculative idea," I said, ruminating. "Especially if you would help me with some of the details. I suppose Tiberius would have become Emperor instead of Drusus. You say he was a good man; so probably he would have done more or less what Drusus did—restore the power of

the Senate, after Augustus and my revered great-great
Julius between them had pretty nearly put it out of
business—"

I stopped there, startled at my own words. It almost
seemed that I was beginning to take Sam's crazy idea
seriously!

On the other hand, that wasn't all bad. It almost
seemed that Rachel was beginning to take *me* seriously.

That was a good thought. It kept me cheerful through
half a dozen more dances and at least another hour of
history lessons from her pretty lips... right up until the
time when, after we had gone back to her house, I tiptoed
out of my room toward hers, and found her butler, Basilius,
asleep on a rug across her doorway, with a great, thick
club by his side.

I didn't sleep well that night.

Partly it was glandular. My head knew that Rachel
didn't want me creeping into her bedroom, or else she
wouldn't have put the butler there in the way. But my
glands weren't happy with that news. They had soaked up
the smell and sight and feel of her, and they were
complaining about being thwarted.

The worst part was waking up every hour or so to
contemplate financial ruin.

Being poor wasn't so bad. Every writer has to learn
how to be poor from time to time, between checks. It's an
annoyance, but not a catastrophe. You don't get enslaved
just for poverty.

But I had been running up some pretty big bills. And
you do get enslaved for debt.

Chapter 4
The End of the Dream

The next morning I woke up late and grouchy and had to
take a three-wheeler to the Hall of the Senate-Inferior.

It was slow going. As we approached, the traffic thickened
even more. I could see the Legion forming for the cere-

monial guard as the Pharaoh's procession approached to open the ceremonies. The driver wouldn't take me any closer than the outer square, and I had to wait there with all the tourists, while the Pharaoh dismounted from her royal litter.

There was a soft, pleasured noise from the crowd, halfway between a giggle and a sigh. That was the spectacle the tourists had come to see. They pressed against the sheathed swords of the Legionaries while the Pharaoh, head bare, robe trailing on the ground, advanced on the shrines outside the Senate building. She sacrificed reverently and unhurriedly to them, while the tourists flashed their cameras at her, and I began to worry about the time. What if she ecumenically decided to visit all fifty shrines? But after doing Isis, Amon-Ra, and Mother Nile, she went inside to declare the Congress open. The Legionaries relaxed. The tourists began to flow back to their buses, snapping pictures of themselves now, and I followed the Pharaoh inside.

She made a good—by which I mean short—opening address. The only thing wrong with it was that she was talking to mostly empty seats.

The Hall of the Alexandrian Senate-Inferior holds two thousand people. There weren't more than a hundred and fifty in it. Most of those were huddled in small groups in the aisles and at the back of the hall, and they were paying no attention at all to the Pharaoh. I think she saw that and shortened her speech. At one moment she was telling us how the scientific investigation of the outside universe was completely in accord with the ancient traditions of Egypt—with hardly anyone listening—and at the next her voice had stopped without warning and she was handing her orb and scepter to her attendants. She proceeded regally across the stage and out the wings.

The buzz of conversation hardly slackened. What they were talking about, of course, was the Olympians. Even when the Collegium-Presidor stepped forward and called for the first session to begin, the hall didn't fill. At least most of the scattered groups of people in the room sat down—though still in clumps, and still doing a lot of whispering to each other.

Even the speakers didn't seem very interested in what they were saying. The first one was an honorary Presidor-Emeritus from the southern highlands of Egypt, and he gave us a review of everything we knew about the Olympians.

He read it as hurriedly as though he were dictating it to a scribe. It wasn't very interesting. The trouble, of course, was that his paper had been prepared days earlier, while the Olympian transmissions were still flooding in and no one had any thought they might be interrupted. It just didn't seem relevant anymore.

What I like about going to science congresses isn't so much the actual papers the speakers deliver—I can get that sort of information better from the journals in the library. It isn't even the back-and-forth discussion that follows each paper, although that sometimes produces useful background bits. What I get the most out of is what I call "the sound of science"—the kind of shorthand language scientists use when they're talking to each other about their own specialties. So I usually sit somewhere at the back of the hall, with as much space around me as I can manage, my tablet in my lap and my stylus in my hand, writing down bits of dialogue and figuring how to put them into my next sci-rom.

There wasn't much of that today. There wasn't much discussion at all. One by one the speakers got up and read their papers, answered a couple of cursory questions with cursory replies, and hurried off; and when each one finished he left, and the audience got smaller because, as I finally figured out, no one was there who wasn't obligated to be.

When boredom made me decide that I needed a glass of wine and a quick snack more than I needed to sit there with my still-blank tablet, I found out there was hardly anyone even in the lounges. There was no familiar face. No one seemed to know where Sam was. And in the afternoon, the Collegium-Presidor, bowing to the inevitable, announced that the remaining sessions would be postponed indefinitely.

The day was a total waste.

I had a lot more hopes for the night.

Rachel greeted me with the news that Sam had sent a message to say he was detained and wouldn't make dinner. "Did he say where he was?" She shook her head. "He's off with some of the other top people," I guessed. I told her about the collapse of the convention. Then I brightened. "At least let's go out for dinner, then."

Rachel firmly vetoed the idea. She was tactful enough not to mention money, although I was sure Sam had filled her in on my precarious financial state. "I like my own cook's food better than any restaurant," she told me. "We'll eat here. There won't be anything fancy tonight— just a simple meal for the two of us."

The best part of that was "the two of us." Basilius had arranged the couches in a sort of V, so that our heads were quite close together, with the low serving tables in easy reach between us. As soon as she lay down, Rachel confessed, "I didn't get a lot of work done today. I couldn't get that idea of yours out of my head."

The idea was Sam's, actually, but I didn't see any reason to correct her. "I'm flattered," I told her. "I'm sorry I spoiled your work."

She shrugged and went on. "I did a little reading on the period, especially about an interesting minor figure who lived around them, a Judaean preacher named Jeshua of Nazareth. Did you ever hear of him? Well, most people haven't, but he had a lot of followers at one time. They called themselves Chrestians, and they were a very unruly bunch."

"I'm afraid I don't know much about Judaean history," I said. Which was true; but then I added, "But I'd really like to learn more." Which wasn't—or at least hadn't been until just then.

"Of course," Rachel said. No doubt to her it seemed quite natural that everyone in the world would wish to know more about the post-Augustan period. "Anyway, this

Jeshua was on trial for sedition. He was condemned to death."

I blinked at her. "Not just to slavery?"

She shook her head. "They didn't just enslave criminals back then, they did physical things to them. Even executed them, sometimes in very barbarous ways. But Tiberius, as Proconsul, decided that the penalty was too extreme. So he commuted Jeshua's death sentence. He just had him whipped and let him go. A very good decision, I think. Otherwise he would have made him a martyr, and gods know what would have happened after that. As it was, the Chrestians just gradually waned away. . . . Basilius? You can bring the next course in now."

I watched with interest as Basilius complied. It turned out to be larks and olives! I approved, not simply for the fact that I liked the dish. The "simple meal" was actually a lot more elaborate than she had provided for the three of us the night before.

Things were looking up. I said, "Can you tell me something, Rachel? I think you're Judaean yourself, aren't you?"

"Of course."

"Well, I'm a little confused," I said. "I thought the Judaeans believed in the god Yahveh."

"Of course, Julie. We do."

"Yes, but—" I hesitated. I didn't want to mess up the way things were going, but I was curious. "But you say 'gods.' Isn't that, well, a contradiction?"

"Not at all," she told me civilly enough. "Yahveh's commandments were brought down from a mountaintop by our great prophet, Moses, and they were very clear on the subject. One of them says, 'Thou shalt have no other gods before me.' Well, we don't, you see? Yahveh is our *first* god. There aren't any *before* him. It's all explained in the rabbinical writings."

"And that's what you go by, the rabbinical writings?"

She looked thoughtful. "In a way. We're a very traditional people, Julie. Tradition is what we follow; the rabbinical writings simply explain the traditions."

She had stopped eating. I stopped, too. Dreamily I reached out to caress her cheek.

She didn't pull away. She didn't respond, either. After a moment, she said, not looking at me, "For instance, there is a Judaean tradition that a woman is to be a virgin at the time of her marriage."

My hand came away from her face by itself, without any conscious command from me. "Oh?"

"And the rabbinical writings more or less define the tradition, you see. They say that the head of the household is to stand guard at an unmarried daughter's bedroom for the first hour of each night; if there is no male head of the household, a trusted slave is to be appointed to the job."

"I see," I said. "You've never been married, have you?"

"Not yet," said Rachel, beginning to eat again.

I hadn't ever been married, either, although, to be sure, I wasn't exactly a virgin. It wasn't that I had anything against marriage. It was only that the life of a sci-rom hack wasn't what you would call exactly financially stable, and also the fact that I hadn't ever come across the woman I wanted to spend my life with . . . or, to quote Rachel, "Not yet."

I tried to keep my mind off that subject. I was sure that if my finances had been precarious before, they were now close to catastrophic.

The next morning I wondered what to do with my day, but Rachel settled it for me. She was waiting for me in the atrium. "Sit down with me, Julie," she commanded, patting the bench beside me. "I was up late, thinking, and I think I've got something for you. Suppose this man Jeshua had been executed, after all."

It wasn't exactly the greeting I had been hoping for, nor was it something I had given a moment's thought to, either. But I was glad enough to sit next to her in that pleasant little garden, with the gentled early sun shining down on us through the translucent shades. "Yes?" I said noncommittally, kissing her hand in greeting.

She waited a moment before she took her hand back.

"That idea opened some interesting possibilities, Julie. Jeshua would have been a martyr, you see. I can easily imagine that under those circumstances his Chrestian followers would have had a lot more staying power. They might even have grown to be really important. Judaea was always in one kind of turmoil or another around that time, anyway—there were all sorts of prophecies and rumors about messiahs and changes in society. The Chrestians might even have come to dominate all of Judaea."

I tried to be tactful. "There's nothing wrong with being proud of your ancestors, Rachel. But, really, what difference would that have made?" I obviously hadn't been tactful enough. She had turned to look at me with what looked like the beginning of a frown. I thought fast, and tried to cover myself. "On the other hand," I went on quickly, "suppose you expanded that idea beyond Judaea."

It turned into a real frown, but puzzled rather than angry. "What do you mean, beyond Judaea?"

"Well, suppose Jeshua's Chrestian-Judaean kind of— what would you call it? Philosophy? Religion?"

"A little of both, I'd say."

"Religious philosophy, then. Suppose it spread over most of the world, not just Judaea. That could be interesting."

"But, really, no such thing hap—"

"Rachel, Rachel," I said, covering her mouth with a fingertip affectionately. "We're saying *what if*, remember? Every sci-rom writer is entitled to one big lie. Let's say this is mine. Let's say that Chrestian-Judaeanism became a world religion. Even Rome itself succumbs. Maybe the City becomes the—what do you call it—the place for the Sanhedrin of the Chrestian-Judaeans. And then what happens?"

"You tell me," she said, half amused, half suspicious.

"Why, then," I said, flexing the imagination of the trained sci-rom writer, "it might develop like the kind of conditions you've been talking about in the old days in Judaea. Maybe the whole world would be splintering into factions and sects, and then they fight."

"Fight *wars?*" she asked incredulously.

"Fight *big* wars. Why not? It happened in Judaea,

didn't it? And then they might keep right on fighting them, all through historical times. After all, the only thing that's kept the world united for the past two thousand years has been the Pax Romana. Without that—why, without that," I went on, talking faster and making mental notes to myself as I went along, "let's say that all the tribes of Europe turned into independent city-states. Like the Greeks, only bigger. And more powerful. And they fight, the Franks against the Vik Northmen against the Belgiae against the Kelts."

She was shaking her head. "People wouldn't be so silly, Julie," she complained.

"How do you know that? Anyway, this is a sci-rom, dear." I didn't pause to see if she reacted to the "dear." I went right on, but not failing to notice that she hadn't objected. "The people will be as silly as I want them to be—as long as I can make it plausible enough for the fans. But you haven't heard the best part of it. Let's say the Chrestian-Judaeans take their religion seriously. They don't do anything to go against the will of their god. What Yahveh said still goes, no matter what. Do you follow? That means they aren't at all interested in scientific discovery, for instance."

"No, stop right there!" she ordered, suddenly indignant. "Are you trying to say that we Judaeans aren't interested in science? That I'm not? Or my Uncle Sam? And we're certainly Judaeans."

"But you're not *Chrestian*-Judaeans, sweet. There's a big difference. Why? Because I say there is, Rachel, and I'm the one writing the story. So, let's see—" I paused for thought—"all right, let's say the Chrestians go through a long period of intellectual stagnation, and then—" I paused, not because I didn't know what was coming next, but to build the effect—"and then along come the Olympians!"

She gazed at me blankly. "Yes?" she asked, encouraging but vague.

"Don't you see it? And then this Chrestian-Judaean world, drowsing along in the middle of a prescientific dark age—no aircraft, no electronic broadcast, not even a printing press or a hovermachine—is suddenly thrown into contact with a supertechnological civilization from outer space!" She was wrinkling her forehead at me, trying to understand what I was driving at. "It's terrible culture shock," I explained. "And not just for the people on Earth. Maybe the Olympians come to look us over, and they see that we're technologically backward and divided into warring nations and all that . . . and what do they do? Why, they turn right around and leave us! And . . . and that's the end of the book!"

She pursed her lips. "But maybe that's what they're doing now," she said cautiously.

"But not for that reason, certainly. See, this isn't *our* world I'm talking about. It's a *what if* world."

"It sounds a little far-fetched," she said.

I said happily, "That's where my skills come in. You don't understand sci-rom, sweetheart. It's the sci-rom writer's job to push an idea as far as it will go—to the absolute limit of credibility—to the point where if he took just one step more the whole thing would collapse into absurdity. Trust me, Rachel. I'll make them believe it."

She was still pursing her pretty lips, but this time I didn't wait for her to speak. I seized the bird of opportunity on the wing. I leaned toward her and kissed those lips, as I had been wanting to do for some time. Then I said, "I've got to get to a scribe; I want to get all this down before I forget it. I'll be back when I can be, and—and until then—well, here."

And I kissed her again, gently, firmly and long; and it was quite clear early in the process that she was kissing me back.

Being next to a rental barracks had its advantages. I found a scribe to rent at a decent price, and the rental manager even let me borrow one of their conference rooms that night to dictate in. By daybreak I had down the first two chapters and an outline of *Sidewise to a Chrestian World*.

Once I get that far in a book, the rest is just work. The general idea is set, the characters have announced themselves to me, it's just a matter of closing my eyes for a moment to see what's going to be happening and then opening them to dictate to the scribe. In this case, the scribes, plural, because the first one wore out in a few more hours and I had to employ a second, and then a third.

I didn't sleep at all until it was all down. I think it was fifty-two straight hours, the longest I'd worked in one stretch in years. When it was all done I left it to be fair-copied. The rental agent agreed to get it down to the shipping offices by the harbor and dispatch it by fast air to Marcus in London.

Then at last I stumbled back to Rachel's house to sleep. I was surprised to find that it was still dark, an hour or more before sunrise.

Basilius let me in, looking startled as he studied my sunken eyes and unshaved face. "Let me sleep until I wake up," I ordered. There was a journal neatly folded beside my bed, but I didn't look at it. I lay down, turned over once, and was gone.

When I woke up, at least twelve hours had passed. I had Basilius bring me something to eat and shave me, and when I finally got out to the atrium it was nearly sundown and Rachel was waiting for me. I told her what I'd done, and she told me about the last message from the Olympians. "Last?" I objected. "How can you be sure it's the last?"

"Because they said so," she told me sadly. "They said they were breaking off communications."

"Oh," I said, thinking about that. "Poor Sam." And she looked so doleful that I couldn't help myself, I took her in my arms.

Consolation turned to kissing, and when we had done quite a lot of that she leaned back, smiling at me.

I couldn't help what I said then, either. It startled me to hear the words come out of my mouth as I said, "Rachel, I wish we could get married."

She pulled back, looking at me with affection and a little surprised amusement. "Are you proposing to me?"

I was careful of my grammar. "That was a subjunctive, sweet. I said I *wished* we could get married."

"I understood that. What I want to know is whether you're asking me to grant your wish."

"No—well, hells, yes! But what I wish first is that I had the right to ask you. Sci-rom writers don't have the most solid financial situation, you know. The way you live here—"

"The way I live here," she said, "is paid for by the estate I inherited from my father. Getting married won't take it away."

"But that's your estate, my darling. I've been poor, but I've never been a parasite."

"You won't be a parasite," she said softly, and I realized that she was being careful about her grammar, too.

Which took a lot of willpower on my part. "Rachel," I said, "I should be hearing from my editor any time now. If this new kind of sci-rom catches on—if it's as popular as it might be—"

"Yes?" she prompted.

"Why," I said, "then maybe I can actually ask you. But I don't know that. Marcus probably has it by now, but I don't know if he's read it. And then I won't know his decision till I hear from him. And now, with all the confusion about the Olympians, that might take weeks—"

"Julie," she said, putting her finger over my lips, "call him up."

The circuits were all busy, but I finally got through—and, because it was well after lunch, Marcus was in his office. More than that, he was quite sober. "Julie, you bastard," he cried, sounding really furious, "where the hells have you been hiding? I ought to have you whipped."

But he hadn't said anything about getting the aediles after me. "Did you have a chance to read *Sidewise to a Chrestian World*?" I asked.

"The what? Oh, *that* thing. Nah. I haven't even looked at it. I'll buy it, naturally," he said. "But what I'm talking about is *An Ass's Olympiad*. The censors won't stop it now, you know. In fact, all I want you to do now is make the Olympians a little dumber, a little nastier—you've got a biggie here, Julie! I think we can get a broadcast out of it, even. So when can you get back here to fix it up?"

"Why—well, pretty soon, I guess, only I haven't checked the hover timetable—"

"Hover, hell! You're coming back by fast plane—we'll pick up the tab. And, oh, by the way, we're doubling your advance. The payment will be in your account this afternoon."

And ten minutes later, when I unsubjunctively proposed to Rachel, she quickly and unsubjunctively accepted; and the high-speed flight to London takes nine hours, but I was grinning all the way.

Chapter 5
The Way It Is When
You've Got It Made

To be a free-lance writer is to live in a certain kind of ease. Not very easeful financially, maybe, but in a lot of other ways. You don't have to go to an office every day, you get a lot of satisfaction out of seeing your very own words being read on hovers and trains by total strangers. To be a potentially *best-selling* writer is a whole order of magnitude different. Marcus put me up in an inn right next to the publishing company's offices and stood over me while I turned my poor imaginary Olympian into the most doltish, feckless, unlikeable being the universe had ever seen. The more I made the Olympian contemptibly comic, the more Marcus loved it. So did everyone else in the office; so did their affiliates in Kiev and Manahattan and Kalkut and half a dozen other cities all around the world, and he informed me proudly that they were publishing my book simultaneously in all of them. "We'll be the first ones out, Julie," he exulted. "It's going to be a mint! Money? Well, of course you can have more money—you're in the big-time now!" And, yes, the broadcast studios were interested—interested enough to sign a contract even before I'd finished the revisions; and so were the journals, who came for interviews every minute that Marcus would let me off from correcting the proofs and posing for jacket photographs and speaking to their sales staff; and, all in all, I hardly had a chance to breathe until I was back on the high-speed aircraft to Alexandria and my bride.

Sam had agreed to give the bride away, and he met me at the airpad. He looked older and more tired, but resigned. As we drove to Rachel's house, where the wedding guests were already beginning to gather, I tried to cheer him up. I had plenty of joy myself; I wanted to share it. So I offered, "At least, now you can get back to your real work."

He looked at me strangely. "Writing sci-roms?" he asked.

"No, of course not! That's good enough for me, but you've still got your extrasolar probe to keep you busy."

"Julie," he said sadly, "where have you been lately? Didn't you see the last Olympian message?"

"Well, sure," I said, offended. "Everybody did, didn't they?" And then I thought for a moment, and, actually, it had been Rachel who had told me about it. I'd never actually looked at a journal or a broadcast. "I guess I was pretty busy," I said lamely.

He looked sadder than ever. "Then maybe you don't know that they said they weren't only terminating all their own transmissions to us, they were terminating even our own probes."

"Oh, no, Sam! I would have heard if the probes had stopped transmitting!"

He said patiently, "No, you wouldn't, because the data they were sending is still on its way to us. We've still got a few years coming in from our probes. But that's it. We're out of interstellar space, Julie. They don't want us there."

He broke off, peering out the window. "And that's the way it is," he said. "We're here, though, and you better get inside. Rachel's going to be tired of sitting under that canopy without you around."

The greatest thing of all about being a best-selling author, if you like traveling, is that when you fly around the world somebody else pays for the tickets. Marcus's publicity department fixed up the whole thing. Personal appearances, bookstore autographings, college lectures, broadcasts, publishers' meetings, receptions—we were kept busy for a solid month, and it made a hell of a fine honeymoon.

Of course any honeymoon would have been wonderful as long as Rachel was the bride, but without the publishers bankrolling us we might not have visited six of the seven continents on the way. (We didn't bother with Polaris Australis—nobody there but penguins.) And we took time for ourselves along the way, on beaches in Hindia and the islands of Han, in the wonderful shops of Manahattan and a dozen other cities of the Western Continents—we did it all.

When we got back to Alexandria the contractors had finished the remodeling of Rachel's villa—which, we had decided, would now be our winter home, though our next priority was going to be to find a place where we could spend the busy part of the year in London. Sam had moved back in and, with Basilius, greeted us formally as we came to the door.

"I thought you'd be in Rome," I told him, once we were settled and Rachel had gone to inspect what had been done with her baths.

"Not while I'm still trying to understand what went wrong," he said. "The research is going on right here; this is where we transmitted from."

I shrugged and took a sip of the Falernian wine Basilius had left for us. I held the goblet up critically: a little cloudy, I thought, and in the vat too long. And then I grinned at myself, because a few weeks earlier I would have been delighted at anything so costly. "But we know what went wrong," I told him reasonably. "They decided against us."

"Of course they did," he said. "But why? I've been trying to work out just what messages were being received when they broke off communications."

"Do you think we said something to offend them?"

He scratched the age spot on his bald head, staring at me. Then he sighed. "What would *you* think, Julius?"

"Well, maybe so," I admitted. "What messages were they?"

"I'm not sure. It took a lot of digging. The Olympians, you know, acknowledged receipt of each message by repeating the last hundred and forty groups—"

"I didn't know."

"Well, they did. The last message they acknowledged was a history of Rome. Unfortunately, it was six hundred and fifty thousand words long."

"So you have to read the whole history?"

"Not just *read* it, Julie; we have to try to figure out what might have been in it that wasn't in any previous message. We've had two or three hundred researchers collating every previous message, and the only thing that was new was some of the social data from the last census—"

I interrupted him. "I thought you said it was a history."

"It was at the *end* of the history. We were giving pretty current data—so many of equestrian rank, so many citizens, so many freedmen, so many slaves." He hesitated, and then said thoughtfully, "Paulus Magnus—I don't know if you know him, he's an Algonkan—pointed out that that was the first time we'd ever mentioned slavery."

I waited for him to go on. "Yes?" I said encouragingly.

He shrugged. "Nothing. Paulus is a slave himself, so naturally he's got it on his mind a lot."

"I don't quite see what that has to do with anything," I said. "Isn't there anything else?"

"Oh," he said, "there are a thousand theories. There were some health data, too, and some people think the Olympians might have suddenly gotten worried about some new microorganism killing them off. Or we weren't polite enough. Or maybe—who knows—there was some sort of power struggle among them, and the side that came out on top just didn't want any more new races in their community."

"And we don't know yet which it was?"

"It's worse than that, Julie," he told me somberly. "I don't think we ever will find out what it was that made them decide they didn't want to have anything to do with us." And in that, too, Flavius Samuelus ben Samuelus was a very intelligent man. Because we never have

The Return
of William Proxmire

LARRY NIVEN

Through the peephole in Andrew's front door the man made a startling sight.

He looked to be in his eighties. He was breathing hard and streaming sweat. He seemed slightly more real than most men: photogenic as hell, tall and lean, with stringy muscles and no potbelly, running shoes and a day pack and a blue windbreaker, and an open smile. The face was familiar, but from where?

Andrew opened the front door but left the screen door locked. "Hello?"

"Dr. Andrew Minsky?"

"Yes." Memory clicked. "William Proxmire, big as life."

The ex-senator smiled acknowledgment. "I've only just finished reading about you in the *Tribune*, Dr. Minsky. May I come in?"

It had never been Andrew Minsky's ambition to invite William Proxmire into his home. Still—"Sure. Come in, sit down, have some coffee. Or do your stretches." Andrew was a runner himself when he could find the time.

"Thank you."

Andrew left him on the rug with one knee pulled against his chest. From the kitchen he called, "I never in my life expected to meet you face to face. You must have seen the article on me and Tipler and Penrose?"

"Yes. I'm prepared to learn that the media got it all wrong."

"I bet you are. Any politician would. Well, the *Tribune* implied that what we've got is a time machine. Of course we don't. We've got a schematic based on a theory. Then again, it's the new improved version. It doesn't involve an infinitely long cylinder that you'd have to make out of neutronium—"

"Good. What would it cost?"

Andrew Minsky sighed. Had the politician even recognized the reference? He said, "Oh . . . hard to say." He picked up two cups and the coffeepot and went back in. "Is that it? You came looking for a time machine?"

The old man was sitting on the yellow rug with his legs spread wide apart and his fingers grasping his right foot. He released, folded his legs heel to heel, touched forehead to toes, held, then stood up with a sound like popcorn popping. He said, "Close enough. How much would it cost?"

"Depends on what you're after. If you—"

"I can't get you a grant if you can't name a figure."

Andrew set his cup down very carefully. He said, "No, of course not."

"I'm retired now, but people still owe me favors. I want a ride. One trip. What would it cost?"

Andrew hadn't had enough coffee yet. He didn't feel fully awake. "I have to think out loud a little. Okay? Mass isn't a problem. You can go as far back as you like if . . . mmm. Let's say under sixty years. Cost might be twelve, thirteen million if you could also get us access to the proton-antiproton accelerator at Washburn University, or maybe CERN in Switzerland. Otherwise we'd have to build that too. By the way, you're not expecting to get younger, are you?"

"I hadn't thought about it."

"Good. The theory depends on maneuverings between event points. You don't ever go backward. Where and when, Senator?"

William Proxmire leaned forward with his hands clasped. "Picture this. A Navy officer walks the deck of a ship, coughing, late at night in the 1930s. Suddenly an arm snakes around his neck, a needle plunges into his buttocks—"

"The deck of a ship at sea?"

Proxmire nodded, grinning.

"You're just having fun, aren't you? Something to do while jogging, now that you're retired."

"Put it this way," Proxmire said. "I read the article. It linked up with an old daydream of mine. I looked up your address. You were within easy running distance. I hope you don't mind?"

Oddly enough, Andrew found he didn't. Anything that happened before his morning coffee was recreation.

So dream a little. "Deck of a moving ship. I was going to say it's ridiculous, but it isn't. We'll have to deal with much higher velocities. Any point on the Earth's surface is spinning at up to half a mile per second and circling the sun at eighteen miles per. In principle I think we could solve all of it with one stroke. We could scan one patch of deck, say, over a period of a few seconds, then integrate the record into the program. Do the same coming home."

"You can do it?"

"Well, if we can't solve that one we can't do anything else, either. You'd be on a tight schedule, though. Senator, what's the purpose of the visit?"

"Have you ever had daydreams about a time machine and a scope-sighted rifle?"

Andrew's eyebrows went up. "Sure, what little boy hasn't? Hitler, I suppose? For me it was always Lyndon Johnson. Senator, I do not commit murder under any circumstances."

"A time machine and a scope-sighted rifle, and me," William Proxmire said dreamily. "I get more anonymous letters than you'd believe, even now. They tell me that every space advocate daydreams about me and a time machine and a scope-sighted rifle. Well, I started daydreaming too, but my fantasy involves a time machine and a hypodermic full of antibiotics."

Andrew laughed. "You're plotting to do someone good behind his back?"

"Right."

"Who?"

"Robert Anson Heinlein."

All laughter dropped away. "Why?"

"It's a good deed, isn't it?"

"Sure. Why?"

"You know the name? Over the past forty years or so I've talked to a great many people in science and in the space program. I kept hearing the name Robert Heinlein. They were seduced into science because they read Heinlein at age twelve. These were the people I found hard to deal with. No grasp of reality. Fanatics."

Andrew suspected that the senator had met more of these than he realized. Heinlein spun off ideas at a terrific rate. Other writers picked them up ... along with a distrust for arrogance combined with stupidity or ignorance, particularly in politicians.

"Well, Heinlein's literary career began after he left the Navy because of lung disease."

"You're trying to destroy the space program."

"Will you help?"

Andrew was about to tell him to go to hell. He didn't. "I'm still talking. Why do you want to destroy the space program?"

"I didn't, at first. I was opposed to waste," Proxmire said. "My colleagues, they'll spend money on any pet project, as if there was a money tree out there somewhere—"

"Milk price supports," Andrew said gently. For several decades now, the great state of Wisconsin had taken tax money from the other states so that the price they paid for milk would stay *up*.

Proxmire's lips twitched. "Without milk price supports, there would be places where families with children can't buy milk."

"Why?"

The old man shook his head hard. "I've just remembered that I don't have to answer that question anymore. My point is that the government has spent far more taking rocks from the Moon and photographs from Saturn. Our economy would be far healthier if that money had been spent elsewhere."

"I'd rather shoot Lyndon. Eliminate welfare. Save a *lot* more money that way."

"A minute ago you were opposed to murder."

The old man did have a way with words. "Point taken.

Could you get us funding? It'd be a guaranteed Nobel Prize. I like the fact that you don't need a scope-sighted rifle. A hypo full of sulfa drugs doesn't have to be kept secret. What antibiotic?"

"I don't know what cures consumption. I don't know which year or what ship. I've got people to look those things up, if I decide I want to know. I came straight here as soon as I read the morning paper. Why not? I run every day, any direction I like. But I haven't heard you say it's impossible, Andrew, and I haven't heard you say you won't do it."

"More coffee?"

"Yes, thank you."

Proxmire left him alone while he was in the kitchen, and for that Andrew was grateful. He'd have made no progress at all if he'd had to guard his expression. There was simply too much to think about.

He preferred not to consider the honors. Assume he had changed the past; how would he prove it before a board of his peers? "How would I prove it *now*? What would I have to show them?" he muttered under his breath, while the coffee water was heating. "Books? Books that didn't get written? Newspapers? There are places that'll print any newspaper headline I ask for. WAFFEN SS TO BUILD WORK CAMP IN DEATH VALLEY. I can mint Robert Kennedy half-dollars for a lot less than thirteen million bucks. Hmm . . ." But the Nobel Prize wasn't the point.

Keeping Robert Heinlein alive a few years longer: Was *that* the point? It shouldn't be. Heinlein wouldn't have thought so.

Would the science fiction field really have collapsed without the Menace From Earth? Tradition within the science fiction field would have named Campbell, not Heinlein. But think: Was it magazines that had sucked Andrew Minsky into taking advanced physics classes? Or . . . *Double Star, Red Planet,* Anderson's *Tau Zero,* Vance's *Tschai* series? Then the newsstand magazines, then the subscriptions, then (of course) he'd dropped it all to pursue a career. If Proxmire's staff investigated his past (as they must, if he was at all serious), they would find that

Andrew Minsky, Ph.D., hadn't read a science fiction magazine in fifteen years.

Proxmire's voice came from the other room. "Of course, it would be a major chunk of funding. But wouldn't my old friends be surprised to find me backing a scientific project! How's the coffee coming?"

"Done." Andrew carried the pot in. "I'll do it," he said. "That is, I and my associates will build a time machine. We'll need funding and we'll need active assistance using the Washburn accelerator. We should be ready for a man-rated experiment in three years, I'd think. We won't fail."

He sat. He looked Proxmire in the eye. "Let's keep thinking, though. A Navy officer walks the tilting deck of what would now be an antique Navy ship. An arm circles his throat. He grips the skinny wrist and elbow, bends the wrist downward, and throws the intruder into the sea. They train Navy men to fight, you know, and he was young and you are old."

"I keep in shape," Proxmire said coldly. "A medical man who performs autopsies once told me about men and women like me. We run two to five miles a day. We die in our eighties and nineties and hundreds. A fall kills us, or a car accident. Cut into us and you find veins and arteries you could run a toy train through."

He was serious. "I was afraid you were thinking of taking along a blackjack or a trank gun or a Kalashnikov—"

"No."

"I'll say it anyway. Don't hurt him."

Proxmire smiled. "That would be missing the point."

And if that part worked out, Andrew would take his chances with the rest.

He had been reaching for a beer while he thought about revising the time machine paper he'd done with Tipler and Penrose four years ago. Somewhere he'd shifted over into daydreams, and that had sent him off on a weird track indeed.

It was like double vision in his head. The time machine (never built) had put William Proxmire (the ex-senator!) on the moving deck of the U.S.S. *Roper* on a gray midmorning in December 1933. Andrew never daydreamed this vividly. He slapped his flat belly, and wondered why, and remembered: He was ten pounds heavier in the daydream, because he'd been too busy to run.

So much detail! Maybe he was remembering a sweaty razor-sharp nightmare from last night, the kind in which you know you're doing something bizarrely stupid, but you can't figure out how to stop.

He'd reached for a Henry Weinhart's (Budweiser) from the refrigerator in his kitchen (in the office at Washburn, where the Weinhart's always ran out first) while the project team watched their monitors (while the KCET funding drive whined in his living room). In his head there were double vision, double memories, double sensations. The world of quantum physics was blurred in spots. But this was his kitchen and he could hear KCET begging for money a room away.

Andrew walked into his living room and found William Proxmire dripping on his yellow rug.

No, wait. That's the other—

The photogenic old man tossed the spray hypo on Andrew's couch. He stripped off his hooded raincoat, inverted it, and dropped it on top. He was trying to smile, but the fear showed through. "Andrew? What I am doing *here*?"

Andrew said, "My head feels like two flavors of cotton. Give me a moment. I'm trying to remember two histories at once."

"I should have had more time. And then it should have been the Washburn accelerator! You said!"

"Yeah, well, I did and I didn't. Welcome to the wonderful world of Schrödinger's Cat. How did it go? You found a young lieutenant junior grade gunnery officer alone on deck"—The raincoat was soaking his cushions—"in the rain—"

"Losing his breakfast overside in the rain. Pulmonary tuberculosis, consumption. Good riddance to an ugly disease."

"You wrestled him to the deck—"

"Heh, heh, heh. No. I told him I was from the future. I showed him a spray hypo. He'd never seen one. I was dressed as a civilian on a Navy ship. That got his attention. I told him if he was Robert Heinlein I had a cure for his cough."

"Cure for his cough?"

"I didn't say it would kill him otherwise. I didn't say it wouldn't, and he didn't ask, but he may have assumed I wouldn't have come for anything trivial. I knew his name. This was Heinlein, not some Wisconsin dairy farmer. He *wanted* to believe I was a time traveler. He *did* believe. I gave him his shot. Andrew, I feel cheated."

"Me too. Get used to it." But it was Andrew who was beginning to smile.

The older man hardly heard; his ears must be still ringing with that long-dead storm. "You know, I would have liked to talk to him. I was supposed to have twenty-two minutes more. I gave him his shot and the whole scene popped like a soap bubble. *Why* did I come back *here*?"

"Because we never got funding for research into time travel."

"Ah . . . hah. There *have* been changes. What changes?"

It wasn't just remembering; it was a matter of selecting pairs of memories that were mutually exclusive, then judging between them. It was maddening . . . but it could be done. Andrew said, "The Washburn accelerator goes with the time machine goes with the funding. My apartment goes with no time machine goes with no funding goes with . . . Bill, let's go outside. It should be dark by now."

Proxmire didn't ask why. He looked badly worried.

The sun had set, but the sky wasn't exactly black. In a line across a smaller, dimmer full Moon, four rectangles blazed like windows into the sun. Andrew sighed with relief. Collapse of the wave function: *This* is reality.

William Proxmire said, "Don't make me guess."

"Solar-powered satellites. Looking Glass Three through Six."

"What happened to your time machine?"

"Apollo Eleven landed on the Moon on July 20, 1969, just like clockwork. Apollo Thirteen left a month or two early, but something still exploded in the service module, so I guess it wasn't a meteor. They . . . shit."

"Eh?"

"They didn't get back. They died. We murdered them."

"Then?"

Could he put it back? Should he put it back? It was still coming together in his head. "Let's see, NASA tried to cancel Apollo Eighteen, but there was a hell of a write-in campaign—"

"Why? From whom?"

"The spec-fic community went absolutely apeshit. Okay, Bill, I've got it now."

"Well?"

"You were right, the whole science fiction magazine business just faded out in the fifties, last remnants of the pulp era. Campbell alone couldn't save it. Then in the sixties the literary crowd rediscovered the idea. There must have been an empty ecological niche and the lit-crits moved in.

"Speculative fiction, spec-fic, the literature of the possible. The *New Yorker* ran spec-fic short stories and critical reviews of novels. They thought *Planet of the Apes* was wonderful, and *Selig's Complaint*, which was Robert Silverberg's study of a telepath. Tom Wolfe started appearing in *Esquire* with his bizarre alien cultures. I can't remember an issue of the *Saturday Evening Post* that didn't have *some* spec-fic in it. Anderson, Vance, MacDonald . . . John D. MacDonald turns out novels set on a ring the size of Earth's orbit.

"The new writers were good enough that some of the early ones couldn't keep up, but a few did it by talking to hard science teachers. Benford and Forward did it in reverse. Jim Benford's a plasma physicist but he writes like he swallowed a college English teacher. Robert Forward wrote a novel called *Neutron Star*, but he built the Forward Mass Detector, too."

"Wonderful."

"There's a lot of spec-fic fans in the military. When Apollo Twenty-one burned up during reentry, they raised so much hell that Congress took the manned space program away from NASA and gave it to the Navy."

William Proxmire glared and Andrew Minsky grinned. "Now, you left office in the sixties because of the cheese boycott. When you tried to chop the funding for the Shuttle, the spec-fic community took offense. They stopped eating Wisconsin cheese. The San Francisco *Locus* called you the Cheese Man. Most of your supporters must have eaten nothing but their own cheese for about eight months, and then Goldwater chopped the milk price supports. 'Golden Fleece,' he called it. So you were out, and now there's no time machine."

"We could build one," Proxmire said.

Rescue Apollo Thirteen? The possibility had to be considered. . . . Andrew remembered the twenty years that followed the Apollo flights. In one set of memories, lost goals, pointlessness and depression, political faddishness leading nowhere. In the other, half a dozen space stations, government and military and civilian; Moonbase and Moonbase Polar; *Life* photographs of the Mars Project half-finished on the lunar plain, sitting on a hemispherical Orion-style shield made from lunar aluminum and fused lunar dust.

I do not commit murder under any circumstances.

"I don't think so, Bill. We don't have the political support. We don't have the incentive. Where would a Nobel Prize *come* from? We can't prove there was ever a timeline different from this one. Besides, this isn't just a more interesting world, it's safer too. Admiral Heinlein doesn't let the Soviets build spacecraft."

Proxmire stopped breathing for an instant. Then, "I suppose he wouldn't."

"Nope. He's taking six of their people on the Mars expedition, tough. They paid their share of the cost in fusion bombs for propulsion."

May 12, 1988—

Greg Benford called me a couple of months ago. He wanted new stories about alternate time tracks for an anthology. I told him that the only sideways-in-time story in my head was totally unsaleable. It's just recreation, daydreaming, goofing off. It's about how William Proxmire uses a time machine and a hypodermic full of sulfa drugs to wipe out the space program.

Greg made me write it.

I called Robert to get dates and other data, and asked if I could use his name. I had so much fun with this story! I made lots of copies and sent them to friends. I sent one to Robert, of course. That was only a few weeks ago.

And now I'm thinking that sometimes I really luck out. "The Return of William Proxmire" hasn't yet been published. Robert's death feels bad enough, but it would be one notch worse if I didn't know he'd read this story.

LARRY NIVEN

About the Editors

Gregory Benford is the author of several acclaimed novels, including *Great Sky River, Heart of the Comet* (with David Brin), *In the Ocean of Night, Across the Sea of Suns,* and *Timescape,* which won the Nebula Award, the British Science Fiction Award, the John W. Campbell Memorial Award, and the Australian Ditmar Award. Dr. Benford, a Woodrow Wilson Fellow, is a professor of physics at the University of California, Irvine. He and his wife live in Laguna Beach.

Martin H. Greenberg is the editor or author of over 300 books, the majority of them anthologies in the science fiction, fantasy, horror, mystery, and western fields. He has collaborated editorially with such authors as Isaac Asimov, Robert Silverberg, Gregory Benford, and Frederik Pohl. A professor of political science at the University of Wisconsin, he lives with his wife and baby daughter in Green Bay.

Editors Gregory Benford and Martin H. Greenberg
ask the provocative question

What Might Have Been?

* if the Egyptian dynasties—and their Hebrew slaves—had survived until modern times?

* if Mahatma Gandhi used passive resistance when the Nazis invaded India during World War II?

* If Lawrence of Arabia faced Rommel in North Africa?

These star-studded anthologies include stories by some of the most imaginative authors writing speculative fiction today, including Poul Anderson, Gregory Benford, George Alec Effinger, Harry Harrison, and Tom Shippey, Barry Malzberg, James Morrow, Larry Niven, Frederik Pohl, Robert Silverberg, and Judith Tarr to name a few. Here are stories that will engage the mind and challenge the imagination!

☐ Volume One: **Alternate Empires** (27845-2 • $4.50/ $5.50 in Canada)

☐ Volume Two: **Alternate Heroes** (28279-4 • $4.50/ $5.50 in Canada)

Buy **What Might Have Been?** on sale now wherever Bantam Spectra Books are sold, or use this handy page to order:
